The shining splendor of
cover of this book reflects
story inside. Look for the
buy a historical romance.
the very best in quality and

PASSION ON THE HIGH SEAS

The pirate's finger slid off Miranda's chin to caress a trail down her neck.

"I wish you wouldn't look at me like that." Jack didn't mean to say the words; they were simply out of his mouth before he could stop them. But she was studying him with languid blue eyes that made him want to forget everything but taking her in his arms.

"I was just wondering," she whispered.

"Wondering what?" he asked.

"Do you suppose you could kiss me like you did before? Simply as an experiment," Miranda added because she feared she was acting very bold.

Jack bent toward her. "One kiss shouldn't hurt."

"No," Miranda said in all seriousness. "I don't think it will."

The touch of their lips was explosive. One moment, Miranda's mind was attuned to documenting the experience; the next she couldn't think at all. It was as if her whole being was engulfed in a tidal wave of sensation.

FEEL THE FIRE IN CAROL FINCH'S ROMANCES!

BELOVED BETRAYAL (2346, $3.95)

Sabrina Spencer donned a gray wig and veiled hat before blackmailing rugged Ridge Tanner into guiding her to Fort Canby. But the costume soon became her prison—the beauty had fallen head over heels in love!

LOVE'S HIDDEN TREASURE (2980, $4.50)

Shandra d'Evereux felt her heart throb beneath the stolen map she'd hidden in her bodice when Nolan Elliot swept her out onto the veranda. It was hard to concentrate on her mission with that wily rogue around!

MONTANA MOONFIRE (3263, $4.95)

Just as debutante Victoria Flemming-Cassidy was about to marry an oh-so-suitable mate, the towering preacher, Dru Sullivan flung her over his shoulder and headed West! Suddenly, Tori realized she had been given the best present for a bride: a night of passion with a real man!

THUNDER'S TENDER TOUCH (2809, $4.50)

Refined Piper Malone needed bounty-hunter, Vince Logan to recover her swindled inheritance. She thought she could coolly dismiss him after he did the job, but she never counted on the hot flood of desire she felt whenever he was near!

CHRISTINE DORSEY

SEA FIRES

ZEBRA BOOKS
KENSINGTON PUBLISHING CORP.

*To my firstborn Ben, my only blond child,
as he prepares to leave the nest — this
golden haired hero is for you.
And as always to Chip . . . my safe harbor.*

ZEBRA BOOKS

are published by

Kensington Publishing Corp.
475 Park Avenue South
New York, NY 10016

First printing: September, 1992

Printed in the United States of America

Prologue

September, 1686
Port Royal, Carolina

"'Tis a shame he sleeps so soundly. Perhaps a good prod would get him moving." Jack Blackstone leaned out, balancing his body along the curved limb of the live oak that spread gracefully over the salt marsh. He and Nafkebee had shinnied up the trunk to get a better look at the alligator nearly hidden by the cordgrass below.

A red-tailed hawk soared overhead, and Nafkebee followed its flight with his dark eyes. He was a Cheraw and, at fifteen summers, older and more cautious than his friend. "Be careful he does not use your arm to break his fast, Jack," he warned in his native tongue.

Swiping back hair burnished gold by the sun, Jack boasted with the cockiness of youth, "Yon gator would have a fight on his hands before I'd let him feast on my arm." He squirmed around till he could reach the leather pouch slung over his back. He withdrew a handful of stones from inside and threw them within inches of the alligator's head. Not even a flicker of movement showed in the animal's eyes, which were all that was visible above the murky water.

Shrugging, Jack sidled across the limb. "I best get back. Father thinks I'm chopping wood." He had been, until he'd heard Nafkebee's call, so near that of a wild turkey that all who heard it in the Scottish settlement of Stuart's Town, save Jack, thought it was. But Jack knew the prearranged signal and, with one last downward swipe of the axe, had headed toward the pine woods.

"Elspeth caught me at the edge of the clearing," Jack said as he leaped onto the spongy ground. "She wanted to come see you, but I assured her 'twas too dangerous." The boys shared a grin. Jack's sister was only five, not much more than a babe, but she could be a pest. The one time Jack had brought her with him on his rendezvous with Nafkebee, she had nearly driven the reticent Indian crazy with her chatter.

After leaving Nafkebee and arranging to meet him again in three days, Jack made his way back to the settlement along an Indian footpath.

Since 1683 Jack had lived in Stuart's Town. In that year his father, a Scottish nobleman, and Whig, fearing persecution at the hands of James II decided to leave his homeland. Along with nine other families they came to the southern border of Carolina. They were each granted twelve thousand acres in

Port Royal and the chance to live free from an arbitrary government.

Life in the colony was hard. Sickness weakened the body, and lack of promised protection from Charles Town disheartened the spirit. There was a constant threat from the Spanish to the south and pirates from the sea. But Jack's father assured him the land was worth it.

Jack had discussed his father's philosophy with Nafkebee, who simply shook his head and stated that the land did not belong to man.

Thoughts of his friend made the corners of Jack's mouth curve up. But in the next instant his smile froze. Shots rang out through the forest, flushing a covey of doves into the blue September sky.

Jack took off at a lope, then as the shooting intensified, ran faster. Branches tore at his clothes as he left the path seeking a quicker way to Stuart Town. His lungs burned, and he gulped air that tasted strongly of fear.

He heard screams now, and as Jack broke into the clearing his own cry of denial escaped his lips. In the harbor were three ships, Spanish by design. Smoke hung over the village, acrid and stinging as Jack ran to his cabin.

His mother lay in the doorway, her once white apron stained crimson. His own blood pounded in his ears as he dropped to his knees. A sob caught in his throat but was forced down by a burning rage. Jack sprang to his feet and raced toward the dock, toward the Spanish soldiers.

Bodies lay everywhere. As his gaze skimmed

across the scene of horror, Jack spotted his father. He stopped only long enough to grab the musket from his limp, lifeless fingers.

He burst onto the Spanish soldiers with a fury that shocked them. His father had died before reloading the gun, so Jack used it as a club. He swung repeatedly, feeling the satisfying crunch of flesh and bones.

Words were yelled at him in the heathen Spanish, but he didn't stop. He fought like a man possessed, not like the lad he was.

Someone grabbed him from behind, and Jack swirled about. And saw his young sister. She was crying hysterically, struggling with her meager strength in the arms of a burly Spaniard. Jack lunged toward them.

But this time his attack was cut short. Pain exploded through his head. He hit the sandy ground with a thud. A booted foot rolled him over, and just before Jack's world went black he looked into the face he would remember through hell and eternity.

"I am a free prince and have as much authority to make war on the whole world as he who has a hundred sail of ships . . ."

— Captain Charles Bellamy, pirate

Chapter One

May, 1699

"Look at them flyin' the Cross a St. George, Cap'n. It's just like the bloody Spaniards, pretendin' to be somethin' they ain't."

Lowering his spy glass, Captain Jack Blackstone dragged his attention from the brigantine dancing on the white-capped south Atlantic to his quartermaster. Phineas Sharp, his expression indignant, stood beside Jack on the *Sea Hawk*'s quarterdeck. Jack gestured toward the red and white flag flying from the yardarm of the vessel they pursued. Pursued across an ever narrowing span of sea. "We're hardly in a position to fault that ploy." He chuckled.

Both he and Phin knew England's red ensign snapped smartly above the deck of their own sloop.

And the British Admiralty would be the first to confirm the *Sea Hawk* was not an English vessel.

"That's different, Cap'n, an' ye knows it. Rules ain't for the likes a us." Phin screwed up his walnut brown face at the word "rules" as if the very act of saying it was bitter on his tongue.

" 'Tis true enough." Jack leaned bronzed forearms on the polished rail. Rules were something he'd given up years ago. No, not given up. Been forced to give up. He took a deep breath of salty air. "But as it happens yonder ship *is* flying its own colors."

"She's English?" Phin's tone was incredulous.

"Aye." Jack pushed away from the rail.

"But—" Phin scurried after his captain down the ladder to the main deck. Here the noise and bustle of the crew as they positioned cannon through gunwales and piled extra shot drowned out the whip of the wind in the square-rigged sails.

Phineas caught up with Jack near the thick pine mast. "But if she's English, then why—"

"No rules, Phin. Isn't that what you said?"

"Aye, but, Cap'n, 'tis different. Not that *I* care, mind ye. I mean, I've attacked me share a British ships, I have. But ye—"

"Drew the line at pirating the British," Jack finished for him, then raked lean, tanned fingers through sun gold hair. Phineas had a right to be surprised. From the moment Jack became captain of the *Sea Hawk* he had insisted they steer clear of the British. Spanish galleons they hunted with relish. French privateers fell prey to their pirate guns. But never the British. Until today.

Jack looked down at his quartermaster. The man, for all his fierce looks and gravel-rough voice, had a soft streak a league deep, especially where Jack was

10

concerned. He'd first shown it eleven years ago when Jack, frightened and alone, had scurried up the side of the *Sea Hawk* and stumbled unceremoniously to the deck. He still showed it in the concern of his deep-set black eyes.

" 'Tis rumored there's a Spaniard on yon ship . . . bound for St. Augustine."

"Ye think it might be de Segovia?"

Jack's fingers tightened into a fist. " 'Tis possible. According to Nafkebee, he's expected to return from Spain to take charge of the garrison at the Castillo de San Marcos." He spoke calmly, belying the turmoil inside him. Could revenge possibly be at hand? After all these years?

"We're running alongside, sir."

Jack acknowledged his head gunner, King Tabrue, with a nod. King, his sweat-slicked muscles bunched beneath ebony-black skin, turned back to tightening the cannon tackle.

Jack raised his arm, then hesitated. He could feel Phin beside him, watching him, his body tense. A coil of doubt in his own gut tightened Jack's jaw. What was he, a pirate with a conscience? Jack almost laughed at the irony.

The ship might be British, but if there was a chance that she carried Don Diego de Segovia, a chance Jack might find him at last. . . .

Unbidden came the echo of screams. His mother's . . . his father's . . . Elspeth's . . . his own. Jack swallowed and shut his eyes, trying to force away the time-faded images. When he opened them again his green stare was piercing.

11

The decision to attack was simple—as simple as it had been when he was a lad of fourteen years.

Jack's arm sliced down through the tension-filled air as his order thundered across the sand-strewn deck.

"Fire!"

"So Newton is saying the centrifugal effect causes an equatorial bulge on all heavenly bodies." Miranda Chadwick chewed on the end of her quill a moment, then glanced up from the volume of *Principia* spread before her on the rough-hewn table. Don Luis de Mancera sat perched on the edge of a sea chest in the cramped cabin. The expression on his deeply lined face made her smile. It was so similar to Grandfather's.

Not that the Spaniard looked anything like the man who had reared Miranda. Grandfather had been tall and spare, with thin gray hair that stuck out at odd angles and clothes that neither fit well nor fluttered with bows and lace.

Don Luis stood under five feet and seemed nearly as wide. His long curled wig framed a face folded with flesh, and he dressed more like a court dandy than the earnest scientist he was. When seen together they had made an odd-looking pair, Don Luis and her grandfather. But despite outward appearances and different nationalities, they'd been the best of friends—colleagues of the mind.

"Excellent, Miranda!" Don Luis clapped sausage-like fingers together, sending the rows of ruffles that hid most of his hands flapping. "Your understanding of Newton's theory is superb. Your grandfather would be very proud."

Tears sprang to Miranda's eyes, and she quickly bent back over the book, skimming her finger down the heavy parchment to find her place. Her grandfather had been dead six months now, and reason dictated she should stop mourning. After all, he'd explained everything to her in the most modern of terms.

She understood that the body was simply made up of muscles and bones and blood that changed color as it picked up air from the lungs. She knew from reading Halley's "Mortality Tables" that the death rate was related to age. And Grandfather had been in his eighty-third year when he succumbed to a disease of the lungs.

"Everything can be explained scientifically." Grandfather had repeated that line often. And over the years, as Miranda first tagged along with him to his laboratory near London, and later helped him with his experiments, she came to accept it as the underlying truth of the world.

But it didn't seem to help her grief.

Miranda sighed and, trying to ignore the smells of bilge water and tar that permeated the below decks, squinted at the page. By the oscillating light of the swaying lantern overhead, she translated the next line of Newton's book from Latin to Spanish. For all his mathematical genius, Don Luis's knowledge of languages was limited to his own.

"Do you suppose Newton thought of —"

A thunderous explosion widened Miranda's dark eyes and stifled her question. The cabin and everything in it tilted precariously, and she grabbed for the book before it slid to the deck. "What was that?"

Don Luis lumbered to the door, yanking it open. The passageway was full of noise and confusion as crew members rushed toward the hatch. Slamming shut the door, he leaned heavily against it. His breath came in deep gulps.

"What is it, Don Luis? Are you all right?" Miranda, still clutching Newton's *Principia* to her breast, fell against the bunk as another blast rocked the ship.

"We're under attack." The Spaniard dragged his perfumed handkerchief down his sweaty face.

"Attack! But who would—"

"Pirates!" Don Luis pushed himself away from the door. "I may understand very little English, but that word I do know."

"Pirates." Miranda's voice was little more than a whisper. She knew there were such things, of course. But they seemed so foreign to her orderly life that the possibility of tangling with any had never occurred to her. What did one do with pirates?

"I should never have brought you on this voyage." Don Luis had regained some of his composure, though his breathing still wheezed from his grim-set mouth.

"It was my decision to come," Miranda reminded him. She tensed for another deafening roar of cannon, but none came. "Perhaps they've gone away."

Another sudden lurching of the ship made her realize how naive her words were.

"I think they must be boarding us." Don Luis's eyes shot to Miranda. "Quickly, you must hide."

Hide. Of course, that would be a solution. Miranda turned full circle, her heavy skirts whipping around her ankles. "Where?" Don Luis's cabin was small and filled with crates of equipment and books, but there was no way she could squeeze between them and the bulkhead.

Loud footfalls in the passageway drew their attention. With a flourish Don Luis swished his sword from the scabbard hanging by his ponderous waist. "I swore to your grandfather to defend you to the death," he announced as the cabin door banged open.

Miranda's mouth opened, but the scream died on her lips. Shock momentarily overcame her fear. The blood drained from her face, and her nails dug into the *Principia's* leather cover.

The pirate was huge. He dwarfed the doorway—the whole cabin—as he stood, booted legs braced apart. His breeches were sin black and skin tight. Above them he wore nothing but a leather doublet that revealed a broad expanse of sweat-slick chest and equally bare, muscled arms. His hair was light and wind-tossed and his face hard and fearsome. Miranda had never seen anyone so large and threatening. She didn't even know people like this existed. The pirate didn't seem to notice her as his dark scowl focused on Don Luis.

Miranda could tell his size intimidated the Spaniard, too, for Don Luis swallowed compulsively, his jowls quivering before he lifted his sword.

The movement jolted Miranda, and the scream she suppressed before came out as a blood-curdling screech. The sound caught the pirate off guard. He swung his head, seeing Miranda for the first time, and riveted her with such a hard stare her mouth clamped shut.

The pirate glared at Miranda, and she could do naught but glare back for what seemed long minutes. Then movement beside her made Miranda turn. At first she couldn't believe what was happening. No one in their right mind would start a fight with this pirate. No one except a man who'd vowed to protect her to the death.

Don Luis lunged forward, trying to simulate the lethal movements of his youth. But age and pastries had taken their toll, and his attack was awkward. Though he aimed for the heart, the tip of his sword did no more than graze the pirate's arm. A slender line of crimson welled on the sun-bronzed skin.

"Ouch! Dammit!" Jack feinted to the side, knocking into the woman. He'd barely gotten over his disappointment that this runt of a Spaniard wasn't de Segovia when the damn fool decided to split him open. Now all he wanted to do was get out of here. But the little Spaniard was yelling at him, and though he'd tried to forget the Spanish he'd learned while a captive, he recognized a few words — like "kill" and "bastard."

Jack tried to lift his hands but his arm ached like hell, and when he glanced down he saw blood streaming into the blond hairs on his forearm. Jack

16

swore again and jumped back as the old man tried to make good on his threats. This time he eluded the cool bite of steel but struck his head on the bulwark in the process.

God, he detested the Spanish.

Jack resisted the urge to yank the pistol from his belt. Instead he sidestepped the next thrust and, catching the little man overextended, delivered a fight-ending right to the older man's jaw. The sword clattered to the wooden deck, followed by the mound of ruffle-covered flesh.

With the tip of his boot Jack rattled the old-fashioned basket-hilted sword across the floor. He was reaching down to help the old man to his feet when he heard a barrage of Spanish behind him, and then a sliver of pain shot through his other arm.

"God's blood!" Jack whirled around on the woman so fast she jerked back. But she still held the sword she'd scooped from the floor. He could tell she was frightened. Her eyes were wide and dark, but she kept the blade pointed at his chest. Unlike her father, or whoever the old man was, she didn't seem inclined to attack him.

Jack stepped forward.

Miranda inched back. Her muscles were unsteady from holding the heavy sword. She longed to just drop it and run. But the pirate would catch her. And even if he didn't, she couldn't leave Don Luis alone with this monster.

The pirate glared down at her, powerful arms folded across his broad chest. Blood seeped from the wounds she and Don Luis had inflicted, but the

17

pirate didn't seem to notice as he watched her from eyes the color of deepest sea.

Then suddenly he lunged to his right. With a small squeal Miranda tried to follow the movement with the weapon. But before she realized her mistake, he lurched back and dove at her.

The sword sailed.

Miranda screamed.

The pirate grabbed.

Trying to evade his hands, Miranda jerked to the side. But her feet tangled in her skirts, and she tumbled to the deck. Caught off balance, the pirate followed.

Air gushed from Miranda's lungs as his massive weight crashed onto her. She tried to breathe and couldn't. Tried to move and couldn't. She was smashed between the unyielding wood at her back and the equally hard weight above her. And that's how she would surely die.

Miranda strove to remember that the body was only bones and muscle . . . that dying could be explained scientifically and thus was nothing to fear. But it didn't help. She was going to die — die lying pinned beneath a pirate — and she didn't want to.

Then suddenly the weight above her shifted. Miranda gulped air into her lungs and blinked back tears of relief. She wasn't going to be crushed to death after all.

But there was still the pirate.

Blowing hanks of ebony hair from her face, Miranda focused on him. He stared down at her. Light twinkled from the gold loop dangling from his left ear. The expression on his face changed from annoyance to amusement while she watched. She liked the annoyance better. How dare he make light of her predicament. If he planned to kill her, then obviously there was nothing she could do. But she wouldn't tolerate being laughed at.

Anger flashed through her. Normally she had an even temperament — her grandfather always said it was because she noticed very little of what happened around her. But he also said when temper finally came, it exploded with a vengeance.

It came now.

"Get off of me, you monster."

"I never could understand Spanish," Jack responded. Actually he thought he caught the word monster.

The woman confirmed it by repeating herself in a language he had no trouble comprehending.

"Well, well, the little Spanish princess speaks the King's good English." Jake couldn't help grinning.

"Of course I do. Now get up." Miranda scrunched up her face and summoning all her strength shoved at his chest with the heels of her hands. His skin was warm and smooth.

He didn't budge.

If anything he settled his body more firmly against hers. Miranda tried to wriggle free, but stopped when she heard his deep chuckle.

"As much as I'd like you to keep that up," he said in a voice that vibrated through the hands still plastered against his chest, "I don't think moving like that is any way to be rid of me."

"Oh." Miranda breathed the word in frustration. She couldn't remember ever being so angry . . . and so totally out of control. This pirate couldn't be explained logically or scientifically, or any other way she knew. And she didn't like it one bit.

Her eyes were dark blue, not brown.

Jack didn't know why he even noticed except that when he'd first caught sight of her, he'd thought they were brown. They were so large and dark, and they were staring at him now with such frustrated anger that he couldn't help being amused. She should be scared. Not that he planned to hurt her, any more than their unceremonious tumble already had. But she didn't know that.

Jack had a reputation to uphold. Fear made most of his prey surrender without a struggle, and Jack liked it that way. Less bloody. But if ships' captains had half the spark of this woman, he'd have nothing but fights to the last man. And there'd be a lot more blood. He glanced down at his wounded arms. Like there was now.

"Do you know who I am, my little Spanish princess?" A healthy dose of fear would do the wench good.

"I'm . . . not . . . a . . . Spanish . . . princess." Miranda tried again to dislodge him, then flopped back to the floor with a grunt. She sucked in her breath. "And I don't care a farthing who you are."

"Well, maybe you should." Her softness was having an unsettling effect on his manhood, and Jack felt sure he should get up and out of here — de Segovia wasn't in this cabin. But some devilish streak made him stay. "I'm—"

"Everythin' all right in here, Cap'n?"

Jack swung his head around to see Phin standing in the doorway. His pistol was trained on the old Spaniard, who was slowly getting to his feet. But his eyes were on Jack and the woman sprawled beneath him.

"Sorry, didn't mean to be interruptin' nothin'. Thought you might need some help." Phin's smile revealed three missing teeth. "Shoulda know'd better."

Jack only glared at his quartermaster as he pushed himself up. The woman ignored the hand he extended down toward her, choosing instead to scramble unaided to her feet. She pushed past Jack, rushing to the old man's side. Jack watched her lower him to a chair and brush her hand gently across his cheek. Then she reached up and tugged his wig straight. Turning, she faced Jack, her expression defiant, her chin high.

"Do what you will. But be quick about it."

Jack's brow arched. She was giving him an order. *Him*. And she looked as if she'd steeled herself for the worst he could offer. A sudden vision of tossing her over his shoulder and taking her on board the *Sea Hawk* flashed into his mind. But he just as quickly dismissed it. He might be a pirate, but he didn't ravish unwilling women. Hell, he didn't have to.

Besides, what would he want with this one anyway? Her gown was dowdy, her hair a mess, and she didn't appear to have enough flesh on her bones to make for an exciting exploration.

But he couldn't seem to break the stare they shared.

"What you plannin' on doin' with them, Cap'n?"

"What?" Something in Phin's expression told Jack he realized his captain was having a difficult time keeping his eyes off the woman. "What?" he repeated, his voice stern.

Phin took no offense. The years had taught him his captain's temper quickly passed. Except when he dealt with the Spanish. With them he had no mercy. "I had me a little talk with this tub's cap'n. And he swore this was the only Spaniard on board." Phin ran his finger lovingly along the pistol's muzzle. "I've a mind he was telling the truth." He gestured toward Don Luis. "This ain't the one, is it?"

"Nay." Jack turned toward the door and Phin, whose mouth gaped open.

"God's teeth, what happened to ye? Yer carved up like a Christmas goose."

Glancing down at his arms, Jack gave a snort. "These two." He jerked his head in Miranda's direction. "They decided to put up a little fight."

"They must've been a handful," Phin cackled. "Never known ye to get so much as a scratch."

"That's about all I have now," Jack insisted, though the cuts stung like hell. But he didn't want the woman to know that.

"If'n ye say so, Cap'n. So what ye want me to do with these Spaniards?"

"Nothing." Jack had turned back to see the fire flash into the woman's eyes when she heard Phin's question.

"Nothin'? We ain't doin' nothin' with them?"

"Them or the entire ship."

"But, Cap'n—"

"We're leaving, Mr. Sharp. Gather the men."

Calling him Mr. Sharp was a sign the captain meant business. But that didn't stop Phin. "The crew ain't goin' to like this none, Cap'n. We've captured this here boat fair and square, we have. And she's as plump as a pigeon." Phin's gaze swung around the cabin. "Just look at them crates. Could be filled with gold and jewels."

"Don't you touch these boxes."

She moved so quickly Jack didn't notice until she stood in front of a crate, her stance protective.

In truth he had already decided to leave the cabin and the ship the way he'd found it—regardless of what Phin or the crew thought. But now, the way the woman acted, his avarice was titillated.

He folded his arms. "What's in the crates?"

Her chin notched higher. "Nothing you'd understand."

Not nothing of value, or nothing you'd want, but nothing you'd understand. The woman was daft to speak to him so. Again he considered tossing her over his shoulder, but this time his imagination had him dumping her over the rail into the sea. He pushed the thought aside. When he spoke his voice vibrated from the overhead beams of the small cabin. "I asked what was in the boxes. In that box?" Jack pointed to the crate she shielded with her body.

Blood drained from her face, and Jack suppressed a smile of satisfaction. He frightened the wench but good. Yet her next words made his brows draw together in a frown.

"It's one of Leeuwenhoek's microscopes."

For a moment Jack figured she was speaking Spanish again. But then he realized he understood a few of the words: "it's one of," and the word "microscope" sounded familiar . . . he thought. He had no idea what it was, of course. Educating him hadn't been one of de Segovia's priorities.

"For studying animalcules," Miranda supplied as if she could read his mind.

Jack's eyes snapped from his contemplation of the wooden crate to meet the deep blue of the woman's. "I see," he said, though in truth he didn't understand at all. His jaw clenched. "And where do you find these animalcules?" She must be talking about some kind of animal he'd never heard of before. Probably something that lived in the jungle or—

"Oh, they're everywhere. In a pond, the ocean, even the water you drink."

"God's teeth, what's she sayin'?" Phin exclaimed. "We got maggots in the biscuits true enough. But I ain't never took a gulp of nothin' with animals swimming in it. I'd a seen and fished 'em out."

Miranda laughed despite her predicament. The smaller pirate seemed so appalled that she had accused him of drinking animals. "No. You don't understand. We can't see animalcules."

"Then, how does ye know they're there?"

Excellent question, Jack thought, exchanging a

24

smug smile with his first mate.

"Let me explain. You can't see them with just your eyes. But with a microscope, one of Antonie van Leeuwenhoek's microscopes, they're quite clear. Leeuwenhoek uses a single lens, and he grinds it —"

"Enough!" Jack's bellow startled Phin, the woman and the little Spaniard huddled in the chair. And it certainly got their attention. This was ridiculous. The woman was lecturing using the same tone his tutor in Scotland had. And Phin was hanging on her every word like an enthralled schoolboy. They were pirates, by damn, and they weren't going to listen to a bunch of bilge water about invisible animals.

"Get above and gather the men. Remember I want no looting."

"But, Cap'n. Don't ye think we could take that microscope thing? I'd sure like to get me a look at them little animals."

"Nay!" Jack took a deep breath which didn't dissipate his anger. "We're not taking anything. And for God's sake, Phin, there are no little animals."

"Yes there are. You can see them very clearly with —" The big pirate speared her with a look that made Miranda stop. What was she doing anyway? She didn't want to educate a band of pirates. And she certainly didn't want them stealing her microscope.

And to her great relief, it appeared they were going to leave her things and Don Luis . . . and herself . . . in peace. Miranda watched the pirates back out of the cabin. First the small dirty one. Then the big pirate captain. His eyes met hers. And she thought she saw his expression soften before he slammed the door shut.

Knees that had held her firmly during the encounter with the pirate suddenly turned to mush. Miranda grasped hold of the crate she had protected only moments ago.

"Mon Dieu!" Don Luis slumped farther into the chair. "I thought for certain they would kill us."

"Yes," Miranda agreed. "I feared that myself."

"And with good reason. When I saw what that barbarian did to you . . . knocking you to the floor. Are you sure you're all right? Your face is white as a ghost."

"Yes." Miranda managed a weak smile to prove it. "Are you hurt?"

"No." Don Luis sat as tall as his short frame would allow. With deliberate care he straightened his wig and smoothed the ruffles at his neck. "It will take more than two freebooters to injure me."

Don Luis was regaining his fuss and fluster, and Miranda's smile now came without effort. She pushed away from the box and retrieved the *Principia* from the floor. It had survived the fray as well as she and Don Luis.

When she sat at the table the elderly Spaniard leaned forward and patted her hands. "In a moment I shall go on deck to see how the rest of the ship fared. In the meantime I think we should put this entire incident behind us."

"Oh, I agree." Miranda carefully opened Newton's book. The neat, orderly words explaining the

26

laws of motion calmed and comforted her. Newton explained scientifically the attraction between the Earth and its moon. Universal gravitation.

Miranda shut her eyes and tried to fill her mind with Newton's words. But she couldn't concentrate. A large, golden pirate kept intruding into her thoughts. For a moment when she had been squashed on the floor beneath him, she'd felt stirrings of something close to attraction.

To hide her gasp of shock at this realization, Miranda coughed delicately into her handkerchief. How could she feel anything but loathing for the pirate? He was crude and detestable. Arrogant and ignorant. It just didn't make sense. It couldn't be explained logically.

Thus it didn't exist.

Satisfied that she had solved the problem, Miranda pushed the pirate from her mind and concentrated on something she could explain and understand: gravitational attraction.

Chapter Two

"Is it as you expected?"

Miranda swiped a strand of windswept hair from her face and shrugged. Turning she smiled at Don Luis as he joined her at the rail. She'd clambered on deck early this morn to watch the ship sail into the harbor at Charles Town. "Not really." Her gaze returned to the curved peninsula of land jutting into the harbor as she slipped easily into the older man's native tongue. "But, then, I didn't really know what to expect." Lifting her hand, she shaded her eyes from the glare of the sun-shimmered water. A stiff breeze filled the sails as the ship skimmed toward land.

"I've read Sanford's accounts of his exploration in '66, and my father wrote me of Charles Town several times, but . . . ," Miranda paused as she clutched the polished rail. "What if he doesn't want me here? I think perhaps I should have waited for his reply to my letter."

"Nonsense. He will be delighted to see you. And the town does not seem so primitive. Look! A

28

church spire. Where the Church puts down roots, civilization blossoms."

Miranda laughed at his attempt to cheer her. Don Luis didn't understand the apprehension she felt about seeing her father. He seemed to think her more worried about living conditions in the New World. He also was probably a little confused about the church spire they saw.

Don Luis was a devout Catholic. Though the creed of the Carolinas followed many of John Locke's views, including religious tolerance, Miranda doubted the town had a Catholic church. Spain and England might be allies now against the French, but animosity still ran strong.

Which made Don Luis's friendship with her grandfather and her all the more rare and special. "I wish you could stay here with me." Miranda grabbed the old Spaniard's hand and clutched it between her own.

"You will be fine here with your father."

"But—"

"And we will exchange letters. I will tell you of my planet sightings. And you—"

"—will use my microscope to observe animalcules," Miranda finished, smiling. "And I will study the flora. Just look at all the strange trees." Miranda's expression brightened as she scanned the lush, verdant foliage nestled against the walled town. "I will record my findings—"

"And I will send them off to the Royal Society." Don Luis shook his head, sending his long curls twirling. "A pity you cannot take credit yourself

29

with the Society simply because you are a woman."

Miranda shrugged. "Perhaps someday. For now I shall learn what I can. We're a long way from England and the Royal Society." And right now that august body was the last thing on her mind. She'd come nearly three thousand miles to be with a father whom she scarcely remembered. A father who had left her mother and her when Miranda was no more than a babe in arms to come to the New World. A father who may want her no more now than he did then.

The bellowing of orders and the scurrying of men to obey caught Miranda's attention. Glancing up toward the web of rigging she saw the tars working to trim the sails and took a deep breath. For better or worse, she was in the Carolinas.

"Oh, please do be careful with that. It contains a most valuable microscope. The lenses were ground by van Leeuwenhoek himself." The sailor looked at Miranda as if she'd spoken a foreign language, though she was quite certain she'd used English. His expression betrayed annoyance, but he did seem to take more care as he settled the crate on his brawny shoulder.

Miranda followed him across the plank, pausing a moment as her legs adjusted to solid ground. The dock was packed with men, and Miranda led the sailor, weaving through the crowd toward the cart she'd hired.

Don Luis stood nearby, shaded from the sun by a

huge tree. He fanned his lace-trimmed handkerchief in a feeble attempt to stir the muggy air . . . or perhaps discourage the pestering insects.

"It is warm," Miranda conceded after the tar deposited her microscope in the cart and returned to the ship for her other luggage. She paused a moment under the tree's arched branches. "Do you suppose it's always this hot?" Miranda couldn't help thinking of her secluded garden in Essex. A clear, cool stream meandered down from the wood, emptying into a smooth-as-glass pond.

A pond full of tiny animalcules that couldn't even be seen until placed under the microscope.

Miranda glanced about until her gaze locked on a stagnant pool of marshy water. Just thinking of all the tiny creatures living in a drop of that water made her eyes shine. Her step as she crossed the dock toward the ship was livelier, and she could almost ignore the perspiration soaking into her stays.

Her concentration was such that she missed noticing the captain of the ship she'd sailed on until he called her name. "There she is. That's Mistress Chadwick."

Miranda glanced toward the captain, but her gaze strayed to the man beside him—a man looking at her with blue eyes nearly the same shade as her own. She stood rooted to the spot.

"Miranda?" The man came forward. He loomed over her, though she was considered tall for a woman. He was tanned by the sun and robust. The face seemed fuller and more lined than the likeness painted on china she wore pinned to

31

her bodice. And he appeared stunned.

"Yes." Miranda clutched her hands together and wondered if her father noticed the quiver in her voice. She'd known little fear while traveling thousands of miles across the vast ocean. Even facing the pirate hadn't caused as much anxiety as discovering this man's reaction to her.

Grandfather had told her the story of how she and her mother, Grandfather's daughter, had come to stay with him. Of how her father had left England after the beheading of Charles I. Her father was a stanch Royalist and adventurer, and he had gone to Barbados in search of a better life for his young family. He'd planned to send for his wife and small daughter, but before he did, Miranda's mother died. Then Henry Chadwick had left the crowded sugar island for the Carolinas and apparently given up all thoughts of sending for his daughter.

Miranda swallowed and wiped her hands down her best padded petticoat. Through her lashes she saw her father studying her as closely as she examined something under the microscope.

"But . . . but, what are you doing here? How?" For someone known throughout the Carolinas as a man of many words, Henry Chadwick was stumbling mightily.

"Grandfather died," Miranda blurted out, then riveted her eyes to the dusty street. "I can return to England . . . if you'd rather." Miranda bit her bottom lip. The thoughts of spending another two months entombed in a tiny cabin were not nearly as intolerable as her father rejecting her. And with him just standing there, staring at her, that was precisely how she felt.

Perhaps Grandfather had been wrong those years ago when Miranda had questioned him about her father's reasons for leaving her. "Your father loves you very much," Grandfather had said. "But he couldn't stay in England, and he didn't think the Carolinas any place for a small child. Especially with your mother gone."

Miranda believed him then because in her heart she wanted it to be true. When years passed with hardly a word from her father she blamed the primitive conditions he must face. After all, Grandfather had said her father loved her.

But now as she stood in this alien land, her only friend a Spaniard whose welcome was even more dubious than her own, Miranda remembered how ill-equipped her grandfather had been to understand people's feelings. He hadn't meant to be. But his mind was usually on some lofty scientific experiment or —

Powerful arms engulfed Miranda, and she looked up in time to realize she was being hauled against her father's chest. "I never thought to see you again," he mumbled into her hair. "You are so like your mother."

As abruptly as she was pulled into his hug, Miranda was deposited back on the dusty road. Her father smiled down at her, and she could do naught but return the expression, her heart lighter than since before her grandfather's death.

"Come. We will go to my house and talk. You mustn't be out in this sun for long." Henry's arm wrapped around Miranda's shoulders as he led her away from the wharf.

"Wait. My things and—" Miranda motioned back toward the cart.

"Amos will bring them along directly."

"But they mustn't be broken."

"Don't worry. I've not been away from society long enough to forget how you ladies love your trinkets."

Miranda dug in her heels. " 'Tis not trinkets. I've brought a microscope with me, and though it's very delicate, it's come unscathed through gales at sea and even pirate attacks."

"Pirates!"

"Yes, pirates." Miranda beamed at the concerned expression on her father's face. But she didn't want him to worry needlessly. "They are loathsome creatures. But have no concern. They didn't harm my microscope."

Henry shook his head to clear his mind. He hadn't a clue what she was talking about except that she had risked her life coming to him. "Are you all right? Did these pirates harm you."

"No . . . well, actually one of them did knock me to the floor . . . sort of. But we thwarted him."

"We?"

"Oh, how could I have forgotten?" Miranda swirled around in a flutter of skirts and rushed back to Don Luis. Tugging on his arm she pulled the elderly man toward her father. "In the excitement of

34

seeing you I—" Miranda threw her hands wide. "This is the man who helped save me from the monster pirate. Father, this is Don Luis de Mancera."

Miranda turned to the Spaniard and introduced her father to him, using his native language. When she looked back at her father his smile of welcome was gone, and his eyes, so jovial moments earlier, were as hard as ice.

"He's a Spaniard!"

Miranda's gaze flew around the dock. Her father's pronouncement had captured the attention of several men in the vicinity, and they pressed forward to hear more. Stepping closer to the little man, she laid her hand on his flounced sleeve. "Don Luis is my friend."

"Miranda. In the Carolinas we have nothing but trouble or threats of trouble from the Spanish. I don't think—"

"I can assure you Don Luis will not do you or the Carolinas any harm."

"Aye but—"

"He's my friend, Papa. He was Grandfather's friend. And he accompanied me here. Protected me from the pirate."

Henry stood still for a moment longer; then shrugging he bowed toward the visitor. "All right. I just hope Jack never learns of this." Henry was a man who knew when defeat was at hand. And he recognized it the moment his daughter had looked up at him.

"What do you mean? Who is Jack?"

"Never mind." Again Henry took his daughter's

arm. "Your friend is welcome in my home."

"Thank you, Papa." Miranda translated her father's greeting to Don Luis, carefully deleting any parts that might hurt the older man's pride.

Don Luis didn't stay long. In little over a sennight the ship was unloaded and its hold filled with rice. And Don Luis sailed for St. Augustine, anxious to get his sightings of Jupiter from the New World and compare them with those he'd taken in Madrid.

By the time he left, Miranda wondered why she had ever doubted her father's love for her. Henry couldn't do enough for his daughter. Her room on the upper level of his Tradd Street home was beautifully furnished. He brought light silks and linens from his warehouse and, though Miranda protested, hired a woman to make her a new wardrobe—one more suitable to the warm climate.

Henry was just as generous with his time. He and Miranda spent hours sitting on the piazza, relaxing in the cool southern breeze, talking.

"We have so many years to make up for," Henry said. "You must tell me everything of your life in England."

And she did. He listened intently, though Miranda was not certain he completely understood, as she described the experiments she and her grandfather had performed.

When she finished Henry leaned his chair against the stucco wall and crossed his arms over the paunch of his stomach. "But what of society. Your grandfather was an earl. Didn't he take you to court?"

"Why, no. We lived quietly in the country except of course when Grandfather went to London for meetings of the Royal Society." Miranda smiled at his perplexed expression. "We had visitors, of course. Issac Newton, Nehemiah Grew, the botanist—"

"But no balls? No parties?"

"Why, no." Miranda's shoulders rounded. Her father didn't seem pleased.

Henry pushed out of his chair and walked across the porch to lean against the white-washed pillar. "I left you in England because I thought your grandfather was better prepared to raise you than I." Shaking his head, he glanced back at Miranda. "I knew of this . . . this hobby of his, but I never thought he'd let it take over his life . . . and yours."

"But the study of science is fascinating." Miranda's eyes shone, and she absently brushed a curl from her cheek. "There is so much to learn, and though we already know more than you can imagine, I think there is still—"

"What of marriage?"

"What of it?" Her hands fell limply to her lap.

"Don't you wish to marry and bear children?"

"Well, yes, I suppose so." Miranda cocked her head to the side. "I really never thought about it."

"Never thought about it!" Henry leaned back on his heels, silently cursing the old fool who'd reared her—and himself for allowing it. But one look at her wide-eyed expression told him she didn't see

37

anything remotely strange about not considering marriage.

All these years since he'd left her, Henry had envisioned Miranda in England, feted at balls, collecting suitors by the score. Instead she'd been hunched over a microscope discussing Lord knew what with a man in his dotage.

His dear departed wife would have had a fit had she known. For once in his life Henry was glad she hadn't lived to see this.

Thank goodness Miranda had come to him before it was too late. Softening his voice, Henry reached for her hand. "Someone as lovely as you will have her choice of young men in the Carolinas."

Miranda wasn't sure she wanted her choice of men, but she did wonder at her father's description of her as lovely. Was he just acting the indulgent father? Certainly no one had ever implied her appearance was anything exceptional before. Oh, she realized her features were even, and her skin clear . . . she was not difficult to look at. But beyond that, no mention was ever made of her face. Grandfather had often spoken of her mind, praising her logical thinking, so he hadn't been adverse to flattery. But lovely. . . . Miranda decided to spend some time in front of the cheval glass in her room this evening. Perhaps she needed to make a closer examination of herself.

Had the pirate thought she was lovely?

Miranda didn't have a clue where that had come from. It was just there, suddenly in her brain, the way thoughts of him had managed to slip in at the most unexpected and annoying moments since she'd first seen him. Miranda shook her head in an effort to dislodge his image.

"What's wrong? You look quite distressed."

Miranda stared up at her father, who was watching her with concern. " 'Tis nothing."

Henry pulled his chair over beside his daughter. "It doesn't look like nothing." His voice gentled. "Does the prospect of marrying upset you?"

"No. At least I don't think so." That was something else she'd have to ponder when time allowed.

"Then what?"

"I was thinking about the pirate," Miranda answered honestly, then wished she hadn't. How would her father react if he knew how often that barbarian invaded her mind? "What do you suppose makes a man become such a loathsome creature?" Miranda hastened to add.

"Greed, I imagine." Henry looked out toward the bay, wishing he didn't know the answer to that question quite so well. "I'm sorry you had to endure the pirate attack."

Henry had nothing against pirates, but he couldn't erase from his mind the vision of his daughter suffering at the knave's hand. He also couldn't figure out who the freebooter could be. He had a rather intimate knowledge of the pirates who cruised these waters, and none of them fit the description Miranda had given him. Henry wished he'd thought to question the ship's captain before he left, or better yet, he wished Jack were here.

Yes, Jack would know who'd dared to touch

Miranda. And he'd take care of the bastard, too. As a favor to his partner, Jack would do it.

But Jack wasn't here. And Henry had no idea when he'd return. With a sigh Henry settled back in the chair. "Tell me again about this pirate who attacked you." Might as well have all the information correct for when Jack sailed back to Charles Town.

"I told you, father, I don't remember much. I was very frightened." Miranda took a deep breath and repeated the description of events as she remembered them. "He was large . . . nay huge, with evil eyes and a sneer that would make you quake in your shoes. And he threatened to take my microscope. At least one of them did," she finished, folding her hands in her lap. This last was enough to make them Miranda's enemy.

"And you say the pirate captain knocked you to the deck?"

"Yes . . . well, sort of knocked me."

"Then he tried to kill you?"

"Squash me," Miranda corrected.

"But you can't remember anything else about his appearance?"

Miranda closed her eyes, and a vision of the pirate captain swam before her lids. He was grinning that arrogant smile, and his golden hair framed his bronzed face. He looked wild and savage and very handsome, and it was the most illogical thing in the world for her to think so.

Miranda's eyes snapped open. "No, Papa, I can remember nothing else." Standing, Miranda moved toward the door. "I think I'll read awhile before dinner. Don't worry about the pirates. I'm certain we'll never see them again."

"'Tis good to be home, Phin." Jack stood on the quarterdeck watching his crew dock at the Charles Town wharf.

"Aye, Cap'n, for a while anyway." Phineas grinned. "Gives the ladies a thrill."

"A thrill is it?" Jack chuckled. "Just make sure you keep your thrilling to the wenches in the tavern. We don't want another incident like Barbados."

"Aw, Cap'n, weren't my fault the woman was wild for me."

"Apparently her husband thought so."

Phin screwed up his wrinkled face. "We got away, didn't we?"

"Barely."

"What's this. Ye ain't goin' soft on me now, is ye?"

"Hell no!" Jack glared down at his quartermaster. "But I don't want anything to cause us trouble here. Knowing the collector of the king's revenue is in town makes my neck itch." Jack rubbed at the skin above his Steinkirk cravat.

"Yer thinkin' a John Sparkes again, ain't ye?"

"I'm thinking I don't want to end up hanging from the gibbet at Execution Block."

"God's teeth, Cap'n, yer too smart for that."

"Smart or no, I want the cargo unloaded as quickly as possible. No sense waiting for the revenuer to come snooping around."

41

"You've the right a it there, Cap'n. He might start wondering where we come by all them Spanish gold pieces and bolts of silk."

Jack's grin showed a row of even white teeth. "He might at that." Pushing away from the rail, Jack strode across the deck. "I'm off to see Chadwick and let him know what we've brought him."

"Give him me regards."

"Most assuredly." Jack swept his quartermaster a bow, then caught his eye and winked. "And you save some of the wenches for me. I've a mind to give one or two a thrill myself."

Stepping onto the quay, Jack took a deep breath. The smells of puff mud and oleander mingled with the tangy scent of salt air. It reminded him of the first time he arrived in the Carolinas. He had been a lad of ten, and though the voyage from Scotland had been harsh, Jack could barely control his excitement.

"A new land. A new beginning," his father had said as the colonists settled at Port Royal, south of Charles Town. But the new beginning had ended suddenly. And the new land had run red with the blood of Jack's family.

Jack forced the memories from his mind as he moved along the crushed oystershell path onto Water Street. It did no good to lament the past. He had realized that years ago. Besides, it was a beautiful day, his hold was full of goods that would make him even wealthier than he already was, and by the reception he received from the good citizens of Charles Town, no one cared how he came by those goods.

Jack smiled at a local matron who bid him good-day and turned up Tradd Street. The breeze from the harbor cooled the air as he knocked on the door of Henry Chadwick's single house.

"Why, Master Jack, is that you?"

"And just who else would it be?" Jack swung Henry's servant, Chloe, into a big hug that had the old woman clutching her turbanned head.

"You put me down this instant, Master Jack. Master Henry, he done told you I don't take to pestering." Her toothless grin belied her words as Jack set her back on the floor.

"Is Henry home?" Jack followed the black woman onto the piazza.

"Sure is. And anxious to see you, I'll bet."

"Why so?" Henry Chadwick was a good friend, and together they'd made a lot of money; but Chloe seemed to indicate there was something beyond the welcome he normally received.

"Oh, I think Master Henry be wanting to tell you for hisself," Chloe said, before knocking softly on the library door.

Henry's expression when he entered the room confirmed Jack's notion that something was amiss.

"Jack!" Henry pushed himself from his leather chair. After pulling Jack into the room, the older man shut the door firmly. Then turning he examined Jack critically from the neatly brushed golden hair that skimmed the broad shoulders of his royal blue silk waistcoat, then down the matching breeches and gleaming black boots.

43

Rocking back on his heels, Henry let out a sigh. "I don't think she'll suspect the truth."

"Which is?"

"That you're a pirate, my boy." Henry's tone was hushed. "You really look very little like one, you know."

Jack's laughter rang through the large room, and Henry rushed to his side, making shushing noises.

"Quiet yourself. She'll hear you."

"Who will hear me? What's going on here, Henry? I may not look like a pirate, but you're certainly acting like the fool."

His expression indignant, Henry indicated a wing chair and, after Jack sat, pulled his own closer. "My daughter is here."

"Your daughter?"

"Yes, I'm sure I've told you of her." Henry leaned forward, forearms on knees. "She lived with my wife's father, Lord Waverly."

"So why is she here?"

"Her grandfather died." Henry held up his hands. "I don't know exactly why she came, but the fact is she did. And she thinks I'm an honest merchant."

Jack's brow arched. "You *are* a merchant."

"I said honest, Jack. Miranda was reared very . . ." For lack of a better word, Henry chose, "gently. She knows nothing about the harsher realities of life."

"Like greed and avarice?" Jack questioned sardonically.

"I was referring to the Navigation Acts and the colonies' inability to import even the most basic of products without paying larcenous prices."

"Ah, those realities."

"Save your sarcastic wit for another time." Henry bounded from his chair and began pacing in front of the hearth. "I'm quite in earnest about this."

"That's obvious." Jack's remark earned him another frustrated look from Henry. "Would you light somewhere? God's blood, what are you worried about?" Now Jack was on his feet. "Did you expect I'd introduce myself to your daughter as Gentleman Jack Blackstone, infamous pirate and scourge of the seven seas?"

"Would you keep your voice down?" Henry hissed. "I simply don't want her to know."

"Then, I swear by the pirate's creed, no talk of walking the plank or plundering the Spanish Main will pass these lips."

"Would you be serious for once?"

Jack held up a placating hand. "I am," he announced solemnly. "After all, it's hardly in my best interest to announce myself a pirate." He felt that familiar itching about his neck but resisted the urge to scratch.

"Good." With a sigh Henry sank into his chair.

Amazed at the other man's obvious relief, Jack settled across from him. "Did you really suppose I'd cause you a problem with this?"

"No." Henry dropped his face into his hands. "It's just that I left Miranda when she was a babe."

"I know the story. It was for the best."

"But I've a notion she thinks I abandoned her."

"Did she say that?"

Henry shook his head. "Perhaps it's my guilty conscience making me think she feels that way."

"Henry, you—"

"I don't wish to discuss my reasons for leaving her with her grandfather. The fact is she's here now, and I don't want her to know about me."

Jack paused a moment and studied his friend's determined face, then nodded. "She won't learn anything from me. But I still think you're being too hard on yourself. You're not exactly a—"

"You don't understand. Miranda despises pirates. And with good reason. Her ship was attacked."

"Was she . . . hurt?" Jack didn't know how else to ask a father about the myriad things that could happen to a young girl at the hand of some pirates. Not him, of course. Jack prided himself on his treatment of the fairer sex. He might be a pirate, but no woman sacrificed her virtue to him . . . unless by her choice.

"No, thank God. From what I understand, another passenger saved her from . . . well from. . . . I don't like to think about what might have happened." Henry's gaze found Jack's. "And Miranda doesn't like to talk about it."

"That's understandable."

"But I'd like your help in discovering who did this to Miranda."

"And perhaps in meting out a bit of punishment," Jack added, his eyes twinkling. Henry was acting more like himself.

Henry smiled. "Perhaps. The problem is, I've

very little to go on. Miranda's description of the blackguard doesn't match anyone I know of. Are there any new pirates sailing the area?"

"Not that I'm aware of. But then I've been down in the Caribbean for over a fortnight. What does this man look like?"

Jack listened to the description and shook his head. "Huge and fierce 'tisn't much to go on, but I'll ask around down by the waterfront. 'Tis amazing how much the tavern wenches know," Jack said with a grin.

Henry's expression matched Jack's. "I'm sure if there's anything to be found, you're the man to do it."

"Quite right. Now, am I to have the pleasure of meeting this daughter of yours?"

"Of course." Henry slapped his knees and stood. But before he was halfway to the door, he paused. "Jack, I don't need to remind you that Miranda is my daughter and not . . . not —"

"A tavern wench?" Jack's brow arched.

"Well, you do have a reputation with the ladies."

"Only the willing ones." Jack hurried on before Henry could interrupt. "And certainly not the daughter of my dear friend."

Jack almost laughed at the relieved expression on Henry's face. He could only imagine that this daughter of his was some straitlaced prude to cause Henry so much despair. But for his friend's sake, he'd be cordial and charming — until he could politely make his excuses and leave. There was a certain wench down by the wharf who he was interested in getting more than information from.

While Jack waited for Henry's daughter he absently wandered about the library. The windows were open, letting in a pleasant breeze. As he passed by a mahogany table, Jack noticed a new addition to the room. It was fairly small and cylindrical, and he'd never seen anything like it before.

"What's this?" he asked, running his finger down the smooth side.

Henry glanced over his shoulder. "That's Miranda's. What does she call it? Ah, yes, a microscope."

"A what?" Jack scratched at his neck.

"A microscope. It's for studying — What's wrong with you?"

But before Jack could answer, the door opened. Miranda stepped into the room, a smile curving her mouth. It froze when she saw her father's guest. She looked at Jack, and Jack looked at her. For an instant she seemed unable to comprehend the obvious. Then her eyes widened, and her hand fluttered to her throat. "My God! It's the pirate!"

Chapter Three

"This is your daughter?"

"What's the pirate doing here?"

"How could you, Jack?"

Three voices, raised in agitation, rang through the room.

Miranda looked as if she might faint.

Henry bustled to help her to the settee.

And Jack loosened the cravat that suddenly seemed too tight around his neck.

"I don't understand." Miranda pushed against her father as he tried to force her down on the cushions. "What is he doing here? Chloe said I was to meet a friend of yours."

"There must be some mistake." Henry glanced around frantically, then grabbed a bill of lading from his desk and used it to fan his daughter.

"There's no mistake." Miranda yanked the paper from his hand and tossed it to the floor. "He's the pirate I told you about."

Two pairs of eyes, one set accusing, the other

questioning, turned on Jack. All he could do was shrug.

"You see. He isn't even trying to deny what he did to me."

"What I did to you?" Jack took a menacing step forward, annoyed when Henry jumped up to block his way. "I didn't do one damn thing to you."

"Now, Jack, there's no call for profanity."

"The hell there isn't," Jack said, before stalking out the door.

"Are you going to let him get away?" Miranda stood abruptly. "He's a criminal and needs to be punished."

"Yes, well, um . . ." Henry didn't think he'd ever been more perplexed. "Will you be all right if I leave you?"

"Of course. I'm perfectly fine. Just do something about the pirate. One of his men threatened to steal my microscope."

With those words echoing in his ears, Henry hurried out the door. He found Jack pacing the piazza. "What did you do to my daughter?" Henry demanded without preamble.

Jack looked up, a scowl darkening his features. "I didn't do one damn thing to your precious daughter."

"Well, she said you—"

"I don't give a damn what she said. What in the hell are you doing with a Spanish daughter?"

"She's not Spanish."

"Well, she sure as hell speaks Spanish."

50

"She speaks English and French, Latin, too." At Jack's disbelieving expression, Henry continued, "Her grandfather taught her languages . . . among other things," he finished in a mumble. Straightening his shoulders, Henry advanced on Jack. "But that's not the important thing here. What you did to my daughter is."

"No!" Jack faced Henry toe to toe. "The important thing is why you don't believe me when I say I didn't do anything to her." With that, Jack turned on his heel and slammed out the door into the bright sunshine.

He was feeling sorry for himself.

Jack recognized the symptoms. Knew he should do something about it. Chose not to.

His chair tilted against the wall in the small waterfront tavern, he swirled his ale in the pewter mug, then took a healthy swig. He'd been here for . . . hell, he didn't know how long he'd been here. But he'd consumed a fair amount of ale. Not enough, but a fair amount nonetheless.

Jack smacked the mug onto the rough-hewn table. Sitting here getting drunk was ridiculous. He should be readying the *Sea Hawk* to sail away from Charles Town . . . forever.

Once Henry's daughter finished with his reputation, he'd no longer be welcome in the town no matter how much the people wanted the cargo he brought. The good citizens could overlook his true profession so long as it didn't slap them in the face. But once someone started screeching, "pirate" — and Henry's daughter could certainly do that — they would ignore it no longer.

If he didn't get out of here, he'd end up like old John Sparkes. Jack untwisted the cravat from around his neck. He'd already yanked off his fancy silk waistcoat. It lay across the table in a wrinkled heap.

Slamming the front chair legs to the floor, Jack shook his head. He probably should walk over to Meeting Street and say good-bye to his uncle. Then he needed to sail away.

Jack took another gulp of ale and let his head fall into his palms. Lord he didn't want to leave Charles Town like this.

"What's the problem, Jack?" A pair of hands slid sensually inside the opening of his shirt. "I'll warrant it's not something Lottie can't fix." The hands slipped lower as Jack raised his head.

"See." Lottie rubbed her full breasts against Jack's shoulder as she skimmed her fingers over the bulge forming in his breeches. "You're feeling better already."

"That I am, Lottie girl, but I'm afraid—"

"Jack! I have to talk to you."

Jack looked up with drink-blurred eyes to see Henry standing before him, nervously twisting his hat brim. A stoic expression tightened his handsome features. "You come to arrest me, Henry?"

"Don't be ridiculous." Henry's glance strayed to Lottie, who was still working her wiles on Jack. "I need to talk to you in private."

Jack's hand covered Lottie's, and he shifted on the hard chair to relieve some of the pressure in his groin. "Be a good girl, Lottie, and get my *friend* here a drink."

"But Jack . . ." The girl's petulant mouth grazed Jack's ear. "I was thinking you and me could go upstairs."

"Maybe later," Jack hedged, though he doubted he'd have the time for more than a hasty departure from town.

"I've looked for you everywhere," Henry said while scraping a chair across the floor to sit huddled beside Jack.

"I've been here."

"So I see. How much did you drink?" Henry fluttered his hand in a dismissing motion. "Never mind. That's not important." He blew out a puff of air. "I spoke with Miranda."

Jack arched his brow. "And that *is* important?"

"Enough of your sarcasm, Jack. She means to see you tried as a pirate."

"Well, I hate to disappoint your charming daughter, but I plan to be long gone before that can happen." Jack's eyes shot to meet the older man's. "Unless of course she sent you to see that I don't leave."

"Don't be a fool." Henry released another puff of air and mopped his damp brow. "Though I am supposed to be seeking out the constable."

"What?" Jack's fist smashed into the table, shaking the wood and spilling the drink that Henry had yet to touch.

"Keep your voice down." Henry gave a nervous look over his shoulder. Most of the tavern's patrons were seafaring men, louder and more boisterous even than Jack. "I'm not doing it."

"Well, that's a relief." Jack emptied his ale, backhanding his mouth and keeping his gaze on Henry.

"Scoff if you will, but my daughter intends to see justice served. Something about laws of science or logic . . . or some damn thing like that."

Jack picked up his waistcoat and tried to smooth out the wrinkles. "Well, let her try to serve justice when I'm out on the high seas." Giving up on the wrinkles, Jack tossed the jacket over his arm and tried to stand. Henry's arm stopped him.

"You can't leave."

Flopping back down, Jack stared at Henry in shock. "What the devil are you saying? I'll not stay and have my neck stretched because of that little hellion you call a daughter."

Henry's back stiffened. "Watch what you say about Miranda, Jack."

"Lord save me from fathers."

"You'll understand some day when you become one," Henry shot back.

"And please, Lord, save me from that."

Henry leaned forward. "Would you be serious?"

"Hell, I *am* being serious! Your daughter is planning to see me hanged, and I'm seriously planning to leave." Jack stood. "Come down to the pier with me and we'll work out what you owe me for the goods I brought. I'll wager my men have unloaded a goodly amount."

"No."

"No?" Jack slid back into his seat. "What do you mean no?" He bent till he was nose to nose with Henry. "My men risked their lives for our cargo, and I intend to pay them."

"Oh, I'll pay you. Haven't I always?"

Henry ignored Jack's mumbled comment about that being before fatherdom. "I meant no you can't leave. At least not now. That won't solve anything."

"It will sure as hell solve the problem of my elongated neck."

"Well, what about me?" Henry's voice squeaked on the last word.

"You?" Jack shook his head. "You aren't a pirate."

"True enough, but I deal with pirates—mostly you," Henry added with an accusing look.

"And made yourself quite wealthy by doing it."

"I know, I know." Henry wiped his face again. "But the fact is, Miranda doesn't know. She thinks I'm a respectable merchant. She admires me."

Jack said nothing. He just waited for Henry to continue and tried to ignore the prickly sensation at the base of his neck.

"If she goes to the king's revenuer, he will investigate . . . even if you're gone. And I'll be implicated for sure."

Jack studied his friend for a moment, unable to stop feeling a bit sorry for him. But when all was said and done, Henry would receive nothing more than a mild reprimand—if that. He certainly wasn't in jeopardy of being hanged. Jack told him as much . . . but it didn't seem to brighten his mood.

"But Miranda will find out."

Jack sighed and leaned back. "She's your daughter. She won't believe it if others speak ill of you."

"No, no." Henry shook his head. "I couldn't bear for her to hear rumors about me."

"Then, tell her yourself. Make a clean breast of it and ask for her forgiveness." Jack had found this method of dealing with women effective in the past, but he could tell from Henry's reaction he didn't fancy the idea.

"That wouldn't work. You saw the way she feels about pirates." Henry had the decency to lower his eyes sheepishly. "She thinks they're the scourge of the earth."

Jack took a deep breath, trying to keep calm. "As I see it, it's about time that daughter of yours faced the realities of life."

"I fear she is a little . . . how should I say this—"

"Odd?" Jack offered.

"I most assuredly wasn't going to call my daughter that. After all, she did have a terrible shock. You did attack her ship . . . her English ship. And knocked her to the deck. Jack, that doesn't seem at all like you."

"I didn't knock her; we fell. And as for my attacking her ship, it wasn't exactly an attack;

they gave up. And when I saw your precious daughter she was with a Spaniard."

"Um," Henry agreed, "Don Luis." Henry inched his chair closer. "But this discussion is getting us nowhere. I've thought about the dilemma. And I think I have the answer to our problem."

"Our problem?"

Henry ignored the skeptical arch of Jack's brow. "I want you to kidnap Miranda."

"What? Are you insane?"

"Keep your voice down, and please resume your seat."

Jack absently righted the chair he'd knocked over when he bounded to his feet, and flopped back into it.

"Now, I know you think my plan sounds bizarre, but—"

"Why in the hell do you want me to kidnap your daughter?" Jack whispered his words when Henry shushed him.

"If you'll just be quiet, I'll tell you. It's to—"

Jack held up his hand. "Wait! I don't want to know. I'm sailing with the evening tide."

"Please, Jack. I can't let her find out about me."

The please did it. Jack shut his eyes and wished he couldn't remember his mother calmly teaching him his manners. "I'll listen," he said, spearing Henry with his stormy, sea green gaze. "But I'm not kidnapping your daughter."

Henry settled into his seat. "Miranda plans to see the king's revenuer about your being a pirate."

Since he paused, apparently awaiting a response, Jack nodded. "So you say."

Henry's lips thinned, but he continued. "Joshua Peterson, the revenuer, leaves for England in a fortnight."

Jack leaned the chair back on two legs. "Lock Miranda in her room for two weeks," Jack suggested drolly.

"I can't do that."

Jack merely shrugged.

"At any point, until a new solicitor arrives from England, Nathan Peabody is to take his place."

"Nathan Peabody." Jack laughed. "He has more than a passing knowledge of piracy."

"Exactly." Henry crossed his arms and smiled. "If Miranda went to him, he'd listen politely, agree with her concern and promptly do nothing. Miranda would be happy, she'd never find out about me, and you could continue to trade in Charles Town . . . out of sight of Miranda, of course."

"As I see it, 'tis but a wee problem in this scheme of yours. What am I supposed to do with your daughter for a fortnight?"

Henry threw up his hands. "I don't know. Keep her prisoner . . . but don't harm her, of course."

"Oh, of course. Aren't you the father who just accused me of throwing his daughter to the deck?"

"I never really thought you did that. I did say it didn't sound like you, didn't I? Just keep her in a cabin . . . and give her plenty of sea air. . . ." Henry's face lit up. "And hold her for ransom.

58

That's it. I shall pay the ransom, and she'll know how much I love her."

"And she'll do whatever she can to see me hanged."

"She's planning to do that now," Henry pointed out reasonably.

Jack couldn't argue with that, but that didn't mean he agreed with Henry's plan. Crossing his arms, Jack leveled his glare on his friend. "There are several other things you've failed to consider."

His face a study in bewilderment, Henry lifted his hands, palms up. "Such as?"

"Such as where your charming daughter would stay on a ship full of pirates." A smug smile accompanied what Jack thought an obvious flaw in the plan.

"I'd thought your cabin. It is the nicest, and I wouldn't want Miranda to be uncomfort—"

"Where in the hell am I supposed to sleep?"

"I'm certain you'll find someplace," Henry responded with such conviction that Jack was momentarily speechless.

When he did find his voice, Jack countered with, "And what about my crew? They aren't used to having a woman on board, and they're a lusty lot. God's blood they're pirates!"

"Don't announce it to the whole town." Henry darted a glance over his shoulder.

"No, we'll leave that little chore to your daughter."

"Sarcasm will get us nowhere," Henry pointed out.

"And listening to this foolishness will?"

"It isn't foolishness." Henry paused. "As for my daughter's virtue . . . I shall trust you to keep that secure."

"Hell." Jack slumped back in his chair. "I was afraid you were going to say that." With a sigh he straightened. "Listen, Henry. I don't know how to tell you this. . . . I might as well simply say it. I don't wish to be around your daughter for two weeks. Hell, I don't want to be around her for two minutes."

Jack yanked up the sleeves of his white linen shirt. "Look what she did to me." He thrust his arms across the table. They were bronzed, well muscled and covered with golden hair. And on each arm was a six-inch-long scar.

"Miranda did that?" Henry couldn't disguise the pride in his voice.

"She and her Spanish friend, aye," Jack said indignantly.

Henry cleared his throat, trying to hide a chuckle. "Well, we shall simply have to keep sharp objects out of her hands."

Jerking down his sleeves, Jack made to rise. " 'Tis no 'we' in this, Henry. She's your daughter. You take care of her."

"I was hoping I wouldn't have to remind you of this."

Jack took a step toward the tavern door and, though he hated himself for doing it, stopped. "Remind me of what?"

"Our friendship." Henry cocked his head. "The

times I've helped you. My organizing men to go after you and your sister . . . to take vengeance on the Spaniards who killed your parents."

Jack crossed his arms. Everything Henry said was true. When Jack had finally escaped the Spaniards and returned to Charles Town, he'd learned an expedition had been formed to attack St. Augustine in retaliation for the Spanish assault on the Scottish settlement at Port Royal.

The retaliatory attack had never been made because a new governor, James Colleton, had arrived in Charles Town and forbidden it. But Henry Chadwick had fought the decision and since then he'd done everything he could to help Jack find de Segovia, the Spaniard responsible for killing Jack's parents and capturing his sister and himself.

Knowing this and accepting what Henry wanted as payment for the old debt were two entirely different things. But with a grunt of resignation, Jack fell back into his chair. "What do you want me to do?"

"I knew you'd think my plan a good one. I just—"

"Let's get one thing straight, Henry. I think you're crazy to even suggest such a thing. I have no doubt the whole thing will explode in our faces. And—" Jack pointed his finger at Henry's chest—"I still think as her father, it's your duty to have a stern talk with Miranda, then lock the chit in her room if she doesn't agree. I know, I know." Jack held up his palm. "You don't like me referring to this paragon of womanhood as a chit. From this moment on I shall hold her in the highest esteem. Guard her ladyship with my worthless life. Treat her as I would my own sister."

With that pledge Jack leaned forward. "Now quickly, before I have a change of heart, tell me the details of this idiotic plan of yours."

Miranda couldn't sleep.

She tried to tell herself it was the heat, though a sea breeze fluttered the mosquito netting draping her tester bed.

"The bed's too soft," she mumbled. Though she'd found the feather-filled mattress quite comfortable until tonight.

Finally, because she knew the best way to solve a problem was to first identify it, Miranda admitted the truth to herself. Her mind was too active for sleep to come. Too engrossed in thoughts about the pirate captain.

How did he have the effrontery to walk into her father's house and pretend to be a respectable citizen? It was simply beyond Miranda's understanding. But then someone who would pirate would undoubtedly do anything. Steal, maim, kill.

She had been very lucky during their encounter on the ship.

Miranda scooted up against the walnut headboard and drew her night rail covered knees under her chin. Tomorrow she would go to the royal collector of revenues — her father had promised to take her—and have the pirate arrested. It was too bad her father couldn't contact the constable or any of his deputies today, but she'd sent a servant down to the docks to check. And the pirate's ship was still in the harbor.

Yes, tomorrow he'd be captured. Then he'd be tried—found guilty, of course, and then. . . . Miranda sat up straighter.

She may never have seen a pirate before this one but she did recall a discussion with her grandfather when a notorious pirate was caught and tried.

He was hanged.

In chains.

And his body was left swinging in the harbor as a warning.

Miranda braided her fingers and bit on her thumbnail. Was that going to happen to her pirate? She simply couldn't imagine his large body wrapped in chains. Or his sea-colored eyes bulging from the strain of the rope. Or birds plucking out his beautiful golden hair.

A noise, part gasp, part sob, escaped Miranda as the grotesque mental picture took form. How could she do it?

Swiping aside the gossamer netting, Miranda slid off the bed. She'd go right now and tell her father to forget the entire thing. She couldn't be responsible for another man's death.

Not even taking time to light the bedside candle, Miranda hurried to the door. But when she reached for the high brass knob, a new thought occurred. She was not the one responsible for the pirate's plight. He was. Certainly he knew the consequences of his actions. And he chose to ignore them. Thus, if he was hanged, it was his own fault.

Besides, maybe they wouldn't hang him. Maybe in the Carolinas the punishment for piracy was something else . . . something less — Miranda rubbed her neck — permanent.

With her decision to seek out the customs collector on the morrow reaffirmed, Miranda decided to retrieve her copy of the *Principia* from below stairs and read. That usually brought about sleep.

"Is ye sure ye don't want no help, Cap'n."

Jack leaned against the stucco wall and tried to make out his quartermaster in the darkness. There was only the tiniest slice of moon shining tonight, and Jack thought the lack of light matched his mood.

"Nay. I'll need no assistance bagging the chit." Jack remembered his vow to treat Henry's daughter with respect and scowled. "I can handle the lady," he corrected. "You just wait down here at the foot of the ladder." Grabbing hold of the splintery wood, Jack stepped onto the first rung.

"I'd feel a mite better if you'd let me go with ye."

Jack shut his eyes in frustration. "No, I said. I can handle this myself."

"But the wench cut you up pretty good aboard

64

that English ship."

"God's blood, she came at me from behind with a sword. And it was no more than a scratch. Besides, this time she'll be asleep—that is unless someone's arguing wakes her up."

Apparently the jibe was too subtle for Phin because instead of quieting he proposed another question. "What if Henry or one of them servants comes by?"

"I told you, the servants were sent away for the evening, and Henry is locked in his room until the dastardly deed is done. Now, may I continue?"

"Aye . . . but, Cap'n, ye ain't goin' to hurt her none, is ye?"

"No." Not waiting for another word, Jack deftly climbed up the ladder to the window of Miranda's room. Henry had assured him it would be open. "Miranda fears not the night air," he'd said with what Jack thought foolish fatherly pride.

"Who cares what the chit fears," Jack mumbled under his breath as he carefully lifted the sash higher. Even then he had to squeeze his large frame through the opening.

Jack took a moment for his eyes to adjust to the darker inside. He could just make out a large, ornately framed bed. His smile wicked, Jack stealthily crept toward it, yanking the burlap bag from under his belt. He'd throw it over her head, heave her over his shoulder and be aboard the *Sea Hawk* in time to sail with the morning tide.

He looked down at the bed. He knew she was

small, but she couldn't have disappeared beneath the coverlet. Jack looked again, finally using his hand to pat the bed. She wasn't there.

"Damnation."

Whirling about, Jack peered around the room, trying to spot his prey in some shadowed corner. Could she have heard him coming and hidden? In exasperation he struck the flint and lit the bedside candle.

No Miranda.

He was close to deciding to forget the entire ridiculous plan when he heard a noise in the hallway; then he saw the doorknob turning. Quickly he pinched out the flame, flattening himself against the wall and unsheathing his sword in a single movement.

If this was some sort of betrayal he'd have Henry's gizzard, friend or no. Jack held his breath, poised to leap out and defend himself against the constable and his deputies as the door opened.

But no horde swarmed into the room. Instead he recognized Miranda's voice as she entered singing softly. She wore something white and flowing, and because of her garb he could easily follow her path as she walked toward the bed.

Resheathing his sword as quietly as he could, Jack watched while she appeared to fumble around on the bedside table. "Now, where did that candle go?" he heard her ask herself before he began moving toward her. This wasn't as good as surprising her while asleep, but it didn't appear that anything concerning Miranda Chadwick would go as planned.

Miranda stiffened. There was someone else in her room. And whoever it was, was creeping up behind her. She could hear his breathing, feel his heat. Her mouth went dry. Miranda sucked in a breath to scream and realized no sound came out.

What could she do? The floorboard creaked, and she knew her assailant was ready to pounce. Miranda's hands tightened on the volume of Newton's *Principia*. Then she turned and swung the heavy book as hard as she could. It hit something equally hard with a satisfying thump, and Miranda heard a groan of pain before she dropped the book and raced for the door.

Jack grabbed himself and doubled over. For an instant everything went black; then the shadow of his boots came into focus, and splinters of nauseating pain slivered out from his groin. He moaned. And with the sound came realization. The chit had hit him, flattened him, right in the family jewels.

He twisted around to see her form swing open the door to the hallway. Lunging Jack grabbed hold of her gown. He heard fabric tear, and then her scream spilled through the night air.

Balling the cotton in his fist, Jack managed to straighten enough to seize her arm. Her screeches grew louder, and she batted at him with her free hand.

"Would you be still," he said through clenched teeth. She wasn't really hurting him—now—but it was damned annoying. For a moment Jack thought she was following his order. She went stock still.

Miranda knew that voice. And suddenly a dire situation seemed even worse. Why would the pirate be here except to kill her? And why wasn't her father responding to her screams? Unless he, too, was a victim of the pirate's wrath?

She started hitting the pirate with renewed energy. He may kill her in the end, but she wouldn't make it easy for him.

Damn the wench, damn, damn. She was twisting all around so he couldn't get the bag over her head. And that screaming. He'd suffered through booming cannon battles that didn't rattle his ears as much.

And his groin still hurt. Damn, if she'd done him any real harm. . . ! Jack couldn't even finish that thought.

The worst of it was he could silence her and stop her struggles with one good cuff. But his mother had taught him not to strike women. Henry's daughter raked her nails across his arm, and Jack gritted his teeth. Damn, if there ever was a woman he was tempted to throttle, it was this one.

Miranda knocked into the pirate, then jerked her arm as hard as she could, and for the second time in their brief but tempestuous acquaintance, she and the pirate tumbled to the floor.

He landed on top her—again. And again air whooshed from her lungs. This time he lifted himself more quickly, straddling her, and filling her mind with another awful possibility. "I won't let you . . . ," she wheezed and jackknifed her knee to make good her threat.

"Oh, no you don't." Jack jerked to the side. "Not again." He grabbed both her hands in one of his and stretched them over her head. "And I'm not going to rape you, for God's sake."

He had her now. Beneath his weight and with both her hands bound in his, there was nothing she could do. Her throat ached from screaming, and she squinted her eyes shut as tears welled in them. She didn't want to die a coward.

Muscles and bone and blood and tissue. Miranda tried to tell herself that scientifically that's all a human being was, but she didn't want to die. And to her shame, as she felt the pirate yanking something over her hair, the words slipped out. "I don't want to die," she croaked.

As he covered her face and the world went black, Miranda thought she heard the pirate claim he wasn't going to kill her. But who could trust a pirate?

Chapter Four

So this was death.

Miranda filled her mind with the sensations—quite pleased that she was still capable of rational thought in the afterlife.

She was floating. . . . No, floating wasn't the exact word she wanted. Rocking. Yes, rocking was more like it. And she was hungry. Hungry? And heaven smelled like bilge water, and what was that creaking noise?

Miranda's eyes popped open.

This wasn't heaven. It wasn't even hell—though that was probably closer to the truth. And she wasn't dead! What had made her think she was?

Miranda sat up, swinging her legs over the side of the bunk as memory rushed over her. She'd been in her room in her father's house and the pirate was there. He was trying to kill her, and. . . . Try as she might, Miranda couldn't remember any more.

70

Standing, she glanced around. She was in a cabin, larger than the one she'd had sailing to the New World, but unmistakably on a ship.

Panic hit her. She had to get out of here and off this boat before it sailed from Charles Town. Ignoring the fact that she wore only a torn, dirty night rail, Miranda ran to the door and yanked on the latch.

The blasted thing was locked!

Rushing across the deck to the transom window, Miranda peered out. Tears fogged her vision, but she could still see the endless expanse of ocean churning in the ship's wake. She slumped down on the window seat, her forehead resting against the wavery glass, and sobbed. It was cowardly to give in to tears, to waste valuable time when she could be thinking of a solution to this problem. But she couldn't seem to help herself.

She jerked around when she heard a rattling at the door. It opened, and she stood, wiping her torn sleeve across her face. When a man walked in, her eyes widened. "You!"

Jack couldn't help grinning at the loathing she injected into that one word. He entered his cabin, truly annoyed with himself when his gaze dropped to her hands in search of possible weapons. "Well," he said, relieved to see none. "You're looking charming this morning." Actually she was a disheveled mess, with tangled hair and dirty face. "Did you sleep comfortably?"

"You. . . you . . ." Words escaped her, and

abandoning rational thought, she flew at him.

Jack caught her easily by the wrists and held her at arm's length. "My, my, we are in a temper, aren't we?"

Miranda blew raven hair from her face. "I demand to know where I am." His evil chuckle made her twist her arms, but he only tightened his manacle hold.

"You demand, do you? Where do you think you are?" Jack blamed some perverse streak in his character for enjoying tormenting this woman so.

"I don't kn—" Miranda stopped, cutting short her reply. He was the pirate, so it was only logical she was—"Oh, no." Her shoulders drooped forward. "I'm on a pirate ship."

"Aye. The good ship *Sea Hawk*," Jack said with some pride.

"Where are you taking me, and why did you kill my father?" A sob escaped her on the last word.

"Kill your father?" Jack dropped one of her hands and swiped aside the midnight black curls still covering her face. He'd meant to give her a little scare in payment for all the trouble she'd caused him, not to mention her attack with the book, but he didn't like seeing her cry. And he sure as hell didn't want her thinking he'd killed Henry. "Your father's not dead."

"Don't lie to me." Miranda dragged her other hand away and scrubbed at the tears that were falling unchecked now. "I know you killed him."

"God's blood, I did not kill your father!"

"Then, why didn't he respond to my cries for help?"

"Why?"

"Yes, why?" Miranda stuck her chin out, daring him to weasel out of his lie.

For a moment Jack just stared at her and her defiant expression. How was he going to answer her? The real reason was out, of course. Henry would never forgive him if he told the little hellion the truth. That her father had been cowering behind a locked door and that he'd planned the entire kidnapping.

That explanation being unusable, what excuse *could* he give? "I tied him up."

"What?" Miranda cringed back.

"Aye. Tied him up and gagged him." Jack stood, booted feet apart, hands clasped behind his back. He was warming to this scenario. "I warned him what would happen to you if he interfered."

"But why do you want me?" There seemed to be a ring of truth to the story about her father. At least Miranda prayed so. Now all she had to worry about was herself.

"Ransom."

"But I don't understand."

"Ransom," Jack repeated. "I kidnap you. Your father pays my price. I give you back. God's blood, pirates do it all the time." Of course this was the first time he'd resorted to it, and if all ransoms were as difficult as this one, Jack figured he'd stay away from them in the future as well.

"I see."

Jack watched his captive chew on her thumbnail, obviously contemplating his words. He wondered if she realized her nightgown was ripped and that he could easily see the creamy swell of her right breast.

"What if he doesn't pay?"

"He'll pay."

"But what if he can't? Perhaps he doesn't have the money."

"He has the money. Do you think I go around kidnapping people without knowing how much I can collect? I'm a pirate, for God's sake!"

"Oh." It did seem logical. Her father couldn't pay unless he was indeed alive. And the pirate didn't appear to have any other reason for taking her, nor could she think of one. There was one more thing. "How much are you getting for me?"

"What?" He never knew a woman—nay, make that anyone—to ask so many questions.

"For my ransom. How much am I worth?" It was a silly question, but Miranda couldn't help wondering how much her father was asked to pay for her.

Jack was beginning to think two pence was too much, but he refrained from saying it. "That's my business, not yours," he growled. "You stay down here, don't cause any trouble, and before you know it, you'll be back in Charles Town." Then, because she looked entirely too relieved, Jack added, "But if you do anything—I mean anything—to annoy me. . . ." Jack left his threat unfinished as he took a menacing step toward her.

"I understand."

Jack glared at her until he thought her suitably intimidated. "Good. Your things are over there." He motioned toward a pile on his desk. He'd sent Phin around to Henry's before they sailed this morning to gather up some clothes for his captive. And Jack was glad he had. The sooner she changed from that torn night rail that exposed entirely too much of her, the sooner he'd stop thinking of easier ways to close those pretty lips of hers.

Damn, he hadn't noticed before just how beautiful she was. Or maybe he had and just didn't want to admit it. Either way, he'd be glad when he could deposit her back on her father's doorstep.

But for now she was quickly sorting through the bundle on the desk. She looked up at him, her face brightening in a smile. "You brought my microscope."

"I did? I mean, aye, I did." What in the hell was the damn microscope doing here? He'd said clothes. Have Henry pack some clothes for her. That's all. Leave it to Henry to provide his daughter with all the comforts of home. Jack was surprised the older man hadn't insisted his cook and a lady's maid accompany Miranda on her kidnapping.

But the microscope did seem to make her happy, she didn't appear to give a care to the dresses she'd scattered about. And maybe if she was happy, she'd stay out of his—

"What?" he asked. His captive was looking at him with an expression of pure loathing. Jack hated to admit it, but he liked the smile a lot better.

"You're scheming to steal it, aren't you?"

"What? The microscope?" He watched as she clutched the stupid thing to her breast like a mother protecting her offspring. "Don't be a blooming idiot. What would I want that thing for?"

"Why, for one thing it's terribly expensive. For another you could study all manner of insects and plant life and in just one drop of water—"

"I know all about the little animals swimming around in my water," Jack said with more than a hint of disbelief in his voice.

"Animalcules," Miranda corrected. "And they *are* there." He was so insufferably arrogant. Miranda wished she didn't find his face and form so appealing. Lord, what was she thinking?

"So you say."

And ignorant, Miranda decided again. He was totally ignorant, and apparently content to stay that way. "A man with any intelligence would wish to find out for himself." Her delicate raven brows lifted ever so slightly.

Dumb! The wench was calling him dumb! Him! Jack felt anger seep up through him like a rising tide. Maybe he hadn't had much formal education since the Spanish attack on Port Royal, but he sure as hell wasn't dumb. He could sail a ship and outsmart an enemy and calculate his position by the stars, not to mention calculating the worth of the cargo he stole. And he had managed to make her his prisoner.

Unfortunately, Jack wasn't certain he could use that as an example of his intelligence. He was beginning to fear her kidnapping could be used to prove her point.

Regardless, the woman had to be crazy to chide him so, under the circumstances. Jack folded his arms across his chest and leveled his gaze on her. "All I need know of water 'tis that it quenches my thirst and floats my ship." Turning on his booted heel, Jack stomped from the cabin, vowing to have naught to do with the chit until he could bundle her off to Henry.

Miranda stood staring at the door, gnawing on her thumbnail. She'd made the pirate angry—really angry. She had noticed the rise of color under his tanned skin. And the way he clenched his jaw until a muscle twitched.

She thought *him* ignorant, but had proven herself even much more so. Who with any sense would anger a pirate? A pirate who held her very life in his huge hands. Miranda shook her head.

And informing him that the microscope was

expensive was just inviting him to steal it. Miranda sank down in a chair. She really had to be more careful around him.

If she believed him—and Miranda found she did—her father was safe, and she would be, too, as soon as the ransom was paid. Miranda wished she'd asked when he thought that would be. Grimacing, Miranda decided not to press her luck by inquiring.

Besides—she glanced around the cabin—her accommodations weren't too bad, and she did have her microscope. Miranda brushed aside a petticoat, smiling when she saw the parchment. She had everything she needed to work and study.

Satisfied, Miranda stood. First she'd dress. For the first time this morning she looked down at herself. She screeched in horror. Her night rail was torn. She clutched at the fabric, trying to cover her breast, cringing with embarrassment because she knew it was far too late.

No wonder the pirate's eyes had kept drifting lower than her face. The blackguard! The miscreant! The bastard! Miranda couldn't think of enough terrible names to call him.

"Why in the hell did you bring that microscope on board?"

Phin glanced up from tying rigging around a belaying pin and grinned his gape-toothed grin. "Well, good morn to ye, too, Cap'n."

Jack ignored his sarcasm, which maybe wasn't a good idea. What the quartermaster needed was a couple licks of the cat to remind him about proper respect. But there was no use threatening it. They both knew Jack wouldn't have him flogged. Besides, if he were to flog anyone, it would be the little lady below—

Jack forced his mind from such thoughts. He knew he wouldn't do that either. "I asked you a question, Phin."

Phin gave the rope an extra tug. "Was only followin' orders, Cap'n. Yer orders," he added for emphasis.

"I know very well what my orders were, and they did not include bringing that . . . that instrument aboard."

Phin shrugged. "Mr. Chadwick musta packed it up with her things."

"And you had no idea it was there?" Jack's hands rested on his lean hips. "You couldn't tell the difference between some frilly dresses and a wooden crate?"

"Well." Phin squinted his face. "Maybe I did figure it was that microscope thing. But I ain't recallin' ye sayin' *not* to bring it with me."

Jack could do nothing but stare against that sort of reasoning.

"Besides, ain't ye just a tiny bit curious to see them little animals?"

Jack shut his eyes. "God's blood, not you, too." When he opened them again his glare could make even the bravest man tremble. "For

79

the last time, there are no little invisible animals!"

"But she done said—"

"Phin!" Jack took a deep breath. " 'Twill be no more talk of this. Do you understand me?"

"Aye, sir."

The quartermaster's demeanor wasn't as convincing as his words, but Jack let it drop. "Good. Now get below and take our prisoner some breakfast."

"Aye, sir." This response was much more enthusiastic.

"No, wait." Jack reached out to grab Phin's arm. "Give the lady another quarter of an hour before you go." Jack had nothing against seeing his prisoner in a torn nightgown himself. As a matter of fact, he quite enjoyed it. But others seeing her that way was a different thing altogether.

And Jack didn't like to wonder why that was.

Even though this time a hearty knock preceded the rattle of key turning lock, Miranda expected to look up and see the pirate captain standing in the doorway.

She wondered at her flicker of disappointment when instead a small wiry pirate stuck his grizzled head in through the opening.

"Got some vittles for ye," he announced before pushing on into the room. "Ain't much. But then when ye ain't got no time to set in supplies, ye can't be too picky."

The wrinkled little man eyed her as if he thought the entire thing Miranda's fault. He also waited as if he expected some sort of reply. She watched him nearly drop the heavy pewter tray on the desk. A thin, grayish green gruel slopped over the sides of the metal dish. Miranda cleared her throat. "I'm certain it will be fine."

"Ye ain't tasted it yet."

And if she weren't so hungry, she wouldn't. But food had never held much importance to Miranda except to replenish her body, so she waved his comment away. She hoped she wouldn't be prisoner on this ship long.

Miranda assumed the man, whose skin was darkened a nut brown, would leave, but he continued to just stand there. Now his black gaze was riveted to the top of the desk.

"That there, that scope thing?" he asked while rubbing his grizzly chin with a gnarled forefinger.

"My microscope, yes," answered Miranda hesitantly. She'd just recognized this man as the second pirate from the attack on the ship she took from England. The one who had wanted to steal her microscope. Miranda inched her way between the desk and the pirate.

The pirate didn't seem to notice. He was still rubbing at his chin, and now he started shuffling back and forth on cracked and worn boots. "Ye don't suppose I could—"

"The microscope is mine." Didn't the pirate captain just say as much?

Phin's obsidian eyes flashed to hers. "I ain't aimin' to change that. Just wanted to get a look at them animals swimmin' around."

"The animalcules." Miranda's shoulders relaxed.

"Aye, them things. I'm kinda curious to see such a thin'."

"You are? I mean, you are. Of course you are." Could this pirate, this gnarled outlaw from society, be a kindred spirit? All Miranda knew was that curiosity drove her . . . excited her. And from the looks of this man, it excited him, too.

"Wait just a moment and I'll show you." Miranda finished clearing away the maps and charts that were covering the desk and set them in a pile on the floor. Then she set up her microscope. From the bucket near the door she scooped a small amount of water. "If you would light the candles, I think perhaps you can see better."

It seemed like she took forever to move the blasted thing to just the right spot and move the little looking glasses around, but finally she stepped away and motioned for Phin to take her place. "There. Don't be afraid."

Phin straightened. "I ain't feared a no little animals. No biggins neither," he clarified.

"Of course you aren't. I simply meant that sometimes things that we don't understand can be somewhat . . . frightening." Miranda pressed on because she saw she'd hurt his pride again. "It's like that for everyone, I suppose. But the truly brave people are the ones, like you, who do it anyway. Cowards will shy away. Not even take the chance that there might be something there they could learn."

"The cap'n ain't no coward."

"I didn't mean. . . ." Miranda stopped because she had a sneaking suspicion she was referring to the pirate captain, and she didn't like to lie.

"I never seen him flinch in a fight."

"I'm certain he's a wonderful fighter." Obviously this man thought a lot of his captain.

"Even when he was no more'n a lad and just escaped from them filthy, thievin' Spaniards, he never backed down from no man."

She really didn't want to know the pirate captain's history—or anything else about him for that matter. "Come here. Hold this up. Just squint your eye and look through this little hole," she said, trying to stem the flow of information.

The pirate followed her instructions—only a little reluctantly. Miranda could tell the exact moment he focused in on the animalcules. He jerked, his face a mask of incredulity.

"Ye put them in there," he accused.

"No I didn't." Miranda worked hard to smother her grin. "It's just a plain drop of water."

He looked again—longer this time. Then he eyed Miranda suspiciously. "How come I can't

taste 'em. Or feel 'em crawlin' round me mouth."
He screwed up his face, and Miranda thought
for a moment he planned to spit on the floor.

"Because they're so small. You can't even see
them without a microscope. No one can."

"But—"

"Your captain has a spy glass, doesn't he?
Have you ever looked through it?"

"Aye." The pirate nodded for emphasis.

"It makes things that are far away look closer.
By magnifying them. The microscope does the
same thing. It uses specially ground lenses to
make things look bigger." She wasn't sure the pirate understood her explanation. He only
shrugged and squinted to have another look.

"Of course, there are different types of animalcules. They've been discovered in rain water
and sea water."

"Let me see some a them."

"I'm afraid I don't have anything but fresh water here in the cabin."

"Get yourself up on deck. You'll find more
salty brine than you can handle."

"I'm certain I would. However, your captain
has restricted me to this cabin."

"Has he now?" Phin rubbed his chin. "Don't
ye worry none, I'll see to the cap'n." He stole
one more quick peek through the microscope.
"Better be on me way. Name's Phin, your ladyship. I'll be back."

* * *

Miranda didn't know how Phin managed it, but the next morning he returned saying he was to accompany her on deck for her morning outing. "Ye'll be getting an evening stroll, too," he confided.

The sun was bright, the wind was warm and brisk, singing through the sails, and Miranda was very happy to be on deck.

If she didn't know better—which of course she did—Miranda would have thought herself on an ordinary ship. The crew looked perhaps a little more savage than that on the vessel that brought her from England. But not by much.

Miranda shaded her eyes and scanned the deck, stopping only when she realized she was searching for the tall, golden-haired captain. She dropped her hand quickly. What was wrong with her? If anything, she should be hoping she didn't run into the arrogant man.

She hadn't laid eyes on him since yesterday morning, and her day had progressed quite nicely without him. She didn't need or want another encounter.

And she had no idea why she'd dreamed of him last night.

"Is Phin telling it true?"

Miranda swirled around at the sound of the deep voice behind her and came face to naked chest with a blackamoor. She tilted her head until she could see his face, then cringed back until the rail bit into her spine. He was huge—even larger than the pirate captain, though she

85

would have thought that impossible. And his cheeks were tattooed with peculiar markings.

He watched her as intently as she did him, but though he looked menacing, he made no move toward her.

"Can't ye see yer scaring her ladyship." Phin gave the giant of a man a small shove. "This here is King. I done told him about seein' them animals in the water."

Miranda stood as tall as she could and straightened her skirt. "You're not frightening me, Mr. King, truly." Miranda didn't *always* tell the truth. "And, yes, Mr. Phin did see the animalcules in the water. Actually we came on deck to get some ocean water so we can compare them."

By the time Miranda climbed down through the hatch, she'd promised to let not only King but several other pirates see the secrets unveiled by her microscope.

"I never realized the crew would be so interested in science," she observed as Phin escorted her along the companionway.

"After I done tol' 'em what I seen, they was."

"Well, I think it's wonder—" Miranda stopped suddenly when she noticed the cabin door was ajar. Pushing it open the rest of the way, she stepped inside, her hands clamped on her hips, her eyes filled with angry sparks when she saw her precious microscope being manhandled.

"What do you think you're doing?"

Jack straightened and speared the irritating

woman with his stormy gaze. "What am *I* doing? I should think the question is, what are you doing?"

Miranda raised her chin. "I was under the impression my excursions on deck were approved by you. Irregardless, that gives you no right to—"

"I don't give a damn about your *excursions on deck*." Actually he did. When Phin suggested them Jack thought they would be the perfect opportunity to come below to his cabin without running into his captive. "However, I do wish to know what you did with my charts." Each word grew louder, so by the end of his sentence Jack was yelling. And he rarely yelled. He wasn't known as Gentleman Jack Blackstone for nothing.

"They were yours?"

"Aye! They were mine. What did you think? And where the hell are they?"

"Cap'n, there's no call to—"

Jack's stare shifted to Phin, whom he hadn't even noticed till now. "Don't you have duties elsewhere, Mr. Sharpe?"

"Aye, Cap'n, but—"

"Phin!"

Miranda watched as the pirate she almost looked upon as an ally retreated through the door, shutting it quietly behind himself. When she turned back to the pirate captain he was regarding her intently.

"Well?"

"I put them in that sea chest." Miranda indicated the trunk near the foot of the bunk. But before the pirate could move, she continued. "Do you suppose you could put down my microscope . . . gently?"

Jack had forgotten he was still holding the damn thing, but he did as she asked, adding a mocking bow after placing it on his desk. Then he went in search of his maps. They were indeed in the chest in neat stacks and rolls. Glancing over his shoulder, Jack caught her examining her microscope, acting as if he'd done something to it. "In the future," he said, "refrain from moving my things."

She stood and met his stare. "Then, I suggest you remove your things from my cabin."

"Your cabin!" Jack dropped the maps. "This is *my* cabin."

"Yours?"

"Whose did you think it was?"

"I don't know." Miranda gnawed on her thumbnail a moment. "I suppose I thought it was a cabin for people you kidnapped for ransom. You did say it was done all the time, and I can't imagine you like giving up your cabin much."

"I didn't say I did it all the time," Jack corrected. "This happens to be a first. And frankly, it will be my last."

Miranda shrugged. "That's probably for the best."

"I'm sure it is." Jack began rearranging his

charts. "In the meantime, remove your things from my desk so I can—"

"Where am I to put my microscope?"

Jack shut his eyes and took a deep breath. "I really don't know, nor do I care."

Miranda could tell he was angry . . . very angry. And his sheer size made him formidable. Carefully she picked up her microscope and laid it in the crate.

The pirate captain gave her a smug smile, then spread his charts on the desk's surface. With that he straddled the chair and began studying his maps. Miranda stood to the side. She tried not to notice the way his thigh muscles bulged against the fabric of his breeches. But she couldn't seem to look away.

She'd seen copies of da Vinci's sketches of human musculature, but she'd never seen such a fine example. The pirate captain should have been used as a model for the drawings. But since he wasn't, perhaps she could sketch him.

Grandfather always told her she was very good with chalk. She couldn't let the pirate know what she was about to do, but if she carefully kept her eyes on him, she could probably do a good job. Though he wore a white, billowy shirt today, she remembered what his chest and arms looked like without it.

Miranda swallowed. In the past, while studying works on the human body, she hadn't experienced this warm, quavery feeling inside, but now staring at the pirate—

"What are you doing?"

Miranda's eyes snapped to the captain's, and she felt heat flood her face. He was looking at her in a way that made that honey feeling inside hotter and more molten. "I . . . I. . . ." She couldn't come up with any logical explanation for what she was doing because she honestly didn't know.

"Whatever, I suggest you remember that I'm the pirate and you're the captive and stop looking at me that way."

"I . . . don't know what you're talking about." He stood, and Miranda resisted the urge to back up.

"I think you do. And if you don't wish to end up on your back with your skirts flipped over your head, you'll remember my warning."

Miranda's face grew redder. Of all the insulting things. The man was a scoundrel beyond compare. "I believe you assured me I would be safe from rape."

"I'm not talking about rape, Mistress Chadwick. And I think we both know it."

Miranda did take a step back now. And then another. His eyes were narrowed, and he had a self-satisfied expression on his face that she found infuriating. "I have no idea—"

He was beside her so quickly that Miranda had no time to question his actions. "You lie very poorly," was all he said before his mouth crushed down on hers.

She'd heard of kissing before—even the man

and woman kissing that had nothing to do with the way her grandfather and father greeted her. But never had she imagined it to be anything like this.

Those strange feelings she worked to keep under control came blossoming forth. He was hard and hot, and Miranda imagined she could feel all the muscles in his body, while those within her seemed to melt away.

His hands grasped her arms; his mouth moved sensually over hers. And then he pulled away.

Miranda stared up at him, stunned. What in the world had happened? She searched her mind for some rational explanation for what she was feeling, and could find none.

For at that moment she longed to cling to his arm and beg him to kiss her again. He looked as if he might without being asked. But instead he turned and slammed out of the cabin, leaving Miranda to make sense of what happened.

Chapter Five

"Damn!"

Jack hit the heel of his hand against a bulwark and cursed again. What in the hell was wrong with him? How could he do something so stupid?

All right. Perhaps he'd done stupid things before. But kissing Miranda Chadwick had to take the prize as the most stupid.

She was Henry's daughter. And if that wasn't enough, she was strange. Strange and complex. Jack didn't like complex women . . . and he certainly wasn't enamored of strange ones. Give him a nice, simple, good-hearted wench with a full luscious body and he was happy.

So why was he spending so much time thinking of his captive? Perhaps he did find her appearance pleasant. But large, deep blue eyes and a rosy mouth couldn't make up for her weird behavior *or* who she was.

He liked a good tumble as well as the next man, maybe more. But he could control himself.

And he certainly had no intentions of seducing Henry Chadwick's daughter.

So why did he kiss her?

"Maybe I'm just tired of her high and mighty attitude and that damn microscope."

"What's that, Cap'n?"

Jack spun around to see Scar Smite coming along the companionway. The oscillating light from the lantern threw grotesque shadows across the disfigured cheek for which he was named. "Nothing," Jack said, turning back toward the ladder leading up through the hatch. " 'Twas nothing."

Now he was talking to himself. God's blood, nothing had gone right since he attacked that British ship and encountered Miranda Chadwick.

De Segovia hadn't been on board as Jack hoped. Then he'd sailed south to see if he could discover any more about the rumor that de Segovia was returning to St. Augustine — only to learn nothing. If it wasn't for the Spanish galleon the *Sea Hawk* had taken, it would have been a wasted trip.

Then, of course, he had sailed into Charles Town's harbor ready for some peace and quiet, not to mention female companionship, only to be waylaid by Henry and his hair-brained scheme.

Jack shook his head as he came out on deck. No wonder he couldn't keep his thoughts off Miranda Chadwick. He'd been too long without a woman. Something he would remedy the next time he set foot in a port.

With that explanation for the kiss resolved, Jack lifted his eyes to examine the sails. He pushed from his mind the niggling thought that there was more to it than that, and completely ignored the flame of desire he had felt when his lips touched hers.

"Come, look at this." Miranda rose from the chair and motioned for Phin to take her place. King and another pirate, introduced to her by the uncomplimentary name of Scar, stood on the opposite side of the desk.

"Gawd's but it's ugly." Phin screwed up his face in disgust.

"Get your arse outta that chair and give me a look." Scar shoved at Phin's shoulder, and Miranda resisted the urge to grab up her microscope and clutch it safely to her breast. But Phin moved, apparently anxious for someone else to view the horrid creature.

"Yowl." Scar's face registered as much revulsion as Phin's had. "When I think of how many of 'em I done ate over the years, I come mighty close to retchin'. Look at them devils, King."

The huge blackamoor's reaction was similar to the other two's, but at least he didn't threaten to vomit.

When they'd all had their fill of scrutinizing the maggot Miranda had placed beneath the lenses of her microscope, she was offered the chair. After placing a piece of parchment on the desk, she dipped her quill into the ink pot.

"What ye doin' now?"

"Making a sketch of what I see," Miranda explained as the pirates drew closer. For the last four days since Phin first looked through the microscope, pirates had been stopping by the cabin to see if the quartermaster was telling the truth of what he saw.

Most all the men showed a curiosity that Miranda found wonderful. And even if they did ask so many questions and want to take so many looks through the lenses that she barely had time for her own experiments, she didn't mind.

Not all the pirates came to the cabin. The pirate captain remained conspicuously absent. Miranda hadn't seen him since the day he kissed her. Even when she went on deck, he was nowhere to be found. Since the *Sea Hawk* wasn't that large a vessel, Miranda assumed he planned it that way.

And that was fine with her. She didn't want to be around him any more than he apparently wanted to be around her. Just remembering the gall of the man to kiss her like that made Miranda furious. And to imply that she wanted him to do it. Miranda nearly shook with rage. She should have slapped him! Yes, that's definitely what she should have done.

And she would have if not for the total daze that kiss had put her in. She could barely remember the pirate captain leaving the cabin.

Miranda blinked, looked around her and noticed the pirates watching her intently. That's when she realized she was sitting motionless, her quill poised above the parchment. She quickly set about sketching the maggot.

But just as the tip of the quill touched the paper, a bellowed yell startled her, and she jerked, spoiling the drawing.

The pirates from huge King to wiry little Phin stiffened as the roar sounded again.

"Phin! Where in the hell is everybody?"

"Gawd's teeth, I was supposed to be collecting a chart for the cap'n."

"He sent me below to fetch you," King admitted.

Scar shrugged. "I'm to be scrubbin' the deck."

Miranda glanced from one pirate to the other. They'd gone pale beneath their sun-darkened faces—except for King, but he looked equally distressed. And all because they had spent a little time with her. Perhaps it was more than a little, but still. . . .

"I'm certain your captain will understand if I simply explain to him your interest in—"

"Gawd, yer ladyship, don't do that." Phin was busy searching through the charts and maps Miranda had pushed to the side of the desk. She hadn't the nerve to remove them completely again, even if they did interfere with her work.

Phin's expression brightened as he found the chart the captain wanted. "Just stay here, yer ladyship, and draw some pictures of them maggots. We'll be just fine."

There was a grumble of agreement as the three hurried from the cabin, leaving Miranda to wonder what kind of hold the pirate captain had that made these three men quake from fear when he bellowed.

"Where in the hell have you been?" Jack glared at Phin as he scurried up the quarterdeck ladder. "I've almost missed the noon reading."

"Sorry, Cap'n." Phin handed over the chart. "Visited the head. Somethin' I et ain't sittin' right."

Jack shook his head, then sighted the horizon through the quadrant. He supposed part of the fault for the late reading was his own. He could have gone below and retrieved the chart himself. Except he didn't want to see Miranda Chadwick. Lord, the woman was keeping him away from his own cabin.

It was almost—Jack cringed—as if he were afraid of her. God's blood, he was a pirate! He feared no one. And most certainly not a wisp of a woman.

He didn't recall his men being such persnickety eaters. Jack took a healthy bite of beef and chewed . . . and chewed. Granted it was tough as an old rope—they didn't call it salt junk for nothing. But still the way Phin, King and the others were picking at it, you'd think it was poison.

Maybe they always ate this way and he just wasn't here to see it. Before the ill-conceived kidnapping, as Jack had come to think of his taking of Miranda Chadwick, he'd eaten in his cabin. Now the little lady had that privilege.

Of course eating in the crew's quarters on boards hinged to the wall wasn't the worst of it. He had to sleep here, too. When he was younger—and shorter—before becoming the *Sea Hawk*'s captain, he'd slept down here. And he hadn't really minded it. But now that he was used to a bunk, lengthened to fit his stature, with a feather-filled mattress, a six-by-three-foot canvas hammock was hellishly uncomfortable.

Between doubling his six-foot-four-inch body into the canvas and the belches and snores of the crew, Jack had gotten little sleep since the kidnapping.

But he imagined Miranda Chadwick slept just fine, all soft and warm in his bed. Jack took another bite and found his mind wandering to what it would be like to cuddle up with her. To feel her smooth pale skin and smell her warm, womanly smell. Then he'd kiss her like he did the other day. She'd wrap her arms around him and open to him on a sweet sigh. She really did have a nice voice—except when she was screeching at him. Or talking in that heathen Spanish.

Jack jerked himself out of his reverie. God's

blood, he had to stop thinking about that woman. His eyes focused on Phin and narrowed. "What are you doing?"

Phin looked up guiltily and brushed hardtack crumbs to the deck with one sweep of his gnarled hand. "Ain't doin' nothin', Cap'n."

"Well, it looked to me as if—"

"I was pickin' out maggots if ye must know," Phin interrupted.

"What the hell for?"

Phin's expression was incredulous. "I ain't too happy 'bout eatin' 'em."

Jack looked down at his own round of sea bread, could find nothing different about it than the hundreds of biscuits he'd eaten over the years, and then back at Phin. "I don't understand."

"If'n ye could see one of them slimy devils, you'd feel a mite different," Scar piped in.

"What are you talking about?" His crew was acting stranger and stranger.

"Nothin'. He ain't talkin' 'bout nothin'," Phin said. He slid off the bench, giving Scar a kick in the shin as he moved by. "I ain't hungry no more. Better get back on deck."

Jack had a mind to question Scar and King. But they were now stuffing their mouths with hardtack, each looking like he was ready to retch. And suddenly Jack felt a little queasy himself as he stared down at the beef swimming in its greasy broth and the maggot-infested sea bread. Pushing his trencher aside, he stood and headed above deck.

There was barely room in the cabin to move around.

Miranda slid from the chair and allowed a pirate named No Thumb—for obvious reasons—to take her place. She hadn't counted how many men crowded the pirate captain's cabin, but she imagined it was near a dozen.

They'd come to talk about how fast light traveled. Actually they'd come to listen to her explain Olaus Roemer's conclusions about how fast it traveled. Miranda had mentioned to Phin yesterday the Danish astronomer's sightings of Jupiter's satellites and how he came to realize it took longer for light to travel from Jupiter to Earth the farther apart the two planets were. He'd started to question her then, but there hadn't been time for her to answer him completely.

They had agreed she would explain it more fully this morning. But when Phin arrived, he was trailed by a multitude of pirates. "They wants to know, too," Phin said in way of an explanation.

But one of them—No Thumb—had yet to see the animalcules in water, so Miranda set up the microscope for him.

"What's this Phin's saying about light travelin'? It's just there or it ain't," Scar announced once No Thumb finished expressing his amazement at the little animals swimming around in the water.

"It does seem that way," Miranda explained. "But only because it moves so incredibly fast — faster than you and I can even imagine."

"The *Sea Hawk* is a mighty fast ship. When she's sailin' all her canvas, she can outrun any other vessel on the seas. And had to more'n once," Scar added with a laugh.

"Yes, I'm sure it has," Miranda said with a smile. "But the kind of speed I'm talking about is faster than we can see." Miranda held up her hands, palms out, when a general grumble of disbelief broke out in the cabin. "Now, I know what you're thinking," she said, and the men quieted. "If you can't see it, it doesn't exist. However, we all know that isn't true. We couldn't see the animalcules without the microscope, but that didn't mean they weren't there."

"Her ladyship's got the right of it there," Phin said, and several others mumbled their agreement.

"Now, the fact that light does travel is very hard to prove. Galileo tried, but — "

"Who's this Gallo fellow?"

"Galileo. He was an astronomer who lived over fifty years ago. Anyway, he tried to measure the speed of light using lanterns. He and a friend stood on two different hills, and. . . . Well, anyway, it didn't work. But in 1675 Olaus Roemer made a discovery that not only proves light travels, but measures it."

Every eye was on Miranda as she chronicled

the Danish astronomer's surprise discovery made while checking Cassini's timed observations of the eclipses of Jupiter's satellites as they passed behind the planet.

"What is them satellite things?"

"It's like our moon. The moon orbits around the Earth. Jupiter's satellites orbit around it." Watching Phin's expression, Miranda wasn't sure he understood, but she continued. "The point is that Roemer found the eclipses came progressively earlier as the Earth approached Jupiter and later as we went farther away." Miranda finished with a flourish, happy that she could explain this exciting bit of science to the pirates.

For a moment a hush blanketed the cabin. Miranda looked from one face to the next, hoping to see some sort of understanding. Just about the time she realized there was none, a general questioning broke out.

"I don't get it."

"What's she talkin' 'bout?"

"That don't prove a damn thing."

They were all talking at once, and Miranda tried to regain their attention, but without success. Their complaining grew louder, and Miranda tried again to quiet them. She was close to giving up when the cabin door slammed open and a bellowed question silenced everyone.

"What in the hell is going on in here?"

Miranda looked up into the angry face of the pirate captain. His tall stature and wide shoulders filled the doorway. And he seemed very wild and savage with his billowy white shirt open to the waist and tucked into tight black breeches.

Miranda chanced a quick glance around her. To a man the pirates stood, gape faced, staring back at their captain. It was almost comedic.

Phin stepped forward, and Miranda saw his Adam's apple bob as he swallowed. "We was just gettin' ready to leave, Cap'n."

"You were, were you?" Jack's even tempered question belied his stormy expression.

"Aye, Cap'n, we was. Me and the lads were just—"

"Who do you suppose was sailing the *Sea Hawk* while you and the lads were down here having tea?"

"Oh, we ain't had no tea, Cap'n," Scar injected, and Miranda couldn't help cringing. The pirate captain's scowl became even more thunderous.

"What Scar means is . . ." Phin hesitated, then realized he couldn't explain Scar's statement or why they were all here. "We weren't exactly thinkin' right, Cap'n. It won't happen again."

"I should say it won't." Jack let his gaze shift around the room, meeting every pair of eyes, waiting until they glanced away. That is he met every pair of eyes except the deep blue set that watched him wide-eyed. Those he skipped over.

Stepping into the room, Jack took a deep breath. "It's only good fortune that kept us from running into a Spanish galleon or French privateer while you were all down here socializing.

103

You're all guilty of dereliction of duty, and I should have each and every one of you flogged."

"Can he do that?" Miranda meant to whisper her query to Phin, but in the silence that followed the captain's outburst, her voice sounded unusually loud and easily carried to his ears.

He couldn't ignore her any longer. Jack drilled his captive with a searing look. "And you. I should have known you'd be behind this."

"Cap'n, she didn't do nothin'—"

"Thank you, Phin." Miranda lifted her shoulders. "But I can speak for myself. You see, Captain, I—"

"Oh, we'll talk, all right. But in private. The rest of you, get above. There are to be no more visits to this cabin . . . by any of you. And I want this ship shining like a Spanish gold piece."

"Aye, sir."

"Right you be, Cap'n. Like a jewel."

The pirates scurried to follow their captain's orders. All except Phin. He stopped in the doorway, his wizened face more wrinkled than ever. "You ain't gonna hurt her none, now are ye, Cap'n?"

Jack shut his eyes and tried to rein in his temper. What did Phin think? He'd never seen Jack deliberately hurt anyone except in battle. And he never harmed women—not even Spanish women. But for some reason Phin thought he had to protect this particular sea witch from Jack. The woman was coming between him and his crew!

"I won't harm her."

"Ye givin' me yer word as a pirate?"

"Phin!" Jack turned on the wiry first mate, and he hurried out the door.

"You didn't have to yell at him. He was only trying to—"

"I know exactly what he was trying to do. And I don't need your advice in how I discipline my men." God's blood, he couldn't seem to keep from yelling when he was around her.

"If you say so, *Captain.*"

She managed to intone the word captain with enough contempt that Jack narrowed his eyes. But he kept his voice calm—with difficulty. "Would you mind telling me what my men were doing down here?"

"Not at all." Miranda folded her hands. "We were discussing the speed of light."

"The what?"

"The speed of light. I was explaining Olaus Roemer's observations of Jupiter's moon and how they showed that . . . oh, Jupiter is a planet."

"I know what Jupiter is."

"Well, anyway Roemer discovered that the farther away the Earth was from Jupiter, the later the eclipse of the moon by Jupiter occurred. Conversely the closer the Earth was, the—"

"Wait a minute." Jack held up his hand. The damn woman was trying to befuddle him. "You're trying to tell me that Scar and No Thumb and Phin were down here talking about this Roemer's theory about light traveling from Jupiter?"

"Actually they weren't talking; they were listening." And though it appeared the captain could grasp the significance of Roemer's discovery, she wasn't sure about his men. "Truthfully, I can't attest to their understanding of the principals."

Jack couldn't help it. He threw back his head and laughed. When he regained his composure, he realized it was the first good laugh he'd had since this ill-advised kidnapping. He also realized Miranda Chadwick was smiling at him. God, but she was beautiful when she smiled. The thought sobered his expression immediately. What did he care what she looked like. The effect she had on his crew was something else, though.

Jack advanced on her. "You don't really expect me to believe this mess of bilge water you're feeding me, do you?"

Miranda raised her chin, but to her chagrin she retreated a step. "I can assure you it's the truth. Though not all of it."

"Aha!" Now he'd hear what they had really been doing. Though in truth, he couldn't imagine what it was.

"Sometimes your men like to look through my microscope."

Jack's anger flared. She had to be lying. These were pirates she spoke of. Cutthroat scourges of the sea. They had no interest in—

"They especially enjoy observing the animalcules and maggots."

106

Jack felt the color drain from his face. "What did you say?"

"I said, they are curious about—"

"No." Jack took another step toward her. "The maggots. What did you say about maggots?"

"They're quite interested in them."

"But not in eating them." Jack rubbed his chin. It bristled with whiskers that he hadn't been able to adequately shave since giving up his cabin . . . and his looking glass.

"I doubt anyone would harbor a desire to eat a maggot after seeing one under a microscope. They hatch into flies, you know."

Jack let out a sigh of frustration. "Did you tell them that, too?"

Cocking her head, Miranda thought back over her conversations with the pirates. "No, I don't believe so. But I'm sure they'd find it fascinating."

"And refuse to eat altogether," Jack added. "Do you have any idea the chaos you're causing?" Her wide-eyed innocent stare only incensed Jack more. How could she not know the effect she had on his men . . . on him? This last thought made him angrier still.

Hands on narrow hips, he paced the cabin, glancing her way occasionally as he passed. "Phin, King, Scar, hell all of them are crumbling apart their hardtack trying to pick out the maggots. Dead maggots, I might add," he said, turning to face her.

"Well, it's completely understandable. Would

you like to see a sketch I did of a maggot?"

"Hell, no, I don't want to see a sketch! And I don't want to see one under that damn microscope of yours." He bent down till he was almost nose to nose with her. "I don't even want to think about maggots."

His words faded away, and still he stood, staring down at her. Close enough to smell the soft, intoxicating scent of her. Close enough to feel her breath against his chin.

"God's blood!" Straightening, Jack strode to the transom windows and looked out at the endless sea. When he was near her, looking into those blue eyes that reminded him of the Caribbean sky just before sunset, he forgot all about maggots and what she'd done to his crew. Now, with some distance between them, he could try and recapture some of his anger. But even that seemed impossible.

Glancing over his shoulder, he said, "Do you think I enjoy eating food infested with vermin? I don't. But on a ship there's no choice. You eat it or you starve." His voice gentled. "I'm not interested in seeing my men starve."

Miranda didn't know what to say. A flush of heat swept over her as she stared at him. He looked the same, gloriously bronze and golden with a body that made her itch to sketch his musculature; he even still had that arrogant lift to his square jaw, and slight scowl shadowing his green eyes. But in that one moment when he spoke of his men, he seemed different to her

. . . more human and definitely less ignorant.

He'd pointed out something to her that she hadn't considered. Though she was smart enough to know there were many things beyond her knowledge—she missed terribly the explanations her grandfather or some other member of the Royal Society gave her—Miranda never expected to be taught anything by the pirate captain.

And he was right. She hadn't thought about the consequences of showing the maggots or the animalcules to the pirates. She'd known about them for years, and so it didn't really bother her. But these men. . . . Apparently this smattering of knowledge she gave them about their food and water wasn't a good idea.

"I'm sorry."

Jack pivoted around. "What did you say?"

"I apologize for causing trouble with your men. It wasn't my purpose to alter their eating habits, and I am sorry." Miranda's gaze fell to the floor or she would have noticed the surprised expression on the pirate captain's handsome face.

He'd never expected her to apologize . . . to act so reasonable. He also hadn't expected her to look so defeated with her down-turned face and rounded shoulders. Jack resisted the urge to brush a lock of shiny black hair from her face. He balled his fingers into a fist and headed for the door.

Then, because he had to admit that she really wasn't that bad, despite her attempt to have him hanged, he hesitated. "I'm sure they'll stop worrying about the maggots and start eating again."

Miranda glanced up. "I do hope so."

Jack watched as she tucked the wayward curl behind a perfect, shell-shaped ear, then reached for the latch.

"Captain . . . Blackstone, is it?"

"Aye." Jack hadn't realized she knew his name.

"I was wondering . . ." She hesitated, and Jack urged her to continue. "Well, you said that none of the crew was allowed in here again." Her head tilted slightly. "Who is to bring my food?"

For an instant Jack was speechless. Then he wished for a bulwark to slam his fist into. He hadn't thought of that when he'd ordered his men to stay away from the cabin. But apparently she had. That alone was enough to gall him. Add to that the choice of changing an order or . . . or—gritting his teeth, Jack barked out his response. "I'll see that you get fed." Now he was going to have to come below and be around her.

"Thank you. And, Captain." Miranda tried not to cringe when he turned back. The understanding glint had definitely left his eyes. Taking a breath she continued. "Am I still to be allowed on deck?"

"I'll see to that, too," Jack snapped. Now he had to accompany her above deck. God's blood, he wished being near her didn't bother him so.

"I shan't speak to the crew," she offered because he seemed so annoyed with her.

"You can talk to the damn crew. Just not about —"

"Maggots, yes, I know."

"Or those little invisible animals that swim around in water."

"I wouldn't think of mentioning animalcules."

"We're agreed, then?"

"Oh, yes, we're agreed." Miranda smiled, and Jack nearly jerked the door off its iron hinges getting out of the cabin. As soon as he did, he slammed the heel of his hand against a rafter.

Chapter Six

They'd shifted direction.

From the first time she was allowed on deck, Miranda knew the *Sea Hawk* headed north. Now, as she climbed through the hatch and felt the sun on the back of her head, she realized they sailed east.

She took the captain's offered hand and allowed him to help her on deck. Since that afternoon two days ago, there was a quasi truce between them. He allowed her the freedom to roam the ship—after he escorted her above deck—and she uttered not a syllable about maggots or animalcules.

Captain Blackstone could be charming. Miranda didn't like acknowledging it, but it was nonetheless true. Phin confided that the captain was known as Gentleman Jack because of his courtly manners. And Miranda could believe it. He smiled at her now, and she had to force herself to remember he was the pirate who kidnapped her. But remember she did.

"Are we heading toward land, Captain?"

Jack paused and turned back. He had just deposited her near the rail. He had things to do, and he never doubted she could keep herself occupied. She seemed to always be doing something, whether it was sketching on parchment or conversing with his crew.

What she talked to them about, he didn't know. But there was no more trouble with eating hardtack or drinking the water. There'd been no more trouble at all. Obviously refusing to allow any of them to go to her cabin and keeping everything out in the open had solved the problem.

"Aye, we're heading for land. We should spot it before nightfall." He didn't question how she knew.

"Is it a town?"

"Nay, only a small inlet I know of." Jack had decided to follow Henry's advice and have his crew careen the *Sea Hawk's* hull while he waited to return his captive to Charles Town. Scraping the barnacles was a job that needed done, and this way he'd not lose any more valuable time when he could be hunting for de Segovia.

"Is that where you will collect the ransom?"

"What . . . ? Oh, the ransom." How could he have forgotten the rest of Henry's scheme? He was supposed to be holding the little lady for ransom. "Aye, your father will deliver the money there."

"Will I be able to see him? Go home with him?"

"No." Damn, she asked a lot of annoying questions. "He'll just send a messenger."

"Can I leave with him?"

"No, dammit, you can't." Jack felt the grip on his temper slipping away.

"But I don't understand why not. As long as you have the money, I should think you'd be happy to be rid of me."

He couldn't argue with that, but then he wasn't getting any money from this hair-brained scheme. He was just getting annoyed . . . and frustrated.

He hadn't slept well since they left Charles Town, and Jack could no longer blame the small hammock or the snoring crew. It was the dreams—erotic dreams that woke him, hot and hard and almost moaning. And they all centered around Miranda Chadwick. Miranda Chadwick! The very fact left him puzzled.

Not that she wasn't lovely. In her own soft, delicate way she was beautiful. But he preferred women with more obvious curves and certainly ones who didn't make a habit of asking him myriad questions.

Regardless, every night he found himself dreaming of his captive. Holding her. Kissing her. Doing all manner of wild and lusty things to her that would probably shock her speechless—a sight he wouldn't mind witnessing.

To put a halt to the dreams, he'd tried staying away from her. That didn't help. Yesterday he decided to overlook her strangeness and treat her like he would any other female. Perhaps keeping his distance caused him to think of her all the more.

It was too early to know if being around her would alleviate those damn frustrating dreams. But he did know it made him a target for her relentless questions.

He took a deep breath. "You cannot go with the messenger because that's not the way 'tis done." She started to say something, but he held up his hand. "I'm the pirate here, remember. I should know how to handle a kidnapping." He shifted slightly under her gaze. Her eyes looked lighter in the sunlight. More azure than twilight blue. And why he noticed or cared was beyond him.

"Now, if you've no more questions, I'll be about my duties." With that, Jack turned and headed for the quarterdeck. He had to do something to get this woman out of his thoughts, but outside of jumping ship and swimming to the nearest land, he couldn't think what it could be.

"Don't let him bother ye none. The cap'n's bark is usually worse'n his bite."

Miranda looked around at Phin and gave him a smile of welcome. "I know," she said. "At least I think I do." She couldn't help remembering that kiss. There were things he could do to her if she provoked him too much. But she had no plans to do that.

Now she just planned to lean back and enjoy the sunshine on the water and the sea breeze in her hair. She caught Phin's eye. "Your captain tells me we are headed for land."

"Aye, to Snebley's Creek."

"I imagine there is an abundance of flora and fauna there." When she noticed Phin's puzzled expression, she clarified, "Plants and animals."

"Ye got the right of it there, your ladyship. There's plenty of plants and bugs where we're goin'. Skeeters big enough to suck a man's body clean dry."

"Goodness," Miranda said, cocking her head. "I don't imagine I'll need my microscope to study them, will I?"

Phin's walnut brown face flushed red. "Mayhap I were exaggeratin' a mite. But they is big."

Miranda just laughed and clamped her bonnet on her head.

"Ye make any more sketches a them maggots?"

"I told you we can't talk about them anymore."

"I ain't gonna stop eating my vittles."

"That's all well and good, but I did promise Captain Blackstone that I would cease discussing maggots and animalcules with his crew. And a promise is a promise. Even if he is a pirate—" Miranda paused and bit her lip. "I'm sorry, I didn't mean to insult you." Despite his profession, she'd become quite fond of Phin. She liked King and Scar and most of the others, too.

"No offense taken." Phin screwed up his face. "It's just me and the men kinda liked hearin' ye talk about such things."

"I know," Miranda sighed. "But I did give my word and—" Her expression brightened. "There's nothing to stop us from exchanging views on other topics."

"Well, there sure ain't."

"We'll have to hold our discussions on deck, of course. But I don't believe your captain would mind. . . . That is, as long as I don't interfere with your work."

"Maybe you could tell us more 'bout light movin'. Though I still think it's either there or it ain't."

When Jack walked past his captive a quarter of an hour later, she was sitting on a coil of hemp, making a drawing on a sheet of parchment, and Phin and No Thumb sat by her feet.

"Does this drawing help?" Miranda asked, holding up a sketch she made of the sun and its planets.

The wrinkles in Phin's forehead deepened. "I ain't sure I got it yet." He twisted his head to the side and caught sight of Jack. "What ye think a this, Cap'n?"

Miranda's gaze flew to the tall, golden captain, and she sucked in her breath. She really didn't think he had any interest in science in general and what she had to say in particular. And he had just told her he had work to do. He couldn't help but resent the interruption. She waited for the roar of his voice as he told Phin not to bother him with such inconsequential things, but it never came.

Instead he squatted in front of her, so close that his muscled thighs nearly brushed her skirt. After reaching for the parchment, he spread it across his knees. His expression was serious as he examined the sketch.

"This is . . . ?" he asked, and Miranda pulled her attention away from watching his long, bronzed finger point to a circular shape.

"Jupiter." Miranda swallowed. She never before noticed the tiny prisms of crystal green and silver that made up his eyes. "And that's its moon." She reached out and touched the paper.

"And I suppose this . . . 'person' is on Earth." Jack outlined the tiny stick figure she'd drawn standing in front of a long cylindrical shape.

"That's Olaus Roemer looking through a telescope." Miranda paused. "It's not a very good likeness."

"One would hope not. At least for old Olaus's sake." That coaxed a smile from her, and Jack couldn't help grinning in return. "What's he doing?"

"He's timin' an eclipse, Cap'n."

Jack glanced around. He'd forgotten Phin and No Thumb were even there. "Why's he doing that?"

Phin rubbed his bristled jaw. "Now, that's the part I ain't too sure 'bout, Cap'n."

"He's recording the difference in time of the eclipse of Jupiter's moon behind the planet when the Earth is closest to Jupiter and when it's farthest away."

"And?"

The captain was looking at her as if he understood what she said. Miranda leaned forward. "And he found the closer we are to Jupiter—

Roemer was at the Paris Observatory."

"A Frenchie," Phin spat in disgust.

"Oh, no. Roemer isn't French. He's Danish. He only used the observatory in Paris because . . . well, that really isn't important. Anyway." Miranda took a deep breath, surprised she still had the captain's attention. "Roemer found that when the Earth was on the same side of the sun as Jupiter, he could see the eclipse earlier, which meant it took the light from Jupiter's moon less time to travel the shorter distance."

"That make any sense to ye, Cap'n?" Phin squinted down at his captain.

Jack leaned back on his heels and shrugged. "Some." Jack examined the sketch again. He supposed she meant that if light took longer to get from two places that were far apart than two places that were closer, it meant it traveled. Kind of like it took him longer to sail from Charles Town to Barbados, than from Charles Town to Snebley's Creek.

He lifted his eyes and related as much to her. And found himself nearly preening at the admiring look she gave him. By the way her eyes shone, one would think he'd just unlocked the mysteries of the universe. He should have been annoyed with her reaction, but instead Jack found himself asking, "This Dane have any idea how fast light travels?"

Jack could, by "heaving the log" every hour or two, determine the speed of the *Sea Hawk*. Of course, there was no way to travel in the sky between the Earth and Jupiter.

119

"Actually, yes, he does know." Miranda couldn't believe it. She was certain now that the captain not only understood what she was talking about, but he was showing some interest. "By using the differences in the time it took light to travel from Jupiter's moon to Earth, he calculated that it travels about 141,000 miles per second."

Jack whistled through his teeth.

Phin dug at his straggly beard. "Ye believe that, Cap'n? Nothin' can move that fast, can it?"

"I don't know." Jack handed the parchment back to Phin and pushed to his feet. "What is it that's moving?"

Miranda stared up at him in awe at his question. It was something she and her grandfather had debated for hours and hours. "No one knows for certain exactly what light is. Newton, of course, thinks it's made up of particles. However Huygens insists it's waves."

"Like in the ocean?" Phin asked.

"Something like that. Only these waves travel in only one direction."

The captain seemed to ponder what she said; then he leveled his gaze on her. "What do you think it is?"

Miranda felt a flash of surprise and something else . . . pleasure? . . . that he asked her opinion. But her shoulders rounded. "I don't know which it is," she admitted.

Jack shrugged. "Well, whatever it is, it certainly travels fast."

"Oh, it does," Miranda agreed. "Much faster

than we can see. That's why it seems like light is just there, or that it travels at infinite speeds."

"It moves faster than ye can see?" Phin's expression was dubious.

"Yes. Remember there are things that you simply can't see."

"Ah, like them animalcules swimmin' 'round in the water."

Miranda's eyes flashed to Jack's. They were watching her with suspicion. "Nay, I didn't mean that." Phin must have realized what he said, for he shuffled back and forth on his feet and pulled on his beard again.

Jack tried hard to suppress a grin. "Do you wish to return to my . . . I mean, your cabin now?" he asked Miranda.

"Not unless I have to." She wasn't sure how angry he was about Phin's reference to animalcules.

But apparently he wasn't annoyed at all, for he bowed and expressed his desire that she do as she pleased. And Miranda wondered if all captives aboard a pirate ship were treated so courteously.

Captain Blackstone excused himself to go below, and Miranda couldn't help feeling a twinge of regret. It really was nice to discuss Olaus Roemer with someone who understood.

Perhaps she didn't do a good enough job of explaining, because Phin and No Thumb still looked quite perplexed. Miranda began to tell them again in simpler language, but they only threw up their hands and said they'd talk more later.

Both pirates seemed a lot more interested in studying the enlarged maggots and animalcules than in something they couldn't see.

"Oh, well." Miranda flipped through several pages of parchment and smiled when she found the one she wanted. It was a drawing of a man . . . a drawing of Captain Blackstone. No one would recognize it as him . . . at least she hoped not.

The features were indistinct, but then she wasn't trying to paint his portrait. Miranda was interested in sketching his musculature, which she knew must be as superb as any da Vinci had drawn.

Miranda studied the paper. She felt fairly good about her depiction of his chest and arm muscles. And she'd noticed the ridges and valleys in his thighs as he squatted in front of her, but the rest. . . .

If only he would pose for her. Miranda expelled her breath. No matter that the captain showed some interest in the speed of light, she seriously doubted he'd sit still and let her sketch him . . . in the nude.

Miranda squirmed on her seat of coiled hemp. Why should the idea of seeing the pirate captain without clothing make her uncomfortable? After all, she'd seen Borelli's sketches in his book, *De Motu Animalium*. What was the problem with her making sketches of her own? But no matter how she tried to rationalize it, she felt an odd sensation in the pit of her stomach at the thought of seeing all of Captain Blackstone . . . even if he was only made of skin and bone and muscle.

"What ye doin' there?"

Miranda jumped and hurriedly covered her drawing of the captain. Scar was leaning over her shoulder, and Miranda wondered if he'd seen her sketch; but he didn't pursue the subject. He just yanked off a less than clean red scarf and wiped his face.

"Sure is hot today, ain't it?"

"It is quite warm," Miranda agreed. Actually, sitting in the shade of the mast she hadn't noticed the heat that much. But Scar had obviously been working in the sun.

"Don't know as I ever will get used to this heat. Course where I'm from it was more the cold that got to ye, so I guess it's even."

"Where are you from?" Miranda realized that was a question she never contemplated before. These pirates must be from someplace. And obviously they'd been something before they'd become a pirates. One wasn't born a pirate . . . not even Captain Blackstone.

"I'm from London, down by the docks. Had meself a pretty decent lot till '65. Sold pies, s'what my mam baked. But then the death swept through and kilt her and me brothers and wasn't none left but meself." He shrugged and tied the damp kerchief back around his neck.

"So that's when you became a . . . a pirate?"

"Naw." Scar breathed in the salty air. "Had me

a stint on one a His Majesty's ships for a while. Cabin boy I was."

"Why that's wonderful." Miranda couldn't imagine why Scar would give up a career in His Majesty's service to become a freebooter.

"Weren't so grand as all that. The damn captain had a strong likin' for the cat. Whipped the crew on a regular like basis, he did. But that weren't the worst of it." Scar leaned closer. "The man was a damn sodomite, if ye knows what I mean."

Miranda was pretty sure she did. Her smile was wan, and she sank back a bit; but Scar didn't seem to notice.

"That's where I got this here." He ran his finger along the ridge of his scar and grimaced. "He didn't take kindly to me refusin' him. But I just say to him, 'Captain Sherry, beggin' your pardon sir, but I ain't no queer."

"I don't imagine he liked that much."

"Ye got the right a it there, ye do. Zipped out his saber and slashed me good across the cheek." Scar took a deep breath. "Kept me safe from him, though, till we reached Barbados. Then I jumped ship. Joined up with Red McNeil; he was the *Sea Hawk*'s captain before Gentleman Jack. And I never did look back."

Well, she'd wanted the story of how he became a pirate, and he'd given it to her—perhaps given her more than she wanted—but still, it made her see him as more human.

"And you're happy . . . I mean, being a pirate?"

Scar rubbed at his puckered cheek. "I can't say that I never miss ol' England. Like I said 'bout the weather. It can get mighty hot. But I ain't got no complaints." His hands straddled his wiry hips. "Cap'n Blackstone's a good sort. And ye don't have to worry 'bout him being no sodomite." He said the last with fierce determination.

"No," Miranda agreed. "I don't imagine you do."

After she was escorted below, Miranda sat thinking . . . wondering what Captain Blackstone's story was. Surely he had some reason for being a pirate. But she knew she'd never ask him, and she didn't imagine any of the crew would satisfy her curiosity about their captain. Besides, she didn't want them to know she was even curious.

Miranda took out her sketch of the pirate captain's musculature and filled in all she could remember.

The next morning Miranda sighted a shore bird, and by afternoon the verdant shoreline wavered on the horizon. The crew was busy all morning, but after the midday meal of salt pork and pease, several of them including Phin, Scar, King and No Thumb sat on barrels near her resting place.

Captain Blackstone had ventured below deck, but Miranda chose to remain above where the temperature was cooled by the offshore breeze.

"So you're sayin' the Earth ain't round?" Phin's face was screwed up in thought. Even he'd heard of the brave sailors who sailed the whole way around it.

"Not exactly, no."

"It ain't flat, is it?" No Thumb wanted to know.

"Goodness, no." Miranda laughed, and No Thumb looked relieved. "It's relatively round, but it's more an oblate sphere. No, that's not a good explanation." Miranda chewed on the end of her thumbnail. "Think of an egg."

"I'd like to be eatin' an egg 'bout now."

"Hush your mouth, Scar, and let her ladyship finish," Phin said.

Miranda sighed. She wished she had an egg right now, too. Not to eat, though it would taste good after all the salt pork she'd consumed. But she'd discovered the men understood things much better if she could show them.

Instead she cupped her hands, roughly showing them the Earth's shape according to Newton's theory.

"Of course he can't prove it," Miranda continued, "but it makes sense that the Earth is larger around at the equator since the gravitational pull is less there."

"What's this gravinal pull stuff?"

"Gravitational pull, Scar. It's the attraction that keeps us from falling off the Earth."

"Fallin' off? What ye talkin' 'bout?"

"Don't concern yourselves. We aren't going to. Gravity from the center of the Earth keeps everything down on the ground." The relief on their faces was amusing. To further mollify them—

Miranda didn't want them running to their captain with fears of falling into space—she related some examples.

"You've all thrown something into the air, haven't you?" They glanced at each other and nodded. "Well, what happened to it? Did it go flying off into space never to be seen again?"

"Hell, no. If ye don't watch, it will come down and bop you on the noggin."

"Exactly. Gravity did that. Pulled it back to the Earth." Miranda shrugged. "It keeps you on the ground, too."

"Well, I'll be." Phin dug at his beard with gnarled fingers. "That's why them heavy rocks we use for ballasts fall so quick."

"Actually, it doesn't matter how heavy something is. It falls back to Earth at the same speed." Skeptical expressions greeted this new revelation by Miranda.

"Ye mean to tell me a heavy rock don't fall no faster than a light one?"

"I know it seems it should, but it doesn't. Galileo first proved it—"

"Din't we hear 'bout this fellow before?"

"Yes, I believe we did discuss him. He was a very interesting scientist . . . and quite brilliant. Anyway, he showed that two objects fall at the same speed regardless of their weight. Later, after Otto von Guericke invented the air pump, he proved—"

"How'd he do that?"

"Do what, No Thumb?"

"How'd that Gallo fellow show a heavy thin'

and somethin' light dropped the same? 'Cause I just don't believe it," he finished, crossing his arms over his barrel chest.

"Well, he went to the top of a tall tower and he — Wait a minute." Miranda shaded her eyes and glanced skyward, a smile spreading across her face. She knew what the best way to teach them was.

Turning her attention back to the pirates, she ticked off the things she'd need on her fingers. "Two pouches, some hardtack. . . ."

Jack finished writing in his log and stretched. Leaning back, he crossed his booted ankles on the edge of the desk. He was tired of being below, but at least this time in his cabin was put to good use. He managed to cipher how much Henry still owed him on the cargo he hadn't had a chance to unload in Charles Town. He smiled thinking of that figure

. But even though he'd done pretty well, Jack was getting the uncomfortable feeling that times were changing. Spanish galleons weren't as plentiful or as easy picking as they once were. And the French. . . . Jack curled his mouth in derision. It was hardly worth his while to expend the shot on them. They rarely carried anything of much value.

Jack folded his arms and inclined the chair on its back legs. Phin was always talking about heading for the Indian Ocean. Attacking Mogul shipping was easy and profitable.

But Jack didn't like the idea. For one thing the Indian Ocean was a long way from St. Augustine, or Spain for that matter. And if he ever hoped to find his sister or de Segovia, he couldn't leave. The other reason had something to do with the itch at the base of his neck. He'd even spoken to his uncle a while back when he was in Charles Town, about giving up the life of a freebooter. It wasn't as if he needed the money. There was the plantation.

Jack shook his head. He wasn't going to hang. He did everything he could to keep from getting caught. Hell, hadn't he proven just how far he was willing to go to avoid the gibbet when he kidnapped Miranda Chadwick?

A scowl darkened his handsome features. Tomorrow morning they'd dock in the creek. A few days after that they'd head back to Charles Town, and he could be rid of her.

Jack decided he'd unload his cargo as quickly as possible; take on supplies and fresh water and head for St. Augustine. Someone had to know where his sister was, and this time he wasn't returning until he found her.

Running his fingers through his shoulder-length hair, Jack righted the chair and stood. He gave one last longing look at his bunk and shook his head about the picture he noticed on his desk—the picture of a man with lines and ripples all over his skin. With a shrug he left the cabin.

Miranda Chadwick certainly did find strange things to do with her time. When he first noticed the sketch under his log, he thought she was drawing someone's portrait. But a closer inspection showed that the face was only a blur of lines. It was the body she'd drawn in detail—but not too much detail. Mistress Chadwick obviously didn't know everything, Jack thought with a chuckle. Because she sure didn't know what a man looked like under his breeches.

Jack climbed through the hatch and glanced around, wondering where everybody was. A bucket of salt water and a holystone lay on the deck by his feet. Granted, none of the crew were wild about scrubbing the deck, but they'd all agreed it was a chore that needed done.

Hearing noises behind him, Jack turned around. To a man, his crew was standing in a semicircle around the mast.

"What the hell is going on?" Guilty faces turned at the sound. As Jack strode toward them they parted, allowing him inside the circle of men. Phin met his stare with an expression on his wizened face that Jack could only describe as sheepish.

"What are you doing?" Jack repeated. "Who in the hell is steering the ship?"

"Er, Cap'n, sir . . . uh . . ."

"I want an answer and I want it now!" A thought sprang into Jack's head. He glanced around nervously. "Where's Mistress Chadwick?"

The slight lifting of Phin's eyes was subtle, but Jack caught it. He raised his gaze and felt his heart leap in his chest. God's blood!" he bellowed. "What's she doing up there?" Jack didn't wait for an answer but repeated the same question for the benefit of his errant captive. "What the hell are you doing up there?"

Miranda Chadwick was at least thirty feet above the deck, clinging to the rigging. Her hair was whipping in the breeze, and her skirts were tucked up through her legs showing an indecent amount of bare skin.

Jack thought she yelled something down about gravity and Galileo, but he didn't stand around to listen. Grabbing hold of the hemp, he swung himself into the rigging. "Don't move! Just don't move!"

Years of practice made Jack's assent up the ratlines quick and smooth. With each swaying motion of the ship he glanced above to see how Miranda was faring. And with each foothold he noticed the distance down to the solid oak deck.

He'd never worried about the height before, but now that there was a chance of Miranda Chadwick falling, he couldn't think of anything else—except how he was going to skin every member of his crew for letting her do such a fool thing. And how he was going to throttle her.

When she was safe on deck, of course.

Miranda couldn't believe how quickly the captain covered the space from the deck to her. She also couldn't believe how angry he looked. She had the strongest desire to climb higher still. But she could only go so far, and she had no doubt he could climb faster . . . and well, there was no sense making him more enraged than he already was.

So she stayed where she was, clutching the rigging with one hand. In the other she held two pouches. One contained sea biscuits. The heavier one was full of small iron balls called grapeshot. She had planned to drop them both at the same time to prove Galileo's theory. Instead she watched the sun turn the captain's hair a brilliant gold as he came toward her.

"I can explain, Captain Blackstone. You see—" The rest of her words were lost as he grabbed her around the waist with one of his steel-band arms.

"Hold on to my neck," he ordered, in a tone that left no room for argument.

She clung as he reached across for the tar-covered backstay. Wind whipped about them, and his smell enveloped her as readily as his body. The sensations were overwhelming. Then he wrapped his powerful legs around the rope, and they slid, nearly flying toward the deck. The rush was exhilarating, but it ended abruptly when the captain's feet hit the deck.

Without a word he bent and tossed her over his shoulder. Blood coursed to Miranda's head, but she didn't dare fight him. He yelled a hasty command to his crew that had them scurrying. Then still holding the back of her thighs, he headed for the hatch.

Chapter Seven

"Oh, you brute! You cretin!" Miranda landed on her feet inside the captain's cabin one moment; the next she flung back her ebony hair and lunged toward him. She had never been so humiliated in her life. As a matter of fact, she didn't think she'd *ever* been humiliated—that is, until she met this pirate.

Captain Blackstone grabbed her hands, effectively thwarting her blows. In frustration she jackknifed her leg and kicked him, forgetting until her toes slammed into his leather boots that she'd removed her shoes before climbing the rigging.

"Ouch! Oh. . . . Oh, look what you've done." Miranda danced around on her other foot—but only as far away as his shackling hold would allow.

"What *I've* done! What *I've* done?" Jack had the strongest urge to take her creamy smooth neck between his fingers and squeeze. Instead he flung her hands down and paced to the transom window. The placid sea kept his attention for only a minute before he turned on her. "What about what *you've* done?"

Miranda stopped hopping around on one foot long enough to face him. "I didn't do anything."

"You didn't—" Jack dug ten fingers through his hair in frustration and paced across the room. "What do you call climbing the rigging?"

Miranda crossed her arms, ignoring the pain in her toes. The ribbon had come loose from her hair when the captain threw her over his shoulder. With a flip of her head she shook a lock off her cheek. "I was demonstrating the law of falling bodies."

"Did you *have* to use your own?"

"I had no intention of falling from the rigging." She wished the captain would calm down. He stalked the small cabin like a tiger in a cage. "I intended to drop these pouches." Miranda unfolded her arms and showed him the leather bags she still clutched in her hands. "There are sea biscuits in one, and in the other, I have balls."

Stopping in his tracks, Jack stared at her through narrowed eyes. "You certainly do."

Ignoring his comment, which she didn't understand anyway, Miranda continued her explanation. "It was a simple experiment. No harm would have come from it."

Jack leaned toward her till their noses nearly touched. "No harm? Do you have any idea what would have happened to you if you'd fallen?" Jack could still feel the panic that had engulfed him when he'd looked up to see her clinging to the rigging.

"But I had no intention of falling," she repeated. When the captain snorted and walked away, Miranda followed. "I'm a very good climber. Back in England I often scaled trees to gather specimens for my grandfather's experiments."

Jack's head whipped around, and his stormy gaze met hers. "Well, on my ship you're my responsibility and you scale nothing. Is that understood?"

Miranda lifted her chin. "I was in far more danger when you threw me over your shoulder than when I climbed the ropes."

"Is that understood?" he repeated.

She wanted to argue the point further, but the captain seemed in no mood. He stood, his booted feet spread, his muscled arms crossed, looking every bit the ruthless pirate, and waited for her reply. Reluctantly Miranda nodded. "I understand."

"Good." His granite chin clenched. "And from now on you are to have no discourse with my crew."

"What?" Miranda dropped the pouches. She didn't bother to notice if they hit the floor at the same time or not. "But that's not fair!"

"I warned you that—"

"You said that I was to refrain from speaking of maggots and animalcules. Which I have."

"Aye, but you seem unable to stay out of trouble when you're around them."

"For the last time, I wasn't in trouble." Miranda's shoulders drooped. "And they have such an interest in science."

"More likely, their interest extends to your anatomy."

His gaze slid downward, and Miranda felt a trail of warmth follow. A flash of passion lit his eyes, and Miranda glanced down to see her skirts tucked up to show her legs from the knees down. Hastily she yanked the garment down.

"You're disgusting," she said, looking away.

"True enough. But at least I don't pretend this great curiosity about Jupiter's moons so I can sit around and gaze into your big blue eyes."

Miranda's big blue eyes widened in shock. "They don't do that."

God's blood, maybe they didn't. Maybe *he* was the only one who couldn't get enough of looking at her. But hell, she'd been up on those ropes, her long, slender legs there for all his crew to see.

"They don't," Miranda insisted again. "Phin is interested in things like the speed of light. And so is Scar and King and No Thumb." Miranda's chin notched defiantly. "They all are."

"All right, maybe they are." Damn, she could be prickly. "Unfortunately, they're going to have to forgo any more knowledge for the rest of your captivity. I'm responsible for you and that's the way it's going to be."

"But I think—"

Jack's mouth covered hers in a kiss that effectively cut off her argument . . . whatever it was going to be. He hadn't planned to use that technique to quiet her. One minute he was just standing there, and the next he was crushing her against him, burying his hands in her luxurious hair.

She felt wonderful, so soft and sweet, and the tightly coiled frustration he'd known since looking up and seeing her in the shrouds dissipated. He—a pirate—had been scared to death when he saw her so far above the deck. It took wrapping her in his arms to assure himself she was safe.

Miranda knew she should stop him, but when she raised her hands to push him away they clutched the front of his shirt instead. He was so hard and strong, and the sheer size of him overwhelmed her in such a delightful way. Surely she should let the kiss continue—if only as an experiment.

But when his tongue nudged her lips apart and she opened to him, Miranda lost all thoughts of scientific research. She moaned and stretched up on her toes, wrapping her arms around his neck.

His lips left hers and rained kisses across her cheeks and nose and over her fluttering eyelids. His tongue trailed down her neck, and Miranda had the strangest sensation in the pit of her stomach. Her head fell back, and she tried to catch her breath as he nipped at her ear.

Miranda's knees felt weak; she thought she might fall but for the hands that skimmed down her body. Then suddenly he was lifting her. Not in the infuriating way of before, but against his hard chest.

His lips found hers again, urgently, hungrily. Jack laid her on the bunk, following her down with his body. She clung to him, drove him wild with her innocent movements and the soft, sweet noises she made.

He cupped her breast through the silk of her gown and sighed when the nipple hardened beneath his hand. He teased it with his thumb, and she arched off the mattress toward him. Jack groaned, rubbing his manhood against her, nearly losing himself when she squirmed beneath him.

God, he shouldn't do this. The thought came out of nowhere, and Jack tried to push it aside. He nibbled at her lips, gently teasing, pleased when she opened for him. Jack's tongue met hers in a rhythmic motion that drove him wild.

He ached. He wanted. He couldn't drive away the nagging regret that he shouldn't do this. *He couldn't do this.*

With a groan Jack pushed himself up, and turned to sit on the edge of the bunk. His breathing was shallow and gasping, and he dropped his head into his hands, trying to regain some control.

She made a small noise, and Jack twisted his head to look at her—and almost forgot his resolve. Her inky black hair spilled across his pillow in abandon. Her eyes, heavy-lidded and dark from passion, questioned him. But unlike the verbal queries she constantly made, this one didn't annoy him. She deserved an answer to this one.

Unfortunately, he had no answers. He couldn't tell her why he had started kissing her. And he sure as hell couldn't tell her why he had stopped.

Closing his eyes, he sought a deep breath. "I apologize." Jack lifted his hands, then let them drop between his knees.

"I . . ." Miranda pushed up on her elbow. "I don't know what to say." This was all so new to her. Miranda knew how animals—how humans reproduced. Grandfather had explained the entire process to her once when they were discussing Nehemiah Grew's discoveries about plant sexuality.

Miranda had been almost eleven at the time. She'd listened with her usual curiosity, asked a fair number of questions and decided it didn't sound too appealing. Oh, she'd been certain that one day she would participate in the procedure. It was important to populate the Earth.

But never did she think she might do such a thing with a pirate. And though the act itself had very little in common with the explanation her grandfather had given her, Miranda was pretty certain that was what she'd almost done with him.

And Lord help her, she would have continued if the pirate hadn't stopped. Even now she had niggling feelings of regret that he had.

Jack studied her a moment, then stood. "There is nothing for you to say. This was entirely my fault. God's blood, I am a pirate, after

139

all." Hell, pirates raped and pillaged all the time. Just because Jack didn't have a taste for it didn't mean he couldn't if he wanted to.

But this had been no near rape. Jack knew it. He shot her a quick glance. And he had a feeling Miranda knew it, too.

God, he was going to have to stay away from her.

Shaking his head, Jack paced to the door. "I should never have kidnapped you, but since I—"

"Why did you . . . kidnap me, I mean." Miranda swung her legs over the side of the bunk.

"Well, it sure as hell wasn't my idea." As soon as the words were out of his mouth, Jack knew he said the wrong thing. The woman worked on his mind as well as his groin.

"Whose idea was it?"

"Nobody's." Jack held up his hand. "I mean it wasn't one of my better ideas. Never mind. Just try and forget this happened. I'll have you home in a sennight." Before she could question him further, Jack left the cabin.

"Ye weren't too rough on her was ye, Cap'n?" Jack had barely cleared the hatch when Phin sidled up to him. "Ye know she didn't mean nothin' by what she done."

"I don't imagine she even knew how dangerous it could be up there in the shrouds with the wind blowing." Jack's voice was calm. "But you knew, Phin, and you let her climb up there anyway."

"Aw now, Cap'n, she said she was a good climber. And damn if she weren't. Why, you'd a been right shocked at how fast she scurried up there. And I swear on my mother's grave she didn't tell us what she was up to before she done it. Just grabbed hold of a ratline and up she went."

Jack let out a deep sigh. Knowing Miranda, it was easy to believe Phin's explanation. "What's done is done. Thank God no harm came to the wench." The memory of lying with her on his bunk and of what he wanted to do flashed into Jack's mind. Henry would have a fit if he found out.

Shaking his head, Jack watched the shoreline of pines and palmettos pass by. They were sailing into the all-but-hidden inlet, toward a narrow, deep-channeled creek that Jack had discovered one time while evading a British frigate. Since then he used the landing often. It offered a safe, protected area for his crew to refit the *Sea Hawk*. This time he'd see the work done as quickly as possible. The sooner he had Mistress Miranda back in the loving arms of her father, the better off she'd be. And the better off he'd be.

By five bells in the forenoon watch the *Sea Hawk* was anchored near shore. The creek's bottom was hard and gravelly, and at low water, the men began graving the ship's hull. Scrubbing the barnacles from the ship's timbers was hard work; but a pirate ship demanded speed, and to accomplish that, the hull needed frequent cleaning.

Miranda observed what she could from the

transom windows. At first it was interesting watching the pirates hanging over the side and scraping at the wood. But she soon found her gaze shifting to the shore where lacquered leaves and cord grass swayed alluringly in the breeze. Miranda bit the end of her thumbnail and wondered what riches of discovery she might find beyond the cloak of green.

If only she could explore . . . like the naturalist, John Ray. Miranda's shoulders dropped. She needed to do something . . . anything to take her mind off her encounter with Captain Blackstone. A wave of excitement rushed through her, and she curled her arms about her waist.

This was terrible. All she could think about was him. How he looked. How it felt to be held by him, to be kissed by him. Why he pulled away so suddenly.

Miranda paced to the door. Her mind was usually full of such lofty thoughts and notions. She wondered about the universe. She wondered about animals and plant life, and gravity and light and all manner of important and fascinating things.

And now the only thing that occupied her mind was a pirate captain. Something was wrong. Something was very wrong. And the only thing she could think of to change it was to immerse herself in a new project. Like exploring the vegetation on shore.

Miranda strode back to the window and flopped onto the window seat. It wasn't as if the captain forbade her to go ashore. Miranda turned and stuck her head out the open window. They were almost close enough to the sandy beach to wade through the water. Besides, she knew how to swim even if they weren't.

Gathering up her parchment, Miranda headed for the door. She would simply ask the captain. He'd told her she was to have nothing to do with any of the crew, but he hadn't said anything about staying in the cabin.

The captain wasn't on deck. No one was. Shading her face from the afternoon sun with her hand, Miranda walked around the railing, glancing over the edge as she went, for some sign of the captain. She noticed Phin hanging over the side and came close to calling down to him, but decided the captain wouldn't like that. Instead she continued to search.

She finally found him aft of the main mast. Like the other men he was scraping at the overlapping shells stuck to the hull. He seemed so busy with his sweat-slick muscles gleaming in the sun that Miranda hesitated to yell down to him. But when she remembered that the alternative was to go back to the stifling cabin and spend her time ruminating about him, she gained courage.

"Captain Blackstone?" Miranda called twice before he looked up. "May I have a word with you?"

God's blood, what did she want now? Jack took another vicious swipe at the hull. "What is it, Mistress Chadwick?"

"I was wondering if I might go ashore?"

143

"Nay."

Nay? Just nay? No let me think on the matter. No please be so kind as to explain why you wish to go ashore. Just nay.

Miranda squeezed in beside the belaying pins and leaned farther over the rail. "I wanted to collect some flora . . . to study under the microscope.

Jack shut his eyes, and took a deep breath. When he regained some of his control, he squinted up at her. She'd braided her hair, and the thick, woven curls hung down over her shoulder as black and shiny as a crow's wing. Jack tried to ignore his desire to dig his fingers into the sweet-smelling mass. Instead he concentrated on all her annoying little habits . . . like pestering him while he worked.

"I don't recall asking why you wished to go ashore, nor do I care. 'Tis all I can manage to keep my eye on you while you're confined to my ship."

"I didn't know you thought it necessary to keep your eye on me." After all, she'd been below in his cabin until a moment ago. The pirate captain made no comment. Like the rest of the pirates, he sat on a small, wooden swinglike contraption at the end of a long rope. Ignoring her, he started scraping again.

Miranda was used to discussing differences of opinion, thrashing them out with facts and logic. Captain Blackstone's method of dealing with something—to simply pretend it didn't exist—she found most annoying. Besides, she didn't like being treated like a child who had to ask permission to do anything. Grandfather had never interfered with her studies.

With renewed zeal Miranda hung farther over the side. "Actually, it would be easier to watch me if I were on the beach. See?" She leaned over until only the tips of her shoes touched the deck. "You'd have naught to do but turn your head to monitor my whereabouts."

He didn't intend to, but Jack swung his head around toward the creek's edge. He did have a clear view of the sandy beach that served as a buffer between the pine forest and the gently lapping water. But just because he could see the beach didn't mean he was going to let her get off the ship. He glanced up to tell her, and his mouth went dry.

"What are you doing? Do you want to fall into the creek?" She was leaning over the side so far, Jack thought any moment she might topple over into the water.

Miranda slid back over the rail. "You needn't worry. I know how to swim."

"That's truly a comfort." Jack's heart seemed to be steadying to its regular pace.

"Actually, I could swim to shore if you'd rather not be bothered to take me."

"Hell, yes, I'd rather not be bothered. But that does *not* mean I want you swimming to the beach." Jack stuck his scraping tool into his belt and grabbed hold of the rope. If he was going to get any work done, it probably would be best if he took her to the shore. She could sit in the shade, do whatever it was she did, and be out of his hair.

Miranda watched him pull himself hand over hand up the hemp. It brought back vivid memories of when she'd clung to him and he'd shimmied down a rope . . . and of what had happened in the cabin after that.

He bounded over the rail and landed on deck. As with every time she saw him, Miranda was struck by his size. Or maybe this time it was because he wore no shirt. His smooth, bronzed chest shone slick with sweat. And Miranda couldn't help watching a droplet run down the flat plane of his stomach and soak into his cotton breeches.

He turned, walking away on bare feet, and Miranda followed. "Gather whatever you wish to take with you. I'll lower the boat." They actually were close enough to shore to swim, but he wasn't having Henry think Jack didn't treat his daughter with utmost respect.

The whole time he'd ben scraping at the barnacles, Jack had thought of his vow to his friend. He'd said he would treat her as he would his sister. Well, he sure hadn't been thinking of his sister when he kissed Miranda.

"I'm ready."

Jack turned and scowled down at her. She had a straw bonnet perched atop her head and her parchment and charcoal. At that moment Jack thought to ask her about the strange drawing he'd found on his desk, but decided against it. He didn't want her thinking he was interested in

146

whatever she was doing.

Jack used the short row to shore to emphasize the rules she was to follow. "Stay on the beach. Do not go anywhere. Do not do anything. Oh, and stay out of the water," Jack added. He remembered her words about knowing how to swim and could just imagine her trying it.

"I'll come back for you in two hours. If for any reason you wish to return to the ship before that, just yell."

"Thank you, Captain. I shall be fine." Miranda spread a blanket out on the sand and seated herself beneath the shade of a large live oak draped with gossamer veils of Spanish moss.

The pirate captain pulled the boat onto shore and, after giving her one more reminder to stay put, waded into the water and swam to his ship. Miranda watched as he returned to his spot near the anchor. His powerful arms caught hold of the rope, and he hoisted himself onto his wooden plank. Before he set to scraping he turned his head and stared at Miranda.

She waved; he didn't.

Miranda had plenty to keep her busy in this new setting. Species of plants she'd only begun to explore before her kidnapping lined the beach in seemingly limitless variety. She had only to reach out to trace a leaf's serrated edges or outline the meandering of a vine. Everywhere she looked there was something new and exciting to see. Then, why did she spend the majority of her time watching the pirate captain?

Telling herself she only wanted to examine his

musculature, she studied his form as he bent over his task. She picked up her charcoal and decided to do a series of drawings of him, not just the one. When Miranda caught herself concentrating on just the right way to sketch his aristocratic nose, and the shape of his generous mouth, she knew this had gone way beyond scientific research of anatomy.

In exasperation Miranda tossed aside her charcoal. What was wrong with her? She was the pirate's captive. If anything, she should be thinking of ways to escape him. After all, she only had his word that he planned to take her back to Charles Town.

What if her father couldn't pay the ransom? Or what if the messenger couldn't find this place? She glanced around. It was certainly remote, seemingly inaccessible except by sea. And she certainly had seen no indication that a messenger had arrived . . . or even that anyone was expecting one. Yet, the captain had clearly said that here was where he was to receive the money.

But who would bring it? Miranda stood and walked along the edge of the small beach. It was completely surrounded by dense forest and underbrush. She couldn't even find a path. It was perplexing to consider how a messenger would find this place. Miranda shook her head. It just wasn't logical.

But then nothing about Captain Blackstone was . . . including her own reaction to him.

With a sigh, Miranda went back to her blanket. The sun's angle threw most of the woolen square in bright light, so she pulled it back farther into the shade. Sitting down, she set to sketching the palmetto tree off to her right.

It was warm even in the shade, and Miranda found her eyes drifting shut. She didn't want to sleep, so she shook herself and straightened her back. That's when she noticed the small lizard sitting on her blanket. She'd seen them before in Charles Town but never this close.

It was about three inches long, a vivid green in color, with a tongue that whipped out periodically. Slowly, Miranda moved toward the lizard for a better look. She reached out her hand just as it darted off the blanket into the sand.

Miranda pushed to her feet and watched it scurry into the underbrush. Without a thought other than studying the lizard more closely, Miranda followed.

"What's all this yelling about?" Jack bounded over the rail and wedged his way through the circle of men to Scar and No Thumb. The two pirates, one large and dark, the other scrawny and fair, glared at each other beneath lowered brows. These two had their share of squabbles, and usually Jack let them work through them without his interference.

But this time the noise from the rest of his crew was so great that he couldn't ignore it. He'd been over the side careening when he'd first heard them. Just to make certain Miranda Chadwick wasn't at the center of this brouhaha, he'd glanced toward shore. She was sitting innocently on her blanket, and he'd had to smile at the pretty picture she made as she bent over something near her.

But he didn't watch her long, because the men on deck recaught his attention. What were they doing on deck anyway? Everyone had orders to be cleaning the hull so that they could get the job finished and get back to Charles Town.

Now he found the men were not only slacking off their jobs; they were nearly having a free for all.

"All right, I want to know what this is all about." Jack shouldered between the two pirates. "Well?"

No Thumb jutted out his bristly jaw. "This good-for-nothing son of a whore says we're gonna be sucked into the ground."

"What?" Jack could barely believe his ears. His crew had some pretty strange ideas sometimes but this. . . . "Scar, you know better than that."

"Weren't me sayin' it. Mistress Miranda told us."

This announcement set off a barrage of yelling, most of which was directed at Scar. The scene was so ridiculous that at first Jack could only stand and stare at his men in amazement. Then he took a deep breath. "God's blood, would you be quiet! All of you."

Mouths clamped shut, and all eyes turned toward Jack. He met their stares, then let out his breath. "Now, Phin, tell me what this is about," he asked his quartermaster when he thought things had calmed a bit.

"Ain't sure, Cap'n. Scar here says Mistress Miranda said we was goin' to be sucked down—"

"I already heard that part of it. When did she say this?" Jack's fist clenched. So help him if he found out she'd gone behind his back and told this rubbish to his men he'd . . . Lord help him, he didn't know what he'd do.

"That's just it, Cap'n. She ain't never said no such thing. She talked to us 'bout gravity." Phin paused to make certain everybody noticed his use of the scientific word. "But that was the day she climbed the . . . well, ye know what she climbed."

He did indeed. That moment he'd looked up to see her hanging on the shrouds was etched forever in his mind. "And she hasn't been spouting this . . . this nonsense since then?"

"Hell, no, Cap'n. None of us done more'n seen her. Which to my thinkin' is the problem."

Jack couldn't believe what he was hearing. "What are you talking about?" His crew listening to her had caused all this mayhem.

"If'n she could explain stuff to us, maybe Scar wouldn't be so all fired mixed up."

"I ain't mixed up. She said—"

"Quiet!" Jack's hands rested on his hips. "Let me get this straight. You all want to hear what this . . . woman has to say. Even though she talks about maggots and being sucked into the ground?"

"She didn't say nothin' 'bout being sucked in.

And, aye. We do want to hear what she has to say 'bout stuff."

There was a general mumbling of agreement that even Scar joined. Jack could only shake his head. What in the hell had come over his crew? God's blood, they were pirates, not green school-boys. But if they wanted to listen, Jack didn't see what he could do about it. He sure didn't want Miranda Chadwick to cause a mutiny on the *Sea Hawk* by not talking.

"All right, men. I'll allow her to come on deck and talk to you again. But you still have to do your work." Their nods and smiles were almost humorous. "I'm going to fetch her and see what she has to say about this agreement."

"Where is her ladyship, Cap'n?"

"She's right over—" Jack turned to point to the shore, and his jaw dropped open. There on the beach was the blanket, a straw hat . . . and nothing else.

"Oh, my God!" Running to the side, Jack vaulted over the rail and dove into the creek.

Chapter Eight

There was a path.

As soon as Miranda cleared the first tangle of underbrush, she found it: a footpath leading farther into the woods. By this time she had lost track of the lizard, but was sure there was much more to see.

Blocked from the sea breeze by the veil of leaves, the air hung heavy and thick. Insects droned about, dancing slowly among the beards of Spanish moss drooping from the trees.

Miranda stood in the middle of the trail and gazed about her. Slivers of sun filtered through the pine needles. This was so different from the forests in England. Everything . . . the flora, the insects, the birds squawking in the branches begged to be investigated.

Gnawing on her thumbnail, Miranda looked back where she'd pushed through the bushes, then forward along the path. She wasn't foolish enough to explore where she could get lost. When she followed the lizard, she'd broken off twigs so that she could find her way back to the beach. But now she didn't even have to do that. There was a path . . . obviously well used. All she had to do was stay close to it and she wouldn't lose her way.

She thought of Captain Blackstone, and indecision seized her. What if he noticed she was gone? But he probably knew about the path and would figure she just went for a stroll. She wasn't going to be long. And she probably would never get another chance like this. Her father was much more protective of her than Grandfather had been. Papa didn't allow her the freedom to simply explore.

Miranda started along the sandy footway. Besides, it wasn't as if she owed the pirate captain anything. He did kidnap her, for heaven's sake. And it wasn't like she was trying to escape. She'd come back.

In the meantime she could collect all sorts of wonderful samples. Miranda pinched some leaves off a vine tangling up around a live oak trunk. For lack of her sample pouch, she gathered up her skirt in front, forming a sack where she deposited her finds. She only wished she'd thought to bring her parchment so that she could record her findings. Instead, Miranda spoke softly to herself, describing the texture of the tree trunks and the knobby way the roots stuck out of the soil . . . trying to store these facts in her memory.

All the while, Miranda kept to the trail and

estimated how far she'd come. She was beginning to feel uneasy about the time she'd been away. Pirate or no, she didn't like to worry Captain Blackstone. Besides, she'd been on the receiving end of his temper, though she had to admit she could find no fault with the way he'd expressed his anger the last time. Yet, she supposed she couldn't count on being kissed whenever he was upset with her.

With a sigh she crouched down to pick her last specimen, a crimson wildflower, before turning back. She twisted to put the blossom in her skirt.

And saw the feet.

They were large, a coppery brown, and as she allowed her gaze to rise she found them connected to sturdy bare legs. Her eyes flew upward, and she gasped, falling back on her bottom and nearly spilling all her plants.

The man was tall, almost as tall as the captain, and he wore almost nothing on his body—nothing, that is, except the drawings that decorated his chest and face. He said something in a low guttural language that Miranda didn't understand, then crossed his arms as if waiting for her to respond.

"I don't understand," she said in English, then French, then Spanish. The man's dark brows rose when she said the last, but other than that he gave no sign that he comprehended what she said. He just continued to stare at her from eyes as dark as midnight. And Miranda wished she'd

155

stayed on board the *Sea Hawk*.

"Who are you?" Miranda finally asked. His response could have been a name, or it could have been anything else. Miranda had never come up against a language quite like this one.

The man was an Indian; she was sure of it. She'd read accounts of Indians and had even seen a volume of *The Drawings of John White* in which he'd sketched Indians who looked amazingly like this one. If only she could communicate with him, perhaps they could—

He grabbed her so quickly that Miranda didn't have time to do more than let out a squeal of protest . . . that is, till she noticed her collected specimens floating to the ground. Then she turned to let the Indian have it, but he clamped his hand over her mouth and dragged her back into the underbrush.

Suddenly the loss of her collection seemed unimportant. She was going to be killed by this Indian. She tried to fight him, but his arms lashed around her and his hand tightened over her mouth. Miranda blinked at him over his hand, and he nodded his head in the direction of the path.

Miranda could swear he was trying to tell her something. But what?

He hunched over behind the bushes and pulled Miranda down beside him. Thorns tore into her bodice, and tears welled in her eyes. Oh, God. First captured by a pirate, now an Indian. She waited for him to do something, but he had become still, his dark head cocked to one side as if listening.

Miranda concentrated, and she could hear something, too. Someone was running, pounding down the path toward them. Hope sprang to her breast. Could it be Captain Blackstone? But if it was, would the Indian kill him? The footfalls came nearer . . . louder, and Miranda's heart seemed to pound with the rhythm.

And then they were passing, going beyond where she and the Indian hid. She couldn't even see if it *was* Captain Blackstone. Maybe it was another Indian. She was sure it was when her Indian stood, dragging her up behind him, and called out a greeting.

The footsteps stopped, but Miranda didn't want to see any more Indians. She shut her eyes and prayed her captors would give her a quick death.

"God's blood!"

That voice. Those words. Miranda's eyes snapped open. But if she was hoping to see a welcome sight, she was to be disappointed. The pirate captain scowled at her as ominously as the Indian had. Still, she sagged against her captor in relief.

The Indian spoke again in his guttural language, and to Miranda's amazement, Captain Blackstone answered him in kind. When the Indian loosened the hand over her mouth, Miranda's jaw dropped open. They acted as if they knew each other.

The Indian spoke again, and the captain crossed his arms and nodded, albeit reluctantly. He said something that made the Indian laugh and release Miranda. Her feet hit the sandy soil, and her knees buckled. And the captain did nothing. Miranda was forced to grab hold of the Indian's arm for support.

Both the pirate and the Indian seemed to find this amusing. Miranda locked her knees and jerked away, but she stopped short of rushing to the captain's side. Besides, he was now in what appeared to be a serious discussion with the Indian. And it was extremely frustrating not to understand what they were saying.

Miranda tried to pick out a word here or there but couldn't. She thought the captain might turn to her and explain whatever negotiations were going on, but he ignored her completely, as did the Indian. She finally decided they weren't discussing her.

Were they getting ready for some horrible form of combat between them? Miranda watched the pirate's face. Though he was definitely in a rage, and growing angrier with every second, his hostility didn't appear to be directed toward the Indian.

Now that she thought of it, neither man had drawn a weapon. Of course, it didn't appear the pirate had one. He wore only wet breeches that clung to his lower body like a second skin. The Indian wore even less, but she did notice a knife handle sticking from a leather case lashed to his waist.

Miranda inched away from the Indian, thinking she was moving unnoticed until the pirate speared her with his stormy green gaze. She stilled. Apparently Captain Blackstone was more aware of her than she thought. That knowledge was strangely reassuring . . . even if he was angry with her.

Their discourse continued, punctuated by hand movements, until suddenly the Indian turned and began loping down the footpath away from the creek. Miranda watched wide-eyed as he disappeared around a bend into the forest. Then she twisted her head to look at Captain Blackstone. He, too, was gazing after the Indian, an inscrutable expression on his handsome face.

Seeing her chance, Miranda sank down to her knees and began recollecting the specimens she'd lost when the Indian grabbed her.

"What the hell are you doing?"

The question was so abrupt and loud that Miranda dropped the flora again, only barely suppressing a scream. She looked up to find the captain looming over her, his hands clasped at his lean waist.

"Well?" He glared down at her, obviously expecting an answer.

"I . . . I was . . . well, you see I'd collected some leaves and flowers and I dropped them, so . . ."

"Leaves and flowers. Is that what you were doing out here? Picking leaves and flowers?"

His voice rose with every word. Miranda simply swallowed and nodded.

"God's blood!" He threw his hands into the air as if beseeching a higher power to explain such behavior to him. "You take a chance on being taken by Indians, not to mention scare me near to death, all for a few leaves and flowers." Jack dropped his arms and paced a few feet down the footpath. Pivoting, he pointed his finger at her. "You are insane."

Miranda stood, carelessly brushing aside the few leaves that had managed to stay in her skirt. "I am not!"

Jack stepped closer. "You are."

Marching up to stand in front of him, close enough so that she could smell the salt water that glistened on his body, she crossed her arms. "I am not." For someone whose only knowledge of arguments—before she met the pirate—consisted of discussing the merits of scientific theory, Miranda was definitely getting into the spirit.

Jack lowered his head till their noses almost touched. "You are. You're crazier than a bat, to wander off alone when there are Indians around."

Miranda raised her chin. "There is no scientific evidence that a bat is crazy."

Jack only snorted. Leave it to this crazy woman to say something like that.

"And," Miranda continued. "No one told me there were Indians in the area."

Taking a deep breath, Jack glared down at her for a moment. What she said was true, still. . . . "You didn't have to know if you'd just stayed where I put you."

Miranda's eyes narrowed. She wasn't something to be put somewhere and expected to just stay like a . . . like a dog. "I did stay—"

"Ha!" Jack's laugh was loud and short. "Are you trying to tell me you were sitting on the beach minding your own business and Nafkebee captured you? And before you answer, let me tell you he said he found you on the trail."

"What I started to say was that I stayed on the beach for a while. Then I decided to take a short walk."

"Short? We must be a mile from the creek."

Miranda ignored this outburst. "The Indian . . . what did you say his name was?"

"Nafkebee."

"Nafkebee," she repeated. "Anyway, Nafkebee didn't *find* me because I wasn't lost. I was simply minding my own business and he grabbed me."

"Nafkebee was right." Jack shook his head. "He said you need someone to watch out for you." Actually he'd chided Jack for not watching out for his woman. When Jack had vehemently replied that she was *not* his woman, the Indian had merely shrugged in that way he had when he didn't trust what Jack was saying.

"I do not need someone watching out for me." Miranda turned on her heel and started back down the path.

"Oh, no?" Jack fell in beside her.

"No!"

"What about what just happened?"

"What *did* happen?" Miranda stopped and looked up at Jack beneath her lashes. "How come he let me go when he saw you?"

"Nafkebee's a friend of mine. But you could've just as easily been kidnapped by a savage Indian."

"You mean like I was kidnapped by you?"

Jack had the good grace to look chagrined, but only for a moment. Then his expression hardened, and he cupped her shoulders, turning Miranda toward him. "It's not the same thing at all."

"It isn't? And just why not? It appears the same to me. A pirate steals into my bedroom in the middle of the night and spirits me away to—"

"I'm not going to hurt you, for God's sake."

"So you say." Miranda tossed her head, sending the raven curls that tangled around her shoulders flying. "You tell me all sorts of things, yet I see no evidence of them."

"Like what?" Except for his little indiscretion in his cabin, Jack felt he'd held to his part of the plan pretty well . . . at least as well as Miranda would let him.

"Like the messenger who's to bring my ransom money. I think you made that up." Miranda tilted her chin. "I think you have no plans to return me to Charles Town."

"Oh, are you wrong there. We're leaving tomorrow morning for Charles Town." God's blood, the chit didn't honestly think he wanted to keep her.

"Tomorrow? We are?"

"Aye."

"But your ship? You couldn't have finished careening the entire hull."

"I haven't." Jack let go of her and started walking. Why was it that every time he got close to her he felt like pulling her into his arms and kissing her? Especially now. He had more important things to think about like—

"Why?"

"Why, what?"

She stopped again and Jack faced her. "Why are we going back so soon? *Did* the messenger come with the money?"

Damn, the woman was full of questions. Jack sighed deeply. "No, the ransom didn't arrive." He held up his hand. "But there's been a change of plans. I'm taking you back now and that's all there is to it." After what Nafkebee just told him, he wasn't going to sit around here for another week. Henry would simply have to see that his daughter stayed away from the king's revenuer. Jack resisted the urge to rub his neck.

"Is it because I wandered off, because if it is—"

"It has nothing to do with that." Jack raked his fingers back through his hair. "Listen, I thought getting back to Charles Town was what you wanted."

"It was . . . I mean it is. It's just that—"

"Then, no arguments."

Miranda lowered her eyes at his loud demand. "I just don't understand."

"God's blood, woman, it isn't necessary for you to understand everything." Her face lost its color, and she stared up at him with large, deep blue eyes. Jack groaned. As angry as he'd been with her before when he didn't know where she was, he didn't want to upset her.

"Hell." Jack groaned again and turned away only to twist back. "Part of the reason I think it's better to take you back now is this." He waved his hand between them.

"What?" Miranda was perplexed. He wasn't acting like the arrogant pirate now.

"This," Jack stated louder. "This thing between us. This . . . attraction." He rubbed his hands down over his face. "God, don't tell me I'm the only one that feels it."

Miranda bit her thumbnail, then shook her head. "No. You're not the only one."

Jack laughed self-consciously. "I don't know whether that makes me feel better or worse."

Lowering her eyes, Miranda looked away. "I don't understand it."

Jack laughed again. Leave it to Miranda Chadwick to need an explanation. "It's not that complex. I'm a man and you're a woman."

"Oh." Miranda's brows furrowed as she

thought about his words. "That's all there is to it?"

Jack shrugged. "More or less." He searched for words to explain it. "It's lust I suppose."

"You mean the desire to fornicate?"

Jack's mouth dropped open. "Aye. You could call it that." Would she never cease to amaze him?

"I understand about the human need to reproduce. It really doesn't differ that much from animals such as—"

"God's blood, what are you talking about, woman? I've no desire to reproduce. I simply meant—"

"Do you feel this way about all women?"

"What way?" She was the most exasperating person.

"Do you have this desire to for—"

"No, don't repeat yourself." He rubbed at his chin. "No . . . I mean yes. Not all," he finally admitted. "But a goodly number."

"I see."

"Well, I *am* a pirate."

"Yes, of course."

God, was he making excuses for himself for enjoying other women? She didn't appear pleased by the idea, but what did she expect? But in truth, Jack admitted to himself, he never had felt *exactly* this way. Was it because Miranda was beyond his reach? There could be no other explanation. The women who usually attracted him were of a different ilk than Miranda

165

Chadwick. They understood the allure of a small flirtation. They not only wanted him as frantically as he wanted them; they were willing and able to do something about it.

"I *do* understand," she said more for her own benefit than his. Miranda couldn't help it. It was illogical and totally irrational, but she didn't like the idea of his desiring other women. She'd certainly never felt anything like this for any other man. But perhaps it was because the only men she was ever around were older, and it was their minds she admired, not the way moisture glistened on the bronze of their skin. Or the way the gold ring in his ear tangled with his equally golden hair. Miranda swallowed and tried to glance down, but his finger caught under her chin. Again her eyes met his.

"You understand what?"

His touch made her so warm she almost lost her train of thought. "About reproduction and forni—"

"How do you know about that?" Until they started this foolish discussion, Jack would have bet his share of the *Sea Hawk*'s booty that she was completely naive and innocent. But now. . . .

Her eyes widened. "Why, I've read about it, of course. And then there was van Leeuwenhoek's discovery."

Jack groaned. "I don't want to hear about it."

"As you wish, but it's very interesting."

"I'm sure 'tis." Jack had never had a stranger

conversation with anyone. He could hardly credit that they were standing in the middle of a footpath talking about making love in the most unromantic way he could imagine . . . and it was making him desire her all the more. "We need to get back to the ship."

"I suppose so."

"Aye, that's what we should do." He was saying the words, but Lord help him, his feet hadn't moved one inch along the sandy trail. "Now that we both understand this thing between us, we can manage it with no trouble."

Miranda didn't think she understood anything. The way she felt had naught in common with the descriptions of reproduction she'd read. The pirate's finger slid off her chin to caress a trail down her neck, and Miranda's breath caught.

"I wish you wouldn't look at me like that." Jack didn't mean to say the words; they were simply out of his mouth before he could stop them. But she was studying him with languid blue eyes that made him want to forget everything but taking her in his arms.

"I was just wondering . . ."

"Wondering what?"

She swayed toward him, and Jack caught her shoulders in his hands.

"Well, since we can handle this so well, perhaps we could. . . . I mean, do you suppose you could kiss me like you did before? Simply as an experiment," Miranda added because she feared she was acting very bold.

"One kiss shouldn't hurt." Jack bent toward her.

"No," Miranda said in all seriousness. "I don't think it will."

The touch of their lips was explosive. One moment, Miranda's mind was attuned to documenting the experience; the next she couldn't think at all. It was as if her whole being was engulfed in a tidal wave of sensation.

The world smelled of him, musky and male. His taste overwhelmed her, drove her to want more. And the feel of him, hard and hot against her body as he crushed her in his arms, made her burrow deeper into his embrace.

Her fingers dug into the coiled muscles of his shoulders, then up to tangle in his golden hair. And all the while the kiss deepened, drowning her in its drugging power. His tongue thrust, first possessively deep, then shallow and taunting. But always in rhythm with the blood pulsating through her veins.

As his lips left hers Miranda sighed in disappointment, but the sound was quickly drowned out by her shivering moan. His mouth wet a path down her neck, a soft counterpoint to the rasp of his chin across her flesh.

She arched, trembling when he continued his foray to the pulse at the hollow of her throat. Her body ached, burned to feel more of him. The hands cupping her head slid down to press her closer. And his mouth roamed lower.

He nudged her bodice, making her wish herself rid of the cumbersome cloth separating them. But the fabric did not stop him. His greedy mouth nuzzled deep between her breasts, then clamped first on one taut nipple, then the other. He wet her through the gown, through the shift, as Miranda's head fell back.

Her groan as he bit down on her nipple sounded sensual in her ears. He yanked her against him, grinding his hips and making Miranda's mouth go dry. All her fluid seemed to well in one place, and the spot at the apex of her legs throbbed as he rubbed his hardness against her.

She neither knew nor cared how he managed to unhook her gown, but suddenly her flesh was free. The warm, humid air whispered across her naked skin heralding his hot mouth. He devoured first one delicacy, then the next, suckling and soothing, tightening the spring of desire that engulfed her.

His tongue was like a flame, igniting her passions. As the gown caught on her upper arms, Miranda fought to free her arms, jealous of the time spent unable to run her hands over the ridges and valleys of his muscled chest. Touching him, his sleek, smooth skin was such a wonder.

Her gown skimmed lower, nudged on by his impatient fingers. And each bit of new skin he discovered received the lavish attention of his burning kisses.

Jack peeled the petticoat away and sank to his knees on the sandy path. Her skin was pale and

169

soft, sweet to the taste, and he couldn't stop feasting on her, skimming the slight ridge of her hip bone, exploring the indentation of her navel.

His hands clamped over her buttocks, squeezing, kneading, caressing. Drifting lower till his fingers stroked the flames of need between her thighs. Moist heat greeted him, and he moaned, burying his face in the tight raven curls guarding her womanhood.

Miranda cried out when his tongue touched her. She shivered, slipping softly to the sand, her limbs no longer able to support her. His mouth never stopped loving her. Sand warmed her back as she twisted and writhed, grasping at his brawny shoulders to press him nearer.

His tongue ravished her again and again, forcing small whimpers of pleasure from her parted lips. Lifting his head, Jack slipped his finger into the moist haven, leaving it reluctantly to fumble with the buttons of his breeches. His breathing was shallow, his body slick from sweat as he slid up her body. His mouth fused with hers, open and hungry, as with one plundering thrust, he entered her.

Pain stabbed through her, sharp and bittersweet. Miranda gasped, but the pirate gave her no time to think of anything but the wild wonder of his body joining hers. Her body stretched, accepted, revelled in the feel of him, hard and huge inside her.

He grasped her buttocks, driving himself deeper and deeper, stronger and stronger.

Miranda arched, meeting his thrust with lusty abandon. Her legs, still encased in cotton stockings, instinctively wrapped around his lean waist as their movements became more frenzied.

She clutched at him savagely, grasping his shoulders in her small hands and gasping for breath as her world began to tilt. What started in the heart of her womanhood, spread over her entire being, tightening her breasts, and washing her in wave after wave of inconceivable pleasure.

Miranda soared. And just when she thought herself earthward bound, she found the sensation anew. She trembled. She convulsed. Her body defied all reason and logic. And she held him tight as his ragged yell heralded his explosive climax.

They collapsed in a tangle of arms and legs in the sand. Jack could barely catch his breath, and a lazy lethargy engulfed him; but he managed to support his weight on the elbows bracketing Miranda's head. Reality, the realization of what he just did, started seeping into the forefront of his passion-drugged mind.

God's blood, this was Miranda Chadwick beneath him, still joined with him in the most intimate way. Henry's daughter for God's sake. The woman whose virtue he swore to protect with his life! And Lord help him, spent as he was, Jack had an almost uncontrollable urge to take her again . . . and again.

He shook his head to help clear away such ridiculous thoughts, and the motion brushed his hair across her cheek. Slowly Miranda opened her eyes. They were a deep, smoky blue, and they stared at him guilelessly.

Her pink tongue slipped out and carefully wet her lips. Then she sighed and asked, "What happened?"

Jack's eyes widened, and despite his guilt and self-derision he chuckled . . . then laughed. Leave it to Miranda Chadwick to end the most amazing lovemaking he'd ever had with a question.

Chapter Nine

What happened? Miranda's question hammered away at his mind. Jack sobered as quickly as he'd been overtaken by mirth.

What *had* happened? One moment he was trying to explain this strange attraction they had for one another. And the next, all reason was swept away. He'd seen powder kegs blow less explosively. And all from the touch of her lips.

Jack looked at her kiss-swollen mouth now, and fought the urge to taste her again. "God's blood!" He rolled away, and yanked up his breeches. Sitting, he scrubbed his hands down across his face.

Glancing around at her he could tell — God he could just tell by looking at her — that she was going to ask another question. To stave her off he began to explain, trying not to let guilt color his words. At least she didn't want to know why it happened or how . . . all the questions he was asking himself.

"We made love," he stated simply, knowing there was nothing simple about it at all.

"Yes, I know that." Miranda leaned up on her elbows, and Jack reached over and pulled the thin cotton shift and her silk gown over her breasts. His hand shook. "I understand the act of reproduction, of forn—"

"Aye, so you said. Then what—"

"The other thing." Miranda rose, twisting onto her knees until she faced him. "The flying. It's quite impossible I know, but I actually felt as if there was no gravity holding me down." She paused, her head cocked to one side. "You didn't experience it?"

God's blood, was she talking about what he thought she was talking about? Jack swallowed. He'd brought women to climax before, even been told in vivid detail by some how accomplished he was as a lover. But he'd never, *never,* been complimented so innocently . . . so honestly. "Aye." He turned away to hide an uncontrollable grin of male satisfaction. "I felt it."

She seemed relieved by his answer, but it didn't stop her next question. "What was that? Do you suppose Isaac Newton knows of it?"

Jack could only stare.

"Isaac Newton," Miranda explained. "He's—"

"I know who Isaac Newton is." Did she think he forgot all the crazy things she talked about?

"Oh."

"I just don't know what in the hell he has to do with what just happened here."

Miranda lowered her eyes. It was obvious the captain was becoming agitated. "Most likely nothing," she admitted.

"You're damn right nothing." Jack pushed to his feet and paced across the path. He turned back so abruptly that Miranda winced. "Do you have any idea what we did?" *What I did,* he added to himself. Jack raked frustrated fingers back through his hair when she opened her mouth to speak. "And I'm not talking about some theory about gravity."

"Yes, I know." Miranda's words were soft, and when she raised her eyes, the deep blue shimmered with unshed tears.

Jack shut his eyes against the sight. After a deep breath he dropped to his knees in front of her. He'd wanted her to accept the reality of what they'd done . . . to not think of it in terms of some scientific experiment. But now that she had, he was sorry. Sorrier than he'd ever been. He reached out to touch her, but let his hand drop.

" 'Tis entirely my fault." Her expression didn't change, and Jack continued. "You can't expect much better from a pirate, I fear."

Miranda swallowed. "It wasn't entirely your . . . I mean, I did nothing to stop you."

"I doubt 'twould have done any good." Jack wished he could feel otherwise. Wished he knew that if she'd asked him to stop, he would have . . . he could have.

"Still. . . ." Miranda tried a wan smile. She felt tears threaten again and couldn't fathom why. She understood the reproductive act. It could be explained quite rationally. Then, why was she so emotional? After clearing her throat, she admitted, "I did ask you to kiss me."

"I would probably have done it anyway." He held her gaze for several heartbeats before glancing away. "I am a pirate after all," he said, repeating the only excuse he could seem to manage.

Miranda thought it a very unsatisfactory explanation and was about to tell him so when voices sounded in the distance.

"Cap'n! Cap'n, ye find her?"

"God's blood," Jack hissed through his teeth. He jerked to his feet, tugging Miranda up beside him and giving the bodice of her sand-covered gown an upward pull. Warm, soft skin brushed his knuckles, but he forced himself not to notice. Instead, Jack twirled her around, ignoring her resistance, and swatted dirt from the back of her rumpled skirt. Pine needles sprinkled from her raven curls as he gave them a quick brush with his fingers.

Jack just managed to twist her back around when Phin and Scar came loping into sight.

"There ye are, Cap'n. See's ye found her."

"Aye." Jack reached his arm around her waist, thought better of it, and grabbed her hand instead. "She was taking a stroll, collecting . . . what did you call them?" She looked at him a moment with those large, deep blue eyes of hers, and Jack felt color darken his face. He wished he knew what she was thinking. Hell, he wished he knew what she was going to say. He should never have given her a chance to say anything.

One word from her and Phin and Scar would . . . God's blood, what would they do? Of course it would be nothing to what Henry Chadwick,

176

damn his fatherly hide, would do. Just one word.

But she didn't say it. Instead she smiled sweetly at Phin and Scar. "Specimens. I was collecting specimens to study under the microscope."

Phin's eyes dropped to Miranda's hands—one still clutched by Jack, the other knotted into a tight fist. "Well, where might they be?"

"I . . . um." Miranda glanced to the side of the sandy path, and heat flooded her face. All the leaves and flowers she had collected where scattered there. Most were hopelessly crushed. It didn't take much imagination to realize she had been lying on them when she and the pirate captain—

"She dropped them. I came up behind her. Frightened her I'm afraid, though it seems a small price to pay for running off like she did. Anyway." Jack stopped and cleared his throat. "She dropped them." God, he was acting like a green youth caught with his hand up the maid's skirts.

"Guess me an' Scar can help ye gather 'em back up." Phin started to kneel, but Jack's hand on his arm stayed him.

"That won't be necessary. We need to get back to the *Sea Hawk*."

Miranda came close to arguing; but the captain must have sensed it, for he shot her a look that made her clamp her mouth shut. And surprisingly it stayed that way as they walked back along the path, Phin and Scar leading the way, then Miranda followed by the captain. She could feel his eyes on her at every step, but she didn't turn around. She didn't even meet his gaze when he handed her into the long boat, though his touch made her breath catch.

Once aboard the pirate ship, she sought refuge in the captain's cabin, glad for the opportunity to be alone with her thoughts, uncharacteristically scrambled as they were.

Jack took a deep breath, then rapped on the door. Damn, he shouldn't feel so nervous about entering his own cabin. But when he heard her softly spoken "you may enter," he had to force himself not to turn away.

She looked up when he walked into the room, and Jack saw her face flush a soft rose shade that he found most becoming. Dismissing that thought, he shut the door behind him.

"I thought we should talk. But if you're busy with your microscope, it can wait." She was sitting at his desk with an array of papers scattered on the oak surface.

"No, I . . . please." Miranda stumbled over her words. She rose, then flopped back in the chair when he started toward her. She'd gathered and sorted her thoughts, had decided her earlier actions were totally illogical . . . until she saw the pirate captain again. Now Miranda felt that same odd sensation in the pit of her stomach that he always seemed to illicit.

She could understand her reaction if he were wearing nothing but his breeches. But his broad chest was covered by a snowy white shirt and waistcoat of finest blue silk. There was no familiar gleam of gold under his ear. He looked more a courtier than pirate. Until she caught a glimpse of his eyes.

"You needn't look so frightened. I have no intention of hurting you." God, he almost said, "Again."

"I didn't suppose you did." Miranda notched her chin higher. She wasn't afraid of him. *She wasn't.*

Jack paced to the transom windows and stared out over the verdant shore. It would be high tide soon, and then the *Sea Hawk* would sail for Charles Town. He didn't care that they'd arrive back in the harbor in less than the fortnight he'd promised Henry he'd stay away. If Miranda planned to go to the king's revenuer—which she most assuredly did—there was nothing he could, or would, do to stop her. Of course he had no intentions of waiting around to stretch a noose.

"We're sailing with the evening tide." Jack slanted Miranda a look, discomforted to see she was watching him.

"For Charles Town?"

"Aye."

Her expression was disbelieving, and Jack decided she had reason enough to doubt his word. He had promised no harm would come to her. But it still provoked his ire. "We're going straightaway. Should reach there in two days, three at the most."

"Why did it take us near a sennight to come here from Charles Town and only two days to return?"

Jack clenched his teeth. He had meant to reassure her and received a damn question for his trouble. "It just did. I was in no particular hurry to reach the creek." Though he should have been. If he'd known what Nafkebee was going to tell him, he would have made haste and cleaned the damn hull of barnacles, too.

"But you are in a hurry to return to Charles Town?"

"Aye."

"To be rid of me?" Miranda didn't know why she blurted that out. It made no difference why he took her back . . . simply that he did. And certainly the sooner the better.

"Nay," Jack answered, then for the sake of honesty added, "Not entirely." He'd have taken her back now even if he hadn't received the message from his uncle . . . the message brought to him by Nafkebee. Jack's hands tightened into fists, and his eyes narrowed as he recalled Nafkebee's words about de Segovia.

"You're forgoing the ransom, then?"

"Ransom?" Jack tilted his head, brought back to the present by her words. For a moment he didn't understand what she was asking, his mind still hearing the long-ago screams of his parents, his sister . . . his own. "Aye, the ransom." He shook his head to clear it. One problem at a time. And for now his problem was Miranda Chadwick.

"Nay, I'll not sacrifice the coin. Your father will pay." That's the way Henry wanted it. Though why Jack should care what Henry wanted after all this, he didn't know.

"But you said earlier that—"

"Enough." Jack turned his green gaze on her, and apparently it and the tone of his voice were sufficient to silence her . . . for the moment. Besides, he couldn't remember exactly what he had told her. Something about meeting a messenger who didn't arrive, he thought.

Lying was one thing. He did it often, and usually well—to the royal revenuer, to the citizens of Charles Town who looked upon him as a privateer at worst, even to certain females of his acquaintance when he whispered hollow words of love. Sometimes Jack thought his entire life was a lie . . . had been since he'd encountered de Segovia.

But lying to Miranda Chadwick was an entirely different thing than the norm. She accepted nothing on face value. She questioned, latching on to the least discrepancy like a ferret, not letting loose. It was a trait he found most annoying. And one, in spite of himself, he admired in her.

But that wasn't the only thing he admired about Miranda Chadwick. He liked the slight tilt of her deep blue eyes and the line of her neck. The soft cloud of raven hair and the feel of those slightly pouty lips on—Jack caught himself. God's blood, what was he doing? This sort of ruminating about his captive was exactly what led him to take her upon the sandy path in the forest.

And *that* was the reason he was here now, fumbling for words like a callow youth.

He looked at her now and found her watching him with an odd mixture of anxiety and bravado—false he assumed. "I'm not going to hurt you." The words were out of his mouth before he

181

could stop them, before he realized how they echoed his earlier claim. The one he'd already proven false by his actions.

She realized it, too. He could tell by the darkening of her expression, by the way her chin rose ever so slightly. Jack cleared his throat. "I mean, I do intend to return you to Charles Town."

"So you said."

"Aye." Jack gave a curt nod and clamped his hands behind his back. He knew he was repeating himself, and making a mess of an already messy situation. "We need to discuss what happened on shore," he said, before he could change his mind and simply leave the cabin. He might be a pirate and a rogue, but he did have some conscience left. He couldn't help thinking that this very same thing had probably happened to his sister.

"Why?" Miranda stood.

"Why, what?"

"Why must we discuss it?"

God's blood, must there be a reason for everything? "Because . . . because, I took your maidenhood, and . . . and . . ."

"I wish we could simply forget it ever happened."

So did he, but Jack didn't think it possible. "But it did," he said softly.

"True." Miranda paced toward the window, seemed to realize that was where the pirate captain stood and turned back toward the desk. "It is an indisputable fact. However, I think it better for all concerned if we ignore it."

Miranda bit her bottom lip. She didn't tell him

that she couldn't think about it in a logical way. Every time she remembered the feel of him, the way he made her soar to the heavens, her emotions engulfed her, forcing reason aside. And she couldn't deal with something that didn't involve reason. Which meant she couldn't deal with the pirate.

"Ignore it?" Jack dug his fingers through his hair.

"Yes." Miranda folded her hands. "As I said before, pretend it never happened." Another thought came to her, one that surprised her. The pirate seemed worried, or at least concerned about what they'd done. That in itself did not seem very much like what she'd heard of pirates. Perhaps he feared his ransom would be less since she was no longer an innocent. Maybe he feared it wouldn't even be worth his while to return her.

"You needn't concern yourself that I shall tell . . . what happened. To my father, I mean. It was partially my fault." She dropped her gaze.

"It wasn't your fault. And as for your father, that's not my concern." God's blood, another lie. But to Jack's credit, it wasn't his *main* concern. "I am a pirate."

"Precisely." Miranda nodded her agreement. "This sort of thing must happen to you all the time." She seemed to wait for his agreement, so Jack gave it to her.

"Upon occasion." Actually, nothing remotely like this had ever occurred before. Because he had never kidnapped anyone before. And if not for Henry Chadwick and his daughter, it wouldn't have happened this time.

"As I thought. But you see it has never happened to me before." She bit the end of her thumbnail, and Jack winced. In the short time he'd known her, he'd come to realize that that gesture preceded a question. "I imagine you know that, don't you?"

"Know what?" Just once he'd like to be able to answer one of her myriad questions.

"That I had never forni — I mean experienced the act of reproduction."

"I knew."

"I assumed you did because you must have noticed when you rent my maiden — "

"I said I knew!" For heaven's sake. He expected recriminations or crying, or all manner of things, but never, never this cold, unemotional discussion.

"Oh." Miranda took a step back despite her earlier resolve to meet the pirate head on. She didn't like it when he yelled. Her grandfather had never yelled, except perhaps when he'd discovered some new scientific truth. But his had been a joyful yell, not one filled with anger and frustration like the pirate's. What did he have to be irate about? By his own admission this sort of thing happened to him all the time. She on the other hand. . . . Miranda sucked in a calming breath, trying to remember that reproduction was a natural, scientifically explained act.

Jack leaned into the window seat under the windows, trying to regain his calm. When he turned from the view of untamed shore, he kept his voice level. "I don't think — "

"Yes, but I do. And what I think is that I don't want to discuss this anymore." Miranda's throat tightened, and she felt silly, emotional and, worst of all, illogical tears burn her eyes. She blinked them back. "There is nothing to be gained by arguing this further. Well, is there?"

"Nay," Jack answered, realizing she'd finally asked him a question he could reply to. Yet finding no solace in the truth of it.

"Then, it is as I said earlier. We shall just forget it happened."

Jack stared at her for long moments, noticing the bottom lip that quivered ever so slightly and the deep blue eyes that tried but couldn't quite meet his. She wasn't as immune to what they'd done as she tried to pretend. Still, he couldn't argue with her logic. There was nothing to be done for it. He let out his breath slowly. "As you wish."

"Thank you." Miranda wiped her damp palms down the sides of her skirt, hoping above all else he would simply leave the cabin. He must have understood her silent entreaty, for he unclasped his hands and strode to the door.

"There's one thing more."

Would he never leave her to shed the tears she kept at bay with such difficulty?

"I spoke with the men . . . Phin and Scar, and the rest."

Miranda's eyes shot up to meet his, all thoughts of crying forgotten. Had he told them what she and the pirate had done? But no, Captain Blackstone was saying something about the pirates wanting the chance to talk with her again about

185

gravity and light. "And you agreed to this?"

"Aye. Of course there is to be no more climbing the rigging or showing the men disgusting little animals swimming about in their grog."

"Of course."

"And you don't have to speak with them if you'd rather not."

"Oh, no. I want to." If anything could take her mind off the pirate captain, it was discussing science with his men.

She seemed so pleased with his announcement that Jack could do naught but turn and leave. He'd taken care of his first problem as best he could. At least that's what Jack tried to tell himself.

By the time he reached the deck, the tide was up and his crew was busy unfurling the sails that would skim them to the creek's mouth. From there they'd head to Charles Town and then on to St. Augustine.

After Don Diego de Segovia.

"Ain't she somethin'?"

Jack turned, focused on his quartermaster, and mumbled an annoyed, "Who?"

Phin's expression assured Jack he wasn't fooling a damn soul, at least not the wily old pirate. "I seen ye watchin' her, Cap'n. If'n I didn't know'd she weren't your type, I'd swear ye was smitten."

"Thank God you know she's not my type." Jack ignored Phin's snaggle-toothed grin, and leaned on the rail of the quarterdeck. He *had* been

186

watching Miranda as she sat on a roll of hemp in the shade of the mast. She was sketching on parchment, intent on her work, but not seeming to mind the frequent pauses she had to make. Each time a member of the crew passed her, he stopped to say a few words.

Hell, every single pirate on this damn ship seemed smitten with her—except himself, of course. He was just perplexed, and annoyed. And he couldn't really figure out why.

Under the circumstances things were working out better than he expected. Her reaction to their lovemaking surprised him. But then, everything about her surprised him. When she'd come on deck, shortly after they sailed, Miranda Chadwick hadn't mentioned their encounter in the forest. God's blood, she showed no sign it even happened! Not that he wanted crying or gnashing of teeth—God no. But this was ridiculous.

Since the moment he'd left his . . . her cabin, Miranda had acted as if nothing had happened. As soon as she'd come above deck she began asking questions, and had barely stopped since. Not of him, of course.

He couldn't really say she ignored him, but damn close. That was for the best. Hadn't he already decided that getting through the next few days, until he could foist her off into her proud papa's arms, was going to be difficult? Well, they'd be a hell of a lot easier if he didn't have to speak with her.

"Ye know, Cap'n . . ."

Jack glanced back toward Phin. He'd come

close to forgetting the man was even there.

"Yer claim that she ain't yer type a woman would be a lot more convincin' if ye didn't look at her like some love-sick lad."

Jack's eyes flashed to Phin's. "I'm doing no such thing."

Phin only screwed up his face and hunched his shoulders in a poor imitation of a shrug.

"Well, I'm not!" A quick glance about the deck showed several heads turned his way, including the creamy-skinned one of the lady in question. Jack lowered his voice. "You don't know what you're talking about. That woman 'tis nothing but trouble."

"Don't know." Phin rubbed his beard. "I'm kinda fond a her meself."

"Good. Fine." Jack emphasized his words by placing his hands on his lean hips. "Care about her all you like. It makes no difference to me. Personally I can't wait to return her to Charles Town and end this farce of a kidnapping."

"That why ye had us leave 'fore we even got the hull cleaned?"

"Nay." Jack leaned against the rail and watched a gull swoop through the air. High tide had filled the channel so that they sailed easily toward the creek's mouth. But he hadn't told anyone why they sailed. Jack let out his breath. "De Segovia is back in St. Augustine."

Phin's eyes widened, then narrowed till there was naught but the dark pupils showing through the lids. "How do ye come by this?"

Jack leaned on his forearms. "I met Nafkebee in

188

the forest. He had contact with a tribe from farther south, down in land claimed by the Spanish. They told him de Segovia has returned to St. Augustine as the new head of the garrison there."

Phin scratched at his chin. "But how did Nafkebee know how to find ye?"

"Robert told him."

"Yer uncle?"

"Aye. Before we left Charles Town I told Uncle Robert of this . . . kidnapping." Jack grimaced. "And that we were headed for Snebley's Creek. When Nafkebee couldn't find me in Charles Town, he sought out Robert, who told him where I was." Jack paused. "Robert sent his own message that we should return to Charles Town immediately."

Phin seemed to absorb that information; then he shook his head. "So that's what had ye actin' so strange."

"What the hell are you talking about?"

"Ye, Cap'n. Ever since we came upon ye and Mistress Miranda in the forest ye been actin' all crazy like."

Jack's jaw clenched. "I'm anxious to find de Segovia and hopefully my sister."

"I know's that, Cap'n."

Phin's expression was so solemn, Jack had a sudden urge to explain that there was more than de Segovia bothering him. But that wouldn't be fair to Miranda, and besides, Jack didn't know what Phin's reaction would be. They both had their share of women whenever they were in port. But in Phin's own words, he was fond of Miranda.

Fond of her in a fatherly way, if Jack didn't miss his guess. The kind of fondness that wouldn't take to someone hurting her, even if that someone was his good friend Jack.

"God save me from fathers," Jack mumbled under his breath.

"What's that, Cap'n?"

"Nothing." Jack shook his head. "We simply need to get back to Charles Town quickly."

"But what 'bout Henry?"

"What about him? And keep your voice down." Jack shot a quick glance to where Miranda sat. She appeared to be deep in conversation with Scar. The fact that Scar could be deep in conversation about anything was a marvel.

"She can't hear me, Cap'n."

"Maybe not. But Henry wouldn't be happy if his daughter found out how well we know her father."

"So what's he gonna say when we bring her back to Charles Town early? What if the king's revenuer ain't sailed yet?"

"That's going to have to be Henry's problem," Jack said. But in the end he knew it would be his, too. He loosened his cravat. "Certainly he can keep his daughter from telling about us for a few days."

"I don't know 'bout that, Cap'n. She's likely to be hoppin' mad when we get her home. Most folk don't take kindly ta kidnappin'."

"True enough, Phin." *And you don't know the half of it,* Jack finished to himself. Once Miranda Chadwick had a chance to think over their encounter in the forest, she might not be so willing to pretend it never happened. Jack's eyes strayed to her calmly smiling at something Scar said. This dispassionate facade could shatter soon. And then Jack hated to see what would happen.

Maybe he'd be gone to St. Augustine, a small, cowardly voice reminded him. Then Henry would have to take care of everything. Of course, Jack could forget ever returning to Charles Town after that.

Braiding his fingers, Jack dropped his head on the cushion of his hands. "What is it, Cap'n? What's wrong? Ye sick?"

"Nay." Jack straightened. "It's just—"

"Sails ho!" The call from the lookout interrupted Jack. He squinted his eyes and looked up at the sailor. What in the hell was he talking about? They were headed toward the mouth of Snebley Creek—the creek that damn few people knew about. How could the lookout have spotted sails?

Jack opened his mouth to question him, when the sailor in the rigging surprised him further. "Looks Spanish, Captain."

Chapter Ten

"What is it? What's happening?" Miranda pushed through the pirates, who'd quite suddenly started moving about the ship. Some were rushing below while others grabbed muskets from a long wooden box and climbed the rigging. They all seemed in a hurry, and to a man they ignored her.

Clutching the rail to the steps, Miranda held up her skirts and scrambled to the quarterdeck. The pirate captain didn't notice her until she grabbed his arm. He stood, brass telescope against his squinted eye, searching the horizon.

He jerked around when she touched him.

His expression was hard, the bronzed skin stretched taut over his chiseled features. There was not a hint of softening when he looked at her. If anything, his jaw clenched tighter. "What the hell are you doing up here?" God's blood, didn't he have enough to worry about without this? In truth, he'd been so engrossed in the

Spanish vessel, Jack had all but forgotten his beautiful captive.

Taken aback by the vehemence of his words, Miranda forced herself not to cower. "I want to know why your men are running about. What's happening?"

Jack stared at her while he worked to control his anger—not at her this time, but at the situation he found himself thrown into. "They're preparing for battle," he answered simply.

"Battle?"

"Aye. Or retreating . . . or whatever we can do to make it past yon Spanish ship."

Miranda sucked in her breath, but she shaded her eyes and stared in the direction he indicated. She could see little through the veil of trees and late-afternoon mist except sails. "How do you know it's Spanish? Perhaps it's simply an English vessel sailing up the creek."

Jack didn't mention that to him an English ship blocking the mouth of the creek was almost as bad. He simply passed her the telescope. "You seem to fancy seeing things larger than life, Mistress Chadwick."

Miranda spotted the Spanish ensign and lowered the spyglass, her eyes catching the pirate's. "We aren't at war with Spain."

"Perhaps you aren't." Jack let out his breath. "But I can assure you, I am. And—" he swiped windblown hair off his forehead—"the feeling is mutual."

Noise from the deck below momentarily distracted Miranda. Her gaze swept across the fore-castle to where pirates were pulling and shoving at large black cannons. She spotted Phin yelling at some men, their shirts stripped from sweat-gleaming torsos, who were piling cannonballs on the deck. Still others were spreading a layer of sand over the oaken floor.

Anxiety curled in her stomach. "You're going to fight them?"

She looked so frightened, with her deep blue eyes as large as gold coins, that Jack was tempted to lie to her. But knowing Miranda he decided she'd figure out the truth sooner or later. Besides, though she appeared alarmed, she stood her ground, and that defiant little chin was held high.

"I'm not going to fight unless I have to," Jack said, then added honestly, "But I don't see any way around it."

"We could sail back up the creek. Surely they wouldn't — "

"Follow?" Jack shook his head. "You're prob-ably right. Except that when the tide goes out we'll be beached as we were before. They'd only have to send some men upstream in small boats to overrun us. We haven't many men.

"The same holds true of staying where we are, or even sailing closer to the Spanish frigate. Un-less we can reach deeper water, open sea, by low tide, we're vulnerable."

"But what of the Spanish ship? Doesn't it have the same problem?"

"Nay. It's in the channel where the water's deeper. And 'tis blocking us from getting there." And from the looks of its position, the Spanish captain knew exactly what he was doing. Again Jack wondered how the Spanish had found this inlet. It had proven such a safe haven before, Jack could have sworn he was the only one who knew of it. Of course, his crew knew, and he'd told a few people close to him. His uncle . . . Miranda's father.

Jack gave his head a quick shake. What was he thinking? Henry wouldn't have said anything.

"Do we have a chance in a battle?"

"There's always a chance," Jack answered, still distracted by thoughts of Henry Chadwick. He glanced down at Miranda when he heard her gasp. "Don't worry. I've fought my way out of tighter scrapes than this." Jack took a measure of comfort realizing what he told her was true. He had faced long odds and come out the victor. But he preferred a surer thing.

"Go below." Jack yanked a pistol from the waistband of his breeches. "And take this with you."

"But—"

"I doubt there will be call to use it. However, if there is, a gun is a lot more effective than a rusty sword."

Miranda colored at his reference to her ludicrous attempt to fight the pirate captain the first time they'd met. She examined the heavy pistol and caught the glint of polished brass as the

195

late-afternoon sun reflected off the muzzle. "I don't know how to use one of these."

" 'Tis primed and ready. Just set the lock to full-cock." Jack covered her hands with his, showing her how to do that, then returned the lock to the safety position. "Aim and squeeze the trigger. But don't use it unless you've no choice. Chances are good that even if the Spanish manage to . . ." Jack paused when he realized he was thinking in terms of losing this battle. "You will most likely be safe no matter who wins the day."

Jack cupped Miranda's shoulders, gently turning her around. "Now, go below and stay in my cabin . . . no matter what happens. Do you understand?"

Of course she understood. Did the captain think she couldn't comprehend a simple order? An infuriating one, perhaps, but a simple one nonetheless. With a quick nod, Miranda descended the ladder onto the main deck. She dodged the men who all but ignored her passage and ducked through the hatch.

Jack watched her disappear down the ladder, then turned his mind back to the ship blocking the entrance of the creek.

"Ev'ry man's at battle stations, Cap'n. And we kept the gunwales closed like ye said." Phin stuck his grizzly head above the quarterdeck floor. "What ye got in mind ta do? Fer sure they seen us by now."

"I imagine they have." The *Sea Hawk* had just

196

cleared the last bend in the creek and could now see — and be seen by — the ship that lay less than a league to the south.

"What ye think they're doing there?" Phin screwed up his face and studied the enemy vessel.

"Exactly what it looks like they're doing. They're trying to keep us from sailing out into the ocean." The ship was anchored at an angle, her great guns, black as pitch, peeping through opened gunwales. It stood as large and formidable as a fortress guarding a harbor.

"But how'd they find out 'bout this place? We ain't never had a speck a problems here before."

"I don't know." Jack brushed the question aside. This was not the time to worry about it. Later he would ponder the hows and whys. Now he needed to get the *Sea Hawk* out of this trap. "Furl sail and drop anchor. I want it to appear as if we stopped the moment we spotted them."

"Cap'n, we ain't got much time left till the tide's gone. And ye know what will happen to us then."

"Aye." They'd be grounded and easy prey. Vulnerable to whatever the Spanish had in mind. Vulnerable like Port Royal and its Scottish settlers had been those many years ago. Jack unrolled a chart and checked some figures. "We still have some time." But not much. Jack lifted his head, face into the breeze, and smiled. As the shadows lengthened the wind picked up, a fair, freshening blow from the north. It followed the flow of the creek and would carry a ship under full canvas skimming swiftly toward the open sea.

"Put every tar who's not manning a gun in the top masts. When I give the signal, I want sails spilling down from the spars. And I want it fast."

"Ye thinkin' to run through 'em?"

"Aye. That's just what I'm thinking." Jack peered through his glass. "She's sitting there so cocksure of herself, thinking we're trapped." Lowering the telescope, Jack tapped it against his open palm. "It will be a tight squeeze getting by her."

"And a damn bloody one. What ye figure, Cap'n? Twenty guns?"

"Aye." Jack blew air through his teeth. "Near as I can tell. But hopefully we'll be by her before she can do us much harm." Jack looked away and shut his eyes. He wasn't much for praying—hadn't been since that afternoon the Spanish wiped out his family—but he said a short one now. And if it came out more demand than supplication, he hoped God wouldn't hold it against him.

Shadows from the tall pines on shore fell across the deck as the sun shifted lower behind the spit of wooded land separating the *Sea Hawk* from the sea. Crickets and locusts started their raucous noises, but aboard the pirate ship there was nary a sound. All were at their posts, ignoring the cramping of muscles and the tension that seemed to shroud the vessel.

And all awaited the order that would send them scurrying to put the *Sea Hawk* in motion, toward the formidable Spanish blockader. Within range of her murderous guns. To a man, they knew what lay ahead was a calculated risk. And though their way of life might indicate otherwise, risks were not something pirates sought. Sure things were more their style. But there was no sure way out of this mess, and they trusted their captain to make the best of a bad situation.

Jack trusted fate and perhaps some divine intervention, and the luck that seemed to ride on his shoulder. When the breeze stiffened as much as he thought it might, and the first filming of dusk settled over the lowering tide on the creek, Jack turned toward Phin.

Hopefully the *Sea Hawk*'s inactivity had lulled the Spanish ship into believing she planned nothing for this night. Immobilizing fear was so easy to accept in an enemy, partly because it so easily took hold of men. But it hadn't seized Jack or the *Sea Hawk*'s crew.

"Now, Phin!" Jack gave the order in a hushed voice, and Phin raised his arm in the prearranged signal. The sign was passed from one pirate to the next, till all knew the time was at hand.

Then in unison the fore and aft sails whipped down the rigging, rattling out through the wooden blocks. At the same moment, King, using a boarding axe, severed the cable, leaving the anchor near buried in the bottom mud and freeing the pirate ship.

The *Sea Hawk* yawed and groaned, then lurched forward as the great sheets caught the wind. They were under way, skimming toward the Spanish ship.

Jack squinted through the spyglass, trying to make out through the gathering dusk the enemy's reaction to the sudden movement of the *Sea Hawk*. They didn't seem to realize at first what the pirates were about, but soon, Jack noticed the frenzied motion of the small figures as they readied the guns.

Tongues of orange spewed from the muzzles well before the *Sea Hawk* was in range, but Jack assumed the Spanish captain was showing but a sampling of things to come.

"Keep your course steady, Phin." Jack lowered the glass and gave his quartermaster a hard stare. "Whatever happens, keep us heading for the alley between the Spaniard and the shore."

"Aye, Cap'n." Phin's gnarled fingers gripped the wheel. "And I'm assumin' the wash is deep enough."

"You're assuming right," Jack answered, hoping against hope it was. He yanked from his waistband the pistol that matched the one he'd given Miranda.

They were fast closing range. The ever-narrowing space of brackish water that separated the two vessels swelled with splashing cannonballs and shot. Sprinkles of water, turned diamondlike by the last rays of the setting sun, sprayed over the *Sea Hawk's* hull.

Jack waited until a thundering blast sent a ball falling mere feet in front of his ship. Then, with one last warning to Phin to keep her steady, Jack bounded down to the main deck. "Fire!" he yelled at the top of his lungs. "Fire at will!"

The resulting roar was deafening. Jack spread his legs, steadying himself against the sudden jolt of the ship. Smoke swirled and billowed around the men, obscuring them from sight. But Jack could hear them, panting for breath, scurrying to swab out the muzzle and reload.

His eyes blurry from saltpeter and sulphur, Jack peered through the rising smoke to the strip of water between the Spanish vessel and the waving green swamp grass of shore. The channel was deep there, cut in the sand by hundreds of years of tides, but it was narrow, thanks to the length of the blockader.

And there was hell to pay getting to that passageway to the sea.

They were well in range now. The moment after Jack realized that, he felt the *Sea Hawk* lurch as the first shot exploded on deck. Grabbing a bucket, Jack rushed toward the spot and along with a tar managed to smother the flames. But there was no respite as another, then another volley hit the pirate ship.

"Fight! Fight!" Jack roared encouragement to his men as they sailed through the rain of shells and fire. His throat burned, and his voice came out as a rasp; but he continued to dive from one gun to the next, sponging here, touching the spark to powder there.

They didn't bother to aim. The *Sea Hawk* and the Spanish ship were nearly side by side now, shooting point-blank at each other. Easily within small arms range.

Jack emptied his pistol but didn't take the time to reload. Sharpshooters in the shrouds were keeping the Spaniards busy, giving Jack's men a chance they wouldn't have otherwise.

They were slipping through, had survived the worst of the frontal attack. Though the *Sea Hawk* continued to fire, the stable Spanish ship could do almost nothing. She was without stern ports to shoot cannon through. It was like the eye of a hurricane, this momentary reprieve from the deadly fire. Jack allowed himself to think that they might perhaps make it, when the *Sea Hawk* listed violently to stern. Jack's first reaction was that they were sinking. But then he realized the ship had hit the shore.

"Phin! Phin!" Jack hurdled over one of his men who lay bleeding and screaming in pain near the main mast, and raced across the slippery deck toward the ladder. Yanking himself up, Jack cursed violently when he saw his quartermaster draped over the wheel.

But there was no time for sentimentality. Untangling Phin, Jack slid him to the deck and put all his strength into straightening the wheel.

Jack's muscles, soot-covered and slick with sweat, strained as he worked. The ship groaned and complained, skimming along the mud-lined shore. Then, with one giant, wind-powered lurch, she broke free. Settling back into the deeper channel, the *Sea Hawk* righted and surged toward the sea.

Within seconds the *Sea Hawk* skimmed into range of the Spaniard's leeward guns. But the angle was not as deadly, and by this time the pirates had maneuverability and the rush of water to the open sea on their side.

A rousing cheer echoed through the rigging. They'd made it! They'd squirmed out of the trap and now raced into the white-tipped waves off the coast. Jack cast a glance behind to where the crew on the Spanish vessel scurried about unfurling the sails. They still posed a threat, but Jack didn't think a very serious one. By the time they raised anchor and maneuvered the ship out of the creek, night would blanket the sea. By morn, Jack intended to be far from here.

As soon as the pirates quieted, Jack yelled down to the main deck for someone to come help Phin. The quartermaster rolled to his side, moaning, and Jack saw blood puddling beneath his body. "Someone get up here. Now!" Jack needed to keep his hands and mind on steering the ship, but if someone didn't get here quickly, he'd—

"What is it, Captain? Are you hurt?" Miranda pulled herself up the ladder, gasping when she saw Phin. Gathering up her skirts, she rushed over to where he lay. "What happened to him?" Carefully she turned the older man over.

"He's been hit. By splintering wood, I think. What the hell are you doing up here?"

Miranda ignored the last as she settled the old man on his back. "Yes, here it is," she said, gently pulling aside the torn and bloody shirt. "Phin, can you hear me?"

Phin's eyes slitted open, but the dark irises were clouded with pain. "Your ladyship," he murmured before biting his bottom lip.

"I know it hurts, Phin. But you'll be all right. I promise." Miranda lifted her skirt and tore off yet another strip of petticoat, hoping this was a promise she could keep. There were several jagged slivers of wood, spar she assumed, protruding from Phin's shoulder and chest. She couldn't tell how deeply they pierced into the flesh, but as she cautiously tugged on one, fresh blood spurted out.

Mopping at the wound with her petticoat, Miranda found a better handhold on the splinter and pulled harder. Phin moaned before losing consciousness. With a final yank, Miranda removed the wood, and quickly plugged the gaping hole with more ruffled linen.

"God's blood, what's going on?" Jack strained to see around Miranda's slim back to what she was doing to his friend. "Where's the surgeon?"

"Dead, I'm afraid." Miranda glanced over her shoulder. The captain appeared truly shaken by her remark. Miranda realized she should have told him more gently. But she really didn't have time.

"Don't tell me you know doctoring, too?" The woman seemed to have an unlimited font of knowledge.

"Not exactly." Miranda gripped another shard of wood. "But I do know something of anatomy."

By the time she'd removed all the wood and wrapped Phin in more petticoat, King had arrived on the quarterdeck. He took the wheel as he gave the rundown of losses to Jack. Two dead, including, as Miranda said, the surgeon. Actually he hadn't been a physician at all, but a carpenter. But he was the closest thing the *Sea Hawk* had to a man of medicine. Little it mattered since he was usually only called on to saw off shattered arms and legs. And he'd been a good sailor, as had Charley Stone, the other casualty.

Jack supposed with the odds against them as they were, losing only two men was the best he could expect. But he still didn't feel good about it. His crew's casualties only added to the hatred for the Spanish that consumed him.

And the number of dead could increase. Phin lay on the sun-bleached deck, as white as the canvas that billowed overhead. Jack swallowed. "Is he . . . ?"

"I think he'll be all right." Miranda wiped bloody hands down her gown. It was then that

Jack noticed her . . . really noticed her.

"My God! Are *you* hurt?"

"No, why?"

"You're covered with blood and—"

"Oh." Miranda stared down at her dress. "It's not mine. I've been helping out. Several other men are wounded."

"You mean Phin isn't the first you've worked on?" Jack's voice was deceptively calm.

"Why, no. I've bandaged up Ed Snively and—"

"But we've only been out of the Spaniards' range a few minutes. Each word grew louder as realization hit Jack. "Do you mean to tell me you were on deck when fighting was going on?"

Miranda simply stood, her eyes dark and as large as saucers, her mouth shut. But it was admission enough for Jack.

"God's blood, woman!" He raked his hands back through his tangle of golden hair. "Do you have any idea what could have happened to you?"

"The same as happened to Charley Stone, I imagine," she answered quietly.

"You're damn right the same that happened to him, or to Doc, or Ed."

"Or Phin," Miranda continued for him. "Don't you think we should carry him below deck?"

"Hell, yes, I think we should carry him below deck." Jack stood, hands on hips, and glared at Miranda. Admittedly he hadn't thought of her during the battle—there hadn't been time. But just before the fighting when his mind had slipped to thoughts of her, he'd imagined her relatively safe in his cabin.

Certainly not on the blood-slick deck exposing herself to the shelling. Thinking of it now, he could barely keep from throttling her.

"Uh, Captain, sir. I can take Phin below if you'd rather."

Jack took a deep breath and looked back at King. "Nay. I'll do it. You—" Jack pointed a long finger at Miranda—"come with me."

"I think I should see to the other men first." She moved across the quarterdeck. "Some of them might need—"

"Miranda!"

Barely restrained anger in his voice made Miranda pause on the top rung of the ladder. She flung back her hair and took a deep breath. "I shall come below soon. After I've seen to the other men." With that, she disappeared over the quarterdeck's side.

And Jack continued to stare, open-mouthed, at the spot where she'd been.

"She's a mind of her own, that one."

Jack clamped his mouth shut and turned toward King. "That woman needs to be taught a lesson in following orders."

King shrugged, the muscles rippling under his ebony skin. "One of you does."

"And just what the hell do you mean by that?"

"Nothing." King's grin gleamed white against

his skin. "It's just, I think you feared for her safety and that made you give orders she wasn't likely to follow."

"You're damn right I feared for her safety." Jack bent over and carefully scooped Phin in his arms. "Who in their right mind wouldn't?" he mumbled as he headed down the ladder.

Set up in the afterhold, the surgery consisted of planks placed on smooth casks. There was one man, a boy actually, sitting on the edge of the board, his skinny legs dangling over the side. When Jack entered the area carrying Phin, Miranda was already there. She was trying to get the boy to lie back down.

"This will be a lot easier, Nat, if you just let me see what the problem is."

"Ain't got no problem, and I sure as hell don't want ye lookin' at me."

"Nat!" Jack settled Phin into a berth that was made up for the wounded and rounded on the boy. "Watch your language in front of a lady."

"Aw, Cap'n. Didn't mean nothin' by it."

"Perhaps not, however. . . . What are you smiling about?"

Miranda tried to sober her expression. How could the pirate captain, of all people, find fault with anyone's language. He nearly singed her ears whenever they were together. But she wasn't going to point that out, especially not in front of the boy.

"I'm not smiling about anything. I simply wish to take a look at this lad's wound."

Hell if he didn't know a smile when he saw one . . . especially one of Miranda Chadwick's, but Jack decided not to pursue it. "Show her your wound, Nat." After giving the order, Jack strode over to where Phin was struggling to sit up. "How are you feeling, you old sea dog?" Jack tried not to think about how panicked he'd felt when he saw Phin lying bloodied and pale on the deck.

"How in the hell ye think I'm feelin'? Damn Spaniards."

"Well, we got by them." Jack twisted around when the low rumble of voices near the makeshift table grew louder. "What's going on over there?" Nat was on his feet, blood running down his leg, and Miranda had hold of his arm. Something that Nat was obviously trying to change. He tried jerking his elbow, but the woman held firm.

"What in the hell is it?" Jack clamped his hand over Nat's shoulder.

"I don't want her lookin' at me, Cap'n," the boy pleaded, his narrow blue eyes looking up at Jack imploringly.

"But he's wounded . . . and bleeding," Miranda countered logically.

Jack studied each in turn, then let out his breath. "She's right, Nat. Now just let her—"

"I ain't! I ain't gonna do it. And ye can't make me."

"The hell I can't." Jack had had enough insubordination for one day. True, on a pirate ship the captain was not an absolute ruler, but he sure had say over a cabin boy and most certainly over a captive. Yet in the space of less than an hour both had defied him. Well, he'd put an end to it.

Grabbing the boy under his arms Jack lifted him, ready to slam him down on the plank. Nat's fervent whisper stopped him. "But, Cap'n. My cut. It's on a part o' me body ain't right for no woman ta see, leastways not no lady."

"Oh, but that's ridiculous," Miranda said. "It's not as if I haven't seen—"

"Enough!" Lord help him, what was she about to say? Would she actually admit to their love-making just so that she could care for the boy? The possibility seemed too likely. "You!" He pointed to Miranda, who seemed taken aback by his tone. "Look after Phin. He's awake."

"But, Captain Blackstone—"

"I'll see to the lad." Jack waited till Miranda whirled around; then he motioned for Nat to drop his baggy breeches.

"It ain't hardly more'n a scratch, Cap'n. Don't know why her ladyship was gettin' so bothered 'bout it."

"It must be some woman thing," Jack mumbled under his breath. But he was wishing back his words when he saw the boy's bloody hip. "Looks like a bit more than a scratch to me."

Jack cleaned up the cut as best he could . . . which with his lack of experience, wasn't very well. But when Jack suggested Miranda should look at it after all, Nat made such a fuss that he let it go. When he finished, Jack told Nat to get some rest; then he checked on Phin, who was sleeping, and went above deck. Miranda, he noticed, was no longer in the surgery.

Some of the pirate crew were busy "fishing" damaged spars. They splinted them with oars, then lashed the whole with hemp. Others were swabbing the decks, cleaning the blood and sand away. On the quarterdeck, wrapped in canvas, were two bodies.

"Thought we'd wait for ye to give them a proper burial." Scar came up behind Jack and motioned toward the bodies. "Don't wanta wait too long though, 'cause a the stench."

The funeral was brief, with Jack and several of the men saying a few words, and then the bodies slipped slowly into the indigo sea.

"Guess we gotta be glad weren't more kilt than them two."

The fact that he'd thought the same thing earlier didn't make Jack feel better about Scar's words. He didn't answer—only stared out over the moon's reflection shattered over the myriad waves. One day, he supposed, they'd bury him at sea—that was if a hangman's noose didn't get him first. Jack rubbed at his neck.

"How's ol' Phin doin'?"

Jack forced his attention from the watery grave. "I think he's going to be all right. Probably too ornery to die."

Scar chortled, running his finger down the

crest of his scar. "Ye got the right a it there. Course, havin' her ladyship on board ta help was a blessin'."

"I don't know if I'd call it that."

"I would," Scar countered. "Don't know what we'd a done without her taking care a the wounded, 'specially after Doc died."

Jack caught Scar's eye. "Just how long was she up on deck?"

"Well, I don't rightly know for sure." Scar rubbed his chin. "I seen her over by the forecastle soon as that Spaniard started shellin' us."

"You did, did you?" From the very beginning of the battle. She'd disobeyed him and put herself in danger from the very beginning of the damn battle. Jack's jaw clamped shut, and his hands fisted.

"Where ye off ta, Cap'n?"

Jack didn't stop walking. "To have a talk with Mistress Chadwick," he said, before crawling down through the hatch.

Chapter Eleven

"Oh!" Miranda whirled around, clutching her blood-stained gown to her breast as the cabin door slammed open. Only one man on this ship dispensed with the nicety of knocking. She wasn't surprised to see the pirate captain standing in the doorway.

But by the expression on his handsome face he was surprised. "I apologize for. . . ." Jack felt heat surge up his neck, and that embarrassed him more than walking in on her while she was undressing. He cleared his throat. "I've something to discuss with you."

"Perhaps we could wait until later?" Miranda could feel his eyes on her, and everywhere they touched, her skin seemed to burn. The rumpled gown hid little of her linen shift from his view, and the linen shift hid little of her body.

"I think we should talk now."

"But I'm changing my gown." Miranda couldn't believe she had to state the obvious. But even that didn't phase the pirate. "The door to the passageway is open." Surely he could see how inappropriate his actions were.

Jack turned and shut the door, remaining inside the cabin.

When he looked back, Miranda's mouth was hanging open.

"I need to finish dressing."

"This won't take long." Jack was determined to prove to himself that he had some self-control where Miranda Chadwick was concerned. He'd say what he had to say and then he'd leave. He cleared his throat again, wondering why his voice sounded so hoarse. "Now, if you'll recall I gave you a specific order to stay below during the—"

"That's what this is about?" Miranda let out a sigh of relief, unconsciously relaxing her hold on the gown. Jack tried not to notice the swell of her breasts above the ruffled drawstring neckline of her shift.

"Aye, it's about your disobedience. What did you think?"

"Well, the way you came in here." The gown dropped lower. "I feared . . . well, I thought perhaps Phin had . . . had. . . ."

She was on the verge of tears—Jack could see them shimmering in her midnight blue eyes—thinking about an old salt of a pirate dying. Jack stepped forward. "He's doing fine. Awake the last I checked and hollering for something to eat."

"I'm so glad. Not that he's hollering, of course, but that he's going to be all right."

"Aye. Well, we all are." The damn dress was

hanging by her side now. She didn't seem to notice that it no longer shielded her. Jack could clearly see the outline of her firm breasts, the dusky nipples that tasted like honey, and the delta of dark curls at the apex of her thighs. Blood rushed to his groin, thickening and hardening his manhood. He nearly groaned before turning on his heel and heading for the line of transom windows. So much for proving himself immune to her.

Jack kept his back to her. "I think perhaps you should dress yourself." He could tell the exact moment Miranda realized her state of undress. She gasped, then grabbed up another gown.

He could hear the sensual sound of silk skimming over flesh as she pulled on the dress. Closing his eyes, Jack tried to control the desire shooting through him. After a moment, when he decided perhaps he could think again, he opened them. But the night had made a looking glass of the window panes, as good as any mirror. He could see her reflected against the churning sea, her slender arms held high, her body taut as it waited for the gown to slide over it.

He did groan this time. Then coughed to cover the sound. Hands clenched in fists Jack turned abruptly. "You cannot continue to simply do as you please on this vessel." His words were sharp edged, and he saw Miranda's eyes widen as she clutched at the gaping bodice of her gown. "And for God's sake cover yourself."

Had he ever sounded more unreasonable in his

entire life? Jack doubted it. He watched her fumble with the back lacings, then with a sigh moved around behind her. "Let me do it," he said when she tried to pull away from him.

His knuckles brushed against the warm, soft skin of her back, and Jack felt it down to his boots. She shivered, and his mouth went dry. "Now, about your not listening to me," he began. "During battle, the ship's captain has absolute authority."

"You don't all the time?" Miranda twisted her head, and dark curls brushed across Jack's hand.

"Not entirely. A pirate ship isn't like most. The men are very independent. 'Tis more like a brotherhood. But during battle—"

"The other pirates seem to bow to your will most all the time."

"Aye, they do." Jack absently followed the slope of her shoulder with his thumb. "But they listen to me by mutual consent. They do as I ask because for the most part 'tis what they'd do anyway . . . or at least what they know should be done."

"I see." Actually, Miranda "saw" very little. The feel of his work-roughened fingers across her flesh was doing strange things to her ability to reason.

"The *Sea Hawk* 'tis no elitist vessel with a tyrant for a captain and sniveling tars afraid to open their mouths lest they get whipped within an inch of their lives." Jack tried to concentrate on fastening Miranda's gown, but his fingers seemed unable to accomplish the simple task.

MORE PASSION AND ADVENTURE AWAIT... YOUR TRIP TO A BIG ADVENTUROUS WORLD BEGINS WHEN YOU ACCEPT YOUR FIRST 4 NOVELS ABSOLUTELY *FREE* (AN $18.00 VALUE)

Accept your Free gift and start to experience more of the passion and adventure you like in a historical romance novel. Each Zebra novel is filled with proud men, spirited women and tempestuous love that you'll remember long after you turn the last page.

Zebra Historical Romances are the finest novels of their kind. They are written by authors who really know how to weave tales of romance and adventure in the historical settings you love. You'll feel like you've actually gone back in time with the thrilling stories that each Zebra novel offers.

GET YOUR FREE GIFT WITH THE START OF YOUR HOME SUBSCRIPTION

Our readers tell us that these books sell out very fast in book stores and often they miss the newest titles. So Zebra has made arrangements for you to receive the four newest novels published each month.

You'll be guaranteed that you'll never miss a title, and home delivery is so convenient. And to show you just how easy it is to get Zebra Historical Romances, we'll send you your first 4 books absolutely FREE! Our gift to you just for trying our home subscription service.

BIG SAVINGS AND FREE HOME DELIVERY

Each month, you'll receive the four newest titles as soon as they are published. You'll probably receive them even before the bookstores do. What's more, you may preview these exciting novels free for 10 days. If you like them as much as we think you will, just pay the low preferred subscriber's price of just $3.75 each. *You'll save $3.00 each month off the publisher's price.* AND, your savings are even greater because there are never any shipping, handling or other hidden charges—FREE Home Delivery. Of course you can return any shipment within 10 days for full credit, no questions asked. There is no minimum number of books you must buy.

4 FREE BOOKS

TO GET YOUR 4 FREE BOOKS WORTH $18.00 — MAIL IN THE FREE BOOK CERTIFICATE T O D A Y

Fill in the Free Book Certificate below, and we'll send your FREE BOOKS to you as soon as we receive it.

If the certificate is missing below, write to: Zebra Home Subscription Service, Inc., P.O. Box 5214, 120 Brighton Road, Clifton, New Jersey 07015-5214.

FREE BOOK CERTIFICATE

4 FREE BOOKS

ZEBRA HOME SUBSCRIPTION SERVICE, INC.

YES! Please start my subscription to Zebra Historical Romances and send me my first 4 books absolutely FREE. I understand that each month I may preview four new Zebra Historical Romances free for 10 days. If I'm not satisfied with them, I may return the four books within 10 days and owe nothing. Otherwise, I will pay the low preferred subscriber's price of just $3.75 each; a total of $15.00, *a savings off the publisher's price of $3.00.* I may return any shipment and I may cancel this subscription at any time. There is no obligation to buy any shipment and there are no shipping, handling or other hidden charges. Regardless of what I decide, the four free books are mine to keep.

NAME

ADDRESS   APT

CITY   STATE   ZIP

(   )
TELEPHONE

SIGNATURE   (if under 18, parent or guardian must sign)

Terms, offer and prices subject to change without notice. Subscription subject to acceptance by Zebra Books. Zebra Books reserves the right to reject any order or cancel any subscription.

GET
FOUR
FREE
BOOKS
(AN $18.00 VALUE)

ZEBRA HOME SUBSCRIPTION
SERVICE, INC.
P.O. Box 5214
120 BRIGHTON ROAD
CLIFTON, NEW JERSEY 07015-5214

AFFIX
STAMP
HERE

Hell, he'd dressed and undressed his share of women before but never with this much difficulty.

"But during battle it's different? You do have complete authority then?" Was that breathless voice hers?

"What . . . ? Oh, aye." She had the softest, sweetest skin he'd ever touched. "Complete authority." Jack gave up all pretense of hooking Miranda's gown. His hands curved over her shoulders, then down her smooth arms to cross under her breasts. At the same time he surrendered to the urge to taste her as his lips pressed the hollow beneath her ear.

"Oh." The word escaped her on a breath of air. Miranda let loose of her gown, and the bodice gaped open. She leaned back, her head resting against his hard chest, tilted to the side so that he could have access to the whole of her neck. His lips nibbled, his tongue dampened and his teeth sent tiny shivers of excitement down her spine.

Miranda barely noticed when his thumbs hooked on the laced fabric of her neckline, gently tugging it below her breasts. The shift followed, catching briefly upon her distended nipples before the linen was replaced by the firm heat of the pirate's large hands.

Her knees buckled, but somehow she remained standing, pressed against the pirate, supported by the strength of his sturdy arms. His wet tongue traced the swirl of her ear, and Miranda moaned long and deep. Her breasts ached, and she arched, thrusting them more fully into his palms.

He squeezed. He lifted and weighed and swirled his fingers in an ever-tightening circle toward the tips. He tempted and teased, and Miranda shifted, pressing back toward the rock-hard length that rode high on her buttock. When his fingers, light as a bird's wing, traced over her nipples, Miranda sucked in her breath and groaned again, a sound that seemed to spur him on to even more delicious forms of torture.

With one hand Jack shoved the gown over her hips. It fluttered to the deck on a whisper of silk as he found the moist heat at the juncture of her long legs. He ground the heel of his hand against her, feeling dampness through the linen shift.

Miranda's breath came on a sob. She couldn't believe what was happening to her. Her lashes fluttered open as she saw a reflection in the wavery window glass. It was a man and woman. The pirate, oh, she would recognize him anywhere. He was tall and muscled, golden and wild against the backdrop of the churning sea.

But the woman. How could that be her? Yet, Miranda knew the dark-haired creature, writhing erotically against the pirate, must be her. Because she could feel everything the pirate did to her, every time he touched her. His fingers skimmed along her thighs, pushing aside the shift, and Miranda's eyes drifted shut.

Bright colors swirled before her eyelids. It was happening again—that strange, wonderful trip through the heavens. Reality slipped farther away as Miranda clutched at the hand that held her. He moved faster, sliding over her till her legs opened and she cried out.

Jack held her tightly as her slim body tensed, then trembled. For a moment he rested his chin atop the crown of her raven hair, enjoying the sensation of having her sensual body pressed to his. But the pain of his arousal was too great to ignore for long. He wanted inside her. He wanted the same breath-shattering relief he'd given her.

With one hand still cupping her feminine mound, Jack fumbled with his breeches. She made a small, whimpering sound as he pulled back; but he breathed soft, soothing words in her ear, and she relaxed. What he said Jack didn't know. He barely knew anything but an overpowering desire to be one with her.

He yanked down his breeches, and his sex sprang forward, large and hot and straining. Blood pounded in his ears as he leaned forward, grabbing her hips. Pounded loud and insistent.

Jack stopped, jerking around as the sound of someone knocking on the cabin door filtered through to his brain.

God's blood, what was he doing? One moment he was fastening Miranda's gown, telling her why she needed to obey him, and the next she was nearly nude and he was a hairsbreadth from making love to her—again.

"Who is it?" Jack strove to make his voice calm but knew he failed.

"It's me, Cap'n, Scar. Bringin' her ladyship somethin' to eat."

"Oh, God," Jack moaned into Miranda's hair. He stepped back, trying to pull up his breeches. He also tried to keep his eyes on Miranda's face as she turned toward him. She yanked up her shift and dragged her dress up over her hips, sticking her arms into the sleeves. And all the while she stared at him with a dazed expression in her blue eyes.

"This tray is gettin' damn heavy, Cap'n, and the last I looked I ain't no lady's maid."

"I'm going to eat with the rest of the crew." Miranda pulled away when Jack grabbed for her arm. He was shaking his head no, but she ignored him and cracked open the door. "I'm sorry you had to bring that down here. I must have forgotten to tell Simon in the galley."

"Well sure, your ladyship, it ain't nothin'. I'm glad you'll be takin' your meals with us."

Miranda smiled. She closed the door, then leaned against it and shut her eyes. Her moment of relief was short-lived.

"What in the hell are you saying? You can't eat with the men."

Taking a deep breath, Miranda pushed away from the wood. "Why not?"

"They're pirates, for God's sake."

"So are you." Miranda reached behind her back, trying to fasten her gown.

"My point exactly." Jack moved to help her, but she jerked away. He couldn't blame her for that. "We're all pirates, scourges of the seven seas. You don't belong with any of us."

"Perhaps you should have thought of that before you kidnapped me." The pirate captain said nothing—what could he say? "I hope we are returning to Charles Town so that—"

"We are," Jack assured her.

"Good. I think it would be best if we stayed away from each other until then."

Jack couldn't agree more ... or quickly enough. He couldn't explain what happened between them, and this time he didn't even try. He simply turned and left the cabin.

If she wanted to eat with the crew, that was her business. They seemed to like her, and for some reason he couldn't begin to fathom, she liked them. Not that his crew wasn't a decent sort ... for pirates. But they weren't likely companions for ladies.

But then Miranda wasn't the usual sort of lady.

She was the kind that could easily drive him crazy.

Jack told himself he'd eat his meals in his cabin, or on deck or sitting on coiled hemp, or any damn place Miranda Chadwick wasn't.

Except, when the time came, he decided he better go to the galley ... just to keep an eye on his captive.

She was sitting at the rough-planked table between Scar and King, drinking from a pewter mug and talking about gravity. Jack sat at the end of the plank and watched the lantern light shine blue in the deep waves of her hair. He was thinking about the way making love with him made her feel like she was defying gravity. Heat seeped through his body and settled in his groin.

He couldn't get her back to Charles Town fast enough.

Rolling to her side did no good. Miranda clutched at her hair in frustration and tried to find a comfortable spot on the bunk.

She hadn't slept well in two nights. And it was all Captain Blackstone's fault. Every time slumber claimed her, she dreamed of him . . . of the marvelous things he could do to her. It befuddled her mind. Why, today Nat had asked her to explain again how she knew light traveled, and she couldn't do it. She'd started to tell him but couldn't remember.

It wasn't like her. Not at all.

She supposed with everything that had happened to her she could forgive herself a slip of memory. But it would soon be over. The pirate captain had told her this evening that tomorrow they'd be in Charles Town.

She'd be able to forget all this as soon as the pirates returned her to her father. Miranda was sure of it. Closing her eyes, she must have drifted to sleep because she found herself snug in the pirate's arms. He was touching her and kissing her and making her feel warm all over.

Miranda smiled when he called her name, his breath tickling warm across her cheek. Her dreams might be frustrating, but they were very pleasant.

"Miranda. Miranda, wake up."

She fought it as long as she could, but the reality that this wasn't a dream finally stirred Miranda. She jerked away, clutching at the sheet and scooting back in the corner of the bunk.

"What are you doing here? What do you want?" This was no dream.

"We're in Charles Town. I'm going to take you back to your father."

Miranda blinked. "In the middle of the night?"

"I can't think of a better time." The *Sea Hawk* had slid into the harbor under cover of dark, and that was exactly how Jack intended to return his captive. "Now get up and dress yourself."

"Are we really in Charles Town? I don't understand. You said we'd be there tomorrow."

"Aye, we're in Charles Town and we're here now, and if you would simply stop asking questions and get ready, you will soon be in the loving arms of your father." And he could be on his way and hopefully stop thinking of her.

"What about the ransom?"

Jack shut his eyes. Good Lord, would she never cease with the questions? "I will collect the ransom when we reach your father's house."

"You're certain?"

"Of course I'm certain." Jack gritted his teeth. "After all, I'm a—"

"Pirate, yes I know. But I simply don't understand how my father will know to have the coin

223

there. You're taking me to his house, aren't you?"

"If you ever ready yourself." Jack leveled his gaze on her. "However, if you persist with this inquisition, I'll be forced to assume you have no desire to leave the *Sea Hawk*. In which case I'll be happy to take you with us to St. Augustine."

He was jesting. Miranda was almost certain, even though the expression on his handsome face was anything but jovial. Still, she didn't think it was a good idea to push him too far. She inched toward the edge of the bunk, hoping he would move.

He did, seeming almost as nervous being near her as she was being close to him. Not that she didn't enjoy what happened when they touched. It just wasn't—

"Are you going to get up or not?" Jack set the lantern down and strode to the bank of windows across the ship's stern. Clasping his hands behind him, he stared out into the darkness. Damn, he had half a mind to climb into bed with her and forget about this midnight stroll into Charles Town.

Jack shook his head. What was he thinking? What he wanted to do, *must do,* was be rid of the wench, quickly take on provisions and fresh water, and head for St. Augustine. His hands balled into fists as thoughts of de Segovia filled his mind.

Twelve years he'd waited to have his revenge, to hopefully find his sister. Twelve years. And if what Nafkebee told him was accurate, Jack wouldn't have to wait much longer.

Someone clearing their throat behind him made Jack turn. Miranda stood in her white night rail, a woolen shawl bundled around her. Dark hair swirled around her shoulders. She looked sweet and innocent, and Jack took an involuntary step toward her only to stop when he noticed something flare in her eyes.

"May I have some privacy to dress?" Her request was accompanied by a defiant lift of her chin.

He crossed his arms to keep from taking hold of her and reminding her that he'd seen nearly all of her, and what he hadn't, his erotic dreams had imagined. But in the end, he gave a curt nod, then abruptly left the cabin.

In less time than it took him to pace the passageway a dozen times, he heard the door and looked up to find her standing in the opening. She was dressed in a gown of deep rose, one he hadn't seen before. It was fancier than the ones she normally wore. This gown had a ladder of bows down the front and a stiff quilted underskirt. Her glorious raven hair was hidden beneath a bonnet that framed her pretty face and made her skin appear pale in the light from the swaying lanterns.

"Are you ready?"

"Yes."

Jack turned to lead the way, but her hand on his arm stayed him.

"Do you suppose you could help me?" Miranda motioned back toward the cabin. Jack grimaced when he saw the pile of her belongings. "If it's too much, we can leave the gowns. But I simply must take my—"

"Microscope," Jack finished for her. "I know." He went back into his cabin and scooped up the wooden crate containing the microscope, then piled the gowns on top of it. "We'll take it all," he said, following her along the passageway.

"I can help you with some of that."

"Nay," Jack gritted the word between clenched teeth as he peered over layers of lace.

Miranda pushed up through the hatch and smiled broadly when she saw Phin. He held a lantern aloft with his good arm. The other arm was still caught in a sling. "I was afraid I wouldn't get a chance to say good-bye." Miranda moved aside so that Jack could climb up.

"Aw now, your ladyship, ye didn't think I'd not see ye off, did ye?"

Impulsively Miranda hugged the wily old man, careful not to hurt his shoulder. "I shall miss you, Phin."

"Now, no need to get all slobbery." Jack couldn't tell for certain in the dim light, but he thought Phin was blushing. Phin rubbed at his chin. "You're a right decent sort, your ladyship."

"Thank you, Phin." Miranda felt close to tears, which was so illogical. She should be elated to finally put this experience behind her.

She was able to say her farewells to Scar, too. He and the captain rowed the longboat to the dock, guided by the lantern lashed to the bow of the boat and the lights twinkling from the dockside buildings.

Once ashore they left Scar and headed along Water Street, Miranda carrying the light, the captain everything else. No one was about, which made Miranda wonder how late it was. The captain only grunted something she couldn't understand when she questioned him.

Captain Blackstone seemed to know the way to her father's house better than she. When they arrived at Henry Chadwick's front door, Miranda raised her hand to knock, but Jack stopped her.

" 'Tisn't the practice for pirates demanding ransom to go announcing their arrival," he said, before lowering his bundles to the grass and fidgeting with the latch. The door swung open.

"How did you do that?" Miranda asked as she picked up the box containing her microscope. Jack noticed she once again left the dresses for him to carry.

"It wasn't locked." He followed her through the doorway, but once inside he caught her arm. "I'll lead the way if you don't mind." He dropped the gowns in a frilly heap and motioned for her to do the same with her microscope. She lowered it carefully, then gasped as he yanked her along. His only comment was a muffled, "Shhh."

The pirate captain pulled her through the sleeping house, and up the carved stairway, with nary a glimmer of light to guide him. He paused outside her father's door and leaned close to Miranda.

By now her eyes were adjusted somewhat to the darkness, but she could only see the gleam of his eyes against the dark shadow of his face. "Stay behind me," he said, before stealthily turning the doorknob.

A filtering of moonlight bathed the room in a silvery glow. Miranda could make out her father's bed draped in gossamer layers of netting. She crept closer, never more than an arm's length from the captain, who now had a manacle hold on her wrist.

He drew aside the mosquito netting, and Miranda saw her father. He was sound asleep, his nightcap ajar and his mouth open. Her smile froze as the pirate captain pulled something from his waistband.

A pistol!

Miranda didn't know whether her gasp or the feel of cold steel against his neck woke her father. But suddenly his eyes gaped open, the whites bright in the darkness.

"What the—"

"It's me, Gentleman Jack Blackstone, and I have your daughter with me." Jack's voice was as smooth as the doldrums at sea.

"Jack?" Henry rubbed his eyes and tried to sit up.

"I'll be collecting my ransom now." Jack dropped Miranda's hand and fished in his pocket for a scrap of parchment. "Here's the amount."

The paper fluttered to the counterpane, and Henry grabbed it. "But I don't understand. You were supposed to—"

"I have your daughter right here," Jack said, dragging Miranda in front of him. That seemed to jolt Henry into action. He sat up, knocking the pistol aside.

"Miranda, are you all right?"

"Yes. Yes, Papa, I am." Miranda smiled when her father grabbed her shoulders and studied her in the shaft of moonlight. Then suddenly she was in his arms, smothered in a gigantic hug.

"I've been so worried about you," Henry lamented.

Miranda sniffed back tears.

Jack rolled his eyes.

"Now, do you suppose we can get on with this ransom," Jack said.

"Of course, the ransom." Henry fumbled with the flint, finally managing to light a candle. He held it up toward Miranda, bathing her in the golden light. "Are you certain you're all right?"

"Yes, Papa . . . I'm certain."

"Well then, perhaps you should go to your room while Ja—I mean this disgusting pirate and I discuss the ransom."

Miranda slid her gaze to the captain. He stood, arms crossed, pistol casually pointing toward the floor, leaning his hip against the washstand. It suddenly occurred to her that she'd never see him again. And though that was certainly what she *should* want, Miranda felt undeniable regret.

"Did you hear me, Miranda?" Henry slipped from the bed and yanked his nightshirt over his bony knees. "Just go and rest and I will take

229

care of everything."

"All right, Papa." Miranda turned and walked to the door. But her path took her right past the captain, and she couldn't seem to stop herself from pausing.

God, he wanted to touch her. He wanted to reach out his hands and pull her into his embrace and . . . and kidnap her all over again. Jack crossed his arms to keep from doing it. Had he lost his mind? For long moments he just stood there, his eyes locked with hers, and Jack knew it to be a strong possibility.

But then Henry took her elbow and bundled her out of the room, and Jack forced himself to think of de Segovia and all the trouble Miranda Chadwick could still cause. By the time Henry latched the door behind her, Jack had regained some of his balance. "What's the idea calling me a disgusting pirate?"

Henry didn't answer, but simply stood, candle in hand, staring at Jack. "What exactly happened between you and Miranda?"

Each word of his question seemed to hit Jack like a fist. He swallowed. "I don't know what you're talking about. I kidnapped her, as you requested and—"

"Don't play false with me, Jack. We've known each other too long." Henry took a deep breath. "I'm not blind. I can read the kind of looks you two were passing each other."

"I don't know what you think you saw . . . ," Jack began, but his voice trailed off. Turning, he crossed the room, leaning out the open window—

sill. What could he say to this man? There were no excuses he could offer for what he'd done. There *were* no excuses.

Jack closed his eyes for a moment, then faced Henry, who still stared at him in disbelief. "Henry, I—"

"I trusted you, Jack."

"You did," Jack admitted. "And I abused that trust."

"Why?"

Why? The same question Jack had asked himself countless times. Unfortunately he could come up with no better answer now than he had before. Jack shook his head slowly.

"Christ!" Henry swiped the silver brush from his bureau. It landed on the floor with a loud thud. "God, I can't believe you did this."

"I take full responsibility for what happened." Jack felt like he was twelve years old again and getting a tongue lashing for tying his sister's braids in knots. Though tangling curls could hardly be put in the same category as taking a young woman's virtue.

"You're damn right you do. What did happen? No wait, I don't want to know. Oh, God." Henry buried his face deep in his palms. "Did you rape her?"

"Hell no! What do you think I—" Jack stopped. It suddenly occurred to him that it might be better for Miranda if her father thought he did force her. But apparently Henry had already rejected that idea.

"What was it, Jack? Were you trying to prove

you can seduce any woman?" When Jack didn't answer, Henry continued. "Well, I expect you to do the right thing by Miranda."

"I am doing the right thing. I brought her home. And I'm getting out of her life. Let her turn me in as a pirate. I don't care. I intend to keep the hell away from Charles Town in the future anyway." With that said, Jack strode to the door.

"Oh, no. You're not getting away that easy. You're going to marry her."

"Marry her!" That stopped Jack in his tracks. "Are you crazy? You don't want your daughter marrying a pirate."

"You're right about that. But I don't seem to have any choice." Henry paced across to the fireplace. "You made it so that I don't have any choice, Jack."

"Henry, I—"

"I haven't been a very good father to Miranda, but I'm not going to let her down now. You *are* going to marry her."

Jack jerked at his cravat. *"This* is your idea of being a good father? Forcing a marriage on your daughter with a pirate? Good Lord, Henry, I'm sailing off to St. Augustine as soon as I can get the *Sea Hawk* provisioned. I could get killed . . . or captured and hung." Jack refused to scratch his neck.

"Fine."

"Fine? Fine!" Jack faced Henry. "What are you talking about 'fine'?"

"I had no intentions of your living with her

232

anyway. I don't care what the hell you do after you marry her. But you *are* going to marry her."

"God's blood." Jack sank into the chair beside the hearth and dropped his head into his hands. "There's just no reasoning with you. It was the same thing when you came up with this scheme to kidnap your daughter. 'Take her off for a fortnight. Keep her from going to the constable because I don't want her to know I'm your partner,' you said. 'What could go wrong?' Well, plenty went wrong."

"And just whose fault was that?"

"Mine. Mine. It was all my fault."

"Then, marry her."

"Nay."

"You tarnished her virtue."

Jack's head whipped up. He wished more than anything he could deny what Henry said. But he couldn't. He could only stare. And the next time Henry insisted that he marry Miranda, he didn't protest.

"Good." Henry nodded curtly. "I knew you'd see the right of it. You're not a bad sort, even—"

"If I am a disgusting pirate?"

Henry didn't see fit to respond to that. He pulled on a silk wrapper and motioned toward the door. "Let's go tell Miranda what we've decided. I'm certain it will relieve her mind."

"Oh, she's certain to be pleased," Jack said, but was sure the sarcasm was lost on Henry. Things were not working out at all the way he wanted. But in truth they hadn't since he first

233

set eyes on Miranda Chadwick. And now he was going to marry the wench.

Jack had half a notion to bolt out of the house and never set foot in the Carolinas again. But he guessed Henry had a point. Marrying Miranda probably was the right thing to do. But damn it galled him.

With a sigh of resignation Jack preceded Henry to the bedroom door. He yanked it open and found himself staring down the barrel of a pistol.

Chapter Twelve

"Miranda, put down the gun." Jack took a tentative step toward her but stopped—abruptly—when she thrust out her arm, aiming right at his chest.

"Miranda." Henry took up the gauntlet. "What are you doing, child? Give me the pistol. I'll take care of this disgusting pirate for you." His voice was soft and placating. "Actually, we've already worked out something that will soothe some of the pain he's caused you."

"A forced wedding?" Miranda was pleased to see the shocked expressions on both their faces. "I don't think so." She motioned them back with the muzzle. "Now, would you both please be seated? The bed will be fine. Oh, and Captain Blackstone, lay your pistol on the bedside table."

Jack yanked the gun from his waistband, disgusted with himself. The shock of looking down the barrel of a pistol held by Miranda Chadwick had made him forget he was even armed. Would the woman never cease to surprise him? He laid the weapon aside. It certainly wasn't as if he would use it on her. Any more than she seriously planned to shoot him . . . he hoped.

But accidents could happen. And the way she held onto the gun butt, her delicate fingers strained white around the trigger. . . . "Miranda." Jack tried to keep his voice calm. "I suggest you put the gun down before someone gets hurt. You don't even know how to use it."

"Oh, but I do. You told me, remember?"

"You taught my daughter to shoot a gun?" Henry twisted on the bed to fix Jack with his incredulous stare.

"We were attacked by a Spanish ship at Snebley's Creek." If Jack had ever suspected that Henry had informed the Spanish about the secret cove, his distrust dissipated when he saw the expression on his partner's face.

"Yes, he taught me." Miranda brought their attention back to herself and the weapon she held. "But even if he hadn't, I could have figured it out. Firing a pistol is a rather simple principal actually. The friction of the metal hitting flint causes a spark to ignite the gunpowder which in turn. . . ." Miranda lifted her eyes to see both men staring at her. "Never mind. Suffice it to say, I know how to fire a gun."

"But knowing how to fire it and killing a man with it are two different things, Miranda." Jack held her gaze for a long moment.

"I realize that. And I have no intention of shooting anyone." Again she aimed the gun at

Jack's chest. The motion effectively stopped him from sliding off the bed. "Unless you make it necessary."

"Now, Miranda, this thing has gone far enough. As your father I demand that you put down that weapon and listen to reason."

"What reason is that, Papa?" The gun didn't lower so much as an inch.

"Well I . . ." Henry sputtered, then started again, "this wedding, I suppose. Though how you know of it is—"

"I listened at the door of course."

"Miranda!" Henry ran his hand over his sparse hair. "That is not something a lady does."

"Perhaps not. However, after having been subjected to this mockery of a kidnapping, I thought it only—"

"What are you talking about mockery? Why, I—"

"Give it up, Henry." Jack let out his breath on a sigh. " 'Tis obvious she knows."

"Of course I know." Miranda tried to keep her anger from spilling into her words. "Who with any intelligence and using Frances Bacon's theory of inductive reasoning couldn't have figured it out?" She began pacing the room but turned abruptly when she sensed movement on the bed. Jack lifted his palms in submission.

"What's she talking about?" Henry wanted to know.

"I have no idea. But knowing your daughter, I'm sure she'll explain it to us."

Miranda lifted her chin. "Perhaps I won't."

"No, please, enlighten us." Jack didn't try to hide the sarcasm in his tone. "Perhaps the knowledge will help the next time I stage a . . . what was it? Ah, yes, a mockery of a kidnapping."

The smile Miranda gave him was too sweet to be sincere. "I simply made a generalization based on specific observations."

Jack's golden brow lifted. "Such as?"

"First of all you two obviously know each other and, more to the point, seem to be friends. How could you not have known he was a pirate, Papa?" Henry sputtered again, but Miranda gave him no time to respond. "It's not logical to assume you didn't."

"So I'm kidnapped from my own home, and my own father does nothing to stop it." She caught Jack's eyes. "The story about tying him up was convincing at first . . ."

Jack gave a slight nod to acknowledge her remark.

"However, taken with everything else it didn't reason true."

"What else gave it away?" Jack couldn't help being impressed by her figuring out the ruse . . . even if she did have a gun trained on him.

"The ransom for one thing. First it was to be collected at the creek, then not. Your concern for the money seemed incidental. I don't think in a true kidnapping that would be true.

"You also seemed overly concerned with my

238

well-being. Granted I've had little experience with pirates—you and your men are the only ones I've known—but I doubt that my safety would be a pirate's main priority if I'd been abducted only for the coin."

"Perhaps I was merely protecting my investment," Jack offered.

"Perhaps. Of course, I really began to wonder after we forni—made love. You appeared so distraught."

"God's blood, I was not distraught!" Jack jumped off the mattress despite the pistol. How in the hell could she bring *that* up?

Miranda merely shrugged. "You seemed so to me."

"Do you see what I've had to contend with?" Jack faced Henry, who still sat perched on the bed. "Do you see?"

"It appears to me that *I* am the one who has had to withstand adversity . . . and at both your hands."

"Miranda, I'm your father. . . ."

"Which is probably why what you did to me hurts the most. All those years while I was in England I imagined you here wanting me with you . . . loving me—"

"I do love you. I do." Now Henry joined Jack beside the bed. "I just couldn't bare for you to know . . . to know the truth about me."

"That you have a partnership with a pirate?"

"Dammit Jack, you told her!"

"Nay, I didn't tell her anything." Jack crossed

his arms. "Haven't you discovered by now there is little that escapes your daughter . . . especially when she listens at doors." His golden head turned. "I think the question now is what you intend to do?"

"I'm not certain." Miranda wished she had some time, some quiet, solitary time to think this problem through. She was sure of one thing. "I have no intention of marrying you."

"If you were listening carefully through the keyhole, you must know that wasn't *my* idea." She didn't have to act as if being his wife was the worst fate she could imagine.

"That's fine, because I will not do it. Though perhaps it would be a just punishment for you."

"Pirates are normally hung, not imprisoned." Jack spat out the words, but as he saw the color drain from her face, he wished them back. Despite the gun, *and* that she seemed to view marriage to him as a fate worse than death, he didn't want to hurt her. Besides, he supposed she had a right to feel the way she did about this whole thing. Jack just wished he weren't in the middle of it.

Especially when Henry continued to play the outraged father.

"I still think marriage between the two of you is the solution," Henry said, before shuffling barefooted to the window. "It's the only way to right the wrong Jack did to you."

"It wasn't entirely Captain Blackstone's fault." Miranda had her reasons for being angry, but she also intended to be honest.

"It sure as hell was," Jack insisted. He was going to be gentleman enough to take the blame for his seduction. Though he certainly hadn't set out to ravish Miranda, the result was the same.

"This arguing is getting us nowhere." Henry lifted pleading hands toward his daughter. "I just want what's best for you. And I want to know if you can ever forgive me."

Miranda opened her mouth to speak, though in truth she didn't know what she planned to say. But a pounding on the downstairs door startled her. She swirled around and, in the same moment, felt the pistol yanked from her grip.

"I don't think you'll be needing this anymore," Jack said, before slipping the gun into his waistband.

"Who in the hell could that be?" Henry padded into the hallway and looked over the banister.

"Scar's the only one who knows I'm here," Jack said, racing down the stairs. He wanted to get to the door before the noise woke the entire street. "And he wouldn't come here unless there was trouble."

Jack rounded the newel just as Chloe came shuffling out from the back of the house. "What's all this racket?" the old black woman mumbled. "Loud 'nough ta wake the dead."

"Don't you worry yourself about it." Jack headed her off as she reached for the doorknob. He turned her, giving her plump shoulders a hug. "You go on back to bed."

"Mister Jack! Shoulda know'd ya had somethin' ta do with this," she said, before retreating back to her bedroom.

Jack jerked open the door to the piazza, ran across the wooden porch and yanked on that door—so quickly that Scar's shocked expression seemed frozen on his face as Jack dragged him inside.

"What the hell are you doing? I thought I told you we were sneaking Mistress Chadwick back to her home."

"That's just it, Cap'n. They knows about it. And they're comin' for ye."

"Who's coming? What are you talking about?" Jack had Scar by the lapels of his scruffy jacket and was lifting him till only the toes of his salt-crusted boots touched the flooring.

"Joshua Peterson, the king's revenuer."

Jack lowered Scar and sliced a quick glance toward Henry.

"He's still in Charles Town. You didn't stay away long enough. I told you a fortnight." Henry scurried onto the piazza, followed by Miranda.

"But that doesn't explain why he'd come after me. Unless. . . ." Again his eyes found Henry's. "Did you tell people your daughter was kidnapped?"

"No. I said she was down with the fever. There was never any question that she was anywhere but in her room."

"The servants?"

"Didn't know the truth. Besides, they're all loyal."

Jack couldn't argue with that. But if Henry didn't tell, that left. . . . Jack's eyes narrowed and fixed on Miranda. "Is that why you were holding me there at gunpoint? Were you waiting for the king's men to get here?"

"No." Miranda couldn't help squirming under that green gaze of his, even though she knew she was innocent. "I was with you, remember."

"Not after I brought you home. You were sent off to your room."

"And listened at the door instead, except for when I ran downstairs to get the pistol from Papa's desk," Miranda reminded him.

Jack dug his fingers back through his hair and let out an exasperated breath. "All right." He addressed this to Scar, who was still busy straightening his clothes. "Tell me what you saw."

"Didn't *see* nothin' 'ceptin' some tars down at the Rusty Pelican. But I done *heard* me an earful. Word is that someone done seen the *Sea Hawk* in the harbor and sent for the customs officer and the constable."

"What in the hell for? We dock in the harbor all the time."

"Kidnappin'." Scar spit the word out. "They was all talkin' 'bout it. Knew 'bout her ladyship bein' with us and 'bout Henry here, too."

"What about me?" Henry asked.

" 'Bout ye bein' in on it. And 'bout ye bein'

243

hooked up with Jack."

That all-too-familiar itch was back at the base of his neck, but Jack was too busy thinking to scratch it. He paced across the porch, then back. Someone . . . and he couldn't imagine who . . . was trying their damnedest to get him hung. But he didn't have time to worry about who it was right now.

Jack grabbed Scar's arm. "We need to get back to the ship and hope we can get her under sail before—"

"What of me?" Henry hurried to block the door with his body. "If they know I'm involved, they'll figure out the rest. I'll be tried for piracy."

"Come with us then." Jack lifted him out of the way.

"And Miranda?"

"God's blood, bring her, too." This was unbelievable. The constable and his deputies could be at the *Sea Hawk* right now. Or on their way here, and—

"No one is going anywhere."

Jack cringed when he heard that voice. He turned and saw exactly what he feared he'd see. "Miranda, put down that gun." His gun. The one he'd carelessly left on the nightstand beside the bed.

"Not until you listen to me. There's no reason for anyone to go running off. I shall simply tell the constable that I wasn't kidnapped."

Jack leveled a look on her. "You'd do that?" It was still fresh in his mind that the motive for kidnapping her in the first place was to prevent Miranda from talking to the authorities. Could she be trusted now?

"For my father, I would. It appears that he is enmeshed in this thing with you. I can't let anything happen to him."

"Miranda." Henry wrapped his arms around his daughter. She made sure the pistol was still trained on Jack.

Disgusted, he stuck his hands on his hips. "This display of paternal love is charming, but I still think Scar and I will leave. You have your proof, Henry. Your daughter is safe and sound and says she wasn't kidnapped."

"I said you're not going anywhere," Miranda reminded him. "I need you to make my story credible."

"What the hell." Jack started toward her. He'd take that gun from her and be on his way. She wouldn't pull the trigger. He was *almost* certain. Scar's frenzied yell stopped him.

"They're comin', Cap'n. A whole passel a 'em."

"God's blood!" At least ten men hurried along the street heading straight for Henry's house. They carried burning brands, and they didn't look in a pleasant mood. Jack recognized Joshua Peterson, the royal collector of revenues, and the constable among them. They crowded around the doorway to the piazza. Jack shoved Scar toward the back of the house with orders to get to the *Sea Hawk*.

"Henry Chadwick, you in there?"

Miranda squeezed her father's arm. "There's nothing to worry about."

Then, why did he have this almost uncontrollable urge to dig at his neck, Jack wondered. But it was too late to run. There was nothing to do but face the men and hope that Miranda Chadwick was true to her word.

Jack nodded toward Henry. "Let them in."

Henry opened the door and stepped into the puddle of light thrown off by the torches. There was an angry rumble from the group followed by a hush as Henry held up his hands. "Gentlemen," he said, his voice betraying no fear. "To what do I owe this visit?"

" 'Tis for Jack Blackstone we've come. Our understanding is that he's here." This from Graham Hicks, the town's constable.

"Jack? He's here. But it's a little late for calling, don't you think? Perhaps morning would be better."

"And have him sailing full speed for the Spanish Main by then," grumbled someone in the crowd, and others joined in the protest.

"It's not a social visit we're paying," Constable Hicks added after hushing the crowd.

"We've reason to believe Captain Blackstone is guilty of kidnapping . . . among other things," Joshua Peterson said. "And I demand to see him in the name of the king."

"Well, certainly, if it's in the king's name." Henry threw open the door, allowing the royal revenuer and the constable inside. He slammed the door on the rest of the rowdy throng. "There's no need for any more men." Henry motioned toward the drawing room. "Jack's in there." At least he hoped he was.

It occurred to Henry that Jack might have made an abrupt departure under cover of all the commotion. That is if Miranda didn't keep a pistol trained on him.

But when he followed the two men into the room, there sat Jack, looking as relaxed as you please. Beside him, her deep blue eyes wide, was Miranda. There was no gun in sight.

"How are you gentlemen? This is certainly a surprise." Jack stood and gave a formal bow. "I realize the hour is late, but would you care for some refreshment . . . some Madeira perhaps?"

" 'Tis not wine that brought us here."

"I'm arresting you in the name of the king." Joshua Peterson stepped forward. He was a small man, near a head shorter than Jack, but he puffed his barrel chest out in importance. "You won't get to slip away this time, Gentleman Jack. We know all about you and Miranda Chadwick."

Jack arched his brow. "You do?"

"Aye, we do. And once we have you in chains I'm certain we'll find many other things about your *profession* of interest to the Admiralty."

Jack wished he hadn't tied his cravat so tightly. But he didn't loosen it. He only smiled, the humor not quite reaching his smoky eyes.

"My dealings with Mistress Chadwick are private. But as you can plainly see, she is here and perfectly safe."

"Only because you brought her back," Peterson countered.

"You know, then." Miranda stood and pressed a lace handkerchief to her eyes.

Jack turned and gawked at her. He barely resisted grabbing her around her slender neck. They had agreed—actually, he'd demanded—that she be quiet unless it was absolutely necessary for her to speak. And it sure as hell wasn't necessary now. Besides, she sounded as if she planned to corroborate what the king's revenuer was saying. "Miranda." Jack stepped toward her, annoyed when the runty Peterson made a move to protect her. "You needn't say anything."

"Oh, but I must." She lowered the handkerchief enough for Jack to notice there wasn't a tear in her eyes. But she also kept prudently out of his reach. "I must tell the truth, Jack."

God's blood, he could hardly breathe. Jack couldn't help it. He yanked on the stylish Steinkirk knot of his cravat. "Henry." Jack's tone was tight. Surely he could do *something* about his daughter.

"Miranda, dear, perhaps you should go upstairs and rest," Henry suggested.

"No." Miranda managed to evade her father's hands. "I intend to tell them." She sniffed delicately, fighting the smile that tugged at the corners of her mouth. The pirate and her father seemed ready to explode. Miranda turned away from them and faced the king's men. "I ran away with Jack Blackstone."

"What?"

Miranda could swear four voices echoed the same word.

"Jack didn't want anyone to know." She sniffed again. "He's so concerned for my reputation, you know. However, that's the truth of it. I'm a wanton woman."

Her announcement left the room momentarily silent. Joshua Peterson was the first to speak. "But I had word from someone very reliable that there'd been a kidnapping."

"Jack himself probably," Miranda said. "He was adamant about protecting me. He's the reason we're here now. The reason we slipped ashore in the middle of the night. Jack insisted upon bringing me back to my father." Miranda slanted the pirate a look, pleased that he seemed so unsure of what was going on. She decided to make him a little more bewildered, and possibly retaliate just a little for what he'd put *her* through.

"He, of course, insisted that we marry." His expression was all she hoped for. "And perhaps we shall . . . someday."

"There will be no someday about it." Henry stepped forward. "The agreement was tomorrow."

"Tomorrow?"

"Tomorrow!"

Jack and Miranda turned toward Henry as one.

"God's blood!" Jack swore.

"Now, Papa, we didn't actually decide upon a date." She'd only mentioned marriage to give the pirate captain a fright. Regardless that his touch could make her feel as if she'd taken flight, she had no intention of actually wedding the rogue.

"I'm not seeing what the problem is here," Graham Hicks said as he accepted the wine Henry offered. "You ran away to be with Captain Blackstone, did you not?"

"Well . . . yes. I did."

"And it nearly broke my heart, too," Henry injected, before handing a goblet to Joshua Peterson. He ignored the angry look his daughter gave him.

"Captain Blackstone." The king's revenuer took a sip of Madeira. "You brought Mistress Chadwick back to marry her, didn't you?"

Jack looked at Peterson, then at Hicks. He scratched his neck. "Aye. That was my intent."

"Then, I see no reason for delay." This from Henry, who had positioned himself between the two defenders of the law. "Especially under the circumstances."

Lord, protect him from fathers. Jack clenched his jaw. That's what this was all about. He had ravished Henry's daughter, and now he was to pay the price. Marriage. And if they all weren't careful, he might pay with his life.

He'd already accepted the idea of marrying

Miranda Chadwick, if only because of the guilt he felt, but she didn't seem to embrace the notion at all. Her earlier refusal still rang in his ears. And by the looks of her—her eyes as wide as saucers and her round chin angled up—she was close to voicing her rejection once again.

And what would be the consequences if she did?

Neither Joshua Peterson nor Graham Hicks were stupid men. If Miranda shied away from marriage, they'd wonder why. And eventually come to the fairly obvious conclusion that she was lying about running away with him. Who in their right mind would run away on a pirate ship anyway?

Smiling, Jack stepped closer to Miranda. He ignored her sudden jolt when he draped his arm around her waist. Her eyes shot up to meet his. Hers were dark with impotent anger. His, he hoped, were understanding.

"This is for the best, sweetness," he said, nearly laughing at her shocked expression.

"Best? But I don't want to—"

"Aye," Jack agreed. " 'Tis a bit rushed. And I know how you ladies like to gossip and plan such affairs, but I *am* a sea captain."

"I've never gossiped in my life," Miranda countered indignantly. Gossiping was for silly chambermaids with nothing better to occupy their minds. Whereas her own thoughts were lofty and . . . and what did she care about that? For heaven's sake, the pirate captain and her father were maneuvering her into a marriage she did not want.

Miranda sighed. She'd done her share in bringing herself to this point, too. The question was, how could she get herself out of this tangle? She could think better if Captain Blackstone weren't holding her quite so close.

"Aye, she's right." Jack bent to brush his lips along Miranda's forehead. "She never gossips. Isn't she a treasure?" His fingers tightened about her waist. " 'Tis a pity you gentlemen were dragged out in the middle of the night like this. But as you can plainly see, there was no need."

"Especially since there's to be a wedding on the morrow," Henry said; adding, as he turned the two visitors toward the door, "I hope you will stop by tomorrow afternoon for the celebration. Hell, come to the wedding, too." Henry was feeling magnanimous.

Henry closed the door behind the constable and the royal revenuer. The three in the house listened to the grumbles of the men as the constable explained they were leaving empty-handed. The group obviously wasn't happy, but a suggestion that they visit a dockside tavern quieted most of them.

Jack watched through the drapes as the men wandered off down the street. When he turned, it was to fix his stormy gaze on Henry. The older man took a sip of amber liquid and swallowed before carefully placing his goblet on the mantel. "That was a tight knot we managed to squirm through," he said.

"Aye," Jack agreed. "Except some of us didn't manage to squirm through as easily as others."

"Papa, how could you?"

"What?" Henry held his hands up beseechingly. "How could I what?"

"You know exactly what I'm speaking of. This farce of a wedding you've arranged."

"If I recall, daughter, you were the one to first bring up the idea of marriage in front of the constable."

"You knew I was simply playing a scene to save your partner here from the gallows." Miranda's skirts fluffed out as she sank into a chair. "I already made my feelings about the matter known to you."

"The question now is, what's to be done?" Jack paced across the room, his hands clasped tightly behind him.

"I think that's obvious. The two of you will marry tomorrow."

Jack halted abruptly. "God's blood, would you stop saying that?"

"Why should I? You already agreed to the match if you recall."

He had, good Lord, he had. Jack couldn't argue, so he simply stated the facts. "I'm leaving Charles Town as soon as we've taken on fresh provisions."

"I've no quarrel with that."

Miranda stood and marched over to Jack. "That's it. You're agreeing to this?"

"I don't see as I have a choice."

"But there must be some way around it. If I could only think on it awhile, I'm sure I could come up with a solution."

Jack shrugged. He'd already given this entire matter too much thought and time. "I need to get back to the *Sea Hawk*. We've cargo to unload." Jack pointed toward Henry. "The paper I gave you earlier is a fair estimate of what you owe me."

"I'll have it for you tomorrow."

"Aye, tomorrow," Jack said, unlatching the door and disappearing into the night.

"That's it, then." Miranda crossed the room to peek out through the curtains. "The solution."

"What are you talking about, daughter?"

"The pirate left. You can't really expect that he will be back tomorrow."

Chapter Thirteen

"Jack *will* be here tomorrow."

Miranda turned to study her father. He took another sip of Madeira, his eyes never leaving her. "How can you be so certain of that?" Miranda was counting on Captain Blackstone stealing out of the harbor under cover of the predawn mist.

"I know Jack."

"How can you say that? I mean granted, you and he are partners." She gave her head a shake, as if trying to sort that out in her mind. "But he's a rogue of the worst kind."

Henry's expression sobered. "Did he hurt you badly?"

"Nay." Heat surged toward her face, and Miranda clasped her hands. The act of reproduction was as natural as eating or drinking. When her grandfather had explained the process to her, Miranda felt no embarrassment. However now, with her father, she could barely meet his gaze. She wondered if this difference was because with the pirate it had seemed much more than natural. The act of reproduction had seemed wondrous.

Miranda cleared her throat. "Captain Blackstone didn't cause me any pain. However, he did lie to me and he tried to fool me."

Henry sank into a chair, and let his head drop back against the crimson velvet. " 'Tis my fault, not his. Jack wanted nothing to do with my scheme at first."

"I doubt his reasons were particularly noble." Considering his initial, very obvious dislike of her, he probably didn't wish to be bothered by her presence.

"Perhaps not. But this doesn't change the fact that I must bear the blame for all that's happened."

"Papa." He spoke the truth, though Miranda wasn't as willing as he to spare the pirate all the culpability. But Miranda couldn't stand seeing her father so dejected. She sank to her knees beside his chair. "It will be all right. Nothing so terrible happened. I met some very interesting men, who were quite curious about my microscope. And I was able to observe some fascinating fauna and flora." Miranda let out a breath. "Of course, I lost all of that when the Indian grabbed me—"

"My God!" Henry jerked up. "You were attacked by Indians?"

"Not attacked actually. As it turned out the man knew Captain Blackstone, so there was no problem. Except I did lose all the specimens I'd collected."

Henry leaned forward and grasped his daughter's hands. She was a mystery to him, but he loved her. "Miranda," he began softly. "You lost something more important than a few plants. You lost your maidenhood." Henry clasped her tighter when Miranda tried to stand. "I blame myself for this. Perhaps if I'd brought your mother and you with me, this would never have happened. But instead I allowed you to grow up around a man who obviously knew naught about raising a child."

"Grandfather was a wonderful man. A great scientist. He had an amazing mind."

"Of those things I have no doubt. I also know that he loved you dearly. But you should have been exposed to more than books and studies. Perhaps then you would have known how to handle Jack."

Miranda took a deep breath, and forced herself to be honest. "Captain Blackstone did not force me, Papa."

"No. I rather assumed he hadn't. 'Tis not Jack's way."

"I asked him to kiss me. As an experiment. After that—"

Henry jumped to his feet. "A father does not have to hear everything, Miranda. The point is, Jack will be here on the morrow, as he said he would. And you *will* marry him."

Miranda knelt, staring up at her father, wide-eyed. She wasn't used to orders. Grandfather had occasionally *suggested,* but he'd never commanded. "But, Papa—"

"You *will* listen to me!" Henry shut his eyes, trying to block out his harsh tone. "Miranda, dear. Charles Town is a small community. By tomorrow everyone will know of your . . . of your liaison with Captain Blackstone. It was generous of you to sacrifice your reputation for me and for Jack. But it was also foolish. You have no choice but to marry him."

Henry watched his daughter's head bow and touched the shiny, raven hair at her crown. "But you needn't be around him. Jack will be sailing to St. Augustine within days, and until then. . . ." Henry hesitated, not knowing exactly how to explain to his daughter that this would be a marriage in name only.

"Until then what?"

"Er . . . until then he'll be busy refitting his ship." Henry smiled, pleased with himself.

"I see. So he'll be leaving me." Miranda raised her eyes. "Much like you did my mother." She stood, then went to him. Standing on tiptoe, Miranda kissed him good night.

Henry watched her leave the room. He wanted to call her back and explain to her why this was nothing at all like what he had done to his wife. But Miranda's marriage was tarnished enough as it was. No need reminding her that there was no mutual affection, much less love, between her and her intended.

"Yer bloody well pullin' me leg."

"Do I look like a man caught up in a jest?" Jack carefully swiped his razor down the side of his jaw and turned to face Phin.

The snaggle-toothed smile slowly left the quartermaster's face. "Damn, Cap'n, ye sure don't. Ye look a might sickly."

"I'm not sickly. This is the expression of a man resigned to his fate." Jack peered back into the small looking glass nailed to the bulwark. He'd slept last night in his own bunk—finally—but his slumber had been anything but peaceful. Jack had woken this morning with the same niggling question on his mind. How did he get himself into this?

"Well, Cap'n, this is more than I can fathom this early in the morn." Apparently Phin was starting to believe his captain's words. "I mean, ye marryin' her ladyship. It just don't seem likely." Phin scratched at his grizzled chin. "I mean, I never woulda believed she'd have ye."

"What?" Jack winced when he turned, nicking his cheek. "God's blood." He grabbed a rag and blotted at the cut. "What do you mean you can't believe she'd have me?"

"Meanin' no offense ta ye, Cap'n, but well, Mistress Chadwick is a fine lady an' all."

"Aye, well. . . ." Jack wasn't sure what he planned to say about his betrothed, but it sure as hell wasn't complimentary. Yet he found he just couldn't say anything against her. Clamping his mouth shut, Jack stuck out his chin and finished shaving.

"Not that ye ain't a fine specimen a manhood yer own self, Cap'n. It's just—"

Jack held up his hand. "You needn't explain yourself. I don't expect a cataloguing of my virtues . . . however short that list might be." With a linen towel Jack cleaned the remaining soap from his face. "I simply told you so you'd know where I was today."

"And tonight, eh, Cap'n?"

Jack's face felt flushed, which was ridiculous, because pirates sure the hell didn't blush. He grabbed for a clean shirt. "Nay," he said, as matter-of-factly as he could. "We'll be sailing on the morning tide. Too much time has already been wasted getting to St. Augustine. I'm anxious to have my revenge on de Segovia."

Phin scratched at his chin. Do ye think we can trust Nafkebee that de Segovia is back?"

Jack paused in tying his cravat. "Aye, *Nafkebee* can be trusted."

"Ye say that like there's some that can't."

"Oh, there's a traitor in our midst, all right. I've just yet to figure out who it is." Jack brushed back his hair. "It's hard for me to believe that Spanish galleon just happened upon Snebley's Creek. And someone did a good job of convincing the royal revenuer that I kidnapped Miranda Chadwick."

"Ye ain't thinkin' it's one a the crew, is ye?

'Cause I'd vouch for ev'ry one a 'um."

"And if you didn't, I would. Nay." Jack pulled on a gleaming black boot. "It's not one of the men." He arched a brow. "Not a one of them is stupid enough to chance getting himself killed during a battle."

"That be true enough."

"And only a handful of people know about the creek's location." Jack slipped his arms into a jewel blue waistcoat. "There's the crew, but we already decided they wouldn't want to risk their own necks." Straightening his full sleeves, Jack turned and caught Phin's eye. "Henry knows."

Phin's dark eyes widened. "Ye don't think . . . ?"

"Nay, even if I didn't trust him for myself, he'd never do anything that would jeopardize Miranda."

Phin rubbed his shoulder, still sore from the battle. "Then, who's doin' the tellin'? And how they doin' it?"

"That, my dear Phin, I do not know." Jack swept up a plumed hat, settling it casually over his golden hair.

"Are ye marryin' her ladyship now?"

"Nay." Jack took a deep breath. "I received a message from Henry, and it's to be this afternoon at four. Right now I intend to pay my uncle a short visit." Jack adjusted his sword.

"Well, there ye go." Phin lifted a finger. "I'm thinkin' yer uncle knows about the creek, too."

"Ah, I do believe you're right about that."

Jack strode along Cumberland Street, trying to convince himself that he wasn't going to question his uncle. He was merely paying a social call on his closest living relative—as far as he knew, his only living relative. After all, Jack normally visited his uncle when he was in port. And today, the day of his marriage, seemed an ideal time to be with family.

The weather was pleasant with a cooling breeze blowing in off the Cooper River. Close by, Jack could hear the metallic clang of hammer hitting nail as the residents worked to rebuild. In February a fire had swept through the town, wiping out nearly a third of the homes. This disaster, following so closely on the heels of an earthquake, had put a halt to much of the town's growth.

But there seemed to be a new prosperity in Charles Town—and though Jack was glad to see it for the town, he feared it pealed a death knell for his way of life.

Profits from trade were rising, and the populace was losing its need for pirated goods. "And thus, its need for pirates," Jack mumbled, mimicking Miranda's logical progression as he turned up the dirt road to his uncle's house.

Built of brick, the Blackstone town house looked prosperous and had been spared damage by the fire. Jack entered, then sent a servant to fetch his uncle before settling into a chair.

"Jack, how good to see you." Jack rose as his uncle Robert entered the room. "I've word this is a big day for you."

Jack's grin was genuine, and he felt the tension ease from his shoulders. How could he have suspected this man, his father's brother, of betraying him? One had only to look at him to see the resemblance to Jack's father . . . the dark auburn hair and light green eyes. If there was one man on earth who hated de Segovia as much as Jack did, it was his uncle.

If not for a strange twist of fate, Robert would have been at Port Royal that fateful day in 1686 when the Spanish attacked the small Scottish settlement. Then he, too, would have been killed or taken prisoner. As it was, he almost lost his life bringing word of the slaughter to the governor at Charles Town.

Jack shook his head slightly. He could not believe it was this man who had betrayed him. There must be some other explanation.

Accepting the crystal goblet of wine, Jack sat in the chair across from his uncle. "So tell me, Jack, how does my nephew come to be taking on the yoke of matrimony?"

After sipping his wine, a fine Madeira he'd brought on his last voyage, Jack arched his brow. "You seem to know about it, perhaps you should tell me."

"As I hear it, there's a bit of a scandal involved. A young woman besot with your manliness, following you to sea, was the version told me by Mistress Denley when she called earlier."

"Ah, Mistress Denley." Jack lifted his cup in mock salute. "The consummate gossip . . . wrong again."

"I doubted it myself."

Jack leaned back in the chair. "I told you of Henry's request that I kidnap his daughter."

"Is your wedding a result of that fiasco? If you recall, I advised against it."

"That you did. And obviously I should have heeded your counsel." Jack paused. For some reason he couldn't fathom, he had a prickle of uneasiness. More to the point, he felt disloyal to his bride to be. An odd sensation when this marriage was being forced upon him. But nevertheless, he couldn't shake it, and he rose, running his finger along the carved marble mantel. "It isn't such a bad match. Miranda Chadwick is quite lovely."

"So I've been told, though I've yet to see for myself." Robert regarded Jack over the rim of his goblet. "You seem fond of the girl."

Fond? Was he? Jack couldn't say for sure. He found her interesting, and certainly desirable, but she'd been more an annoyance than anything else. Jack shrugged away the comment.

"Nafkebee found me. I suppose he told you about de Segovia," Jack said, turning back toward his uncle.

"Indeed. I suppose that's why I was so surprised by your plans to marry."

"One has naught to do with the other. I'm

leaving for St. Augustine on the morning tide." Jack paused, surprised by his uncle's expression. "You doubt my words?"

"I believe that is your intention, however. . . ." Robert stood and carefully made his way to the window.

"What? What is it you're not saying?" Jack knew his uncle well. He was one to usually speak his mind.

"Nothing." His hand beneath the layers of lace fluttered as if in dismissal. He appeared to have a change of heart and continued. "I just wonder how serious you could be about finding de Segovia and punishing him."

"How can you even question my intent, or my commitment, to avenging our family? I have sacrificed nearly everything to that end."

"What you say is true." Robert touched his finger to the side of his nose. "However, you do plan to marry today."

"I already told you that shall have no effect on my quest."

"Ah." Robert's hands lifted. "That is easy to say now, when the blood runs cool. But a night in your young bride's arms may change that. Women have a way of working their wiles upon a man. Your mother for instance—"

"I'm leaving for the *Sea Hawk* immediately after the ceremony," Jack said with determination.

"Excellent."

The hard edge of malice that tinged Robert's

smile did not escape Jack. This man was obsessed with revenge. Almost as obsessed as Jack himself. They indeed had the same goal in life. Still, Jack was glad he'd stopped Robert from expounding upon his mother.

Robert had been in love with Jack's mother. The notion still surprised Jack, even though he'd had nearly a year to get used to the idea . . . a year since Robert had told him of the beautiful Flora. And how she'd at first encouraged the amorous attentions of a noble second son, only to spurn him after meeting his older brother, Jack's father.

It made Jack wonder, after Robert told him of this strange triangle, why his uncle came to the Carolinas with his parents. But Robert had always seemed devoted to Jack's father, and he was still obviously affected by his death.

As was Jack.

Sometimes he wondered if he'd ever get over his own feelings of rage when he thought of de Segovia.

Jack took a deep breath. "Soon, Uncle." He clenched his fist. "Soon I will return from St. Augustine with word that I've killed the bastard de Segovia."

"A day we all await." Robert clasped his nephew's shoulder.

Jack spent the remainder of his visit discussing Royal Oak, his plantation to the south of Charles Town. The land was the original grant given to his father when he'd settled at Port

Royal. Jack was so often away at sea, Robert managed it for him.

During their talk, Jack thought how amusing it would be to inform Miranda that her betrothed, besides being a pirate, was also a wealthy landowner. With a shrug he conceded she probably wouldn't care.

But would she ever want to live on the plantation with him? Jack had played with the idea of retiring from the sea and focusing his energies on growing rice. He'd even discussed it with his uncle. But it wouldn't be until he found de Segovia, of course. And hopefully, his sister. But then, perhaps Jack would consider it. A change in lifestyle would help alleviate the itch at the base of his neck if nothing else.

"Jack, are you listening to me?"

"Aye." Jack searched his mind for what his uncle just said. "You plan to flood more acreage. I think that's a prudent idea. Rice is bringing a good price."

"And it is relatively safe from pirates," Robert added.

"Indeed." Jack laughed. He stood and walked to the window. It was time for him to go to Henry Chadwick's house, but he still had something to discuss with his uncle. "The *Sea Hawk* was attacked by a Spanish ship." Jack couldn't help himself; he studied his uncle's reaction carefully. He appeared surprised.

"Good heavens, when? I thought you did the attacking."

" 'Tis the usual scenario. But not this time. It was three days ago." He paused a moment. "At the mouth of Snebley's Creek."

Robert shook his head. "Dreadful. But it appears you came through it unscathed."

"Aye, but two of my men were killed."

Robert made a clicking noise with his tongue. "A shame. But I suppose that's one of the consequences of being a pirate."

"I suppose." Jack ran his finger along the wainscoting. "But we've always felt relatively safe at Snebley's Creek."

"Because it's well hidden?"

"Aye. And because so few people know of its existence." Jack knew he should let it drop, but some perverse streak made him continue. "You are one of those few people, Uncle Robert."

"So I am. You did tell me its location. And as I recall, you said Henry Chadwick also knew about it."

"He does."

Robert crossed to the table to pour some more wine. Jack shook his head at the silent offer. "Then, I imagine if you found the creek, others could, too. Perhaps this Spanish ship stumbled across your hiding place."

"You could be right." *Except that they were waiting for us,* Jack thought. But he didn't say it. He had an uncomfortable feeling he'd said too much already. It wasn't as if he honestly believed his uncle would betray him. But then who, a small voice asked. "Well, I must be on my way."

"I am welcome at the nuptials, aren't I?"

"Aye." Jack laughed, wishing he could dispel his nagging doubts. This man was his flesh and blood. "Inviting you was one of the reasons I stopped by."

Miranda had never been so pushed and prodded in her life. When all she wanted to do was read or study a specimen under her microscope, two servants twisted her hair into smooth, upswept rolls. They teased a few raven curls onto her forehead before adding a fontange of stiff lace that made Miranda appear several inches taller than she was.

Her stays were laced tightly and covered with a mantua of the finest ruby silk. The stomacher sported bows of ivory ribbon. The same ribbon that ruched, decorated her petticoat. The scarlet overskirt was tied back and trailed along the floor in a train that Miranda thought would surely trip her before the day was through.

"Your ladyship looks ravishing," declared Molly, the servant her father had borrowed from his friend, Mistress Denley.

"Oh, indeed she does," Henry piped in as he stood in the doorway to her bedroom. "May I come in?"

"Of course, Papa." Miranda turned to the two servants. "Are we finished?" she asked, almost frightened that they might have some other form of torture waiting for her. But they simply nodded and, after curtseying, left the room.

"Jack is downstairs."

"He is?" Though her father seemed certain the pirate would show up today, Miranda had secretly hoped and even expected he wouldn't. Oh, maybe a small part of her didn't like the idea of his rejecting her so obviously; however, she thought that preferable to a forced marriage.

Miranda sighed and decided to wage her last battle against what was about to happen. She'd been unable to come up with any way out of this marriage — even using all her reasoning skills. Perhaps if she and the captain joined forces, they could come up with something. "Do you suppose I could speak with Captain Blackstone . . . here."

"In your room?" Henry appeared shocked that she would suggest such a thing.

"Actually, it doesn't have to be in my room, but really Papa, what could possibly happen? I'm so bound up in these clothes, I can barely move." Miranda spoke with more tact when she noticed her father's cheeks turn a dull red. "I really do need to discuss something with him . . . privately."

Her father seemed somewhat disgruntled as he left the room, but a few minutes later he returned, the pirate captain in tow.

Of course, he appeared nothing like the pirate he was. He was tall and handsome, his golden hair neatly brushed and his powerful body dressed in the most stylish of clothes. Miranda's pulse quickened, just looking at him.

He stepped into the room, shutting the door on her father, who mumbled something about remaining in the upper hallway.

"You wished to see me?"

"Yes." Now that he was in the same room with her, some of Miranda's courage failed her. It was much easier to think when he wasn't near her. And she'd been wrong about his not seeming like a pirate. Though he was shined and polished, there was still a wildness about him that all the silk from China couldn't conceal.

Miranda moved toward the fireplace . . . anything to put distance between them. When she turned back, she caught Captain Blackstone watching her, a light in his eyes that she well remembered. Perhaps her father was right about not allowing them too much privacy. Miranda had the strongest urge to wriggle out of her clothes and wrap herself around him—pirate or not.

She cleared her throat. "We must find a way to change my father's mind about this marriage."

"Why?"

Why? What did he mean, why? She was the one who usually asked such questions. "Because neither of us wants it," Miranda said, stating what she thought was the obvious.

"Perhaps," Jack agreed. However, seeing her now, he couldn't remember exactly what he had against this match. "But sometimes we must do things simply because it is the right thing to do."

Miranda's mouth dropped open. "That's a strange thing for you to say."

"Why so strange?"

"Well you're a . . . I mean. . . ." This was not the way she wanted to start this conversation, by insulting the captain.

But he didn't seem insulted. He only shook his head and chuckled. "Because I'm a pirate?"

"Well, yes." She might as well be honest.

"And is that why you're so against marrying me?"

"No . . . yes . . . perhaps it has something to do with it. But it isn't the main reason," Miranda hastened to add.

"Which is?"

"I simply don't wish to marry." Miranda lifted her hands. "I don't believe either of us does. There must be another way to solve this problem. We need to do some deductive reasoning."

"I'm afraid reasoning of any sort is out." Jack had to grin at the expression on her face when he said that. You'd have thought he suggested she jump out the window.

"But that's ridiculous. Logic and reasoning—"

"Don't always work when you're dealing with people's feelings. And that, Miranda, is what we're dealing with here." Jack took a deep breath and tried to think of the best way to explain. For all her knowledge about planets and gravity and little invisible animals, his bride to be knew very little about human nature.

"What we did together—and I assure you I take full responsibility for it—is usually reserved for people who are married. Now, sometimes a man and a woman do make love without the sanction of a wedding." Jack held up his hand when he felt she planned to interrupt. "However, it is not something that is openly spoken of."

The captain paused, and Miranda continued to stare at him. When he said nothing else, she prodded, "And?"

"And because you told the constable and the king's revenuer that you ran off with me, they assume we . . . well, what we did."

Miranda whirled about, brushing her hands over the scarlet silk in frustration. "I still don't understand—"

"God's blood! Your reputation will be ruined if we don't wed. And your father, who loves you very much, will be devastated." Jack clenched his teeth. "That's all you need to understand."

Couldn't he hold a rational conversation without yelling? Miranda stuck out her jaw, and kept her voice as low as she could. "Don't forget that my lie about running away with you won't be believed if we don't marry."

"There's that, too," Jack admitted. "But if saving myself was all that concerned me, I would have sailed away last night rather than tonight."

"You're leaving tonight?"

Her words were spoken softly, and Jack felt a tightening in his chest. "Aye. You won't have to concern yourself that I will—I mean, after the ceremony I'll be leaving."

"Off pirating?" she asked. Miranda couldn't understand it, but she felt disappointed. He wasn't going to stay with her at all.

"Aye, pirating," he said; but he'd hesitated before answering, and Miranda could swear he wasn't telling her the truth.

Miranda watched in silence as he turned abruptly and left the room without further explanation. Her last hope gone, Miranda realized she was actually going to have to marry him.

And then he was going to leave her. The idea should have pleased her, but for some reason she couldn't get the image of her mother from her mind. Her mother who'd been married and left behind.

Of course, that was different. Her mother and father had loved each other. And Father had gone off to make a better life for them, not taking his wife because of the danger.

But that hadn't saved Miranda's mother from dying alone, longing for her husband's touch.

"This isn't the same thing at all," Miranda mumbled. But as she followed the captain downstairs, she decided to find out the truth about where he was going.

Chapter Fourteen

But discovering the truth — if indeed there was something other than the obvious to discover — would have to wait.

As soon as Miranda reached the parlor door her father grabbed for her hand. "I've had the coach brought around front."

It wasn't far to St. Phillips Church opposite the half-moon battery, but Miranda didn't argue about riding. She sat beside her father and across from the imposing figure of Captain Blackstone. He said, nary a word, and Miranda followed suit as she deliberately studied her gloved fingers.

Henry, on the other hand, seemed unable to allow a moment of quiet time. He spoke of the weather, of the rice crop, of anything that might relieve the tension that hung as heavy and damp as the sultry summer air. And he seemed obviously relieved when the black cypress church came into view.

Miranda imagined her father thought one or both of them might suddenly change their minds about this wedding and bolt out a door. Smiling, Miranda imagined herself leaping from the moving coach only to trip over her train and land in an ignominious heap on the dirt road. As soon as the coach rolled to a stop Henry jumped from his seat. Reaching back in, he took Miranda's hand and gave it a tug. Her lashes lifted, and for the first time since the encounter in her bedroom, her eyes met the captain's.

She lost herself in the sea green depths, forcing herself to look away only when Henry gave her fingers another yank.

After the gloomy interior of the coach, the bright sunlight made her squint. When her eyes opened, Miranda thought she must be dreaming. A group of people, perhaps twenty strong, stood in front of the church. Most of them were leading citizens of Charles Town, friends her father had obviously invited. But standing off to the side, conspicuous in rough but relatively clean clothing, stood the pirate crew.

Miranda smiled when they broke into a loud huzza.

"What the hell . . . ?" Jack swung through the cramped doorway to the cheers of his crew. In a half-dozen strides he reached the scraggly group. "What are you doing here?"

"Come ta see yer weddin', Cap'n," Phin said, showing his snaggle-toothed smile. "Yers and her ladyship's."

Before Miranda could say anything, Jack grabbed Phin's upper arm and hauled him off to the side. He bent till his head was close to the quartermaster's ear. "What in the hell are you doing? Who's unloading the cargo and taking on supplies? We need to leave as soon as this . . . wedding is over."

"Don't ye worry none, Cap'n. Me an' the boys done took care a all that. The *Sea Hawk*'s ready ta sail with the tide."

"But—" Jack was about to mention that consorting with the gentry was one way for the pirates to get themselves caught—his neck had started itching the moment he saw his crew—but Miranda stopped him. She elbowed her way between the two men, clutching hold of Jack's hand and pulling. Jack was so surprised he let go of Phin's arm.

"Don't you go bullying him, Captain Blackstone. "I'm glad your men came today. I invited them."

"*You* invited them? You? What gave you the right to do anything with my crew?"

"They may be your crew, but they're my friends, no matter that they're—" The widening of Captain Blackstone's eyes made Miranda stop. "No matter that they are seamen," she finished. "And I certainly have a right to invite whomever I choose to my wedding."

"You do, do you? Well, let me tell you this—" Jack faced his bride nose to nose. But something, perhaps Henry frantically clearing his throat, made him broaden his focus.

Lined up behind Miranda, not a single one doing anything to hide their interest in what he was about to say, were some of Charles Town's citizens . . . including Graham Hicks, the constable, and Joshua Peterson, the royal revenuer.

Jack swallowed, then dipped his mouth, brushing it across her cheek. Her expression of shock was comedic. "Sweetheart, you were wonderful to invite them. But then everything about you is wonderful." Before she could do anything but stare up at him, her mouth gaping, Jack took Miranda's arm and propelled her toward the church door. "Let's get on with this, shall we?" he hissed for her ears alone.

The citizenry followed them into the cool sanctuary of the church, and Jack let out a sigh of relief. If he made it through this day without being arrested, he'd feel fortunate. Thankfully things seemed to be progressing satisfactorily.

Henry introduced him to the Anglican minister. He was a prunelike little man with a dour expression, as if he'd just sucked a lemon. But he made no comment about never having seen Jack in church before. Or about the circumstances of this wedding.

Again, Henry took up the task of keeping the conversation going, and for that Jack was relieved. He wished everyone would settle into their pews so that they could begin. He glanced over his shoulder to check on progress and noticed a small group by the door. The next instant he heard the first voice raised in anger: Phin's.

"God's blood," Jack mumbled under his breath. He started back the center aisle, ignoring the clergyman's expression of reproach. "What is it? What's going on?" His men, looking every bit the blood-thirsty pirates they were, despite their fresh

278

scrubbing, stood huddled in the doorway. Constable Hicks blocked their way. Jack clenched his fist to keep from scratching his neck.

"We ain't leavin' him outside, Cap'n. No matter what this here constable says."

Jack thought for a moment Phin planned to spit, but thankfully, he didn't. "Leave who outside? What are you talking about?"

"It's quite all right, Captain. I shall wait here." This from King, who stood tall and straight, his arms folded across his powerful chest.

"This here Negro can't come into the church," Constable Hicks explained.

Jack looked from Hicks to King, and back again. His voice was deceptively low when he spoke. "Mr. Hicks, I don't believe you understand. Mr. King is a member of my crew and an invited guest."

"That don't make any difference. He's a Negro . . . could be an escaped slave for all I know."

"Mr. King is a free man. You have my word on that."

The constable snorted his opinion of Jack's veracity, and Jack's fingers relaxed around the hilt of his sword. Hicks saw the action and reached for his own weapon, but in the next instant, his arm was bumped by an apologetic Miranda.

"I'm so sorry, Constable Hicks," she said, smiling at him. "Jack, dear, what *is* the delay? My father is starting to pace. Oh, hello, King. I'm so glad you could come to our wedding." Miranda talked while maneuvering herself between the men, forcing them apart. Then she took the blackamoor's arm and twined her own under it. "Let me find you a seat," she said, leading him through the group. Constable Hicks stepped aside, and the rest of the pirate crew followed Miranda and her escort.

Jack could only stand and stare.

By the time the ceremony began, Miranda was tired and irritable. She wanted nothing more than a quiet corner where she could read, or perhaps study a specimen under her microscope. The Anglican minister's voice droned on, and Miranda sighed. This entire thing was so foolish, so. . . .

Miranda's head turned ever so slightly, and her eyes met Jack's. At that moment, something happened to Miranda, something that she didn't expect and couldn't explain logically or otherwise.

It was as if she just realized exactly what she was doing. Marrying Captain Blackstone before man and God.

She and her grandfather had often discussed religion, mostly how it related to science. She had no strong opinion about which religion was the right one, partly because she'd studied several. Don Luis was Catholic, and though she knew countries fought over such things as religious supremacy, Miranda thought that very foolish. She didn't consider herself by any means devout, and that was probably why the feelings flooding through her were so illogical.

Words drifted through the clergyman's litany. Words such as love and honor and obey. Words she was promising Captain Blackstone. Words he was promising her.

He was holding her hand. It wasn't a romantic act. He'd been told to do it. But no one suggested he squeeze her fingers, or stare intently into her eyes. It was as if he felt it, too, this strange, steadfast sensation that came over her.

They stood before the altar, and the cleric's voice seemed to fade away. Miranda imagined she could feel the captain's heartbeat racing toward her through his hand. And miraculously, it matched her own.

She could smell him, wild and free. Remembered how it felt to be touched by him, to become one with him, and in that moment she realized it was happening. She was becoming one with him. It was a mystical, magical feeling, and quite strange for a woman who believed only in logic and reason.

The minister stopped speaking and folded his hands, and Miranda expected the sensation to pass, but it didn't. She found herself returning the captain's smile, and even leaning into him when he gave her a quick hug.

After that her father came forward to kiss her cheek, and somehow with the mix of people pushing around them, Miranda became separated from her new husband. She saw him again, briefly, on their ride back to her father's house. Again she sat beside her father.

But this time they shared the coach with the captain's uncle, who monopolized Captain Blackstone's attention with talk of St. Augustine. Through the snatches of conversation Miranda was able to hear while pretending to listen to her father, she gathered Robert was very anxious for his nephew to go to St. Augustine.

It was also clear that his going there had naught to do with pirating coin. Through her lashes, Miranda watched her husband's jaw clench and his face grow taut with rage. She'd seen that expression before . . . when he'd listened to the Indian. Right before the captain had decided to return her to Charles Town.

"Are you listening to me, daughter?"

"Oh, yes, Papa . . . what did you say?"

"I said it was a lovely wedding. Now things can settle down."

Miranda was saved from responding when the coach stopped under the magnolia tree in front of the house. Captain Blackstone alighted and almost as an afterthought reached back in for her. It was obvious if he'd felt anything for her during the wedding ceremony, it had faded in the heat of his anger. What could make him so enraged?

She didn't know, but Miranda was certain it had something to do with where he was going. It was like a scientific puzzle. She'd gathered bits of information, and using the rules of logic she'd discover the answer.

Unfortunately, the reception at her father's house didn't seem to be the place to do research. It was an odd mix of people who crowded out into the garden behind the house.

When her mother was still alive, she occasionally held garden parties at the estate in Essex. Miranda was permitted to join the festivities, though even at such a tender age she preferred the stimulation of her grandfather's library to the gaiety of her mother's soirees.

But those parties had been nothing like this one. Probably because her mother had never invited pirates, Miranda decided, as she set off to speak with Phin. He was leaning against a column, Nat by his side. Both men were stuffing sliced ham into their mouths. Miranda noticed their pockets bulged with meat.

"I want to thank you again for coming, Phin, and bringing everyone with you."

"It were—" Finding he couldn't talk with his mouth crammed full, Phin swallowed some of the savory ham and continued. "It were real nice a ye to invite us."

"I thought it only fitting since you are . . . ," Miranda hesitated over the word husband, "since you are Captain Blackstone's crew . . . and my friend."

Phin couldn't suppress a grin, then gathered several sweet cakes into his gnarled hands.

Miranda took a deep breath. "I was wondering about the destination of your next cruise."

"Ye mean, St. Augustine?" Sugar icing whitened Phin's beard.

"Yes, that's the one. Why are you going there?" Miranda hesitated. "It's Spanish."

Phin's eyes watered as he swallowed and gulped. "Aye, it is. And so's de Segovia."

He nearly spat the name and Miranda searched her mind. Where had she heard it before? "Who is—"

"Ye got some real tasty vittles here," Phin said.

His eyes narrowed, though he kept his smile in place. "Ye wanta know more 'bout that damn Spaniard, I'm thinkin' ye should be askin' yer husband."

Phin didn't seem to have any trouble referring to his captain as Miranda's husband. She wet her suddenly dry lips. "Perhaps you're right."

But the pirate captain was now bent toward her father, and neither seemed anxious for an interruption. Besides, she had a better idea. Skirting several ladies of Charles Town who didn't appear to know exactly how to react toward her, Miranda headed for the captain's uncle.

He was tall, like his nephew, but not nearly so large. He watched her approach, his head cocked to one side, and Miranda realized she didn't really care for him. Which was uncharacteristic. She had disagreements with people, of course, and the pirates she'd disliked at first because of what they were, but this was different. It was deep seeded, and totally irrational. He even stepped forward to meet her and bowed low over her hand. But she couldn't shake off her feeling of unease.

Her grandfather would have labeled it an intuition and summarily dismissed it. Miranda tried.

"I didn't realize until today that my . . . husband had an uncle in Charles Town." Miranda didn't add that there were many things she didn't know about the pirate captain.

"Ah, yes. I fear Jack and I are all that's left of the Blackstones who came here from Scotland."

"That's a shame. How many of them were there?"

"My brother, his wife and children." Robert Blackstone smiled down at her. "Jack and his sister," he explained. "We came to the New World seeking a better life, but alas, it ended tragically."

"What happened?"

Robert sighed. "The Spanish from St. Augustine attacked one day, killing most everyone. The rest Don Diego de Segovia took prisoner."

There was that name again. "Were you taken prisoner?"

"No." His smile hardened till Miranda thought it seemed more like a sneer. "I was away from the settlement."

"I see."

"It is something I've had to live with since that day."

"What happened to Captain Blackstone?"

"Why don't you ask your husband that question?"

Miranda stiffened as the deep voice floated over her left shoulder. She turned and tilted her head, staring up at Jack Blackstone. He was smiling, but no mirth touched the stormy green of his eyes. "I was just—"

"I heard you."

"Oh." Obviously he didn't like being the topic of conversation.

"Your father wishes to see you." Jack took Miranda's arm. "Will you excuse us, Uncle Robert?"

"But my father is by the punch bowl," Miranda protested as Jack pulled her along toward the piazza. He ignored her, and made only the briefest comment to several men who offered their congratulations. When he shut the door, effectively sealing them off from the crush of guests, Jack turned to his bride.

"What is it that you wish to know?"

"I . . . I don't understand."

His golden brow arched. "You forget that I'm somewhat acquainted with you. You're asking questions about me—of Phin, of Robert. Perhaps you should simply ask me."

Miranda lifted her chin. "Will you answer them . . . truthfully?" She couldn't forget how he'd lied to her before.

"Perhaps." The corners of his mouth lifted slightly.

"I want to know about de Segovia." She saw the hint of a smile disappear and anger darken his eyes.

"Why?"

Miranda hesitated. She really couldn't answer that. She simply wanted to know. "I think you're trying to find him."

Jack held her gaze a moment. "Again, why should you care?"

"Well, I am your wife." The words were out of her mouth before Miranda could stop them. She could tell they shocked the captain as much as they did her. "I mean. . . ." She tried to come up with an explanation but could think of nothing.

"This really doesn't concern you, Miranda."

"You wanted to know why I didn't ask you." Miranda turned away from him. "This is why. I didn't think you'd tell me."

He caught her before she moved two steps. "He's the man who killed my parents, and captured my sister and myself." Jack answered quickly, then wondered why he bothered at all.

"You escaped?"

"Obviously."

Miranda ignored the sarcasm. "And now you're going back for him. But why?"

"My sister didn't escape."

Miranda bit on the end of her thumbnail. "But anything could have happened to her in — how long ago was this?"

"Twelve years."

"Twelve years?" Her eyes widened. "But surely you can't hope to — "

"You asked why I was going after de Segovia, and I told you."

Miranda had more questions, but with a sweep of his hand, her husband indicated the interview was over. Miranda sighed, having no choice but to lead him back into the garden.

"There ye be," Phin bellowed as soon as the door opened. "I was thinkin' ye done sneaked off 'fore I could raise me hand in a toast."

To Miranda's thinking, Phin had already raised his hand too many times. But he draped one arm about her shoulders and the other around his captain's waist, explaining how it was the quartermaster's duty to salute the health and success of a wedding.

"Phin, I don't think it's necessary to — "

"Now, Cap'n, I knows me duty." Phin untangled his arm from around Miranda, managing to push her toward Jack in the process. She fell against his chest and stayed there. Phin gave a sharp yell, gaining everyone's attention. "To the cap'n and his bride." Phin held up a silver goblet that looked too delicate for his hand, then downed its contents in one gulp.

Most of the guests took a moment to exchange glances, then followed suit.

"Now ye need ta give her a good kiss." Phin tried to shove the newlyweds even closer together.

"Phin, you've had too much to drink."

"And when has that ever bothered ye, Cap'n, 'cepten when I be on duty, and ye knows I don't overindulge. " 'Sides, drinkin's the right of ev'ry red-blooded pir—"

"If it's a kiss you want," Jack yelled, trying to cut off and drown out Phin's last word. God's blood, the man was loose-lipped when he was pie-eyed drunk. "It's a kiss you shall get." Jack swung Miranda around in his arms, hoping against hope that the constable didn't hear the word pirate from Phin's lips.

To the cheers of his men, and the shocked "ahhs" of several ladies, Jack leaned Miranda over his arms and kissed her soundly on the lips. A soft sound escaped her, one of surprise . . . of yielding. Her mouth opened, and before Jack could think, his tongue shot inside. Her body quivered, then seemed to melt into his. He could feel her arms slide up his to wrap around his neck and her fingers dig into his hair. And all thoughts of why he was doing this fled his head.

She was warm and soft and smelled more exotic

than the mid-summer garden. Her scent seemed to envelop him as surely as his body surrounded her. It made him light-headed. Ready to sink with her to the crushed-shell walkway.

He remembered what it felt like to lie with her, to touch her delicate body and sink into her heat. Blood pounded in his ears, boiled and raced to his groin. And all the while Jack's mouth devoured Miranda's, savoring the sweet honey of her.

Jack's hands roamed along her back, the silk warm and smooth like the flesh below, pressing her ever more tightly into his embrace. And she came willingly, ardently.

All he knew was the overpowering need that seemed to invade him, consume him, every time they touched.

Until he felt something hard and clawlike bite into his shoulder. Jack twisted, and reality flooded over him in one fearful and totally embarrassing moment. Henry's hand gripped his shoulder, and the smile on his lips didn't disguise the anger in his eyes. Miranda clung to him, her body limp and flushed, her breathing ragged. Jack could almost see her mind working, trying to formulate the question she would ask.

What happened? That would most definitely be it. And Lord, he wished he knew. One minute he'd been stopping Phin from getting them all hung by blurting out they were pirates, and the next he was soundly kissing his wife in front of a score of gaping people.

Jack's gaze drifted out across them. Every last person gathered under the live oaks shading the garden appeared stunned . . . and that included his crew. God's blood, he'd shocked a band of pirates!

Jack's laugh was forced, and his voice huskier than usual. "Well, you wanted a kiss, a kiss you got."

At first only silence greeted his words; but then gradually a few guests chuckled, then a few more, and eventually most of them drifted off toward the long food-laden table.

But not Henry. He stood his ground like a bulldog. Under Jack's leveled glare he did remove his hand from Jack's shoulder. But his tone was irate and fierce, though low enough not to be heard by the other guests. "Just what did you think you were doing?"

"Kissing my wife." Jack gnashed out the words. He moved to walk away; but Henry blocked his path, and though Jack could have pushed him aside, it would have caused a scene . . . another scene.

"Listen to me," Jack began. "Phin was about to announce to everyone that we are pirates. I didn't think any of us would like that, so I did something to distract him."

"Maul my daughter?"

"Nay." Jack's eyes narrowed. "Kiss my wife." Jack forced himself to remain calm. "If you recall, Henry, the fact that she is my wife is your doing. Now, I suggest you leave it be." With that Jack walked away.

"I'm sorry, daughter." Henry let out his breath, and his shoulders sloped forward. "I never meant for any of this to happen." His eyes met hers. "I never wanted you hurt."

"I know that, Papa. And I'm fine, really." Miranda smiled, though her knees still felt weak. "It was, after all, only a kiss." Her father nodded his agreement, but Miranda didn't think he meant it. And *she* certainly knew better. Captain Blackstone had touched her, and she'd lost all sense of reality.

"And, Papa, Phin *was* about to announce that they were pirates." Miranda whispered the last word.

Henry let out his breath. "I should have told you of my involvement from the beginning. I've caused all this."

"Nothing bad has happened." Miranda touched her father's sleeve. "Really."

Jack stood off to himself and watched Miranda and her father. He should apologize to her. But that would mean being around her, and right now he didn't want to do that. Strange things happened to him when she was close.

"Cap'n."

Jack turned to see Phin — a contrite Phin — standing at his elbow. His head was lowered, and his felt hat was smashed between two gnarled hands. "I'm askin' yer forgiveness for what I said. I nearly got us all hung."

"That you did, Phin."

" 'Twas the drink, Cap'n. Now, I knows that ain't no excuse, but. . . ." He shifted his feet, smashing grass beneath his salt-stained boots.

"Let's just forget it, Phin. Neither of us belong

here, and the sooner we leave the better."

"Like I said earlier, the *Sea Hawk*'s at the ready."

"Good. We'll sail with the morning tide, then." Jack tore his gaze away from Miranda to smile at Phin.

"I knows what ye said earlier, but ain't no reason ye has to be on board tonight."

"What?" A moment ago, he'd forgiven Phin for almost getting them all hung. Now the old man thought he needed to arrange Jack's wedding night. "No. Never mind. Don't repeat yourself."

"Well, I just was wantin' ye to know—"

"I think I can handle this, Phin."

"Sure, and ye can." Phin leered up at his captain. "Never doubted that for a moment."

Not long after Phin offered his bit of romantic advice, the guests started taking their leave. The pirates were the first to go. Jack was congratulating himself that his men had managed to mingle with the upper crust of Charles Town without actually getting arrested for piracy, when he glanced around to see No Thumb and Constable Hicks in a heated discussion.

"God's blood, why didn't he leave with the others?" Jack mumbled as he skirted a portly matron who was busily fanning away the first evening mosquitoes. "Leslie," Jack said, clamping his hand on No Thumb's shoulder. No Thumb jerked around, an angry glare in his pale eyes. He hated being called by his Christian name which was exactly why Jack did it now. If he was going to argue with anyone, let it be with his captain.

"What ye be wantin', Cap'n?" No Thumb's tone was surly.

"I just thought I'd say good-bye. Did you notice the others left for the ship? You should be leaving, too." Jack's tone was authoritative.

For a moment Jack thought the pirate was going to argue—he held Jack's eye a little longer than necessary. But in the end, he heaved a sigh. "Aye, Cap'n. But would ye tell this landlubber about them invisible animals swimmin' in the water. He don't believe me."

"That's what you're arguing about?" Jack felt the itch around his neck subside.

"Aye." No Thumb was indignant. "It ain't as if I ain't seen them with me own eyes."

Jack tried not to laugh. "He's right, you know," he said, turning toward the constable. "They're called—wait." Jack snagged Miranda by the arm as she walked past him. "My wife's the expert. My dear, Mr. Hicks would like to know all about your invisible animals."

Hustling No Thumb off, Jack looked back to see a bewildered constable listening to Miranda's explanation.

By the time the servants lit candles to keep the night shadows at bay, the wedding guests were gone. Only Miranda, Jack and Henry remained, and they'd wandered into the parlor.

It had been a long day, and Miranda was tired. She'd wanted to discover more about her new husband . . . about his reasons for going to St. Augustine, but that wasn't going to happen. He was preparing to take his leave, and he was telling her father that the *Sea Hawk* was sailing early the next morning.

Miranda sighed, inadvertently drawing both men's attention to her. "I . . . I suppose I should retire." This moment of parting seemed so awkward. Especially because she wasn't certain she wanted to part from the pirate. But it was obvious he couldn't wait to leave. He paced between her father's chair and the windows, like a wild animal longing to be free.

Miranda rose, her silk skirt rustling softly. She leaned over and kissed her father on the cheek. "Good night, Papa." Next she faced her husband. "Good-bye, Captain Blackstone. I wish you success in your voyage."

"My name is Jack. We are married . . . and well, I just think it would be better if you called me that."

"All right . . ." Miranda held out her hand, and the moment he took it, she felt the familiar heat spread through her body. It was inexplicable. Miranda tried not to think about it. She pulled away from him and started toward the hallway when she remembered something.

"Jack," she said, smiling over her shoulder. "Constable Hicks actually *was* interested in the animalcules."

Jack stepped toward her, suddenly awash in emotion. He felt a stab of embarrassment because he'd used her to occupy the constable while he'd sent No Thumb on his way . . . and she obviously knew it. But that had nothing to do with the warmth that engulfed him. She was smiling, and he suddenly realized he might never see her again.

He took another step, but before he could follow her into the hall, Henry was by his side, turning him and thanking him for doing the right thing.

"You won't be sorry you did this, Jack. You've made right a wrong you committed. And this marriage needn't interfere with your life."

When Jack looked back, Miranda was gone.

By the time he stepped out onto the street, Jack had again been wished luck on his trip, this time by Henry. He'd also been paid for the cargo his crew had delivered to Henry's warehouse by the dock.

Jack took a deep breath and let the sultry night settle around him. Fireflies twinkled in the dark as he headed away from the house. He could smell the salty scent of the sea on the air and it beckoned, but Jack hesitated.

His fingers balled into fists, and he cursed himself his weakness. But there was something else . . . someone else . . . who held more allure.

Turning on his heel, Jack retraced his steps to the Chadwick front door in long strides.

"What the—" Henry peeked out through the sliver of light he made when he cracked open the door—"Jack, what is it? What do you want?"

"My wife," was all he said, as he pushed through the door and headed for the stairs.

Chapter Fifteen

Jack took the stairs two at a time. He hesitated only once, at the landing, when he heard Henry's plaintive, "You've got no right —"

"I've every right." Jack turned and glared down at the older man, who clung to the newel at the bottom of the staircase. "We were wed before God and man." Jack dragged his fingers back through golden hair. "I've every right," he repeated softly before continuing up the steps.

Henry didn't follow, but Jack had already decided it would do his friend no good. He wanted Miranda, and he intended to have her. He pushed any thoughts that she might not want him from his mind.

Standing outside his wife's door, Jack considered knocking, had his hand raised to the panel, then changed his mind and reached for the latch. Pirates didn't knock, by God. And right now he felt like a pirate. A wild, free buccaneer.

Miranda jumped when he slammed open the

door. She was staring out the window, her gown unhooked and loose around her alabaster shoulders. Clutching it to her breast, she stared, wide-eyed, not knowing what to think.

The flickery flame from the single candle she'd lit glowed over his golden hair and bronzed skin. He was dressed in the clothes of a civilized man, but there was nothing . . . nothing civilized about him. He looked savage and untamed, his nostrils flaring and his jaw clenched.

With the heel of his boot, he kicked the door shut, then strode to the center of the room. Feet spread on the Aubusson carpet, hands balled on narrow hips, he silently dared her to question his right to be there.

Miranda said nothing. Her breathing became shallow, and her skin tingled . . . and she waited.

"I've come to partake of my marital rights," he said, his voice low and rough.

Still Miranda said nothing. She wet her suddenly dry lips, let her gaze roam the length of him, and swallowed.

Then she dropped her gown. Before it puddled to the floor, her arms reached out for him.

Jack didn't remember moving, but suddenly he was across the carpet, lifting Miranda against him. She was soft and warm, and the moment his lips touched hers Jack groaned. The kiss was frenzied and deep, and before it ended Jack and Miranda had tumbled onto her bed. The feather ticking and comforter billowed around them as they rolled across the mattress, first Miranda on top, then Jack.

When his lungs burned for oxygen, Jack raised his head and sucked in air. Her breathing was as ragged as his. And she seemed thoroughly baffled by what was happening. Her hair had come loose from its coils and lay in frantic disarray, vivid black against the pale pink counterpane. Her perfect, moist lips parted, and knowing Miranda, Jack suspected a question lurked behind the languid blue eyes.

But she didn't ask, she demanded. Gathering handfuls of golden hair, Miranda pulled his mouth back down to hers . . . and Jack was lost.

The veneer of control he'd exercised dissolved, leaving only a core of pulsing need. His mouth roamed over her skin, racing down the fragile column of her neck, devouring the petal-soft flesh above her shift. She smelled like flowers, like the sweetest, most exotic flowers. Like magnolia and jasmine, and honeysuckle, and he couldn't get enough.

When the fine cotton of the shift blocked him from her, Jack tore it aside as ruthlessly as the pirate he was. She arched into him when he took her breast in his greedy mouth. She moaned and grabbed his head when his tongue flicked over the nipple.

His teeth nipped and his lips soothed and the pounding in his head matched the throbbing in his groin.

Jack tore at the corset, but though he found the ribbons, they tangled. He couldn't seem to keep his hands off her body long enough to give the ties his full attention. "Can you . . .?" His voice was husky, muffled by the valley between her breasts.

"Let me." The words were no more than a breath of air. She arched up to reach behind her, but the motion pushed her breast farther into his hungry mouth. Miranda moaned and tore at his clothes instead of her own. She shoved the silk jacket off his powerful shoulders. His waistcoat wouldn't budge, but she managed to tear open his shirt and ran her fingers over the sleek skin beneath.

Frustrated, Jack gave up on the stays and skimmed his hand up her thighs. Her legs opened, and moist heat welcomed him, drove him over the edge. He yanked at his breeches, flipped up the hem of her shift and thrust deep inside her.

Their mingled sighs of relief were soon lost in a frenzy of movement. Jack drove deeper, harder, lost in a rush of passion that swept him mindlessly away.

And Miranda met, welcomed, every urgent plunge, shamelessly, wantonly. When she felt herself lifting, soaring beyond the confines of earth, her fingers tightened in the fabric of his shirt. She flew, sailing above the clouds where the heavens exploded into the vibrant colors of the rainbow. Yellows, reds and violets swam behind her closed lids, dizzying in their brilliance.

Jack sensed her release, and his own burst upon him with the force of a broadside.

At first he was too spent to do more than collapse, his legs tangled with hers, his face buried in her sweet-smelling hair. The pounding in his body slowed, and he tried to pull himself up from the abyss he'd just catapulted over.

Control. He needed to gain some. But all he really wanted to do was look into her eyes and kiss her sweet lips. Jack elbowed his weight off her, and studied her face, uncommonly pleased to see her expression of unabashed wonder.

His lips skimmed across hers, once, then because she tasted so very good, again. "No gravity?" he asked, his breath soft on her cheek.

Miranda's lashes lowered, and she took a deep breath. "Issac Newton would be amazed." She felt his chuckle down the length of his body to where they were still joined. Miranda's legs tightened around his.

His body noticed . . . responded to her motion.

"What is that feeling?"

Jack smiled and nipped at the end of her nose. He didn't even mind her questions at the moment. "Heaven," he answered, and it seemed to satisfy her. He brushed his cheek across her forehead, kissed her earlobe and the underside of her chin, and all the while he felt himself expanding and hardening inside her.

His mouth found hers, and before he knew

what was happening Jack was once more slipping out of control. He wanted to undress before they made love a second time. At least shed his boots. But there didn't seem to be any stopping once he began. His body already ached for release, and when he tasted the skin at the base of her throat, her pulse fluttered frantically against his mouth.

Following so quickly on the heels of their last climax, Jack couldn't believe how violently their bodies trembled with each touch. How they clutched at each other, surging upward and riding the tidal wave as it crested and then spiraled downward.

This time Jack levered off her and rolled to the side. She looked delicate and fragile as he gathered her into his arms. He sighed, fluttering the wispy curls along her temple, and tightened his embrace.

She winced.

"What? Did I hurt you?" God's blood, he'd been rough and impatient.

"No. It's just my stays. I'm really not used to them. Grandfather always said our anatomy wasn't meant to be squeezed and shoved about so."

"I think I would have liked your grandfather." Jack leaned up on his elbow. "Turn over and let me untie these."

The ribbons were much easier to undo this time, though Jack found he had to force himself to ignore the rounded curve of her shoulder and the scent of her skin. When he unwound the stays and smiled at her sigh of relief, it only seemed natural to skim the torn shift over her head.

He tried to keep his breathing calm when she lay revealed on the rumpled bedding. "I . . . should I strip off your stockings?"

Miranda nodded, but Jack didn't see. His gaze roamed over her body. He dipped his head, his hair whispering across her flesh as he kissed one knee, then the other.

"Dimples," he murmured while untying the garters and rolling the cotton down her slender calves. Her feet were ticklish, and Jack grinned when she jerked them from his grasp.

She was naked, and beautiful, and Lord help him, he was hard again. Not just hard . . . aching. With a grunt Jack swiveled around and tugged at his boots. He'd had no real plan when he'd come back to Miranda . . . aside from enjoying his husbandly rights. But vaguely, in the back of his mind, he'd thought to stay only a short time with her, then be off to his ship.

Now he wanted to stay the night. To do more than make love to her. To hold her while she slept and then wake up with her, and love her again. It was foolish, he knew, but he wanted it all the same. And what was keeping him from having it?

He'd be on the *Sea Hawk* fair and early, in plenty of time to catch the tide.

His breeches were next. He shucked them down over his hips, unhooking the silk from his swollen sex. His shirt was torn, and he tossed it and his waistcoat aside as he headed for the door.

"What are you doing?"

Jack turned the brass key in the lock. "Assuring our privacy." He couldn't imagine Henry was taking too kindly to his settling in Miranda's room, and he didn't want any unpleasant surprises. He heard a giggle and turned to his wife, grinning. He guessed she was thinking near the same thing as he.

She leaned up on her elbows, and as he watched, her smile faded. Her eyes darkened as they strayed over him, and Jack felt his chest swell with masculine pride.

"You're much more comely than David," she whispered, and his ego deflated.

"Who in bloody hell is David?" In three strides he was across the room, knee on bed, glaring down at her.

"Why, Michelangelo's David. The statue, of course. He's supposed to be the epitome of male beauty, but I think—What's the matter? Haven't you heard of Michelangelo? He was a sixteenth century Italian artist—"

"I know who he was." At least he thought he remembered something about him from his tutor in Scotland. But that was so long ago, and Jack hadn't been the best of students.

He settled onto the bed, pulling the netting

down around them. "Have you studied this David a lot?"

"No."

Jack thought he saw a hint of color seep into her cheeks. He leaned on his elbow and watched her. "You seem to know a fair amount about him."

"I've seen a drawing of the sculpture. He has good musculature." Miranda lowered her lashes. The way he looked at her made her warm all over.

"Musculature, huh?" Jack let his finger drift from her collarbone to the tip of her breast. "I have muscles."

"I know." Her nipple hardened, and Miranda sighed. "Yours are quite large."

"Ummm." His thumb dipped into her navel, then skimmed lower.

"Yes, but then everything about you is . . . large, I mean," Miranda managed as she arched into his cupped hand.

"Are you cold?" Jack pulled the linen sheet up around Miranda's shoulders and snuggled her closer. She lay with her head on his chest, her legs spanning one of his. He'd thought she was comfortable until he felt her tremble.

"Nay." Her voice was drowsy, for the hour was late. The flame had long since guttered into the hot tallow, and only the moonlight filtering through the windows lit the room.

304

" 'Tis only that this night seems unreal."

"And that made you shudder?"

Miranda lifted her head. "It's hard for me to understand . . . the way I feel."

Jack sighed, bringing her head back against his shoulder. "I don't understand it either." He felt less and less the cocky pirate as the night waned. "But I do know that this is unreal. To-morrow—" his fingers sifted through her hair— "with the rising of the sun you will have your reality back."

"I didn't say I wanted it back." Miranda shifted, settling more fully over him. Her legs tangled with his as she ran her hands over the smooth flesh, the hard muscles beneath.

Midnight black curls curtained him and Jack reached up to touch the pale oval of her face. His fingers wound around her neck, pulling her lips to his. He loved her slowly this time, gently, till the passion swept them away.

"No one need know you're a pirate," Miranda said when they were lying cuddled together. "I won't say anything, and I'm certain Papa won't. You could stay in Charles Town."

"Miranda, I—"

"I know de Segovia murdered your family, and I'm sorry; but it will do no good for you to kill him . . . or possibly die yourself." Miranda was close to tears, and she struggled to hold them back. Everything about her reaction to the pirate was unreasonable and irrational and totally fool-ish, but she couldn't seem to help herself. And she was very close to begging him to stay with her.

"I don't want this night to end either," Jack whispered against her temple. "But it must. The Spanish did more than kill my parents and take me prisoner twelve years ago." Jack let out his breath. "They also took my sister. I saw them carry her off."

Jack scooted up and bolstered pillows behind his head. Miranda settled against him. "I never saw Elspeth after that."

"But, Jack . . . ," Miranda hesitated, "she could be dead by now . . . could have died as soon as she was taken."

"No. I heard of her once while I was still in St. Augustine. De Segovia, or someone, must have taken her with him when he went back to Spain."

"What makes you think so?"

"I've been back to St. Augustine." Jack hesitated. "After I became captain of the *Sea Hawk,* we raided the Spanish stronghold. Elspeth was no longer there . . . nor was de Segovia."

"But now he's back in the New World."

"Aye." Jack's fist clenched, and he rubbed his knuckles along Miranda's jaw line. "Now he's back."

He wasn't rational where de Segovia and his sister were concerned, Miranda thought as she lay against her husband, listening to the strong beat of his heart, and she decided she could hardly blame him. However, few things were ever solved without rational thought.

Miranda was good at it, and she'd done nothing but think since Jack fell asleep. She sighed, wishing she could work through this problem. Actually, she had two of them. She didn't want anything to happen to Jack when he recklessly went after de Segovia. And she didn't want to be separated from him. Unreasonable as it was, Miranda wanted to be with her husband—tonight had made her realize how much.

But though he'd kissed her sweetly when she'd told him, he'd made no promises. He was a pirate, after all, he'd mumbled before shutting his eyes and drifting off to sleep.

He snored softly, and Miranda turned her head to glance at him. Stubble, darker than his hair, shadowed his lower face. He didn't seem so fierce in slumber, though there was still a wildness about him.

A wildness she loved.

Dawn pearled the room when Jack jerked awake. God's blood, the *Sea Hawk* was sailing with the morning tide, and here he lay, sprawled on a tousled bed. His first impulse was to leap to his feet, but then he noticed the warmth at his side.

Twisting around, Jack bent to wake Miranda with a kiss . . . and discovered she was already staring at him. "I have to go," he murmured, wishing he didn't.

"I know." Miranda smiled, then sat up. The sheet pooled at her waist, but she didn't notice that or the fact that her shoulder bumped Jack's jaw as he tried to kiss it. "You probably should leave."

"Leave?" What happened to his soft, sweet lover of last night? The woman who didn't want him to go? "Aye. Well, I imagine Phin will be wondering what's become of me."

"Yes." Miranda brushed her hair aside. "Your breeches are over there."

"My breeches." Jack stared to where she pointed at the rumpled pile of clothes. The way she was acting it was hard to imagine they'd torn them off each other last night in a fit of passion. He looked back at her, trying to ignore the way her breasts shone creamy white in the morning light.

She bounded from bed, and Jack groaned as he watched her bend over and toss his shirt to him. Perhaps he had time to tarry a little bit. The idea of jumping up and grabbing her rounded hips from behind and burying himself deep inside her had a great deal of appeal.

But she seemed in no mood. Before Jack could swing his legs over the bed, she'd shimmied into her shift. While he stood staring, his mouth hanging open, she stepped into a simple gown and reached back, struggling to fasten it.

Her eyes lifted, raking his naked form, and finally catching his gaze. Her mouth went dry, and her pulse quickened. But this was no time for sensual thoughts, though from the look of his swollen manhood, her husband didn't agree. Miranda resisted the urge to throw herself into his arms.

She had other things to do.

"Aren't you . . . ?" Miranda paused and tried to speak again. Her voice was so husky. "Aren't you going to dress?"

God's blood, she was a cold wench this morning. He'd never had anyone so anxious to be rid of him. Well, he could act as if last night didn't happen the same as she could. Jack yanked on his breeches, swearing to himself when they rubbed against his straining staff.

His shirt was wrinkled and missing several buttons, but he didn't care as he stuffed the tail in his breeches. Miranda was busy brushing her hair, completely ignoring him, and Jack wished he could do the same.

What had come over her? Did she remember in the light of day that he was a pirate and not fit for the likes of her? Or was she just too busy with other things to give him a second notice? As he watched, she pulled several books from a cabinet. Was she going to start reading before he even left?

He hurriedly stamped into his boots, ramming his arms into the silk jacket at the same time. "There's no need to see me out," Jack said, more to gain her attention than anything else. She was dipping a quill into an ink bottle.

"Oh." Miranda glanced up. "All right." Her

smile was distracted.

"All right? That's it?" Jack dug his fingers through his tangled hair. "After what we did last night, 'tis all you have to say?"

Miranda looked at him, her blue eyes wide. "What do you wish me to say?"

"What do I . . . ?" He was sputtering. The damn wench had him sputtering. What in the hell had he been thinking last night? Had he actually started wondering if he was falling in love with her? With Miranda Chadwick? No, not Chadwick, Blackstone. She was Miranda Blackstone. But for all the attention she paid him this morning, he might as well be married to a book . . . a question-asking book.

After strapping on his sword, Jack reached for the doorknob. She didn't glance up till he yanked the portal open.

"Jack."

"Aye?" Jack cursed the excitement that shot through him when she said his name.

"Good luck on your voyage." By the time she finished the words her shining head was bent over the parchment.

Jack's hands fisted. He turned on his heel and slammed out of the room, angrier than he'd ever been with a woman. He clomped down the stairs, cursing his wife, himself and marriage in general. When he reached the landing and caught sight of the hallway below, he added his father-in-law to the list.

Meanwhile, Miranda chewed on her thumbnail

and stared at the parchment. She'd written one word—*Papa*—on the paper. Tears filled her eyes as she tried to think of the best way to say what she must. Finally she settled on, *My place is with him.*

"Dammit, Henry, what are you doing skulking around the hallway this time of the morning?"

"I should think that is obvious. I'm waiting for you. I've waited for you all night."

"Well, you've wasted your time." Jack skirted around him. "I have to get to the ship."

"I don't care about your damn ship. We need to talk, *now.*"

Few people could have grabbed Jack the way Henry did and lived to tell of it. As it was, Jack's hand tightened around the hilt of his sword. He forced himself to remember the years of friendship that bound them. His voice bore the same steely strength as the blade hanging at his side. "I'm sailing with the morning tide."

"You owe me—"

Jack shrugged off Henry's hold. "I owe you nothing. All debts were paid yesterday."

"Then, what was last night about?"

Jack turned his face away, unable to meet the entreaty in the older man's eyes. "What do you think."

"Oh, Jack, how could you do this?" Henry wrung his hands and walked, slump-shouldered, into the parlor. "I trusted you."

"What the hell." Reluctantly Jack followed. "I married her, didn't I? It's not as if we—"

"But bedding her was never part of the agreement."

"Bedding her was the reason for the agreement," Jack pointed out. He was trying to stay calm, trying to see Henry's side of this. But truth be known, he was getting damn tired of seeing Henry's side. It was seeing Henry's side that got him into this mess in the first place.

"I'll not have you speaking of my daughter like that."

Jack looked heavenward, resisting the impulse to remind him that Henry's daughter was his wife. "Listen," he said, his hands lifted in appeasement. "Miranda is fine." Jack didn't mention that apparently he'd been more affected by their night of lovemaking than she.

"Fine? How can you say that? The poor child is no doubt devastated. This was *never* part of the agreement." Henry paced to the fireplace. "It was to be a marriage in name only."

"Well, now it's a marriage in every sense of the word." Jack's hands balled at his waist. "And for the last time Miranda is not devastated." He thought of her sitting at her desk, barely bothering to nod his way when he left. And after all they'd touched and loved last night. His jaw clenched, and he turned to face Henry.

It was just the move Miranda was waiting for. On tiptoe she scrambled past the parlor door.

Carefully she lifted the latch and hurried onto the piazza. The sun was tinting the sky a soft rose when she scurried onto the street.

Her arms strained with the heavy load she carried, but Miranda didn't stop to rest. She headed straight for the dock. She couldn't be sure how long her father would keep Jack occupied. Her new husband had sounded increasingly impatient with her father's rantings.

Thoughts of her papa brought tears to her eyes, but Miranda blinked them away. He'd understand. He'd have to. How many times had he said he wished he'd brought Miranda and her mother with him when he came to the New World? "A husband and wife aren't meant to be separated," he said, while lamenting his wife's death before he could send for her.

Miranda was simply assuring that she and her own husband didn't suffer the same fate. Not that she expected to die. She felt wonderful, and was rarely ill. But Jack was much too rash and impetuous. Lying in bed last night after he'd drifted off to sleep, Miranda had thought about all the things he might do, and she'd decided he needed her with him . . . to help him.

Unfortunately, she didn't think he'd see things the same way. He could be so stubborn.

She just had to be smarter.

But she knew Jack was going to be angry when he found out. And she dreaded his temper. Miranda tried to bite on her thumbnail, but the motion knocked her parcel of heavy books and boxes against her leg. "God's blood," she mumbled, and hobbled onto the wooden wharf.

Even this early in the morning, there was plenty of activity: sailors hoisting barrels on their shoulders and quartermasters yelling orders.

Miranda recognized the *Sea Hawk,* and rushed toward it.

"Yer ladyship." Phin came bounding off the gangplank. "If yer here to see the cap'n off, well, er . . . he ain't up yet." Not for anything would Phin tell the captain's new wife that her husband hadn't come back to the ship last night. Phin had thought maybe his captain had gotten good sense and stayed with his bride. Her presence here . . . alone . . . proved that false.

"I'm not looking for Captain Blackstone. Phin, could you possibly carry this?" Miranda handed her bundle to the surprised pirate and, lifting her skirts, stepped onto the gangplank. He followed her across onto the *Sea Hawk*'s deck.

"Yer ladyship. . . ." Phin scratched at his beard after Miranda took her belongings back. "I ain't sure what yer doin' here, but—"

"I want you to hide me. I'd thought the hold might be a good place, but you, of course, would know better than I."

Phin's eyes widened, and his mouth gaped open. "What?"

"You can choose the location," Miranda repeated. "But I do think we should hurry because the captain should be along any minute."

314

"I done told ye, he's 'sleep down in his cabin."

"Phin." Miranda touched his arm. "You needn't lie for me. Captain Blackstone spent the night at my house. He got, well, waylaid by my father this morning, so I rushed on ahead. You see, I plan to go with him, but I don't think—"

"Cap'n ain't gonna take ye to St. Augustine."

"I was afraid that would be his attitude, so that's why you—"

"He's got hisself a real good attitude. This ain't no place for the likes a ye."

"Phin, listen to me. I know what I'm doing." Miranda put her bundle on the deck. Several other crew members wandered by and stopped to say hello. Miranda waited till they were alone again. "Your captain needs my help to find his sister."

"But—"

"There are no buts about it. I can help him. And he'll thank you for this later. You know he won't let anything happen to me."

"I don't rightly know 'bout this."

Miranda thought Phin was weakening; but time was running out, and she couldn't afford to quibble. "Phin, you must take me below and hide me."

"Aw, yer ladyship. . . ."

"Do it now, Phin!"

The old pirate responded to the command in her voice as she hoped he would. Grumbling, he reached to pick up Miranda's bag. She beat him to it. Her microscope was inside, along with some other things she didn't want broken.

Miranda followed Phin down the ladder below deck, then lower. Phin grabbed a lantern from an overhead beam and held it out in front of them. It did little to pierce the darkness. Miranda took a deep breath. The hold was dark and musty, smelling of tar and bilge water, and for the first time, she had doubts about her plan. But she swallowed and refused to listen to Phin's arguments.

" 'Tis just for a short time. Till we're out to sea. Then I'll let the captain know I'm aboard." Miranda settled herself on a barrel. "In the meantime, if you'd bring me an occasional meal and tell the others who saw me come aboard to keep their counsel, I'd appreciate it."

"Ain't the others ye got ta worry 'bout. The cap'n, now that's a different matter all together."

"I can handle Captain Blackstone," Miranda said. But later as she sat in the puddle of light from the lantern, alone with her thoughts, she wondered if that were true.

Chapter Sixteen

"Where are you off to?" Jack took a swig of grog. "With a share of meat?"

Phin paused, guiltily glanced down at his pocket, where he was sure he'd discreetly hidden the food, then met his captain's eyes.

After back-handing his mouth, Jack leaned back against a bulkhead. In the crew's mess, the rumble of conversation ceased, and Jack had the feeling that all the pirates who moments ago were devouring their supper, were now holding their collective breath. For three days, since they'd left the harbor at Charles Town, Jack had noticed Phin secreting food in his clothes, till now the pockets were dark with grease.

"Well now, Cap'n, I ain't goin' nowhere special. Just thought I'd get me a breath a fresh air while I finish me vittles."

"I see." Phin wasn't a very convincing liar. "You've been consuming a great deal of food lately."

"I been hungry." Phin's grizzled chin shoved forward. "If you've got some complaint 'bout me holdin' me own, then—"

"Nay." Jack waved that aside. "Your work more than makes up for the extra food you eat."

Phin flexed his shoulders. "That be more like it, Cap'n."

Jack raised the pewter mug in a slight salute. "I was just wondering, that's all."

"Ain't nothin' to wonder 'bout, Cap'n."

"I can see that now." Jack smiled.

"I gotta go."

"Fine." Jack leaned his elbows on the rough-hewn boards that formed a table. As if on cue, the other men in the room continued their conversations.

Jack watched Phin scurry out, then stood.

"We was wonderin', Cap'n." Scar grabbed his sleeve, letting go of Jack's wrist only when he raised his brows.

"What were you wondering, Scar?" If this wasn't an attempt to keep him from following Phin, Jack would dive off the main mast.

" 'Bout our raid on St. Augustine? How much coin ye think we'll be gettin'?"

Jack gave his chief gunner a protracted stare before answering. "I haven't a clue. I thought we already discussed that."

"Right ye are, Cap'n. I musta forgot." Scar turned back to stuffing his mouth with salt pork, and Jack imagined Scar thought it was all right for him to leave now.

Scraping his bench over the hard oak deck,

Jack stood. Not a man seemed willing to meet his eye as he bent over to keep his head from knocking against the beams. Something was amiss. He'd suspected it before, but now he knew it.

He just didn't know what it was.

A mutiny was always a possibility on board ship. But Jack couldn't believe his crew would do such a thing. Besides, if they were planning something, they'd just go ahead and do it. And mutineers had no call to sneak food.

No doubt about it, something strange was happening, and he intended to discover what it was.

One thing about this mystery, Jack thought as he stepped out on deck, it kept his mind occupied so that he didn't think about his wife . . . at least not all the time.

"I'm tellin' ye, he knows somethin'." Phin sat on a water cask and watched Miranda pick at her pork and sea biscuit. They were in the forward hold, between the main and forward hatches. Raised planks covered the ballast below, keeping the area relatively dry of bilge water.

"Tell me again what he said." Miranda gnawed on a piece of unappetizing hardtack, finally managing to break off a piece without splitting a tooth.

"Ask me where I be off to with the meat," Phin began. "I'm tellin' ye he's on to us."

Miranda swallowed, then sighed. "Well, I

imagine I should let him know I'm aboard." She chewed on her thumbnail. "Do you think he'll turn back at this point?"

"Ain't sure. The cap'n is chaffin' to get to de Segovia. But he ain't gonna like takin' ye along. I should never a let ye aboard." Phin scratched at his chin.

"Don't blame yourself, Phin. I'm the one who insisted."

"But yer nothin' but a woman." Phin's voice was firm. "I shoulda know'd better. Just ta see ye sleepin' down here, with nothin' but a moth-eaten blanket to stave off the damp. . . ." He stopped and shook his head.

"It hasn't been that bad." Miranda tried to sound convincing. Actually, being confined down here in the near dark was worse than she ever could have imagined.

"It be my fault," Phin continued as if he hadn't even heard her denial. "I just don't know how I'm gonna make it right with the cap'n."

"You should have thought of that earlier!" The voice sounded at the same instant the musty canvas Phin had strung for her privacy was yanked aside. Miranda and Phin jumped up in surprise.

Jack Blackstone stood, his hand resting loosely on the hilt of his cutlass. It froze, and his mouth dropped open when he saw Miranda. "God's blood!"

"N-now, Cap'n, I can explain everythin'," Phin stammered before he realized the younger man wasn't paying him the least attention.

"What are you doing here? . . . Miranda?"

Her husband seemed unable to believe his own eyes. She actually saw him blink. But when he opened his eyes again, he must have accepted that it was indeed her, for he grabbed her arm and started hauling her along behind him toward the hatch.

"Bring the lantern," he yelled over his shoulder to Phin. "We don't want the powder catching afire along with everything else that's going wrong."

Miranda could only assume he referred to her presence. She scrambled to keep up with him until she remembered her belongings; then she dug in her heels and grabbed hold of a bulwark. It hardly stopped the captain's forward motion, but he must have noticed something, for he glanced around at her.

"My things," Miranda began. "I don't want to leave my books and microscope."

"We'll retrieve them later," he said in a tone that even Miranda didn't question.

He pushed her in front of him, bracketing her hips with his hands, as they climbed to the berth deck. From there it was only a short walk to the captain's cabin.

Jack kicked the door open, yanked her inside and slammed it shut. His temper was near exploding. Of all manner of things he suspected his crew was hiding, he never, *never* thought it might be his wife.

They were sailing to fight the Spanish, on their own ground, by God. You didn't take

321

women into situations like that. Especially gentle-born women like Miranda. You just didn't. My God, she could be killed!

His fists knotted, and in an attempt to calm himself Jack crossed his arms "Now," he said through clenched teeth. "Explain yourself."

He really was formidable. He stood easily a head taller than she and twice as broad. The gold loop peeked through his tousled golden hair, and his expression was stern. Oh, he was every bit the pirate, and Miranda wondered why she had ever considered this silly plan. He didn't look like someone who would need her help. With his strong muscles bulging, he seemed quite capable of taking care of himself.

Miranda swallowed.

"Well!"

"I decided to come with you."

"What?" Jack's bellow echoed through the cabin.

Miranda winced . . . ever so slightly.

"You decided to come with me?" Jack couldn't believe this was happening. "What the hell for?"

Shrugging, Miranda tried to appear more at ease than she felt. She had expected his anger. She just hadn't known it would bother her so much. It really hadn't before. "Well, I am your wife," she began, only to pause when Jack's eyes flew open.

Jack paced to the window, then turned abruptly. His eyes roamed over her, taking in the soiled gown and her tangled hair. She had a smudge of dirt across her cheek that he itched to rub off with his thumb. But he fought back the urge as savagely as he molded his expression. "This marriage your father arranged was to be in name only. There is no need for you to come traipsing after me."

"It didn't appear to be in name only on our wedding night," she said guilelessly.

"That was different. It was . . ." He couldn't find the words to describe to her exactly *how* it was different, so he turned back to stare out at the indigo water.

"I see," she responded as if she really understood, and that annoyed the hell out of Jack.

"Don't act as if *you* are enamored of this marriage. If you recall, your voice was raised in protest as adamantly as mine. For God's sake, you barely took the time to bid me farewell the morning I left."

Miranda's eyes widened. For a moment she thought she noticed a touch of vulnerability. In his expression. In his words. But he quickly masked any trace of it with a stormy glare that made Miranda wonder if she had imagined it. "Actually," she explained after a deep breath. "I had things to make ready. And I knew we wouldn't be separated for long."

"Oh, you knew, did you?" The wench thought she could play games with him. "Well, this time I think it would be prudent to say your good-byes." Jack strode to the door.

"What are you going to do?"

His hand grabbed the latch. "What I should

have done when I first found you. Turn this ship about."

"What of de Segovia?"

"God's blood, I knew I should never have told you anything," Jack mumbled, wondering why it had seemed so natural to do it. "I shall find de Segovia. Have no fear of that." He lifted the latch.

"I can help you," Miranda said softly.

"What?" Jack turned on his wife. "God's blood, woman, what are you talking about? I'm Gentleman Jack Blackstone, captain of the pirate ship *Sea Hawk*. My crew and I are feared from one end of the Spanish Main to the other. We . . . *I* . . . need no assistance from a slip of a girl."

Miranda stood by calmly, waiting for her husband's tirade to end. When it did, she asked, "Do you know where de Segovia is?"

"You know I do. In St. Augustine."

"But where in St. Augustine?"

Jack stuck out his jaw. "I shall find him. If I have to tear the settlement apart, palm tree by palm tree, I shall find him."

"And what will happen to your sister while you are dismembering plants?"

Jack only glared in response. Damn, he hated her never-ending questions. He really hadn't planned on simply attacking the town, but he didn't care for his wife's reasonable tone. His fists clenched. "I shall find a way to get her away from them."

"But I can help you do that." Miranda hurried

324

on before the pirate could argue. "I speak Spanish like a . . . well, like a Spaniard. You even took me for one the first time you saw me. If I go ashore at St. Augustine—"

"God's blood!" Jack advanced on her so quickly Miranda took an involuntary step backward. "Do you think for one moment I'd allow you into that Spanish lair?" The woman was insane. He had suspected it before. Before this wild attraction between them got in the way of his thinking. But now he was certain.

"The Spanish are no different from you and me. One of my grandfather's and my dearest friends is Spanish and—"

"They're a bloodthirsty lot," Jack insisted. He couldn't believe what she was saying, defending the people who had killed his parents.

"Some of them are, 'tis true. But others, like Don Luis, are warm and kind. Just as some English, some Scots, are evil."

Jack opened his mouth to tell her exactly what he thought of her logic, but the pounding stopped him. "What?" he yelled while jerking open the door.

Phin, Scar, King, and No Thumb stood crowded in the passageway. They didn't come forward, nor did they back away when their captain glared at them.

"What the hell do you want?" Jack was in no mood for this interruption.

"Just wonderin' how her ladyship's doin'. Couldn't help but hear some yellin' down here, Cap'n."

"Her *ladyship* is doing just fine. Much better, I might add, than when someone hid her in the hold."

Phin flushed beneath his sun-darkened skin. "Now, that weren't my idea, Cap'n."

Jack glanced toward Miranda. "I'm quite sure of that. However, you *did* go along with her scheme." Whenever Jack thought of his delicate wife sleeping down in that dark, rat-infested hold, he grew angrier. He crossed his arms. "Unless I miss my guess, you were all in on this." And he planned to punish each and every one of them.

"Now, Cap'n, I ain't sure havin' her along ain't a right good idea." This from Scar, who inched himself forward. "She most likely can ferret out de Segovia for ye."

Jack's eyes found Miranda's. "How many people have you discussed this preposterous scheme with?"

"Just Phin . . . and you."

"And Phin took it upon himself to inform the rest of the crew, I suppose," Jack said, impaling his quartermaster with his steeliest gaze.

"Aw, Cap'n. We're just tryin' to think things through logically."

Jack gaped at Phin as he spoke. Good Lord, where had he heard those words before?

"Ye want yer revenge on de Segovia, and none of us can blame ye." There was a general mumbling of agreement among the men. "But ye ain't been havin' much luck so far."

"I didn't know where the man was."

"True 'nough, but ye still ain't sure. Leastways ye ain't sure where in St. Augustine he is. And well, we just can't go on lookin' for him forever."

Jack couldn't believe what he was hearing. "If you recall, we've all made a pretty hefty profit while looking for him."

"Aye, we have." Phin nodded, and the other men joined in. "But pickin's are gettin' slim. Ye knows that as well as me. Just ain't that many pigeon-fat Spanish galleons floatin' round no more. We need to be off to new seas."

"I suppose you're speaking of the Indian Ocean."

"Right ye are, Cap'n." Scar spoke up but after an admonishing look from Phin shut his mouth.

"Now, Cap'n, rumor is a pirate can get hisself richer than Midas pluckin' gold off them Mogul ships."

Jack said nothing. He simply tried to settle the seething inside him.

"Now, we ain't suggestin' we give up on de Segovia. We all know how important killin' him is ta ye. But we been thinkin' the sooner we get it done, the better."

Phin shifted uncomfortably under his captain's silent, scathing stare, but he bolstered his courage, and continued. "And we been thinkin', too, that the best way to do that is to let her ladyship help."

It was a mutiny, a goddamn mutiny. And his wife was the center of it!

Jack turned to her, but she wouldn't meet his

eyes. Phin had the same problem, but he was bold enough not to study the tips of his shoes as Miranda was doing.

Jack's voice was low . . . calm. Anyone who didn't know him would think he found the discussion appealing. But the pirates knew differently, and so did Miranda. "It appears you've all agreed upon this . . . without my thoughts or wishes being considered."

"Now, Cap'n, that ain't true a'tall. We knows how ye feel 'bout de Segovia and yer sister. That's why we're wantin' to help ye."

Jack ignored Phin's explanation. "And you agreed upon this without remembering who's the captain of this ship."

"We ain't forgot," Scar chimed in.

"Good. Then, let's get the *Sea Hawk* turned about and take my *wife* back to Charles Town."

No one moved.

The air in the cramped space seemed heavy, near ready to crackle like the moment before lightning struck. Jack held his ground, but he felt some of it slipping away beneath his booted feet.

It was King who brought up the articles. He stepped forward, and the other crew members let him through, in a move that Jack thought was probably planned. The big black man lifted his hand slowly. He was near the same height as Jack, and though not as broad in the shoulders and chest, still a formidable-looking man, with his fierce expression and his tattoos.

But for all that and the fact that he was a pirate, King had a gentle heart, and a loyal heart, and Jack felt a deep sense of betrayal when he spoke. "According to the articles, we all have an equal vote in the affairs of the moment."

"And you've already had this vote?"

"No, Cap'n, we ain't," Phin said. It was obvious he found this entire encounter upsetting. "But there be little doubt how it would go, if'n we did."

Jack had little doubt either. He turned and walked into the cabin. The pirates followed.

"Don't make us vote, Captain." King put his hand on Jack's arm. "The men can't see beyond the promise of gold in the East."

Jack blew air out of his mouth. "I don't appear to have a choice." He was intimately familiar with the articles that ran the *Sea Hawk*. He had helped draw them up. But they'd never been used against *him* . . . until now.

In the past he'd given his crew ample opportunity to disagree with him, but they hadn't. Their exploits in the Caribbean, exploits that stemmed primarily from Jack's desire to find de Segovia, had made them wealthy.

But now, now when the issue centered around Miranda, they chose to challenge him. And he had no idea what to do about it.

"It ain't that we're shying away from goin' to St. Augustine, Cap'n. We ain't. We're behind ye."

"Aye, Cap'n, ye can count on me cutlass anytime."

But not you, Jack thought, though he said nothing.

"We just be wantin' to get it good and done so's we can move on."

"Aye, that's the right a it," agreed No Thumb. "We just want to get to them Mogul ships 'afore there ain't no more gold."

Jack wanted to tell them to go on, then. To take the *Sea Hawk* and sail off to the Indian Ocean. But he didn't. He'd been a pirate long enough to know they didn't take kindly to a crew member, even if it was the captain, going against the majority.

And Lord help him, he wanted them to go to St. Augustine with him. He didn't think he stood a chance of finding his sister and avenging his parents' deaths without the ship and her crew.

But he didn't care what they said; he wasn't going to endanger Miranda. Even though she *was* the cause of all this.

"Well, I guess we'll be leavin' ye now, Cap'n," Phin said. He backed toward the door, and the other pirates followed. When the latch caught behind them, Miranda turned toward her husband.

"What were they talking about? Voting . . . I don't understand."

He didn't want to talk to her right now. And he sure as hell didn't want to answer one of her countless questions. But Jack forced himself to face her. "Pirates are a free, independent lot . . . not much enamored of rules or rule makers, like the gentry. They gave up most of that when they became pirates." As he spoke, Jack busied himself gathering some shirts and breeches. "They don't like the idea of following orders, from anyone."

"But you're the captain."

"Only because they choose for me to be. They can vote me out at any time."

"That's what they were threatening to do, isn't it?"

Jack glanced up from stuffing his shaving dish into the ditty bag. "How clever you are."

The sarcasm in his voice made Miranda raise her chin. "It wasn't my fault. I never suggested they overthrow you . . . or go to the Indian Ocean, either."

"Nay!" Jack tossed the canvas sack on the bunk. "But you did stow away on my ship and talk my crew into hiding that from me."

"I did it because I wanted to help."

"Well, I don't *need,* nor do I *want* your help." Jack grabbed up the pile of belongings he'd tossed together. "I wish to God I'd never attacked that British ship," he mumbled, before heading for the door.

"Where are you going?" Miranda scurried to block his exit. This wasn't turning out at all as she had planned. She knew he was angry, yet thought if they could only discuss this rationally. . . .

"To the crew's quarters." Jack easily set her out of his way. "This cabin is at your disposal."

"But, it's yours." Miranda felt tears threatening—silly, irrational tears.

"Perhaps, however I can't in good conscience allow you to continue sleeping in the hold. And though I realize you're the darling of the crew, I don't think it appropriate for you to stay with them."

"But I thought . . . I thought we'd stay in your cabin . . . together." Heat crept up Miranda, coloring her cheeks.

He stared down at her and swallowed, wishing the notion weren't appealing. "I don't think that's a good idea," was all he said before he turned, and left the cabin.

"Ye ain't lookin' too chipper this mornin'. I'd a thought bein' outta that dank hole a blessin'."

"Oh, it is, Phin." Miranda was standing on deck, hands clutching the rail, letting the wind gust through her unbound hair. When she woke this morning, she'd felt compelled to come up into the sunshine, and since then hadn't seemed to get enough of the fresh air and light.

But though her body was revived, her spirit was none too "chipper" as Phin put it. She felt very out of sorts as if her humors were all churned up. And there was but one reason for that. Miranda's gaze skittered toward the quarterdeck, then jerked back again when she remembered Phin was watching her.

"Ye and the cap'n have a spat?" he asked, scratching at his beard.

A spat hardly seemed to cover it, but Miranda nodded. "He's very angry with me."

"An' rightly so, I'll wager."

"What?" Miranda blinked up at him. "I

thought you were on my side. You said I should go along to help him find de Segovia. You said—"

"Don't matter none what I said." Phin leaned his corded arms over the rail. He still favored his left side, but it was healing up well, thanks to Miranda.

"But . . ."

"Now, don't go gettin' yerself in a fluster. I *do* think the cap'n could use yer help. And God's teeth, he sure needs to get this de Segovia kilt. But that don't mean he ain't got good reason to be up there on the quarterdeck sulkin'."

Miranda's eyes strayed again. "Is that what he's doing?"

Phin took a deep breath of salty air. "Says he's not, but I know'd the cap'n since he was no more'n a lad. He's feelin' like we all lied to 'im, then deserted 'im to boot."

"But it's only because we care about him," Miranda blurted out before she realized what she was saying.

"Aye, an' that's the truth. Ain't never been a man I been fonder a than the cap'n. Rest a the crew feels the same. But that don't mean he ain't hurtin'. He's a proud man, and he don't like anyone hidin' stuff from him."

How many times could she say that she was only trying to help? The words seemed hollow when she really thought of them, true though they were.

Besides, Miranda knew there was more to her sneaking aboard the *Sea Hawk* than simply helping her husband.

After Phin walked away she tried to decide if she should tell her husband all of the truth. It would make her feel exposed, and Miranda wasn't sure she liked that idea. She was used to dealing with reason and logic, and her feelings for the captain seemed to defy both.

She'd known love before. With her grandfather it had been so much a part of her life that she'd taken it for granted. There had been uncertainty about her father, but that had evaporated after two minutes in his presence.

But this emotion she felt for the pirate captain, she didn't even know for certain that it was love. But she *did* have an overwhelming desire to be with him.

Taking a deep breath, Miranda made her way past the hatch, pausing only a second before climbing the ladder to the quarterdeck. Jack was standing at the wheel, his expression solemn. He didn't notice her at first, and Miranda took a moment to study him, appreciating anew how pleasing he was to the eye, before she stepped forward.

When he looked over at her, his eyes hardened. "Is there something you need?"

"Yes." Miranda floundered, then rushed ahead. "A chance to explain why I—"

"I think you did that last evening." Jack settled his feet more firmly against the roll of the ship.

"But I didn't explain all of it."

"You aren't going to try to unravel the mysteries of gravity for me, are you?"

"No." Miranda couldn't help a small smile, and she thought the corners of her husband's mouth twitched ever so slightly as well. "I thought I might give you my views on marriage."

That got Jack's attention. His head whipped around. "Whose marriage?"

"Our marriage . . . and my parents'." Miranda looked up at him. "I don't know what my father told you about my mother or me, probably noth—"

"He spoke of you often. Frankly, he used to bore me with stories of his daughter in England."

Miranda's smile was broader this time. "Did he ever speak of why we didn't come to the New World with him?"

Jack shrugged. "He didn't feel it was safe. He went to Barbados first, then later to the Carolinas."

"Yes, and he was going to come back for us when he thought the time was right." Crossing her arms, Miranda paced to the rail. "But the time never was right." She glanced over her shoulder. "I wasn't very old, but I can still remember my mother's despair at being without him. She was so sick at heart."

Miranda turned back to Jack. "She died, you know. And I think one reason she couldn't fight the fever was their separation. No, it's true," Miranda continued when she saw his dubious expression. "My father tried to keep her safe, and instead . . . she died."

Jack held her gaze a long moment. " 'Tis not the same thing, you know. This—" he waved his hand to encompass the ship—"or our marriage."

"Perhaps," Miranda said with a sigh.

"God's blood, neither of us wanted this marriage," Jack said softly. "And being on a pirate ship is a hell of a lot more dangerous than emigrating to the New World."

"I agree. And I won't repeat my contention that I can help you with de Segovia."

" 'Tis a good thing."

"I just thought you should know why I stowed away on the *Sea Hawk*. And . . . that I'm sorry for the trouble I've caused you." Before he could say anything, Miranda scurried down the ladder. She climbed down the hatch and hurried to the captain's cabin.

She'd told him too much. She felt exposed. Whenever she shut her eyes, Miranda could see his face as he said that neither of them had wanted their marriage.

It was true. She knew it was true. But still it hurt to hear it.

When Nat brought her meal, a mix of meat and potatoes called lopscouse, she ate little. Someone, Phin she assumed, had brought her books, microscope and the few clothes she'd brought, to the cabin. Miranda tried to read, but couldn't keep her mind from wandering.

Why had she come? Why hadn't she thought it through and realized that the captain didn't want her . . . didn't even need her?

By the time the sea and sky melded into dark

indigo, Miranda was so tired of thinking that she peeled off her gown and tumbled onto the cot. But sleep wouldn't come. She lay awake listening to the creaking of the timbers, the soft lapping of the sea. The sounds were so hypnotic that at first she didn't hear the footfalls in the passageway.

It wasn't till they paused outside her door that she took notice.

Miranda elbowed herself up as the door swung open. Moonlight spilled in the transom windows, throwing silver highlights over Jack's golden hair. His shirt shone white across his broad chest as he stood motionless, dwarfing the entryway. Miranda could not see his expression for the shadows, but she knew he watched her. Her breath ceased, and blood rushed to her head, pounding in her ears when he carefully closed the door behind him.

"I couldn't stay away," was all he said, before crossing the room.

Chapter Seventeen

At the side of the box bunk he hesitated, as if unsure of his reception. Miranda marveled that he thought she didn't want him. Oh, the rational side of her preached prudence. But Miranda was quickly learning that where the pirate was concerned reason rarely prevailed. Her emotions involving him were too strong to ignore. Too passionate to explain away using *any* kind of logic.

Miranda lifted her hand toward him. He grabbed it, enfolding her warm fingers in his as he sat on the edge of the mattress.

"I shouldn't be here," he murmured as he touched her palm to his lips.

Then a veil of memory seemed to cross his features, hardening the handsome mouth. He scowled down at her, his breath feathering her fingers. "Hell, you shouldn't be here."

"But, how could I not come when I knew you needed—" Miranda's words were cut off when his mouth settled over hers. The kiss was slow, and thorough, a prelude of things to come, and Miranda felt herself sinking.

When he finally pulled away, she felt his smile against her lips. "No questions tonight. Please, no questions."

Giving her no time to reply, even if she could indeed come up with one, Jack pushed her down on the ticking, following with his own body. He moaned as she twined her fingers through his hair, guiding his mouth back to hers.

Kissing her was all he remembered it to be. He had paced the deck tonight, chastising himself for even considering going below to his wife. And he'd almost convinced himself that he'd exaggerated in his mind the way it felt to touch her. Even that hadn't kept him away. But now Jack realized his memory didn't come close to the sensations that flooded him when they kissed.

It was the damnedest thing, and one day he was going to ponder it.

But not now.

Now he couldn't keep his hands off her. They followed the ridges of ribs, feeling her warmth through the cotton chemise she wore. Her body seemed to flow toward his, ignite his, till desire overwhelmed him.

Her response was as open and trusting as it had been before. She drew him in, softened for him. Jack broke off the kiss and buried his face in the curve between her neck and shoulder. Her hair smelled so good . . . she smelled so good.

Her scent had haunted him as surely as the feel of her smooth skin, the taste of her mouth.

"Stand up a moment." Jack stood and pulled her with him. He gathered the chemise in his hands, slipping it over her head, and just stared.

"So pretty," he murmured, tracing his fingertip down the gentle curve of her moonlight-limned breasts. Bending forward, he touched a rucked tip with his tongue, smiling at the way she moaned and arched into him.

"Oh, Jack." Miranda's hand skimmed across his cheek, then tangled in the neck opening of his shirt.

Answering her silent demand, Jack yanked the white cotton off. He twisted, shifting reluctantly away from her to sit on the edge of the bed. After tugging at a boot, it thudded to the floor.

Miranda stepped closer, her leg brushing his bent knee. Jack sucked in his breath.

When the second boot hit the deck, Miranda leaned forward, brushing her lips against the silky hair on his bowed head. Jack's hands whipped out, clutching her hips and jerking her toward him.

His open mouth ground against the smooth flesh of her stomach, slid over to nip at her hip bone, then dragged down toward the delta of tight, raven curls.

Miranda could barely breathe. His long fingers slid round to cup her buttocks, and his voice was a mere rasp vibrating through her body as he begged her to open for him.

Her legs spread, and his whisker-rough chin grazed down her inner thigh, moments before Jack lost himself in her moist heat. He pressed his mouth to her in a deep kiss that made Miranda cry out. She clutched Jack's shoulders to keep from falling, then as the hot touch of his tongue sent her soaring, tangled her hands in his hair, pressing him ever closer.

Jack's breathing was shallow and ragged as she slumped into his arms. He lowered her to the bed, following her down when she clung to him, kissing her, touching her. But the pressure of his thick, pulsing shaft against the binding breeches was painful. Jack fumbled with his waistband, freeing himself and plunging into her with one motion.

"Miranda?" he said, because she went very still, and he feared he'd been too rough in his hurry to possess her.

Her lashes fluttered open and she smiled at him, and Jack could do naught but smile back. But the heat of her, the tight way she surrounded him, made the interlude short. He moved, cautiously at first, and then as her legs wrapped around his, more firmly.

She lifted her hips, pressing him to fill her completely, and Jack felt the wild stirrings of release strum through his body. He plunged, taking her mouth in a carnal kiss at the same moment, and she clutched at him, arching her back and crying out.

Her body shuddered and convulsed, milking

341

him with the tiny tremors that squeezed and excited every inch of him. It seemed to last forever, this pleasure too perfect for words. He rode the wave, crested, then finally, slid softly to shore . . . exhausted.

Jack flopped down on the bunk and pulled her warm body into his arms. She was sleek with sweat, as was he, and he barely had the energy to reach for the sheet and pull it up around them. She snuggled closer to him when he did.

Jack shut his eyes, content, only to jerk them open again. "This doesn't change the way I feel, Miranda. You should never have come with us."

"Mmmm."

Tucking his chin down, Jack tried to look at his wife, but all he could see was a tangled cloud of midnight black hair and the tip of her nose. "Do you understand me, Miranda? I may not be able to take you back to Charles Town right away, but I—" Her hand flopped across his stomach, and Jack sucked in his breath.

"Are you awake?"

Again she made a noise, part sigh, part snuffled "yes."

"Good, because I want you to understand that you are not going to set one foot ashore at St. Augustine." There, he'd said it and he was glad. That was until he felt her wriggle away from him. The air chilled his chest as she sat up, pulling the sheet with her.

"Why not?"

Jack tugged gently on her arm, but she refused to budge. "Miranda."

"Why aren't you going to allow me ashore at St. Augustine?"

Jack shut his eyes. Why wasn't he content to simply go to sleep after making love to her? Why did he have to open the door for her questions. It would have been much better if he'd simply waited until they reached the Spanish stronghold to tell her.

He reached up again, this time letting his hand skim over her breasts. "Let's not speak of it tonight."

"But, Jack, I really can be of assistance, if you'd just let—" She quieted, sucking in her breath when his fingers circled her pouting nipple. "Jack?"

"Mmmm?"

After that Miranda was much too busy to worry about St. Augustine.

Jack woke at eight bells of the midnight watch and rolled from the bunk. Not even the barest hint of dawn lit the cabin, and the moon had waned; but he managed to gather his clothes by groping about on the deck. Striking flint to steel and lighting the lantern would have simplified the task, yet Jack hesitated to wake Miranda, who lay cuddled on her side.

Instead, he muffled the sound of his movements as best he could. He made his way topside by instinct and touch, taking a deep breath of heavy sea air as he emerged through the hatch. His chest expanded as the westerly breeze whipped through his hair, and his mouth relaxed into a smile.

He felt good. Despite all that had happened so far on this voyage, he felt good. "No secret as to why," he mumbled to himself after making his way to the rail. He'd always been a lusty sort— he was a pirate, wasn't he? And he'd never pretended not to enjoy the pleasures of the flesh. Since his wife had the most delectable flesh he'd ever encountered, it made sense that he find himself taken with her.

Jack breathed a sigh of relief. Now that he could explain away this attraction he felt for her, he might as well take advantage of it. Granted she had some annoying habits. Her bookishness for one. Her inability to follow a simple order for another. Jack's ire began to rise, and he purposely tapped it down.

She was on the ship. There was nothing he could do about it. So he might as well accept it. Besides, as he'd lain awake beside her on the cramped bunk, he'd decided he could use her help.

Not ashore at St. Augustine, of course. But he'd heard her speak Spanish, and she had a fair knowledge of it. Perhaps she could teach him enough so that he could get by in the town. If only he'd tried to learn the language earlier, when he was a prisoner of de Segovia, he wouldn't need lessons. But he'd so despised anything Spanish that he'd closed his mind to the foreign tongue. Now he could see the advantage of communicating with the enemy.

"Ain't no hard feelin's, is there, Cap'n?"

Jack shifted to see Phin standing beside him. A pale pewter glow separated the sky from the sea, and threw a wash of light over the older man's worried face.

"I know we didn't handle it good, but we—none of us wants any man leadin' us but ye."

Jack stared at him a moment before shrugging. "I appreciate that, Phin." He turned back to watch the ribbons of dawn streak across the horizon. "And I'm not angry." He had been at first, but thinking about his men was something else he'd done last night. Considering he was dealing with a crew of independent freebooters, he decided he was lucky they only wanted him to accept help fighting de Segovia.

"Ye know we wants that bloody Spaniard as much as ye do."

Jack seriously doubted that, but grinned and clasped Phin across the back.

"I know'd ye wouldn't hold a grudge, Cap'n." Phin smiled his snaggle-toothed smile. "You'll see. We'll be doin' great once we head out for the Indian Ocean. Did ye hear tell how much them pirates from the *Amity* took on her last voyage?"

From there Phin launched into one of his favorite subjects: the wealth to be made, with very little effort, from the Moguls. Jack listened politely. But in truth, his heart wasn't in it. Every once in a while, he nodded, or made some remark that expressed interest, but he really didn't care.

And it bothered him that he didn't. The life of a buccaneer had suited him since that day he escaped from the Spanish. At least he thought it did. But he'd been so filled with the need for revenge. Now, with the promise of retaliation at hand, he worried that he lacked the desire to rush off to the Indian Ocean.

Jack shook himself mentally. 'Twould do no good to bother with it now. He still had to find his sister and avenge his parents. And to do that he needed to learn some Spanish. Excusing himself from Phin, Jack went below and toiled over his charts until he thought his wife might be awake.

"You want me to do what?" Jack exclaimed.

He couldn't believe his ears. He came down to his cabin to ask his wife a simple favor, and she . . . she shocked him. Lord knew, he was no prude, but this. . . . Jack raked his fingers back through his hair and paced to the window.

Sighing, Miranda scraped the chair back across the floor and stood. She hadn't expected him to react like this, really hadn't given much thought to what he would think of her request. But seeing him so agitated, she realized it would do her well to remember that the pirate wasn't as enlightened as some.

She reached over and closed the book she was studying. "You really needn't become so unsettled about it. I simply thought, while I was tutoring you in Spanish, you could do something for me."

Jack stopped pacing. "I'm not unsettled," he stated with more assurance than he felt. " 'Tis simply that your request surprised me."

Miranda smiled. "You don't mind, then? I've done a fairly good likeness of your chest and arms, but lower than that I just don't know."

"Miranda," Jack groaned. "You do know. I mean, we've . . . we've made love in the daylight. Surely you've seen. . . ." He was as tongue-tied as a youth, and Jack didn't like it one bit.

"I'm only interested in your musculature."

"My what?"

"Your muscles. They are truly a fine example of what I've studied in—"

"You only wish to sketch my muscles?"

"Of course." Miranda lifted the charcoal drawings she'd done and showed them to Jack.

"This is me?" How could she think he looked like that with little wriggly lines all over his body?

"Your muscles, yes. At least most of them." Miranda bit her bottom lip. "However, if you feel uncomfortable—"

"Nay, 'tis fine. I'll do it. That is, if we can study Spanish at the same time."

"Certainly we can." Miranda settled into the chair and positioned the parchment in front of her on the desk. "I think we should begin with some simple questions, don't you?" She glanced up. "You can disrobe."

"What type of questions? Do you mean take off everything?"

"You wouldn't be nude otherwise, would you?" Miranda asked logically.

"Right. And you did say you wished me to pose for you in the nude." Jack yanked his shirt over his head.

Miranda waited. He toed off his boots, and her mouth went dry. She had to force herself to remember she was doing this for science.

When he reached for the waistband of his breeches, Miranda squirmed in her seat. She searched her mind for a Spanish phrase to teach him, but the most illogical thing had happened. She couldn't remember a thing.

Miranda looked down at her sketch and grabbed up the charcoal; but her hand was damp, and it slipped to the desk top. She heard the whisper of fabric against skin, and her lashes lifted. He stood before her like a golden god. She could barely breathe.

"Well, go ahead and draw," Jack commanded. He had never before done anything so stupid in his life, and if his men found out about this, he'd never hear the end of it.

"Draw . . . ? Oh, yes, draw." Miranda swallowed and clutched the charcoal. Determined, she bent her head toward the parchment and began to sketch. She could do this . . . she could.

But each time Miranda glanced up to follow a ridge or plane with her eyes, her concentration slipped a little more. Until finally she could do naught but shut her eyes.

"Is something amiss?" Jack resisted the urge to cover himself with his hands. He was trying to stand here and let her draw him—to not think about his state of undress—but he couldn't. And as he watched her work, watched the curve of her cheek and fine crow's wing hair at her temple dip forward when she bent over the parchment, he couldn't stop wishing she were unclothed as well.

Miranda pushed away from the desk. " 'Tis the light. It's not sufficient for me to see." She glanced up. "I mean, I can see." Her eyes drifted over Jack, widening when she noticed his arousal. With a jerk of her head she looked away. "It simply isn't bright enough for me to sketch."

With that she edged around the desk, her back to Jack, and began sorting through the papers there. "Oh," she said. "You can put your clothes back on."

She was as embarrassed as he, Jack thought. Except, he wasn't embarrassed anymore. Silently he moved up behind her, smiling when her gasp of breath accompanied his touch. He pressed against her, sandwiching her body between him and the desk.

His arms stole around her, crossing over her chest, and he bent to nuzzle her ear. "You didn't teach me any Spanish," he said, before nipping gently at her lobe. "For instance." His hands crept up. "What's the Spanish word for these?" They closed over her breasts. His thumbs drew delicate circles around her tightened nipples.

Miranda moaned and leaned back into his hard body. "I doubt you need to know that."

" 'Tis possible, you're right." His mouth skimmed down the side of her neck, taking tiny love bites as he went, and Miranda leaned her head to the side, allowing him better access. "Then, what about this?" One hand slid down between her legs.

"Jack." Miranda could barely catch her breath. " 'Tis daytime."

"I know." He bunched up her skirt in front, sighing and rubbing his hardness into her buttocks when he felt the smooth warmth of her naked thigh.

"Oh, Jack." Miranda arched, driving herself more firmly into his palm. His fingers wove through her tight curls, then delved deeper. Miranda's strength abandoned her. Her knees buckled, and she would have slipped to the floor if not for the strong arm binding her to the captain.

"Lean forward."

"What?" The question was a low moan. His finger stroked her, driving any semblance of reasoning from her mind.

"There." With one swipe of his arm, Jack sent charts and papers flying. Miranda was quivering too near the brink to question when he gently pushed her forward. Cradling her cheek on her bent arm, Miranda lay across the desk.

Standing behind her, Jack ran his hands down the slender sides of her rib cage. When he reached her hip, his fingers fanned, then dipped down to flip up her skirts.

His manhood throbbed, hot and heavy, pulsing as he leaned into her. Controlling the urge to slam into her, he caressed her rounded flesh. He kneaded, then slipped lower, gently spreading her entry. His penetration was slow and deliberate, and Jack thought he'd lose his mind before he was fully sheathed in her.

She was so hot and tight, so unbearably sensual, that he hesitated before resuming his thrusts. When he could stand it no longer, his body moved. He grabbed her buttocks, digging his fingers into her, and arched forward.

His movements became frantic, spurred by his own lack of control. She called out his name, and Jack leaned over her. "Give me your mouth," he groaned, brushing her hair aside when she turned her face toward his.

His open mouth covered hers. His tongue speared into her, and he held her while she climaxed. The tightening of her flesh around him ignited his own long, searing release.

When Miranda opened her eyes, she was face to face with the pirate, their heads resting on the

351

hard oak desk top. She hadn't noticed till now how hard and uncomfortable it was. But she forgot her discomfort when his golden lashes lifted and he smiled at her.

His grin deepened. "God's blood, I don't know what came over me," he whispered, before levering himself up. He gave her bottom a teasing pat before lifting her around to sit on the desk.

Miranda shifted her skirt down around her ankles. Her heart was still pounding in her chest as she tried to catch her breath. "What . . . what did we do?"

Jack's laugh made Miranda flip back the long strands of hair which had come undone. Intently, she peered at him.

"We made love." Jack chuckled, brushing a kiss across her swollen lips before reaching for his breeches.

"But . . . but it wasn't like before."

"Ah, Miranda, there are lots of ways." Jack slid his arms into his shirtsleeves. "And I intend to show you as many as I can, but first I need to learn some Spanish."

Miranda sighed. "Say it again. This time let it roll off your tongue." She turned toward the pirate and demonstrated.

This attempt was as poor as his last. Jack leaned his head back against the bulwark. "God's blood, why can't they just speak the

King's English or Celtic. I have little trouble with them."

"Or Indian," Miranda reminded him. "I heard you speaking with the Indian in the forest, and I had no idea what you said."

"Nafkebee is Cheraw. I learned the language when I was a lad, before the Spanish came." He frowned. "I don't know why I can't seem to pick up this heathen tongue."

Miranda settled down on the window seat in the captain's cabin. They'd been working at this for nearly an hour, ever since they'd made love, and were making little progress. " 'Twould not be so much of a problem if you'd only allow me to accompany you."

"M i r a n d a." Jack drew out her name in warning.

She threw up her hands. "You wish to go ashore at a Spanish settlement and find your sister, when you do not speak the language, nor do you look particularly Spanish. And even if you did, and sought out de Segovia, he would probably recognize you."

"I doubt that."

Miranda glanced up. "You've changed so much since your sixteenth year?"

"In actual appearance nay, but there is naught the same about a free man and a slave. De Segovia will not know me until 'tis too late."

"For you or him?" Miranda sighed when her comment earned her a stormy scowl from the pirate. "You are being stubborn."

"Me?" Jack jumped to his feet. "You're the one who stowed away and won't give up this crazy notion of coming ashore with me." Shutting his eyes, Jack forced himself to calm down. She was exasperating—no question about that. But he'd known that from the beginning, and he seriously doubted he'd ever change her.

"I shall think on it," Jack assured her, before settling back in the chair. "Now, may we continue with the lessons?"

Miranda cast him a sideways glance. "You're considering taking me along?"

"I said only that I'd think on it," Jack hedged. "How would I inquire of the whereabouts of a young woman in Spanish?"

Miranda told him, but she didn't believe for one moment that he was honestly contemplating taking her with him. If she knew anything of the pirate, he was not one to change his mind so quickly.

She listened as he stumbled through another Spanish phrase and made up her mind. Regardless of what she had to do, she was going ashore with him.

The *Sea Hawk* dropped anchor late in the afternoon in a secluded cove on the east bank of Anastasia Island, across the bay from St. Augustine. After trimming the sails, most of the crew lazed on deck, drinking or snoozing, or grumbling to each other about the heat. Thinking of the coming events, though none would admit it.

Below decks, his full length stretched out upon the bunk, Jack's thoughts drifted in the same direction. If Nafkebee's information was correct, by tomorrow the blood of Jack's parents would be avenged. Unbidden, the scene of horror at Port Royal invaded his mind, and he shuddered.

" 'Tis something wrong?" Miranda shifted, swiping hair from her face and elbowing herself up beside him.

Jack rolled his head to glance at his wife. She looked thoroughly debauched and seduced, her raven curls tumbling down across her bare shoulders and her eyes glazed with passion.

A fissure of guilt snaked through him.

Not that he didn't find the sight of her delectable. Not that, though he'd made love to her twice already, the feel of her soft breast swelling against his shoulder didn't cause stirrings in his groin. Not that touching her, tasting her, being one with her, wasn't starting to become as important to him as breathing.

But all that aside, he was in his cabin for a reason. And that reason was deceit.

And blast his worthless, pirate hide, he didn't like deceiving her. Even knowing it was for her own good, he didn't like it.

"Nay." Jack realized Miranda watched him, her intelligent eyes searching his face, and he reached up, touching her cheek to reassure . . . to distract.

"You are so beautiful," he said and shut his eyes against the bitter taste the words left. Not because he didn't find her beautiful, but because he knew why he said it.

Miranda's lips brushed his in a fleeting kiss. "You're beautiful, too."

Jack slitted open one eye, amused despite himself. "This isn't an attempt to persuade me to pose for you nude again, 'tis it?"

"No." Her sparkling laughter made him smile. "I think I will leave the drawing of nude men to others."

" 'Tis an excellent idea. Though if I recall, the afternoon was not a complete waste." His grin was lecherous as his hand skimmed down her body.

"Hmmm." She appeared thoughtful, with her rounded chin resting in the cup of her palm. "That was the day you showed me there were other ways to—"

"Aye." With Miranda he was never certain what she would say.

"You're an excellent teacher," she said, her eyes twinkling when his expression nearly beamed with pride. "I never would have guessed 'twas possible to stand against the door and—"

Jack silenced his wife with a kiss. He'd made love to her pressed against the door, when he first came below. He'd caught her just as she was ready to leave the cabin to go on deck. And he couldn't have her doing that.

The kiss left them both breathless and dazed,

and Jack was thinking less of his plan and more of the woman he'd married when he lifted her to lie sprawling on top of him.

Her blue eyes met him, questioning at first, and then they brightened. " 'Tis another way, isn't it?"

"Aye, Miranda, yet another way."

Her legs spread with only the slightest encouragement from him. If he was a good teacher, she was an excellent student. Jack was continually amazed and thrilled by his passionate wife.

His hands rode her hips, settling her on his swollen staff, and she arched back, accepting all of him. Her breasts tasted sweeter than honey as he raised his head to suckle them.

All thoughts save those of her deserted him as the passion mounted. She rode him well, her knees pressed into his sides. He caressed her stomach, then lower, using his fingers to send her soaring. And when she did, she took him along on the wild, untethered flight.

Pulling her down to him was instinctive, as was gathering her closely in his arms. It was only when she squirmed that Jack realized how tight was his hold. Relaxing his muscles, Jack lay her gently on the bunk beside him and pulled up the sheet to cover them.

Night shadows crept across the cabin, but Jack made no attempt to light a candle. Instead he murmured softly to her. "Sleep now. I know you're tired." After all, he'd done all he could to make her so.

Her sigh brought another pang of guilt. "Jack." Her voice was thick with sleep. "Are you going to take me with you when you go ashore?"

He'd hoped she wouldn't ask, but knowing Miranda, he'd expected—and prepared—for the worst. "Aye," he whispered. "Now sleep, for we depart first thing in the morn."

She snuggled closer. "I'll be able to help. You'll see."

Jack made no reply to that. He lay beside her, his body tense as he waited for the moon to appear through the transom windows. Then he carefully inched away from her and slid from the bunk. He soundlessly gathered his clothes, which like hers lay in disarray on the floor. She made no move to awaken as he lifted the latch on the door.

Once in the passageway, Jack pulled on his breeches, then hurried toward the hatch and the crew that waited for him to lead them ashore.

He'd lied to her . . . twice. She would not be going with them; he never intended she would. And they were leaving tonight, not with the dawn. It galled him, those lies, because he cared for her, cared for her deeply. Too deeply to allow de Segovia to harm her.

Chapter Eighteen

The first thing Miranda noticed when she awoke was that the space beside her in the narrow bunk was empty. Poor Jack, she thought. He'd seemed so nervous last night. It must have interfered with his sleep.

She took a moment to stretch, her hands clasped above her head; then she swung her legs over the side of the mattress to the floor. It was barely dawn, but she hurried with her toilette, brushing her hair and twisting it high on her head in coils. Lately, with just the pirates to see her, she'd taken to wearing her curls down, simply tied at her nape with a ribbon. But that wouldn't do today. She wanted to appear like a fine Spanish lady.

The gown she chose was the best she'd brought with her, a silk mantua with a brocaded stomacher in a vivid shade of emerald green. After fastening the gown, wishing all the while Jack would come below to help her, Miranda added a lace fontange and mantilla, and decided she was ready.

It wasn't until she was on deck that Miranda suspected something was amiss. True, the morning watch between four and eight bells was rarely busy on the pirate ship, but today should be different. Today the pirates planned to go ashore. Except, Miranda had a suspicion they were already there. She didn't need to check the longboat's cradle, but she did.

The boat was gone.

"There ye be, yer ladyship. Hope yer feelin' more the thing."

Miranda swirled around at the sound of Phin's voice. "You're still here?"

"Cap'n decided I should stay aboard seein' how me shoulder ain't completely healed."

Miranda took a deep breath. "When did the rest of them leave?"

"Beginnin' a mid-watch."

Midnight. Jack had left the ship around midnight. Not long after they'd made love.

Miranda tried to keep her mind on the problem at hand, but his deceit kept clouding her logical thinking. He'd lied to her before, true enough. But she'd expected it then. She'd known he was a pirate who cared naught for her, so she'd understood, if not condoned, his deceptions.

But things were different now — at least she'd thought they were. Apparently the difference was in her mind alone.

Miranda fought back a feeling of sadness. "You mentioned something about my feeling better?"

"Aye. The cap'n said ye were under the weather and couldn't go ashore. Said ye were upset by it and not to disturb ye."

"I was." Two could play this game of lying. "Last evening I felt faint, but today it's gone. I'm fine. Except . . ."

" 'Cept what? Ye ain't ailin', is ye?"

"Oh, no." Though she knew she didn't have a choice, Miranda disliked lying to Phin. Now, Jack would be different. She wished he were here right now so that she could tell him all manner of untruths. "It's just that I'm worried. If Jack gets caught, it will be my fault because I was ill and couldn't go with him."

"Don't ye concern yerself 'bout the cap'n. He can take care a hisself."

"I know that's usually the case. But he counted on me to translate for him and . . . Phin, do you suppose you could take me into town? Or just ashore? I would feel so much better if I were with him."

It wasn't easy convincing Phin that he should take her. But as she rapped on the plank door, Miranda decided it hadn't been exactly difficult either. She knocked again, harder this time, and thought she heard someone scurrying about inside.

While Miranda waited, she glanced about. The street was narrow, and she felt the need to flatten herself against the walls of coquina rock when a donkey-pulled cart rumbled by. She swatted at the dust thrown up by the wheels and pounded on the door this time.

Overhead she heard commotion and saw Venetian shutters open and then a head pop out the second-story window. "Who is it? I am in the middle of an experiment, and I don't—Holy Mother, is that you, Miranda?"

"*Si*, Don Luis." Miranda backed into the street and squinted up, smiling at her friend's surprised expression. It had only taken a few inquiries in the town to find Don Luis' abode.

"But . . . but, what are you doing here in St. Augustine? Where is your *padre?*"

" 'Tis a rather long story. Do you suppose I can come inside?" Another wagon was heading her way, so Miranda stepped closer to the house.

"Of course. Oh, my dear. Wait right there. I shall be down to let you in."

By the time Don Luis threw open the door, he'd donned a silk jacket and his curled wig—he'd been in shirtsleeves and bald-headed when he'd spoken to her through the window. He grabbed Miranda's arm, then glanced up and down the dusty street. "You are alone?"

"Yes. Sort of." She'd left Phin by the quay, promising to return soon.

"Come in out of the sun. I do believe it shines brighter here than in Madrid. Come. Come." He led her into a large, cluttered room that opened onto a courtyard resplendent with tropical blooms.

"Now," Don Luis began, after clearing books off a chair and seating his guest. "Tell me everything that has happened to bring you here." He handed her a glass of wine.

Miranda took a deep breath. "Perhaps you should also be seated," she said in the Spanish she'd used since setting foot in St. Augustine. She began her tale, stopping frequently to respond to Don Luis' questions.

"The pirate abducted you?"

"*Si*. But 'twasn't a true kidnapping. I told you my father arranged it."

The Spaniard touched his forehead and shoulders in the sign of the cross. "To think I brought you to such a man. No wonder you ran away."

"Actually, I didn't run away from my father. He really is wonderful, and he loves me very much . . . in his own way. Papa didn't want me to know he and the pirate captain were partners." Miranda rushed through that part of the explanation, deciding this could take all day if she let it. But she hadn't gone much farther when Don Luis' exclamation interrupted her.

"You *married* the pirate!"

Miranda inched her untouched goblet across the table toward Don Luis. He reached for it, clutching the silver stem with his fat fingers, and downed the contents in one gulp. He sputtered, touching his mouth with a lace-trimmed handkerchief.

"I'm sorry. 'Tis not my intent to upset you."

"It is you, dear girl, who has been through so much. It is no wonder you ran away."

"Well, actually, I didn't run away from the pirate either . . . whose name is Jack, by the by." Miranda bit on the end of her thumbnail, sighing after she made her decision to reveal her feelings to her friend. "I love him, you see. And that's why I'm here. To help him."

Miranda gave the Spaniard a quick sketch of her husband's history. "So that's why I came to you. I thought you might assist me in find—"

"What kind of man would send his wife to discover the whereabouts of his parents' killer? I do not care if this man is a pirate, he should have more care of you than to do such a thing."

"He does."

"What?"

"I said he does. Jack doesn't know I'm here. He left me on his ship. Actually, he left me in Charles Town, but I stowed away. Then he left me on his ship; but I knew I could help him, so I came ashore."

"Miranda. Your poor grandfather would turn over in his grave."

"Now, Don Luis, you know such a thing is impossible." Miranda reached for the decanter and poured him another glass of wine. This one disappeared as quickly as the other.

When he appeared to regain at least a modicum of composure, Miranda continued. "Now, if you would just tell me—"

"I know of Sergeant Major de Segovia. He is a cruel man. You are no match for him, Miranda."

"Nor do I plan to be. It is Jack's sister I wish to find. Jack will do nothing until she is safe."

"So, does this pirate of yours plan to destroy the entire town? For if that is his design, I cannot allow him—"

"No," Miranda assured, hoping against hope she spoke the truth. "He only wishes to find his sister . . . and destroy the man who killed his family and held him prisoner."

Miranda let out a breath she didn't realize she held when Don Luis nodded. "That sounds just. Though John Locke may not—"

"Don Luis, please." Most times Miranda would love nothing better than to hold a philosophical discussion, but she could not allow it now. "Do you know of Jack's sister?"

The Spaniard leaned back, seeming to take no offense at her interruption. "Let me see. You say her name is Elspeth?"

"*Si,* that is the name her parents gave her, but who knows what happened after she was captured? Truthfully, she may even be dead."

"I don't think so. There is a young woman—how old did you say she'd be?"

"Perhaps seventeen. Jack was fourteen when the attack took place, his sister nine years younger."

"Yes, it sounds like it could be. . . . Is her hair—"

"Red. Jack told me she had red hair, like the color of leaves in the autumn. You know her, don't you? I can tell by your expression."

"*Si*. I know of such a woman."

"Then, take me to her." Miranda jumped to her feet, pausing on her way to the door when she realized Don Luis wasn't following her. "What is it?"

"I will not assist in her kidnapping."

"Kidnapping?" Miranda retraced her steps. "Jack doesn't wish to kidnap her. He wants to rescue her."

"And what if she doesn't want to be rescued?"

"But that's ridiculous. Why wouldn't she?" Miranda sank back into the chair.

"Twelve years is a long time."

Miranda met his glance. "Don't you think the choice should be hers?"

"Can you promise me it will be?"

"Of course." Oh, she wished she wasn't being forced to guarantee so many things. Especially when the final decision was not hers but her husband's.

"Very well, then." Don Luis pushed himself from his chair. "I suppose she has a right to know."

On the short walk toward the outskirts of town, Don Luis spoke of his recent work with his telescope. "And you, Miranda? Have you done anything for me to write the Royal Academy about? I had a letter recently from Christopher Wren. He asked of you."

"Really?" The president of the Royal Society had inquired about her? Miranda couldn't help the surge of joy. But it was short-lived. "Actually I've done very little since arriving in the New World." Which wasn't strictly true if you counted meeting her father, her kidnapping and marriage, but Miranda decided not to go into that again.

"Is this where Jack's sister lives?" They'd stopped in front of a small house set back from the road. A crushed-shell walkway led to the doorway, and Miranda followed Don Luis. "De Segovia doesn't live here also?" she asked, placing her hand upon his sleeve.

"No. Just Isabel Cadiz and her husband."

"Husband. . . ?" Before Miranda could inquire about that, the Spaniard had knocked on the door, and it was answered by a plump woman with streaks of gray fanning out through her black hair.

They were ushered into a large, well-appointed

room, and greeted by a lovely young woman with red hair.

"Don Luis," she said, coming forward. "How nice of you to visit. And you've brought a friend."

"*Sí*. Isabel, this is Miranda Chadwick."

Isabel's smile widened. "You are English?"

"Yes. I've recently come from there," Miranda answered in fluent Spanish.

"I, too, have recently made a voyage . . . from Spain," Isabel said shyly. "Please sit." She indicated a carved chair. "Tell me, what is your reason for visiting St. Augustine?"

Miranda looked around for Don Luis, but he simply shrugged and walked out into the garden, leaving Miranda and Elspeth alone. Taking a deep breath, Miranda forged ahead. " 'Tis you I've come to see." At the young woman's bewildered expression, Miranda continued. "My name isn't Chadwick any longer. I'm newly married."

"I don't understand. What has that to do with me?"

Miranda studied her a moment. She was petite where Jack was large; redheaded, where her brother was fair. But the eyes were the same. The same sea green color. The same shape. Miranda leaned toward her. "My husband is Jack Blackstone."

There was a flicker of recognition in the depths of those sea green eyes. At least Miranda thought there was, but the woman only smiled, and offered her guest a cup of tea.

Miranda accepted the drink, then laid it on the table to her side. "Jack Blackstone," she repeated. "Certainly you remember him. He's your brother."

"I have no brother."

Miranda might have believed her if not for the rattling of Elspeth's teacup against her saucer. "But you do." Miranda dropped to her knees in front of Elspeth. "He survived the attack on Port Royal. The Spanish held him captive for two years; then during a pirate attack he escaped. When he was able to return to St. Augustine he looked for you, but you weren't here."

Elspeth shook her head so violently locks of red hair cascaded down her back. She tried to cover her ears, but Miranda grabbed her hands, making her listen.

"You must remember him. You're Elspeth Blackstone, and your brother is Jack. He's—"

"Enough, Miranda." Don Luis entered the room and put his arm around Miranda's shoulders. "I cannot permit this. Your grandfather would not have permitted this."

"But can't you see she's—"

"I see only that you've upset her terribly. And her father, who is an acquaintance of mine and a man with a great interest in the philosophies, recently told me she is with child."

"Her father couldn't have told you anything. Her father was killed by the Spanish in 1686."

Miranda twisted out of Don Luis' hold on her. Turning, ready to do more convincing if need be, she paused. Elspeth was crying softly, her face buried deep in her hands, and Miranda didn't have the heart to cause her further pain.

When Don Luis suggested they leave, she agreed, making it almost to the parlor door before a tear-thick voice called her back.

"Don't go. Please, I must speak with you." Elspeth pulled a handkerchief from beneath her ruffled sleeve and dabbed at her eyes. "Please," she repeated, motioning toward the chair Miranda recently vacated.

"You're right," she began, when Miranda was seated and Don Luis returned to the garden. "I do have a brother . . . at least I did."

"You still do. He's here in St. Augustine looking for you."

Elspeth's fingers flattened against her lips, and she sniffed back fresh tears. "I thought him dead . . . along with all the rest of them." She shut her eyes, and Miranda reached for her hand.

"He's not dead."

Elspeth nodded once, then let out her breath. "I was but five when it happened. Truthfully, I remember very little except the screams. So many people screaming and I didn't know why." Her gaze sought Miranda's. "I screamed, too, so loud and long." She shrugged slightly.

"When I woke up it was dark and I couldn't find Mama. Later, when I was older, I pieced together what must have happened. But at the time, I only knew how frightened I was. Until Don Carlos and his wife came to me. They treated me as a daughter and helped me forget. When Don Carlos was sent back to Spain, I went with him."

Her hand turned, and she grasped Miranda's fingers. "You must understand. Deep down I knew they weren't my true parents; yet they took care of me and loved me, and I love them."

"I do understand." Miranda covered their joined hands with her palm. "But it's over now. Jack has come to take you home and—"

"But I am home."

"I realize you—"

"No, no, I really am home. I want to see Jack, of course, but I will not leave St. Augustine with him. My husband is here, my family. All I know and hold dear."

By the time Miranda finished listening to Elspeth, she was truly convinced that Jack's sister was happy where she was. The man she thought of as her father was recently widowed and had returned to St. Augustine with Isabel and her husband. Her first child was due in the winter, and she had no intention of raising the baby any place but by her husband's side.

Miranda understood her feelings. She just wondered if Jack, who had spent years searching for his sister, would share that empathy.

"So, what are you going to do now?" Don Luis inquired.

She and Don Luis were in front of Isabel Cadiz's house, and Miranda had been asking herself the same question. "I suppose I'll go back to the quay. Phineas is there, and he may be able to help me find my husband." She sighed. "I wish I knew where Jack was."

"Perhaps you should return to his ship and let him handle his own business in St. Augustine."

"Maybe you're right. I would like to tell him about his sister, though." Miranda turned toward her friend. "Do you know where I might find de Segovia?"

"Sergeant Major de Segovia is the commander of the Castillo de San Marcos." Don Luis pointed toward the large structure to the north of town. "But you are not thinking of going there after him, are you? De Segovia is a very dangerous man."

Miranda shaded her eyes and stared at the fortress made of the native coquina rock. It shone bright in the mid-afternoon sun.

"Miranda, you cannot be thinking—"

"No," Miranda assured him. "I'm going back to the quay, and then to the *Sea Hawk*."

"You are sure?"

"Do not worry, Don Luis. It would be illogical for me to go anywhere else. And you know how logical I am."

The entire time she bid her farewell to Don Luis, Miranda believed she was telling him the truth. She even headed straight for the harbor when she left him. But without conscious thought her feet seemed to veer off toward the north.

When she finally realized her destination was the huge stone structure, Miranda paused. Shaking her head, she decided the pirate's style of veracity must be contagious.

But the truth was, she needed to find Jack. And if she knew him — which she decided, she probably didn't very well — he was somewhere near the *castillo*.

All she intended to do was tell him about Elspeth . . . Isabel . . . and then go back to the ship. Her husband had a very good reason for hating de Segovia; however, she had no desire to witness the confrontation between them. Of course, she had little doubt that Jack would be the victor in a fair fight. But there *were* a large number of Spanish soldiers in the area.

And two of them seemed intent upon staring at Miranda. She'd first noticed them right after saying her good-byes to Don Luis, but hadn't really thought much of it till now. Miranda stopped, pretending interest in some fruit in the market area. When she glanced up through her lashes, the two soldiers, one tall and dark with deep-set eyes, the other smaller and gray, were still watching her.

But what could they want with her?

Miranda said something in Spanish to the old woman behind the stall and moved along, mingling as best she could with the people busy marketing. She didn't look back toward the soldiers, and she nearly convinced herself that she had imagined their interest in her. After all, she looked like any number of women in the market.

Nonchalantly, Miranda meandered toward the *castillo,* ever watchful for some sign of Jack or the rest of the pirates. She didn't see them, but as she rounded the last stall Miranda stood face to face with the two soldiers.

Trying not to show her fear, she pardoned herself and tried to move away. A dirty hand on her arm stopped her.

"Excuse me," Miranda said in her most indignant voice. She twisted her arm, but the soldier's grip did not relax.

"Come with us please." This request came from the taller soldier—the one not clutching her arm.

"I don't believe I wish to accompany you." Miranda frantically glanced around to see if anyone was coming to her aid. Not a soul seemed to find anything unusual about her predicament. By now the shorter soldier was pulling her behind him toward the *castillo.* "I said, I don't want to go! Help!"

With that, the taller soldier grabbed her other

374

arm and twisted it behind her back. Miranda gasped in surprise and pain.

"I do not care what you wish to do," he gritted through yellowed teeth. "You ask many questions. Now you are coming with us."

For good measure he levered her arm up, bringing tears to Miranda's eyes. But she didn't cry. She couldn't even speak. For at the same time the Spaniard revealed their destination.

"You have such a fascination with the *castillo*. Perhaps the inside of the dungeon will interest you as well."

Jack lifted his head, squinting toward the door when he heard the muffled rattle of keys on the other side of the thick cypress wood. A filtering of light through the slit in the coquina stone cast the room in dusky shadows.

Pushing to his feet in the filthy straw, Jack took a deep breath and prepared for another beating. He'd been here a scant five hours by his own calculation, which admittedly probably wasn't too accurate. And already they'd "questioned" him several times.

"Where are your men, Captain Blackstone?"

"Why do you dare to come to St. Augustine?"

Each query he refused to answer was followed by a jab or poke, a slap or a punch by the corporal of the guard, while two other soldiers held Jack's arms. His head hurt and his ribs were sore, but he hadn't said a word, nor did he intend to.

He might be in the familiar position of being a captive of the Spanish, but at least his men were safe. And sooner or later they'd realize he wasn't coming back, and they'd return to the *Sea Hawk* and sail away. Knowing that Miranda and his men were spared this made his spine a bit stiffer as the door opened wider.

Jack blinked into the light, and his resolve faltered. "God's blood," he mumbled as he rushed forward. Jack caught his wife as she fell, thrust forward by the guards into the cell. His arms cradled her an instant before instinct made him turn to rush the men who had shoved her. But they quickly slammed the door, and as he pounded in frustration, Jack could hear their muffled laughter through the wooden planks.

"I don't believe that will help anything."

"No?" Jack whirled around, his face a mask of anger. "As I see it, things couldn't get much worse." His breath left him on a forced gust, and Jack's expression softened. "For God's sake, Miranda. What are you doing here?"

"I'm not exactly certain. I was walking through the market, looking for you, when two soldiers came upon me." With each word Miranda was forced to tilt her head more as the pirate moved closer. By the time she finished speaking, she could no longer see his face, for he had her wrapped securely in his arms, her cheek pressed against his broad chest. She shut her eyes and took comfort in the strong, steady beat of his heart.

"Oh, Miranda, Miranda," Jack whispered into her hair. The lace fontange was askew, tilted to the left, and curls tumbled down her slim back. "Why did you leave the ship?"

Miranda flattened her hands against his silk waistcoat and pushed away, her eyes accusing. "You lied to me."

"What?" He was shocked by the change in her from sweet and cuddly to accusing.

"You lied. You said I could come with you; then you stole off the *Sea Hawk* in the dead of night."

Jack gave a quick, sharp laugh, then paced across the cell, turning to pin her with his stormy gaze. "You're damn right I lied. And let me tell you this." His finger jabbed at the air separating them. "I'd do it again. Though it does me precious little good." His hands spread beseechingly. " 'Tisn't it obvious why I didn't wish you to come?"

Miranda let her gaze wander about the cell, taking in the damp stone walls and filthy, straw-littered floor. He had a point. Sighing, Miranda folded her hands. "Perhaps I could have helped you."

"I doubt it." Giving in to his desires, Jack moved back beside Miranda and draped his arm around her shoulders, pleased when she turned into his strength. "The Spanish surrounded me almost as soon as I stepped foot ashore. It was as if they knew I was coming."

"But how could they? I mean, the *Sea Hawk* was hidden, wasn't it?"

"Aye, I'd swear they didn't catch sight of the ship." As to another reason for them to know about him, Jack had used his time in captivity trying to come up with one. But the only explanation that made any sense, he didn't want to believe.

"What of your crew? Are they somewhere in the *castillo?*"

Jack shook his head. "They're safe as far as I know. We'd split up before I was captured. I'm hoping they managed to make it back to the *Sea Hawk.*"

"But surely they'll come for you. I mean, you're their captain."

Jack shut his eyes, then pulled her closer, reluctant to share reality with her. "Nay, sweetheart. They won't be back."

"But—"

Jack touched the soft swell of her bottom lip. " 'Tis an unwritten rule we follow. No sacrificing the entire crew for the sake of one man." He let the tip of his finger drift across her cheek. "I'm sorry, Miranda. So sorry you're involved in this." Jack sucked in his breath. "God, how could I have let this happen?"

"Don't." Miranda wrapped her arms around

his waist. "There must be some way out of this. If we could only think. . . ."

"Ah, sweet Miranda." Jack kissed her forehead, and eyes, the tip of her nose. He hesitated to tell her that he'd already thought and thought . . . and could think of nothing. He bent to gather her closer, but something she said made him straighten.

"You found my sister?"

"Yes. Do you think she might be able to get us out of here? Of course, the problem is, she doesn't know we're here. Still—"

"Tell me." Jack cupped his wife's shoulders. "Tell me of her."

Miranda looked up into Jack's expectant face and smiled. "She's well and happy. Married and with child."

"What?" Jack dropped his hands as if he'd been burned. "What are you saying?"

"Jack." Miranda touched his arm, wishing he'd look back at her. "Listen to me."

"Nay. 'Tis not true. It must have been someone else you spoke to. Elspeth would not be. . . ."

"Be what? Be happy?" Miranda watched as he shook his head.

"Not with the Spanish. No, by God, she would not!"

"Think, Jack. 'Twas twelve years ago. Twelve years."

"I care not how many years. How many decades."

"But she was just a babe. Time has softened the pain. Mayhap you should let it soften yours."

Jack turned on her abruptly. "Soften? How am I to soften my hate while imprisoned in a Spanish fort? Tell me that, Miranda."

"I know not," she whispered.

He looked at her, and his anger dissipated. "I'm sorry. 'Tis not your fault. I just loathe that I've brought you to this. I've felt the Spanish yoke before." Jack ran his hand over the rough wall. "I helped dig the moat that surrounds us."

Memories came flooding back to him, nearly suffocating in their intensity, but Jack fought them. Reaching out, he pulled Miranda into his arms. There was no reason for her to hear the worst of it now. "We'll get out of this, wife," he said, grinning when she glanced up at him.

It didn't surprise Jack at all when she inquired as to how he thought they'd do that. After all, he *was* dealing with Miranda, and she questioned everything.

However, she didn't question when he brushed his lips across hers, or when he deepened the kiss.

Yet they both knew he hadn't answered her.

Chapter Nineteen

"Comfortable?"

Miranda snuggled deeper into the cradle of her husband's body and sighed her affirmation. Feeling guilty, she levered up, trying to make out his features in the failing light. "Are you?"

"Aye," Jack assured her, then cupped her head back against his chest.

They were huddled in a corner of the cell. As the evening shadows had marked the end of their first day as prisoners in the *castillo,* Jack had prepared them a place to sleep. They'd already scoured every inch of the small enclosure in a futile search for a way out, so Jack knew where to find the cleanest straw.

Using his boot, he'd cleared out a corner, spread straw to cushion them, settled down, and reached up for Miranda. She now sat on his lap, with Jack's arms wrapped around her.

He didn't think de Segovia would do anything tonight. The Spaniard probably wanted to give Jack time to stew and worry about the morrow.

And damn his murdering hide, that's exactly what Jack was doing. His neck was itching something fierce, and worse, he imagined Miranda with the same malady.

His fingers brushed down over the soft skin at her throat, and his chest tightened at the thought of a rope marring that soft perfection.

"Miranda," he said, his voice husky with emotion. "Tomorrow . . . or whenever they come for us." He was sure, knowing de Segovia, that there would be a face-to-face confrontation. "I intend for us to escape."

"But—"

"It won't be easy," Jack continued, ignoring the question in her voice. "And you will have to do exactly as I say." He paused, waiting for her agreement. When he didn't get it, his voice prompted. "Miranda?"

"Yes, Jack, I'll do as you say."

"Good." His hand drifted down her arm. "I'll try to create some havoc."

"What kind of havoc?"

"I don't know . . . something. I'll leap on a guard, or lunge at de Segovia. Anything that will take their minds off you." Jack shifted, taking her face in his hands and trying to see her in the darkness. "Then I want you to run like hell. Do you think you can find your way out of here?"

"Yes, but what about you?"

"I'll follow. Or get away some other time."

"But Jack—"

"Nay, Miranda. You cannot question this. You are to do it. Do you understand me?"

Miranda swallowed. She could not see the pirate's face, but she could feel his intensity, in the strength of his hands, in the power of his voice. "Do you understand me?"

"Yes."

"Good." Jack let go of her face and rested her back against his heart. "When you get out of the *castillo*, hide, then somehow get across the bay to Anastasia Island . . . to the ship. You'll find Scar and the others there." He hoped. "They'll take care of you." Jack paused. "They'll see you safely back to Charles Town."

Miranda said nothing. Jack continued talking, telling her some wild story about how he would get away later and meet her in Charles Town, and she didn't believe a word of it. More, she knew he didn't believe it either. He was planning a way for her to escape, but he knew his own was hopeless.

She swallowed when his arms tightened about her. "Promise me you will do this, Miranda. Promise me."

"I promise." Her voice was soft and low, and her breath wafted across his neck. "Jack?"

He expected an argument and prepared himself to bully her into compliance. He found that he could accept the inevitability of his own fate, but not hers. But her next words surprised him.

"I'm so glad I married you." Miranda heard

383

his sharp intake of breath and continued. "I know I've been a trial to you and—"

"You haven't." Jack shrugged, and honesty forced him to add, "Not really."

"Oh, but I have. Though 'twas never my intent. But I am glad we married and even that you kidnapped me."

"Strange as it may seem," Jack admitted, "I am, too." He settled back against the hard stones and tried to be quiet. There was no real need to say more. But God's blood, he might never get another chance to tell her. He opened his mouth and realized he was scared. He was a bloody pirate, and he was afraid to say three words to a wisp of a woman . . . and that woman was his wife!

"Miranda?"

"Yes?"

Jack took a deep breath and plunged forward. "I love you."

There was no response, and Jack wriggled on the damp floor. God, why didn't she say something? Did she think it foolish that a pirate, a lawless freebooter, could experience such an emotion as love? True, it had shocked him when he'd realized what he felt for her went far beyond lust, far beyond fondness. "Did you hear me?"

"I heard you," Miranda whispered. She'd taken a moment to savor his revelation. "I love you, too."

"You do?" Jack felt absurdly happy, especially considering the circumstances. He'd barely allowed himself to think upon his love for her, let alone hope that she felt the same. He pulled Miranda up higher against his chest, facing him, and brushed a kiss across her forehead. "Then, 'tis good we're wed," he said, before his lips met hers.

When he finally raised his head, Jack's breathing was shallow, and his hands were working their way beneath Miranda's skirts. He cupped the delicious curve of her bottom, basking in her shiver of delight.

" 'Twould appear you've married yourself a lusty pirate," Jack said on a breath of air. His fingers splayed, delving into her moist folds, and she wriggled closer, rubbing her body against his swollen staff.

" 'Twould appear I have," she agreed. "But, Jack—" Miranda pushed away when it became obvious her husband wasn't going to stop with this glorious stroking of her body—"how can we?"

"Shhh. You ask too many questions."

"But I don't know. . . . Oh . . . Jack. . . ."

"Move a little to the side. Ah, there." Jack managed to work his breeches down over his hips, freeing himself in the process. He lifted her skirts, skimming his knuckles along the smooth skin of her thighs.

She could barely see him, the cell was so dark.

Miranda closed her eyes and gave her remaining senses free reign. Her head dropped back, raven curls brushing the naked backs of her legs as he lifted her up against him. She breathed in his musky, masculine smell, knowing there would never be another fragrance that excited her so.

Miranda let her fingers trace down his ruffled shirt to where fabric stopped and hot, hair-roughened skin began. He sucked in air, mumbling a shattered curse when she touched him. Satin-smooth and hard, he thrust against her as if begging for more than her shy exploration. The darkness, the threat of the morrow, made her bold, and Miranda wrapped her hand around his thickened staff. Her fingertips barely touched, but she fondled and caressed till his hand clamped onto her wrist, stopping her sliding motion.

"God, Miranda . . . you'll unman me."

" 'Tis impossible to even imagine." She said the words against his lips, between erotic little forays of her tongue into his mouth. Parry and thrust. Each silken entry delved deeper, till Jack arched forward, capturing the kiss.

His large hands bracketed her hips, sinking into her curves, lifting her. On her knees Miranda was poised above him. The smooth, rounded tip teased her dewy flesh as they both waited, anticipating the moment of joining. Desire shot through Miranda, and she squirmed. Sinking onto him, she took him fully into her body, and the cold stone, the cell . . . the world, seemed to disappear.

Sensual sounds, a medley of breathless sighs and erotic moans, accompanied the sleek movements of their enmeshed bodies. Jack's fingers found taut nipples straining against the bounds of her silk bodice. Deftly he nudged the fabric aside. Her breasts fell into his palms, and he molded them. Arching forward, he took one ardently into his mouth.

The suckling motion accentuated the rhythm of his hips, making the coil of hunger inside Miranda tighten unbearably. Her skin tingled, and a flush of desire spread through her. "Make me soar," Miranda breathed as one hand dropped to tangle in the springy curls meshed with his. His thumb slipped lower, sliding inside and finding the core of her passion. "Make me fly up beyond the clouds."

With his free hand Jack grasped the backside of her knee, yanking her forward, filling her deeper. His thrusts grew bolder, and Miranda was swept up on a tumultuous gust of air. She shivered uncontrollably, spiraled and sailed on the wings of pleasure. And Jack was swept along with her, bursting free of the harsh confines of earth.

It was a powerful joining of bodies and souls, sharper, yet more fragile than anything they'd yet experienced. A beginning, Miranda vowed. Somehow she would make certain this was the beginning of their life together. But her husband, her life-hardened pirate husband, knew it by another name. The end.

When she collapsed on his chest, Jack gathered his wife in his arms. He straightened their clothing and settled her next to his heart. "Sleep, Miranda. We shall both need our strength tomorrow."

But Jack didn't heed his own advice. Long after her soft, even breathing revealed her slumber, he reclined against the stones, his mind actively conjuring up scenarios of the morrow. He wanted to anticipate every possibility, every chance to get Miranda away from here.

He must have slept, for the heavy thud of the door slamming against stone woke him. Jack scrambled to his feet, his body damp and stiff, and pulled Miranda up behind him.

She tossed raven hair behind her shoulders and peered around Jack. Light shone from the lantern one of their captors was holding in front of him. She could make out the shadows of two other men—all of them wearing swords at their sides. The leader motioned them forward, and Miranda grasped Jack's hand.

"Remember your promise," was all he said to her before heading for the door.

Candles stuck in iron mounted prongs lined the dreary hallway as they were led away from the cell. One man, mumbling orders in Spanish which Miranda translated, walked in front of

388

Jack and Miranda, and the other two men followed closely behind.

Jack waited till they neared an open door that led out into the inner courtyard. He took a deep breath, gave Miranda's fingers a final squeeze, and slowed his step. The man directly behind him grunted, poking him in the back. Turning, Jack cursed.

Miranda's hand on his arm kept Jack from lunging at him. "He wants you to hurry," she said.

Jack's head snapped around. "I know what he wants." God's blood, *he* could understand a prod. But it looked like his wife didn't grasp the concept of creating havoc. His eyes shot toward the open door, then back to meet hers, and he had the first inkling that she may have decided against keeping her promise to him. She gave her head a small shake.

Again he stared pointedly at the open doorway, and this time he lurched forward when the guard, obviously deciding he'd had enough of this delay, shoved him.

Miranda turned on the short Spaniard. Her expression indignant and her voice raised, she started giving him what Jack could only guess was a good lambasting. The man appeared shocked, as did the others escorting them down the hallway.

Jack seized the moment.

So quickly that she gasped, he grabbed Miranda's shoulders, turning and thrusting her into the courtyard in one movement. He kicked out and tripped the soldier who leaped after her, and shoved him sprawling toward the other guards. As a group they were knocked off balance and fell against the far wall.

For an instant, before yanking the door shut, Jack considered rushing into the daylight and taking his chances with Miranda. But the soldiers where scrambling to their feet, reaching for their swords, and he knew he had to delay them for her to get away.

"Run," he yelled, before slamming the door and whirling about, blocking the passage with his big body. With a slash of his arm he knocked aside one of the guards, who fell in a rumpled heap in the dirt. But another was bearing down on Jack, sword drawn, his face a distorted mask of outrage.

Jack feinted to the right, conscious of keeping himself between the soldiers and the door, avoiding the angry thrust of steel. The weapon fell from the Spaniard's numbed fingers when the edge of Jack's hand came down on his wrist.

Grabbing the hilt, Jack plunged forward, impaling the soldier with his own sword. With a quick yank Jack turned to face his next adversary. The man hesitated, obviously affected by what he had just witnessed.

Hefting the sword, feeling its balance as an extension of his limb, Jack grinned at his opponent, mocking his reluctance to do battle. Jack felt a rush of exhilaration followed by a glimmer of hope. One more man to get by and he had a chance . . . a chance to make his way to de Segovia and extract his revenge . . . a chance to escape and join Miranda.

The soldier suddenly rushed forward, but Jack was quicker and thwarted the attack. He lunged, flicking the sword tip across the Spaniard's chest and drawing blood. Fighting in the narrow hallway was awkward, but Jack was definitely the superior swordsman. He parried each thrust, backing the Spaniard down the hallway. With each step Jack became more aggressive.

Then with a well-executed flick of his wrist Jack sent his opponent's weapon spinning to the floor. Sweat broke out on the man's florid face as he flattened himself against the stone wall.

Jack leaned forward. "Where is de Segovia?" His sword tip played with the buttons decorating the front of the soldier's jacket. "De Segovia?" he repeated, when the man showed no signs of understanding.

The soldier broke to the side, lunging toward escape, but Jack followed, piercing the man's body with a single thrust.

In that same instant Jack felt the hair at the back of his neck bristle. He whirled about, frantic to prepare himself to face a new adversary. But he was too late to avoid the club already plummeting toward his head.

Blinding pain exploded in Jack's head, then rushed through his body. His knees buckled, and Jack tried to keep his footing; but it was no use. As realization of defeat permeated his brain, Jack felt the packed dirt come up to meet him.

Just before blackness embraced him he conjured up a vision of Miranda. The picture etched on his mind was as he last saw her. She stared at him, her blue eyes filled with love and regret and shimmering with unshed tears.

God's blood, he hoped with all his heart she was able to escape.

Ah, the wages of sin.

Jack languished, racked with pain, certain he'd died and found his way into the depths of Hades. He was a pirate, after all.

"I see you've finally arrived."

Jack stopped lamenting his final destination, and his eyes shot open. He recognized that voice. After twelve years, and though he now spoke a heavily accented English, Jack knew. And though hell was a most appropriate place for de Segovia, Jack hadn't had the pleasure of sending him there.

Focusing his eyes, Jack picked out de Segovia seated on a wooden bench near the door of the cell. Gray now flared out through his dark hair, but other than that he looked nearly the same as that day long ago on the beach at Port Royal.

With a primal roar Jack tried lurching to his feet. The bite of chain links gouging his wrists brought him to an abrupt halt.

"You always were one to cause trouble, weren't you Jack?"

The scorn in the Spaniard's expression made Jack tug against the restraining chains. The motion only caused him further anguish, but it amused de Segovia. He laughed diabolically, a sound that echoed through Jack's head, mingling with the memories of the massacre at Port Royal. The Spaniard had laughed then, too . . . bared his teeth and guffawed at the lad sprawled at his feet.

"You will not escape this time, Jack. I have you, and I won't let you go . . . except of course to embrace a painful death."

"You sniveling—" Gritting his teeth, Jack yanked with all his might, but in the end he could only flop back, exhausted . . . defeated, and listen to more of the fiendish laughter. It seemed to reverberate off the dank walls and surround Jack, creeping beneath his skin.

"I'll kill you, you bloodthirsty bastard," Jack hissed, when the tormenting cackle subsided.

"*You* kill me? You have it all wrong. It is *I* who shall do the killing." He leaned forward, bracing his satin-covered elbows on his knees. "And you have gall, calling me bloodthirsty. Pirates are known for that trait."

"Pirate I may be, but I've yet to slaughter

393

women and children."

De Segovia's expression hardened, and his thick, dark brows lowered. "Your crimes are the ones we are discussing. Thievery, murder, piracy." The volume of his voice rose with each word, till he nearly screamed the last. "Foul deeds all. And all punishable by death."

He stood and walked toward Jack, careful to keep himself out of the pirate's limited reach. "You've caused me anguish since the day I first laid eyes on you. I should have run my sword through you then. But I spared you, more fool I."

"Spared me to slave in your quarry, cutting coquina, or to labor from sunup to sundown digging the moat." Jack remembered vividly the two years he'd spent as a prisoner under de Segovia's cruel thumb. "Tell me, de Segovia. Was I spared to give you practice with the whip?"

"You couldn't be trusted," de Segovia stated simply.

"Aye. And you can't trust me now." The venom in Jack's voice made the bulging vein in de Segovia's forehead pulse, but he laughed heartily.

"Brave words from a captive." De Segovia roamed about the small cell as if to point out the confining walls. "I shall not make the same mistake I made before. There will be no pirate ship's guns to conceal your escape. The *castillo* is complete now. And it can easily thwart any attack by sea."

De Segovia came to stand in front of Jack, and his smile was evil. "Ten years ago, when I realized you were gone, I had hoped the pirates had killed you . . . or if not, that the swamp would do the deed. I left for Spain believing you dead. Then I began to hear tales, tales of a pirate who roamed the Spanish Main at will. A pirate by the name of Jack Blackstone."

"I was seeking you, de Segovia."

"And now you've found me." The Spaniard seemed to find this highly amusing. "Fortunately it shall do you no good."

Jack's fingers fisted, and he longed for the chance to wrap his hands around his captor's thick neck. But Jack could only kneel in the squalid straw, enduring the Spaniard's rantings. De Segovia seemed to truly enjoy Jack's plight, for he paced back and forth, his bulldog body jerking about, facing Jack now and then to make a point.

Jack grew almost anesthetized to his words till he heard the mention of Snebley's Creek.

"Ah, I see that gained your interest. I almost had you there. Unfortunately, you slipped through my fingers. But not this time."

"That was your galleon at Snebley's Creek? But how did you know—"

"Of your secret hiding place? Your safe harbor?" De Segovia chuckled. "I don't suppose there's any harm in telling you now . . . now

395

that it's too late for you to do anything about it." He tilted his head. "I had a message. From someone you would never suspect. You have more enemies than you can imagine, my pirate friend."

Jack listened with a sickening sense of betrayal as de Segovia droned on, finally revealing the traitor. How could he not have known?

The pounding of blood in his ears nearly drowned out the Spaniard's words as Jack thought of his Judas. And de Segovia was right. Now that he knew, it was too late to do anything about it.

It was too late for everything . . . even revenge.

Dawn tinged the musty cell a dingy gray. Dawn of the day he would die.

Strange, Jack thought as he leaned against the rough stone wall, there was no itch at the base of his neck. The tingle that had bothered him since the day he became a pirate was gone. He would have thought today of all days it would be unbearable. Not that he was going to hang, as he had always feared. That was the English punishment for pirating.

The Spanish method, though similar, was more fiendish. Or perhaps it only seemed that way because de Segovia took such relish in describing it in agonizing detail.

Garroting.

They would place him in a chair, wrap a rope around his neck and slowly twist screws that tightened the hemp, strangling the life from him.

Jack took a deep breath, again wondering why he didn't have the urge to dig at his neck. Perhaps the worst part of dying was the worry, the anticipation. Within hours that would be over.

Shutting his eyes, Jack wished he could die with a clear conscience. Wished, too, he needn't die full of regrets. But he had them, and they gnawed at him like the rats that shared his cell.

He had failed. Failed to bring de Segovia to justice, even if it was his own form. Failed to rescue his sister. Failed to recognize the viper nestled close to his breast.

That was his hell.

Jack shuddered, forcing his thoughts away from the morbid. He smiled to himself when they settled on Miranda. His only regrets from that quarter were that he had exposed her to danger, and he didn't know for certain that she had escaped. But he prayed she had. Miranda was resourceful. He'd go to his death hoping against hope she was safe.

When the heavy wooden door creaked open, Jack struggled to his feet. He brushed the prickly straw from his breeches as best he could and straightened his shoulders. He was Gentleman Jack Blackstone, by God, and he'd go to his death with as much dignity as the Spanish would allow.

There were three guards. This time two of them had pistols trained on him while the third unlocked his leg irons. His shackled wrists had momentary relief when the metal bands came off. But they were quickly replaced by twisted hemp. With his hands tied behind his back Jack was prodded forward.

After three days in semidarkness the sunlight hurt Jack's eyes. He blinked, then forced them open. The courtyard was filled with people. A carnival atmosphere seemed to permeate the air. Then, suddenly, someone noticed him, and a hush descended on the gathering. More soldiers joined the guards. As they surrounded him, Jack wasn't certain if they were to protect the crowd from him, or him from the crowd.

The soldiers prodded Jack forward and the throng aside. Slowly, reluctantly, they moved, forming a corridor of humanity. Their faces were filled with hate, and though Jack couldn't understand what they said, it obviously wasn't sympathy for his fate.

"The good people of St. Augustine hate pirates such as you," de Segovia had told him yesterday. "They will declare the day you die a holiday."

His words had sent shivers down Jack's spine. Seeing the proof now made him lift his chin higher. He fixed his eyes straight ahead. And that's when he saw it. A high wooden platform, empty save for the chair and post behind it.

He hesitated only a moment before striding forward to meet his fate.

De Segovia stood at the foot of the platform. He was dressed in full military regalia. The tropical sun reflected off the silver and jewels adorning his short, bulldog body, and the breeze fluttered his plumed hat.

But it was the look on his face that caught Jack's attention. He was obviously very pleased with himself, puffed up and gloating. And Jack would give his last minutes to wipe away that expression.

Instead, he stood there tall and stoically while de Segovia spew taunts that moved the crowd to a high pitch of excitement. When they were shoving against the soldiers that encircled the platform, de Segovia gave the signal for Jack and the hooded executioner to ascend the crude wooden steps.

De Segovia followed. He stood to the side as Jack was shoved into the chair. Then he turned, a smirk on his face. "Knowing you do not ascribe to the true religion, I thought it a waste of time to provide you with a priest."

Jack said nothing.

"Have you no final words? No thoughts on this momentous occasion?"

"Only that I shall await you in hell."

Jack took a modicum of satisfaction in watching the color drain from de Segovia's face. The Spaniard nearly trembled with rage. He turned toward the crowd and lifted his hand. "Let the execution of the despised pirate Jack Blackstone commence!" he shouted, before descending the steps.

Jack forced himself to return the stares of the people as the rope scratched around his neck. They were a mix of peons and gentry, men and women, and Jack briefly wondered if one of them was his sister. But the thought of Elspeth watching him die was so abhorrent, he quickly pushed it from his mind.

His gaze flicked from one face to the next until it met a pair of dark blue eyes. His breath caught.

"God's blood."

Chapter Twenty

Before Jack could begin to fathom what Miranda's presence in the crowd meant, the rope tightened painfully about his neck. He gasped for a breath, thinking it his last. But no sooner had the hemp grown taut, than it loosened and fell away. Jack jerked his head around when he heard a familiar voice muffled by the executioner's hood.

"Ain't nothin' ta worry 'bout, Cap'n."

Then all hell broke loose.

Several explosions rang out almost simultaneously, sending sand and palm fronds flying. People screamed and panicked, running helter-skelter within the confines of the courtyard. The soldiers shouldered their firearms, but were obviously caught up in the hysteria.

Jack's wrists were cut free and a cutlass jammed against his palm. His hand molded about the hilt, and Jack whipped it around, slicing the polished steel through the air.

Another blast sounded, and Jack leaped from

the scaffolding, Phin by his side. Pirates, who moments before had passed for haggard peons, flung aside their raiments, brandishing pistols and swords. Jack's crew had positioned themselves near the soldiers, and now fell upon them with fierce abandon.

"Raise the drawbridge!" The order screamed by a Spanish officer was his last.

"This way, Cap'n." Phin yanked at his arm, motioning toward the gate now jammed with humanity trying to push through. "Don't need ta worry none 'bout them closin' the bridge. Her ladyship done seen ta that."

"Where is she? Where's Miranda!" Jack yelled above the din. "I saw her in the crowd."

Phin shrugged his scrawny shoulder. "On her way ta the ship, I'll wager."

But Jack wasn't about to wager on her life. Breaking free of Phin's hold, he rushed toward the crowd, most of whom fell back as he approached. It seemed none of the civilians wanted to take their chances against the pirate captain.

"Miranda!" Jack thought he spotted her shiny head, and he ran toward the spot.

Miranda glanced up as he approached, taking her attention from the man at her side. "I have him for you, Jack. I have de Segovia." In that instant the Spaniard knocked her arm, grabbing the gun she'd had trained on him, and proving her words false.

With his arm locked around Miranda's throat,

402

de Segovia aimed the pistol toward Jack.

Hesitating only a moment, Jack lifted his cutlass, pointing the tip toward de Segovia's chest. "Let her go, you bastard!"

"I'll kill her." In a wave of panic the Spaniard started moving the gun around toward Miranda.

"De Segovia!" Jack yelled as Miranda rammed her elbow into the Spaniard's side. The spark from the flint exploded in the priming pan, firing the pistol just as Jack lunged forward.

His cutlass met resistance of flesh and sinew, and Jack plunged harder. It wasn't until the echo of the shot faded that Jack realized he wasn't wounded. De Segovia lay sprawled, faceup, the sword centering a blossom of crimson on his jacket. But Jack gave little thought to the man who'd spurred his years of revenge. All he knew was that Miranda lay motionless, her fragile body partly covered by the Spaniard.

"Oh, God, Miranda." Jack dropped to his knees, praying the shot hadn't killed her. He shoved de Segovia's body onto the sand, relieved when Miranda lifted her head. She stared at him, her eyes wide.

"Jack . . . Oh, Jack."

"Are you hurt?" Jack ran his hands over her arms and hips. When they reached her legs she winced. "God, what is it?"

"Nothing really. I just twisted my foot." She attempted to stand and lost her balance. Without waiting for another try Jack bent down, scooped her over his shoulder and took off toward the *castillo's* gate. He elbowed his way through the crowd. As Phin had predicted the drawbridge was still down. A fleeting memory of digging the moat crossed Jack's mind as he pounded across the wooden bridge. Once on the beach he spotted some of his crew and raced toward them.

Farther down the stretch of sand, near a stand of palmetto, Jack saw King, Scar and No Thumb. They were situated behind a hastily constructed barricade of logs. They fired their muskets, and Jack glanced behind him to see several Spanish soldiers pursuing him. One of them dropped to the sand. Another turned on his heel and ran back toward the *castillo*.

"Little farther, Cap'n. Beyond that spit a land. There be a longboat."

"Aren't you coming?" Jack slowed and shifted Miranda.

"We'll be along. Just waitin' ta give ye a bit of a head start." Scar fired his musket at yet another soldier, causing him to dive to the ground. Scar looked up and grinned. "Get her ladyship outta here, Cap'n."

Jack didn't hesitate, promising to come back as soon as he saw Miranda safely aboard. He found more of his men on the beach of a small cove. The *Sea Hawk* was riding at anchor just off shore, and one longboat was already heading across the placid water toward her. Another ketch was pulled up on the sand.

"There ye be, Cap'n." Phin rushed over as Jack settled Miranda into the boat. "Is her ladyship all right?"

"I'm perfectly fine." Miranda took a deep breath and swept hair from her face.

"It's her foot," Jack said, refuting her words. "Take care of her; I'm going back for King and the others."

"No need, Cap'n. See fer yourself." Phin pointed to the three pirates in question hurrying across the beach toward the boat. "Now, come on and get yerself in here, so we can get off this here heathen shore."

As he stepped into the boat, Jack noticed Miranda's face. She was staring past his shoulder. She touched his arm. "Jack," was all she said, but the way her fingers tightened made him wary.

Turning, Jack saw a young woman standing in the sand. She was short and fine-boned, and her hair shone red in the sunlight. Jack's mouth went dry. He didn't need Miranda's prodding to approach her.

"Elspeth?" Jack searched her features, trying to reconcile the child he'd known with the young woman standing before him.

"I wanted to see you before you left," she said in halting English. "To tell you how happy I am that you are safe."

"We're both safe." Jack reached for her hands.

"Come." He pulled gently. "Come with me to Charles Town. You have nothing to fear there."

"I have nothing to fear here," she said, pulling her hands from his grasp. "My husband is in St. Augustine. I will not leave him."

She was confirming what Miranda had said, but Jack didn't think he could accept it. Not after all these years. He grasped her shoulders. "Elspeth, listen to me—"

"It's Isabel, not Elspeth, and I have listened . . . to your wife. She wanted me to leave with you also. But I do not wish to go. Please, do not waste this time we have in foolish pleas. Be content that I am happy."

"But—"

"Cap'n, we need ta be shovin' off!"

"I'm coming." Jack barked the words over his shoulder. When he looked back at his sister his throat felt tight. "I've searched for you for twelve years . . . twelve years. Wondering if you were alive or. . . ." Jack's voice thickened, and he had the uncomfortable feeling he might cry. But that was foolish. He was a pirate, after all. He took a deep breath. "Ever since that day the Spanish attacked, the day you wanted to come with me to meet Nafkebee and I wouldn't let you, I've feared you were dead. I can't just leave you here . . . with the enemy."

"You must." Elspeth grasped his hand. "My life here has been good. Nothing for you to—"

"Cap'n!"

"You must go. I've subjected you to further danger by coming. But I wanted so badly to see you. Now go . . . please." Elspeth smiled and gave him a gentle push. "Go."

He had no choice. With each moment he delayed, he endangered his crew and his wife. But God it was hard. She pushed at his hands again, and Jack turned, taking three strides before he stopped. Whirling about, he retraced his steps, scooping his sister into his arms and hugging her to him. "I love you," he whispered, before putting her down and hurrying back to the longboat. With King he pushed off from the beach.

They were nearly to the ship when Spanish soldiers exploded through the trees and began firing. But the distance was too great, and the musketballs fell harmlessly into the turquoise waters.

Jack shaded his eyes as the others climbed up the rope ladder to the *Sea Hawk*'s deck, searching the shore for any sign of Elspeth.

"She left the beach before you set foot in the longboat," Miranda said. "Don't worry about her. She knows what she's doing. 'Tis she and Don Luis who helped with your escape. Elspeth kept us informed of de Segovia's plans for you. Her husband is de Segovia's secretary. She felt badly using his knowledge, but she could not stand by and let her brother die. And Don Luis was responsible for the explosions. He used just the right amount of powder and fuse to create havoc without really harming anyone. He was really very pleased with the way it turned . . ."

Miranda laughed at the expression of amazement on his face. Leaning across the seat, she touched his whiskered cheek.

Later, when the *Sea Hawk* was under sail, skimming along the waves toward Charles Town, Jack and Miranda resumed their discussion.

" 'Tis inconceivable that Don Luis, a Spaniard, would help me escape."

"I don't think so. After I explained the circumstances to him in a rational way. . . ." Actually, Miranda admitted to herself, she had been anything but rational when she'd escaped from the *castillo* and gone to see Don Luis. She had wept and wrung her hands, declaring her life over if her husband remained a prisoner.

"But, God's blood, he's a Spaniard."

"Jack," Miranda said softly. "Elspeth thinks of herself as Spanish also. Since she was five she's been with a family who loves her very much. They took her to Spain and reared her as one of their own children."

"But she wasn't theirs," Jack said, his chin raised defiantly. "Does she forget her real mother and father, the settlement at Port Royal?"

"No. And she hasn't forgotten you either." Miranda's heart went out to her husband when she saw his bottom lip quiver. He turned away and paced to the windows, and Miranda contin-

408

ued. "She met her husband in Spain, then returned with him to St. Augustine when de Segovia came back. She never liked the commander but didn't know until I told her that he was the one responsible for the raid on Port Royal."

"Her husband. . . ." Jack paused and turned toward Miranda. "There were many Spanish soldiers killed when I escaped. Could one of them have been . . . ?"

"No," Miranda was quick to assure. "Elspeth made certain he didn't go to the *castillo* today." When Jack's brow raised in question, Miranda shrugged. "She is with child. I imagine she used that as an excuse."

Jack nodded, then stared out to sea. "I suppose I shall have a Spanish niece or nephew someday." When Miranda didn't answer, Jack glanced over his shoulder toward her. "What do you think you're doing?"

"I'm getting up." Miranda swung her legs over the side.

"But—"

"Jack, I'm fine." Miranda gave his broad chest a shove as he knelt beside her. "De Segovia landed on my foot when he fell, but it's all right now."

"You're certain?"

Miranda pulled up her skirt to reveal a shapely ankle which she turned from one side to the other. Jack resisted the urge to push her gown higher. Instead he stood and crossed his arms, frowning down at his wife. "Then, I have something to say to you. I recall a promise you made the night we spent in the *castillo*. A promise to get out of St. Augustine. You obviously didn't do it."

Pushing to her feet, Miranda faced her husband, her expression as dark as his. "No. Instead I saved your roguish neck. And this is the thanks I get for it."

"If 'tis thanks you wish, you shouldn't have risked your own neck to save mine. You did promise—"

"What nerve you have, to speak of promises. Or is it just pirates who are allowed to break theirs? What of your vow to take me with you when you went to St. Augustine?"

Jack's chin jutted forward. " 'Twas for your own good that I broke that vow."

Miranda's expression softened with love. "And 'twas for your good that I broke my promise to you." She stepped toward him, and his arms unfolded, then pulled her closer.

"When I saw you with de Segovia. . . . When I thought he might kill you. . . ." His embrace tightened, and Jack buried his face in her raven hair.

"It's over now. You have your revenge."

"But it wasn't revenge. When I killed him, my parents, Elspeth, the hell he put me through, were not foremost in my mind." His thumbs caught under her chin, lifting her face toward

410

his. "I killed him to keep him from hurting you. It was for you."

"Where are you going?" Miranda rounded the landing of the stairs at her father's house in time to see Jack opening the front door. They had arrived in Charles Town less than an hour before. Leaving Phin in charge of the *Sea Hawk,* Jack had hustled Miranda and himself off to the house on Tradd Street. Once there he had suggested Miranda go upstairs and rest.

She'd been tired, but though she'd lain on her bed, she couldn't sleep. Her mind had been too active. And it had not been filled with gravity or the theories of light travel or anything else she learned in books. It had been thoughts of her husband and his behavior that worried her.

On the voyage back to Charles Town he'd been loving—though he'd never repeated the revelation made that night in the cell that he loved her. But mostly he'd been quiet. She'd caught him many times staring out the transom windows, absorbed in thought. Thoughts he'd declined to discuss with her.

Miranda feared he planned to leave her.

She had heard Phin and the others talk of the riches to be had in the Indian Ocean. They were pirates, and the call of wealth and thrill of adventure was in their blood. It was in her husband's blood, too.

Now he was leaving and he was reluctant to face her with the news. So in true rogue form he planned to simply steal away into the night.

Except it was morning, the sun was shining, and Miranda wasn't about to let him leave her like that. She hurried down the stairs.

"Where are you off to," she repeated, because his expression held a trace of guilt.

"For a walk. Down to the docks," he clarified.

"Let him go, daughter. You can't be forever hovering about."

Miranda turned on her father, who'd come into the hallway. "I'm not hovering. I simply questioned."

"I'll be back soon." Jack leaned over and gave his wife a quick kiss before exiting through the door.

"Jack." Miranda reached for the latch, but her father beat her to it.

"Give him some time, Miranda."

"Only if you tell me what's going on. I know 'tis something. He's leaving me, isn't he?"

"No." Her father seemed genuinely surprised. " 'Tis nothing of that sort."

"Then, what is it? I have a right to know."

Henry sighed and taking her hand led her toward the parlor. "I suppose you do."

Jack hesitated outside the narrow brick town house and took a deep breath. The time for con-

412

frontation was at hand. He had both longed for and dreaded this since the day de Segovia had told him of the betrayal.

He knew what had happened.

Now he was going to find out why.

"Master Jack, this is a surprise."

"Hello, Molly." Jack stepped through the paneled door. "Is my uncle at home?"

"Yessir, he's in his library. I'll be tellin' him you're here."

"Don't bother." Jack's hand upon her plump calico-covered shoulder stayed the black woman. "I'll give *him* a surprise, too."

"Whatever ya say, Master Jack." The woman went mumbling off back down the hall. "Whatever ya say."

Jack didn't bother to knock. He simply opened the door and stepped into the room. The furnishings were grand, imported from the mother country at great expense, or in the case of the desk his uncle sat behind, pirated from a Spanish galleon at no monetary cost at all.

"Jack!" Robert dropped the quill from his long, slim fingers. "I didn't expect to see you again so soon."

"Or ever, for that matter."

"What do you mean by that?"

" 'Tis nothing." Jack waved the comment aside with a flick of his hand. "De Segovia is dead," he said without preamble. "I knew you of all people would be pleased by the news."

413

"Dead? Are you sure?"

"Aye. By my own hand."

"Well, that's . . . that's wonderful to hear."

"Now they're avenged. My mother and father. Your brother. All the members of the settlement at Port Royal."

Robert started to rise, but Jack strode toward the desk and motioned him back to his seat. He settled back reluctantly. "You must be very happy."

"As should you. Surely you felt a healthy hatred of the Spaniard who led the attack?"

"You know I did."

"So you always said."

"What is that supposed to mean? Listen, Jack, I'm busy at the moment with the plantation accounts. Perhaps we can discuss this later."

"We'll discuss it now." Jack shoved Robert back into the chair when he tried to stand. "I'll tell you now of my narrow escape from St. Augustine. How without the help of my wife and crew I would be dead by now. Garroted in front of throngs of Spanish onlookers.

"Have you ever had to anticipate such a fate for yourself, *Uncle* Robert? Have you ever had to worry that your wife may not have escaped? Have you ever had what you thought were your last days marred by the knowledge that you'd been betrayed by your own flesh and blood?"

The color drained from Robert's face, and he stared silently at Jack, his mouth grim.

"What, no frantic questions demanding to know what I mean? But, then, you know what I'm talking about, don't you, Robert?"

"I have no idea what—"

Jack leaped forward, grabbing Robert's lace cravat and hauling him up till they were nose to nose. "Don't lie on top of everything else." Jack's voice raged through clenched teeth. "He told me. De Segovia told me about your letter when I was his prisoner awaiting execution. That you told him of Snebley's Creek, and that I was coming to St. Augustine after him. Pox take you, he told me!"

In a fit of anger, Jack shoved the older man back into the chair, then spun around and strode across the room. "I know what you did. 'Tis why that now concerns me." He turned back. "Why, damn you?"

The question was barely out of his mouth before something near the surface of the desk caught his eye. He glanced down to see the gleaming barrel of a pistol aimed at his middle.

"It's loaded, and ready to fire in case you're wondering."

"Do you plan to kill me outright now?"

"As a matter of fact that's exactly what I intend to do. You've become a nuisance to me."

"Because I know of your duplicity."

"In part." Robert kept the gun leveled at Jack as he stood. "But, then, my wish to be rid of you is long-standing. You needn't appear so

415

shocked. My missive to de Segovia was merely the first time I took any action. Till then I had counted on your impulsive nature and reckless profession to handle the problem for me.

"But unfortunately, it didn't," Robert continued. "It seemed to matter not, how many sea battles you fought or how many times you tweaked the Spanish nose, you survived, even flourished."

"Is that why you decided to help fate along?"

"I decided to shove it along the day you came to me with your foolish talk of retiring. Of taking up your rightful place on the plantation. Ah, I see you remember the conversation."

"It was months ago. And it was merely the glimmer of an idea."

"Aye, but you were growing tired of your lifestyle. I, on the other hand, was not tired of mine."

"Meaning?"

"Meaning, I had no desire to hand over the management of Royal Oak Plantation to you. I've done as I saw fit since right after your parents died. I've built the plantation into a thriving business."

"With the help of money I've gained through piracy," Jack interjected, but his uncle failed to acknowledge his words.

"I won't have you coming back after all this time and taking it away from me."

"But it never was yours. Royal Oak has always

belonged to me."

Robert's smile was evil. "It won't after today."

Jack snorted. "You plan to simply shoot me. Here? In your house? Don't you think the constable will find that suspect?"

"Not after I explain how you barged in here, a bloodthirsty pirate, demanding that I give you money. I'll be believed. After all the effort I've put into convincing people of your freebooting ways." He raised the pistol, balancing it in his hand. "Thanks to my not-so-subtle hints, I had the constable convinced you had kidnapped Miranda Chadwick."

"So that bit of trouble was yours, too."

"Indeed. But I think we've talked enough." Robert's eyes narrowed, and his finger tightened on the trigger. His gaze was intense, but he snapped his head around when he heard the commotion at the door.

"Master Robert, this here woman insists that she—" Molly's mouth clamped shut when she saw the gun.

Miranda pushed by her, but Jack only caught a glimpse of her before he dove across the desk, slamming into his uncle.

Jack was stronger, but the gun still aimed at him more than compensated for that. Jack knocked his uncle's arm, shoving the barrel up, but not far. It was aimed just above Jack's face. And Robert fought to bring the muzzle back, inch by deadly inch.

Jack kept his fingers biting into Robert's palm, and his muscles bulged as he lay sprawled across the desk. Robert, pushed back against the leather chair, grunted and his teeth gnashed. Sweat broke out across his upper lip, and his eyes bulged.

But he held on.

A noise sounded behind him, but Jack didn't look. Robert, however, did, and Jack used the break in his uncle's concentration to raise onto his knees and shove with all his might. The chair fell backward, Robert and Jack with it. As it hit the floor, the gun fired.

"Jack! Jack!" Miranda skirted around the desk and slid to the floor beside her husband. Grabbing his shoulders, she tried to pull him up. Tears welled in her eyes when he did not help her. Blood was everywhere, scarlet and flowing freely onto the carpet, and Miranda couldn't find the source. Her hands skimmed over him, but jerked away when she heard the moan.

Jack groaned again and lifted his groggy head. Miranda threw her arms about him and nearly knocked him back onto the floor. His temple hurt, and he lifted a hand to rub the bump caused by the fall.

"Oh, Jack, you're all right."

Miranda was crying in earnest now, and Jack stood, pulling her up beside him. A quick glance revealed Robert lying in a puddle of blood, his sightless eyes staring at the ceiling. Jack pressed

418

Miranda's head against his chest and moved away from the desk.

"Papa told me where you were," she whispered into his jacket. "He told me of your uncle's treachery."

Servants rushed into the library. Jack sent for the constable, and when he arrived Jack and Miranda met him at the door.

" 'Tis all right now," Jack murmured to Miranda. But as he watched Graham Hicks look first at the body on the floor, then up at him, Jack just wished he knew for sure that he spoke the truth.

Chapter Twenty-one

"'Tis late, Miranda." Jack brushed aside the curls trailing down her neck and gently kissed her nape. She turned in the chair, a smile of welcome on her lips.

"You're finished going over the accounts, then?"

"Aye. For the night." Jack started to pull his wife to him, then paused. "Are you ready to stop reading?"

Miranda laughed, and reached up to him. She'd seen that lusty gleam in his eyes before—often. He wanted her. Now. Reading be damned. And she wouldn't want him any other way. Still, she found it endearing that he asked. "I only opened the book because I was waiting for you."

"Mmmm." Jack nuzzled the warmth of her neck while fumbling with the tiny buttons down the front of her night rail. "'Tis a waste for you to don this thing."

"Would you have me sit about in the nude?"

Jack cocked his head, pretending to ponder

the question. "Aye. That would suit. Mayhap I could sketch you."

"You can't draw." Miranda stilled his fingers and took over the task of unfastening the white gown.

"So I can't." The playful bite he took of Miranda's exposed shoulder made her giggle. "Then, perhaps I can do other things."

Oh, and he could, Miranda thought as her head fell back. Her husband knew just where to caress, to nibble, to suckle, to make her melt inside. She tangled her fingers through his golden hair as he carried her to the large tester bed. He laid her on the sheet, then followed her down.

His lips found hers, and she opened for him, drowning in sensual delights. She clutched at his shirt, shoving it aside to feel the smooth, muscled skin beneath. Miranda basked in his heat.

When he sat up to pull off his boots Miranda curled around him, her palm curving down his broad back. She couldn't stop touching him. His smile was wicked as he paused between boots to run the tip of his finger across her breast.

"We repaired the bridge across the creek today," Jack said as he watched Miranda's nipple tighten. When he and Miranda had come to Royal Oak the day after his uncle died, they'd both been surprised to find the plantation so poorly maintained. Apparently Robert had been using much of the money Jack gave him, the money from his pirating, to live a life of ease in

Charles Town. There were fields planted with rice, but the main house and outbuildings were in a sad state. For the past eight months, Jack had worked hard to rectify that.

He trailed his fingers lovingly down Miranda's stomach before standing to remove his breeches. "The bridge got me thinking. I recall that day in St. Augustine that Phin said not to worry about the drawbridge closing, that you took care of that. I never asked how you did it."

"The drawbridge?" Miranda's brow furrowed. She was so engrossed in watching her husband undress, it took her a moment to think. "Oh, that wasn't difficult. The bridge could only be raised by lowering the counterweights." She sat up, brushing raven curls behind her shoulder. "You most likely didn't get the chance to study the mechanism, but it was fairly simple. As someone turned the windlass, gravity pulling on the counterweights helped raise the drawbridge. No gravity—" she shrugged—"the bridge can't be lifted."

"But how did you get rid of the gravity?"

"I didn't. Not really." She wriggled around to face Jack, who now sat on the bed. "The counterweights needed to be lowered into a deep hole, as deep as they are long, so that gravity continued to pull them down. I had some of your crew nail the trapdoor over the hole shut."

"So the weights just rested on the wood?"

"Exactly. Without the force of gravity on the

counterweights, the men didn't have enough power to raise the bridge. And with all the commotion and gunfire, they didn't have the time to get the trapdoor open."

"Very clever, wife," Jack said as he lowered her down beneath him.

"I do have my uses."

"You do indeed." Jack had settled in with a kiss of carnal delight when a noise in the drive outside their bedroom window gained his attention. He sat up. "What in the hell is that?"

"It sounds like a rider." Miranda's eyes met Jack's. Neither of them spoke a word as Jack jerked on his clothes.

"You stay here," was all he said before hurrying out the bedroom door.

"Who was it?" Miranda crouched on her knees in the center of the canopied bed. She peered through the fine gauze of mosquito netting toward her husband, who stood in the open doorway.

" 'Twas a messenger . . . from Charles Town," he answered, then said no more as he turned to shut the door. He held Miranda's gaze as he crossed the room. He sat on the bed, placing the letter on the rumpled counterpane. They both studiously ignored it.

"His pounding at the door woke Missy," Jack said, referring to the cook's helper. "She's giving the rider a meal; then he's going to bed down in a spare bedroom before heading back to town."

"Perhaps I should help." Miranda moved to leave the bed, but Jack's hand stopped her.

"Missy can handle it." His gaze dropped to the rolled parchment bearing the royal seal, then skittered away.

Miranda saw the action, and her heart went out to her strong, golden husband. "Jack, we have to open it to find out what it says."

"I know." He sighed. "I just want a moment to pretend everything is as it's been these last months."

Miranda could certainly understand his feelings. Life for them since the day Robert died had been idyllic, but fragile. A respite from reality.

Their initial fear that the constable would charge Jack with his uncle's murder proved false. With Miranda's testimony, corroborated by the servant Molly, that Robert had pulled a pistol on his nephew, Graham Hicks had had no choice but to believe Jack.

But Jack's explanation had raised suspicions about his possible piracy. And questions Jack didn't want to answer. So he'd packed up Miranda and headed for Royal Oak.

But not before sending off a plea to the king.

Since then he and Miranda had worked hard on the plantation. Jack rose early to supervise the flooding of the rice fields, and worked late learning the intricacies of the accounts. Miranda studied the management of the household with the same fervor she once reserved for her scientific pursuits. She learned to care for the sick and oversee the making of candles. And she still had time to use her microscope and read her books. Jack had set aside a sunny corner of their bedroom for her to use.

The life suited them. They were in love. They were happy. And the reality of Jack's past was like a sword, ever threatening to swoop down and destroy them.

They lived each day to the fullest. And with the night they retired to the large tester bed and made love.

"There's no help for it," Jack finally said, scooping up the parchment. He broke the seal, pausing only when Miranda's hand settled over his.

"You know I shall love you no matter what the king's decree. And I shall follow you anywhere."

"Aye." He knew she would, but his gaze strayed to the slight bulge of her stomach, and he thought of the child, his child, nestled under her heart. He wanted more for his family than the wandering life of an outlaw.

His eyes raced along the letter; then he bent toward the candle and read more slowly. A grin spread across his features.

"It's a pardon," he yelped. "He granted me a

full pardon." Tossing the paper aside, he gathered her up in his arms and twirled around the room, slowing only when she squealed with joy.

"I knew it." Miranda laughed. "I knew everything would be fine."

"More of your logical thinking?" Jack kidded as he set her back on the bed.

"Maybe." Miranda scooted over, making room for her husband. "Why would the king wish to punish a respected planter such as yourself?"

"Why indeed? But I think 'twas more my promise to stop pirating that swayed him." Jack laughed and Miranda joined him. But as he leaned against the bolster of pillows, pulling her down with him, Miranda's expression sobered.

"Jack?"

"Hmmm?"

Miranda leaned up on her elbow. "You aren't going to miss it, are you? When Phin and the others took the *Sea Hawk* and sailed to the Indian Ocean I feared you might have regrets."

"What, that I wasn't going with them?" Jack touched the tip of her nose when she nodded. "Nay. I've found my safe harbor right here." He drew her back into his arms.

Snuggling down, Miranda smiled, then admitted, "There are some things I shall miss."

"Really?" Jack tucked his chin to look at his wife. "Such as?"

"Being married to a lusty pirate for one."

Shifting, Jack managed to pull her under him.

His grin was devilish. "Have I given you any reason to think I'm not just as lusty being a planter?"

"In truth you haven't."

"Nor shall I," Jack said, and trailed kisses down her neck in way of proof.

"What of your gold ear loop?"

Jack lifted his head, his eyes meeting hers. "What of it?"

"I like it."

"Then, I shall wear it. At times. For you." He punctuated each sentence with a whispery brush of his lips across hers. "'Tis that it?"

"Yes."

"No more questions?"

"No. . . . Except, did I ever tell you of the animalcules Antonie van Leeuwenhoek discovered in your manly fluid?"

"My what?" Shocked, Jack stopped tracing the delicate curve of her chin.

"Well, not yours exactly. But when he observed a drop of the fluid through the microscope he discovered tiny —"

"God's blood, Miranda. Must we speak of this now?"

Pulling his lips back down to hers, Miranda agreed there were other things she'd rather be doing.

To My Readers

I hope you enjoyed the tale of Miranda and her roguish pirate, Gentleman Jack Blackstone. I loved researching and writing it. Though the Blackstone family is fictional, some of the events in the story actually did take place.

In the early settlement of the Carolinas and Florida, there were often raids between the English and Spanish. Lord Cardross's Scottish settlement at Port Royal was destroyed by the Spanish from St. Augustine. Captives were taken, and there are accounts of prisoners being used in the building of the Castillo de San Marcos.

Miranda's interest in science — called the philosophies in the seventeenth century — is typical of the time. It was an exciting Age of Science. With the exception of Don Luis and Miranda's grandfather, all the scientists and discoveries mentioned in this book are factual. Newton, van Leeuwenhoek, and Wren helped change mankind's understanding of the world.

But it was also a violent time. A time when pirates flourished . . . and as I indicated in this book, were actually accepted in some cities. The reasons were primarily economic. The Navigation Acts forced the colonists to trade only with England — at prices set by English merchants. This meant the English colonists had to sell their exports at lower than world-market prices and buy manufactured goods at relatively high prices. And that doesn't even take into account the customs duties.

Enter the pirates and privateers who brought "imported" goods into the colonies and sold them at much more reasonable prices. After all, the pirates were assured a hefty profit, for the cargo had cost them no more than shot and sweat, and the chance of meeting a pirate's death.

Most pirates were an independent lot. They ran their ships by articles that they drew up, and they bowed to no authority, not even that of their captain. The pirates' version of democracy was way ahead of its time.

And yes, through the years, pardons were granted to pirates. In 1699, King William offered a general amnesty to those pirates willing to accept an oath to plunder no more. Many, like Jack Blackstone, took it. Many more, like the rest of the *Sea Hawk*'s crew, tried their luck in the Indian Ocean.

Jack and Miranda Blackstone are typical of the intrepid souls who pioneered the New World. Together they built a powerful dynasty in the Charleston area.

In my next book, due out in the spring of 1993, I tell the story of their great-grandson, Jared Blackstone, a patriot and privateer during the American Revolution. He becomes involved in the colonies' attempts to gain French support for their fight against England. It's a tale of espionage and love as Jared matches wits with Lady Merideth Bannister.

The Blackstone trilogy winds up with a Civil War novel that pits Devon Blackstone, a rake of a blockade runner, against feisty Felicity Wentworth. When Felicity decides she needs Devon's help with her Underground Railroad activities, the sparks fly.

I hope you enjoy the Blackstone family, men of the sea all, and the women who love them. Let me know what you think. For a newsletter and bookmark please write to me care of:

Zebra Books
475 Park Avenue South
New York, NY 10016

A SASE is appreciated.

To happy endings,
Christine Dorsey

CATCH A RISING STAR!

ROBIN ST. THOMAS

DISCOVER DEANA JAMES!

CAPTIVE ANGEL (2524, $4.50/$5.50)
Abandoned, penniless, and suddenly responsible for the biggest tobacco plantation in Colleton County, distraught Caroline Gillard had no time to dissolve into tears. By day the willowy redhead labored to exhaustion beside her slaves . . . but each night left her restless with longing for her wayward husband. She'd make the sea captain regret his betrayal until he begged her to take him back!

MASQUE OF SAPPHIRE (2885, $4.50/$5.50)
Judith Talbot-Harrow left England with a heavy heart. She was going to America to join a father she despised and a sister she distrusted. She was certainly in no mood to put up with the insulting actions of the arrogant Yankee privateer who boarded her ship, ransacked her things, then "apologized" with an indecent, brazen kiss! She vowed that someday he'd pay dearly for the liberties he had taken and the desires he had awakened.

SPEAK ONLY LOVE (3439, $4.95/$5.95)
Long ago, the shock of her mother's death had robbed Vivian Marleigh of the power of speech. Now she was being forced to marry a bitter man with brandy on his breath. But she could not say what was in her heart. It was up to the viscount to spark the fires that would melt her icy reserve.

WILD TEXAS HEART (3205, $4.95/$5.95)
Fan Breckenridge was terrified when the stranger found her near-naked and shivering beneath the Texas stars. Unable to remember who she was or what had happened, all she had in the world was the deed to a patch of land that might yield oil . . . and the fierce loving of this wildcatter who called himself Irons.

Available wherever paperbacks are sold, or order direct from the Publisher. Send cover price plus 50¢ per copy for mailing and handling to Zebra Books, Dept. 3899, 475 Park Avenue South, New York, N.Y. 10016. Residents of New York and Tennessee must include sales tax. DO NOT SEND CASH. For a free Zebra/ Pinnacle catalog please write to the above address.